The Piano's Key

Book Two of The
Fairy Godmother Diaries

IZOLDA TRAKHTENBERG

Copyright © 2016 Izolda Trakhtenberg

Editor: Pamela Potter

Cover artist: Magdalena Adic

All rights reserved.

ISBN: 0-9802298-5-5

ISBN-13: 978-0-9802298-5-1

DEDICATION

To Rich, Emily, Golda, Kristen, Mike, Sondra, Petra, Alec, Kimba, Pyro, Ninja, and Hatha for your support and love.

To my teachers: my singing teacher, Mary Alice Powell, for teaching me how to sing and how to teach, my violin instructor, Abe Levine, for helping me discover the violin, and my sixth grade English teacher, Linda Gutman, who nurtured an immigrant kid's nascent interest in reading, until it blossomed into a life-long love affair.

CONTENTS

Acknowledgments	i
Chapter 1	Pg 1
Chapter 2	Pg 19
Chapter 3	Pg 26
Chapter 4	Pg 32
Chapter 5	Pg 55
Chapter 6	Pg 62
Chapter 7	Pg 68
Chapter 8	Pg 77
Chapter 9	Pg 81
Chapter 10	Pg 94
Chapter 11	Pg 115
Chapter 12	Pg 123
Chapter 13	Pg 132
Chapter 14	Pg 176
Chapter 15	Pg 184
Chapter 16	Pg 188
Chapter 17	Pg 201
Chapter 18	Pg 213
Chapter 19	Pg 219
Chapter 20	Pg 235

Chapter 21	Pg 241
Chapter 22	Pg 251
Chapter 23	Pg 281
Chapter 24	Pg 291
Chapter 25	Pg 297
Chapter 26	Pg 303
Chapter 27	Pg 312
Chapter 28	Pg 329
Chapter 29	Pg 354
Epilogue	Pg 363

ACKNOWLEDGMENTS

This book would not exist without the Fairy Godmother Diaries Brain Trust: Kristen Hughes Evans, Petra Mayer, Katie van den Heuvel, Dayle Hodge, Kathy Zottmann, and my sisters Emily Altman and Golda Noble. Thank you for your generous feedback and encouragement. You helped me more than you can know.

To my Facebook friends and family: you have come through with opinions and ideas on everything from plot points to music playlists. You have taken my surveys, held my hand, cheered me on, and surrounded me with care and love.

To my editor, Pamela Potter: thank you for helping my writing sing. To cover artist Magdalena Adic who brought my ideas to glorious and vibrant life. Thank you, and I can't wait to work on the next cover with you.

To Ethnomusicologist Alan Lomax: You presented your database of recorded music to the National Geographic Society when I worked there. You showed us the history of the routes music has traveled, and you changed my life.

I thank the ABC Writing Collective, especially my Little Brother, Mike Dougherty for your friendship and great ideas.

To my husband, Rich Potter, I am grateful for your support, confidence in my endeavors, and love.

Finally, I am blessed to share this story with you. Thank you for reading.

CHAPTER 1

"This is our last night," Evie murmured. She pushed herself off the worn couch and paced Daniel's tiny living room.

"Only for a little while," Daniel replied. "Then, you'll be back."

"I don't know how you can be relaxed about all this," she vexed. "We're not going to see each other for months, and I've gotten used to you. I'm going to have a talk with the Tribunal about getting more vacation time."

"Well, we'll write. Wait, can we write?" Daniel sat up.

"There's no cell service in Core City. So, no, we can't text, if that's what you mean." Evie replied. "I could write to you, no problem," she giggled. "You know, spooky writing in the steam on the bathroom mirror and strange lights in the sky. But you can't exactly do SnapChat over to Fairy."

"Well, you'll be really busy anyway. You have all sorts of new magic to learn, right? And that will be fun."

"You have a seriously twisted idea of fun," Evie pouted. "I'm going to be learning healing and battle magics. Believe me, neither of those can even remotely be called fun. If you manipulate healing wrong, you can screw everything up. If you do battle magic wrong, you can blow everything up. The tiniest mistake and everything goes kerfuffled. It takes pinpoint accuracy and me, I'm more of a ..."

"Rock 'em, sock 'em girl. I know, Evie." Daniel smiled. "But I'm sure you'll be great. And battle magic comes in very handy, I'd imagine."

"Yeah, actually, that will be awesome. It would have been really awesome to have those when Zeke was messing with Joanna and with you." She stopped there. By tacit agreement, they kept silent about Daniel's brush with both Zeke and death. "In the end though," she continued. "I'm glad I didn't know battle magic then. I would have killed him too quickly, and he deserves to be roasted alive while chipmunks feast on his eyeballs."

"Now Evie, you don't mean that," he admonished.

"Yeah, I do. He came this close," she put her index finger and thumb together, "to destroying everything. And by everything, I mean everything. In Ireland, it was Joanna who saved us. If she hadn't been strong and able to deal, he would have succeeded in getting the Ramrocks to kill her and then where would we be? No, I should have done it when I had the chance because then ..." she trailed off.

"Then what, Evie?" Daniel asked.

"Then, nothing," she said. She had no desire to remind Daniel of Zeke's threats. She had vowed to protect him at all cost and her charms and protection spells ought to hold while she was gone. If Zeke tried to mess with Daniel in her absence, heads would roll.

"You know, the trouble with it is that Wisteria is teaching," she changed the subject.

"Wisteria?"

"Yeah, Wisteria Flamethrower. She's the battle magic instructor this term."

"That's quite a name."

"No doubt. And just so you know, they named the weapon after her and not the other way around. She was a consultant to some high mucky muck when it was being developed."

"See? I'm sure you'll have a great time, learn lots of new things, see friends, and be back before you know it."

"Wisteria isn't exactly what I'd call a friend. She's more like an old bulldog with a sore paw and a bad attitude." She sagged against the cushions. "And to top it all off, I won't see you graduate."

"Hey, it's okay. I'll send you pictures. Good ones, I hope," he laughed.

"You'd better since you're getting your Photography Master's," she sat in his lap and nuzzled at his throat.

"Besides, I won't get to see you graduate either," Daniel mumbled into her hair. "But at least I'll get to see your Juilliard recital, and that's even better."

"Crap!" Evie jumped up. "I have my last practice session with Professor Weingart at two o'clock."

She pulled him up for one last kiss. "I'll see you at the recital tomorrow night."

She reached into her backpack, touched her wand, and disappeared.

EVIE

"Evie, you're not concentrating," Professor Weingart tapped her pencil against the sheet music in irritation. "At this rate, you will have quite the challenge to get ready for your recital." She glanced at her copious notes on my performance. "You must languidly flow with the legato. It must glide on gentle wings of love and light. Then, and only then, you must pick up the spark and spirit of the mosso like the joyfully spinning, delightedly flirtatious, moving rapture that it is. You only have one day to discover and adorn yourself with the gilded nuances of this most adored of Chopin's waltzes. Your ardor for the composition must shine through as if you are both musician and dancer, lover and beloved." She caught her breath, smoothed her slate gray skirt, and patted down her chignon.

I tried to calm my ragged breathing. I had to hand it to her; she still had the best inspirational descriptions of music that I'd ever heard.

"I'm sorry, Professor. I just, well, I have a lot on my mind right now. I'm graduating soon, and then I have to go get trained in battle ... I mean," I changed course before I let something slip. "I mean I have to catch the train to Baton Rouge. I'm, um, attending a friend's wedding this weekend, and I'm not much of a flier. And I'm not even close to being packed and ready to go."

"You aren't leaving tomorrow night," the professor admonished. "Tomorrow night, you're performing Chopin, Beethoven, and Rachmaninov. You have plenty on which to focus right here and right now. So, lock it up."

My eyes shot up, startled. Professor Weingart, bane of pop culture, staunch supporter of Tradition, fervent advocate for everything Victorian and Romantic, had just uttered a phrase from the current vernacular. She meant business!

"Wow, Professor. I've never heard anything so, er 'hip' from you before. It feels disquieting and maybe even disturbing."

"I'm not above utilizing popular vernacular when I deem it appropriate. And my dear, you in many ways epitomize these modern times. You have the vibrant passion of youth and the curiosity that encapsulates this current era of music." Here she paused and a faraway look came into her eyes. "And yet ... and yet, you possess some spark, some tie to history. It is as if you resonate with the ardor and drama that compelled those who composed these masterpieces to begin with...."

Hold the phones, this was new! She could somehow see that my feet were planted in two worlds—this modern one and the ancient one. She couldn't have any idea that I was alive back when Chopin was composing this waltz, could she? Nah, that'd be ridiculous. What was this then? Did everyone in New York have some connection to magic, or was I just getting lucky in my choice of companions?

"I believe that is why you normally have such a kinship with these pieces," she continued. "And yet, today, something feels lacking. Best we get back to work." She checked her watch. "We have time for one more run-through of the Chopin. Pick it up from the beginning and remember to find the lilt and sway of the piece before you throw yourself onto the altar of the racing titillation of the mosso." She sat back down and folded her hands in her lap.

I composed myself at the piano, as if I were sitting in front of Steinway's first Grande, and placed my fingers on the keys. I pressed myself into the first few simple notes and chords of this most extraordinary waltz. As usual, I lost time, the world, everything as the music that flowed from the instrument overwhelmed me.

The echoes of the last run of notes riding up the length of the keys still rang in the air as I returned to the here and now. I pressed my fingers to my cheeks and wiped the tears of delight from my face. I'd always meant to ask dear Frédéric how he'd composed that particular vertical sweep and tender swoosh to the end of the piece. No one could hear it and not want to leap up and waltz around the room. Even Reverend Moore, Footloose, who outlawed dancing would have had a tough time not tapping his toes to this tune. Keeping my eyes closed, I checked in on the professor with my other senses. She breathed rapidly but showed no outward signs of displeasure. So, I took a chance and cracked one eye open.

The silence lengthened until finally I lost my nerve. Sure, I had plenty of years on her, but the Professor knew the piano as well as the best of them. Since I knew most of the "them" in question, this was really saying something. "Well, Professor? What do you think?"

Her eyes opened and brightened like she'd just been on a lovely magic carpet ride. "What do I think? Evie, I think ... I think you're quite prepared for tomorrow night. I think when you concentrate, you are well nigh unstoppable. So, don't you let anything stop you." She stared at me fiercely. "Don't you let anything stop you."

"No, ma'am," I said. "I won't." On that note, we tacitly agreed that rehearsal had ended. I gathered my bag and various bits of sheet music and left the room.

I made it back to the thirteenth floor of the Rose building without incident and let myself into the suite I shared with Joanna Brennan. Yeah, you remember her. She's the one who almost ended the world last year. Well, technically, that's not exactly true. Her devastation when Marcus the Twinkie cheated on her almost ended the world. Actually, that's still not exactly true. Zeke Dunne, a Bane and the bane of my existence, manipulated events to make sure she remained anguished and then the poop hit the fan, big time. But, we managed to fix things and in the process kick both some Ramrock and Bane ass.

Joanna is bright, beautiful, talented, and made almost completely of magic. So, when she's happy, the rest of us tiptoe through the tulips. But when someone messes with her calm, bad things happen, on an epic scale not unlike Armageddon. (You know, Bruce Willis can still do a badass better than just about anyone.) Yep, Joanna is a sweet, talented, walking, talking, magic-impervious asteroid. She floats on by in the universe and basically helps everyone else feel great just by being around her and her playing is out of this world. Just don't make her angry.

"Hey Jo," I called out as I entered the suite. The shades were open to welcome in the afternoon sun and various dust mites, or imps masquerading as them, played on the warm air currents. I dropped my books on my small, scarred, faux wood desk and plopped on the tiny, lumpy couch. My time here had whisked by and after tomorrow's show, I'd be leaving the dorm forever. Yeah! I didn't care for dorm life the first time I went to school. Repeating the Dorm Cafeteria Food Era while living in the city with the best collection of cuisines on the planet insulted my sense of, well, everything.

I had just closed my eyes to check for pinholes when Joanna stirred from within her room.

"Hi Evie," she called from the doorway. "How did practice go?"

"Oh, you know. Despite my many decades of experience and despite the fact that I have several centuries on her, Professor Weingart has the infuriating ability to make me feel like I'm an incompetent and tone-deaf four-year-old playing 'London Bridge is Falling Down,' while my every note is making nuns weep into their habits."

"Come now, Evie. It couldn't have been as bad as all that now, could it?" Shane McDuggan, lovely Irish guitarist and Joanna's boyfriend, stuck his tousled and gorgeous blond head out of her bedroom. After Joanna beat Zeke at his own game and defeated the Ramrocks in Ireland, she and Shane had stayed together. He moved to the States to work at his uncle Tully's pub while he made a go of it as a New York musician.

"Shane, you don't know the half of it," I grumbled back. "She was vicious and harsh and most maddening of all, she was right," I smiled. "I worked those keys like I was stomping a good ol' polka on 'em when the delicate touch of a ballerina was called for. Not that she said anything actually cruel, you understand. But she might as well have since the recital is, oh, tomorrow night, and I'm going to sound like that cranky four-year-old. She actually told me to 'lock it up.'" I looked to Joanna for corroboration that this was indeed extraordinary.

"She said, 'lock it up?' Professor Weingart? Really? She wouldn't say something like that unless ... Wow, she meant business," Joanna replied.

"That's all I'm saying. And that's why I'm going to have to really bring my 'A' game' tomorrow. Or Liszt will never forgive me." Not that I was going to back in time and tell him about my lack of polish and passion or anything, but I liked to think that he still took an interest in his old pupils' progress, and I wouldn't want to disappoint him, or for that matter, Professor Weingart.

Luckily, Shane didn't notice my little slip about Liszt since he was too busy canoodling with Joanna. He nuzzled her long honey blond hair and grinned into her kiss as she stood on tiptoe and planted one on him.

"Okay, you two. Get a room," I said. I love viewing good, healthy, lusty PDA as much as the next person, but I had work to do.

Joanna giggled and snuggled closer into his strapping frame. "Actually, we're headed down to Tully's. Shane has to work, and I'm going to play in the session."

"Are you now," I batted my lashes at her. "Then, don't you think you might want to bring your violin?"

"Oops," she laughed. "Shane's been distracting me."

"I'll bet he has. Now, off you go before I change my mind and go with you." I could resist neither a Tully's Pub music session nor one of his world famous subs. Honestly, the man made Babette's Feast look like a poorly-stocked, drive-through, fast food joint. What he could do with a sub could make angels weep and had on more than one occasion.

Joanna reentered the room cradling her treasured violin in its case. "Should we bring you back a Tully's Special with the works?"

"You know you should," I agreed as I stretched on the couch and prepared to review my pieces one by one. "And don't forget the extra pickles. You know, I love me some pickles."

"Yes, both old and new ones." Joanna agreed as they walked out.

I meant no disrespect and normally I adore both Joanna and Shane. But tonight, I needed all of my meager powers of concentration. I had about twenty-four hours to eke out the mysteries within four of the most challenging piano pieces ever written. I reached into my tattered tote bag and withdrew the sheet music for tomorrow's show. I propped open the Chopin waltz and began a gorgeous 'air piano' rendition of its lilting notes. I would rehearse and reinvigorate each piece until it was in my ear, in my body, and in my spirit. I would interpret each bit of music as if it had never been performed before, as if I were the first pianist who had ever dared put fingers to keys to play these masterpieces.

"Yeah, baby. Yeah." I quoted Austin Powers as I pumped the air with my closed fist. I was going to rock. Those composers were not going to know what hit them. I was playing with fire, and I knew it. These guys might be dead but they could still ring my bell if they felt like it, so I'd better watch my step. And I'd better do them proud. Beethoven, Chopin, Rachmaninov and a special surprise from the master himself, Liszt. Oh boy. I had some serious work to do.

I grabbed the keyboard from my bedroom, and I got to it.

The next day dawned bright and cheerful—the little bugger. I staggered out of my bedroom as Joanna sashayed into the suite bearing a tray full to the rim with delectable breakfast dishes that had definitely not come from the cafeteria.

"Whatever magic you cast to bring this here, I applaud you." I said as the delicious aromas lifted me out of my catatonia and into a state of perfect grace. I plopped down on the couch, cleared the little coffee table of books and other detritus, and prepared to relish this feast.

"Well, it's your big day," she said as she set the tray in front of me. "And I wanted to make it special. Besides," she teased. "I know you have a lot to do today and nothing will wake you up like breakfast from Good Enough to Eat.

"You're not wrong," I replied as I unrolled the napkin she had twisted into a swan shape. The silverware sat underneath and I grabbed knife and fork and dove in. The first dish contained delectable fruit. A rainbow of grapes, sliced watermelon, kiwi, strawberries, cantaloupe and honeydew adorned a generous dollop of Greek yogurt. Granola made of slivered hazelnuts, almonds, oats, brown sugar, and raisins topped the entire thing. That bowl alone would have satiated me, but Joanna had other delights up her culinary sleeve.

"Mmm," I barely managed to keep my teeth in my head as I spied the next treat. Good Enough To Eat, had achieved fame for a few dishes that provided gastronomical nirvana to foodies, the world over. But their signature sauce, their hollandaise, looked like a Hawaiian sunset and tasted like heaven with a bit of devilish hell thrown into the mix. Rich, creamy, zesty, spectacular—a secret spice rounded out the flavor. It fell somewhere between savory and piquant and at the end it grabbed you by the teeth and rattled you around, but it was all okay because the way it articulated the dish it accompanied made you want to weep tears of ecstasy. Do you think I'm kidding or exaggerating? Go there sometime and try their vegetarian Eggs Benedict. Then, you'll know.

"Oh, Jo," I moaned as I licked the plate clean. "This was a major slice of heaven pie."

"Chef Leo couldn't be stopped, especially once he heard that your recital is tonight," she replied.

"Aiee," I leaned back against the couch and licked my lips of the last vestiges of hollandaise sauce. "Don't remind me. I can't believe I'm about to say this, but I'm actually nervous."

"What!" her brown eyes widened in surprise. "Impossible! The great Eveningstar Songbottom, staunch defender of all things Liszt and Rachmaninov, how can you possibly be nervous? No, wait," she amended. "I get it. It's your last one. It means something."

"It so does," I sighed. "And I'm going to have to kick ass, and make the Professor proud since I won't be able to warn her that I have take off, right afterward. Hopefully, my playing will rock enough that by the time I'm back she'll have forgiven me."

Jo leaned over and picked up the tray and carried it to the doorway. She tidied up the room. "Look, Evie. You will be brilliant. Now, why don't you go relax. I'm going to get the tray back to the cafeteria. See you in a bit." She left our suite balancing the tray on her hands.

"Relax," I sniffed. "Hah! Like that's going to happen." I jumped off the couch and grabbed my conductor's baton wand. I needed to get to a Time Keeper and speed things up a bit. Generally, we are required to log all such requests through the Portal Keepers. Heck, we're not even supposed to ever have contact with the Time Keepers themselves. But, Morrick owed me a favor and this was as good a time as any to collect. A trip to visit It was definitely in order.

Concentrating on the Palace of Time, I transported myself onto the Ley Lines and walked the few steps to the marker for the Palace. Ley Lines are an efficient way to travel. A whole mess of intersecting blue neon-like lines that crisscross the entire planet and then some, they allow us to move swiftly over great distances. Getting to them is pretty simple. We just have to look sideways and we can spot 'em, grab one, and hop onto the Ley Line Highway.

I jumped off the Lines and stood before the gate of the Palace. I rang the large brass bell. Within seconds, I was pounding on the door with fists and feet. "Come on, Morrick!" I cried. "I just need one small favor, pretty please? Just speed it up a little bit."

I had a bad feeling not even the biggest bribe I could bring to the table, a year's supply of Jumping Cow ice cream would get Them to speed up time an iota. I hoped that Morrick, Time Keeper, First Guard, would remember It owed me one, but sometimes these Time Keepers can be selective about what stays in what passes for Their heads. I tried one last time and raised the trunk of the enormous Elephant Head Brass Door Knocker. I threw the trunk at the eighteen-foot tall door with all my might.

In the resounding quiet, I studied the door. It depicted carvings of all the ways we have told time over, er time. Sundials, Rolexes, a veritable cornucopia of horological wonders; heck even a gorgeous carving of the Mayan calendar, adorned it.

The door glided open and Morrick stood before me.

"Your nervousness is insufficient reason to accelerate time," It rumbled.

"But Morrick," I cajoled. "Don't you want some Mother's Milk Ice Cream from the Jumping Cow? I'd even bring it to you and everything. And you could slow time down enough that it wouldn't even melt before you got it."

Morrick's clock face eye blinked at me and narrowed to a slit. Its minute hands folded over the clock face like a strange set of eyelashes. Its long, wood-like body resembled an Art Nouveau grandfather clock. Small articulated butterflies, owls, and praying mantis adorned its sides. It watched me. Its second-hand circled slowly across Its white clock face eye.

"Evie," Morrick said. "Despite the fact that few things in this universe are as delectable as Mother's Milk ice cream, there is nothing We can do. On the first hand, We cannot change time for you, or for anyone, unless there is a good reason. And on the second hand, you are just nervous. The recital will go fine. You will, as you say, 'rock the house.' The Professor will forgive you for ducking out after the recital. And besides," It continued. "You will soon have bigger things to wor- think about."

Recital forgotten, I rushed forward and stared at the Time Keeper.

"Wait a minute," I cried. Morrick stilled. "Just exactly what do you know, Morrick?"

Morrick stood in silence for a minute. It could not lie to a direct question. "I know a great many things," It replied. "I know that a light year equals the distance light travels in one year. I know that the Earth resides eight light minutes from the sun. I know Mars orbits the Sun every 687 Earth days. I know …."

I had made a rookie mistake. I wasted my One Important Question. If I'd worded the OIQ carefully, I could have gotten the keys to the kingdom.

"Jupiter's Giant Red spot wasn't always red-" Morrick intoned.

"Okay, Morrick. Okay. You win," I held up my hands. "I get it. You're not going to spill the proverbial beans. But is there anything you can tell me?" I wheedled. "A little hint?"

Morrick stilled and gazed at me. "Keep your friends close and your enemies closer. But Evie, don't keep your enemies too close." It closed Its eye and disappeared.

"Dammit!" I stomped my foot. I waited for a few minutes, but It did not reappear.

"Fine," I grumbled. I jumped back on the Lines and headed back.

Room 309, the main student recital room at Juilliard, was full by the time I reached it, and I'd taken my time to get ready. Hair purple. Dress purple. Nail polish purple. If I could have invited Prince to come and hang out wearing his customary color, I would have done it. Besides, he would have drawn some of the attention away from me. The butterflies were playing Chinese jump rope in my belly.

My favorite professors sat in the front row of the long rectangular space. Music history professor Beringer and I shared a love for the great composers and for a certain deli in Ann Arbor, MI. We had spent a good few hours over the last year discussing the lesser known works of Menotti, Brahms, and Percival, while reminiscing about the #36 sandwiches from Zingerman's.

Then there was Professor Weingart. The Professor gave me an appreciation of music and the performance of it that I had not thought possible. Her erotic descriptions of the pieces and how to play them had carbonated the hormones of hundreds of students over the years. None of us who had heard her description of Beethoven's Ninth would ever be the same. We would expect more from ourselves as musicians, performers, and people. Unfortunately, for all our future partners, we would expect more love, passion, romance, and up-against-the-wall hoopty than we would have had we never heard her riotous and luscious lectures.

I needed to make them proud, especially since I had to blip out right afterward, and I'd be gone for at least a year. It takes time to learn battle magics so you don't blow yourself up and take everyone else with you. And healing workings take almost as much time. Classes would start in Core City tomorrow morning. And if I knew Wisteria, I'd better not be late.

For the umpteenth time today, I sighed.

"Evie!" Joanna hurried toward me with her arms extended. She enveloped me in a tight hug. "You look beautiful!"

"Thanks, love." I smoothed my shimmering skirt and ran my hands up and down my arms.

"Are you cold?" Daniel appeared as if by magic and draped his jacket over my shoulders.

"Daniel. Hi." I turned my face to his, and we kissed.

"You are going to own this place, tonight," he whispered. "You will do the Professor proud."

"Oh sweetie, you always know just what to say," I wrapped my arms around him and inhaled his spicy scent. I released him and smiled at them. "All right you two, it's not like I am about to walk the plank or anything," I laughed.

I walked to grand piano that waited at the end of the small room. I caressed its exquisite black finish and paid my respects.

Professor Weingart met me in front of the grand. Her iron-gray hair sat in a bun at the back of her head. She wore a tailored suit, and looked the stern patrician. Then, she held her hands out to me and smiled. And, I noticed a discreet flower tucked behind one ear.

"Evie," she took my hands. "Congratulations. You have done so very well."

"Ladies and Gentlemen, welcome," she turned to the audience. "Today, we will have the pleasure of hearing the last Juilliard recital of one of our most dedicated students, Ms. Eveningstar Songbottom. The winner of last year's Mason Tripplehorn Piano Competition, she has prepared a wonderful program for this evening. We expect many more performances from her unparalleled perspective. You will see that her interpretations of the compositions herald the great composers themselves. It is as though they have been whispering in her ear," she gave a small laugh.

I looked around to make sure no one noticed any of the composers hanging about the room. Likely, Joanna would see

THE PIANO'S KEY

them but everyone else would remain oblivious. Since Joanna was made of magic, she could see all of us from the Magic Realms and she easily accepted all the fairies, elves, ghosts, and brownies. When she stopped being able to see them last year, all hell had broken loose. It had been a job to set it all back to rights. Luckily, she'd done it, but still ....

"Without further ado," the Professor continued. "Ladies and Gentlemen, Please welcome, Ms. Eveningstar Songbottom."

"Thank you, Professor," I said.

As she returned to her seat in the front row, I rounded the piano and sat down on the black, rectangular bench. I looked up and acknowledged the maestros. Liszt, Rachmaninov, and Chopin, my three favorites of all time, floated near the ceiling in the corner of the room. Dressed in various fashions from the last few hundred years, they were translucent but visible, if you knew how to look for them.

"Thank you," I mouthed at the ghosts of my mentors and friends. Contrary to popular opinion, ghosts aren't here to haunt us. In fact, generally, they're taking a vacation from wherever they have been since they stopped being tangibly three-dimensional. Sometimes, they're pissed and have a bone to pick with someone. Sometimes, they exhibit a warped sense of humor and prank those still living on this Earth plane. But usually, they're tourists.

My three favorite composers had made the journey to hear me play their stuff. That knowledge brought a tear to my eye and a few more hundred butterflies to my belly. Now I had to be great, or they would never let me hear the end of it.

I placed my fingers on the single E that begins the ride and took a deep breath. "Here goes nothing."

Chopin's "Winter Wind Etude:" a waterfall of rushing, dissonant sound, driving blizzard, sometimes a geyser that wings you up and then crashes you to the ground. It drops you over a cliff when the wind howls and the driving snow engulfs everything. Runs of notes flooded out of my fingers. The storms flung me like a rag doll being thrown by an enraged child.

And now, for a last surprise: Liszt's "Totentanz." It begins where it ends, on a simple D. But, oh the ride! Roiling, boiling, frenetic motion – it is underscored by the heavy, pounding footsteps of some giant devil and a fairy's lightest touch upon your cheek. Those are juxtaposed with striking, throbbing heartbeats. The echoes of simple country melodies float into and through the infernal sounds. The last minute of the piece climbs melodic mountains. They rise craggy and rough into the heavens. The notes soar across turbulent skies. No wonder they call it "Danse Macabre." It does that most terrible of things. It gives you a scrap of hope.

I struck the last unison octaves on D keys and released the keys immediately. Liszt once mentioned to me that he never intended for the notes to be held. "That is why I wrote it as a quarter note. You strike the keys and then you must allow the music to be complete. To do otherwise, is to belabor the point," he once said to me over a cognac. When it's done, let it be done. "To do otherwise, is to belabor the point." Words to live by.

I took my last bows at Juilliard. Smiling, the Professor approached the small stage.

"Just wonderful, Evie," she said. "And thank you for my surprise. The passion with which you flew on the Totentanz will sustain me for a long time." She wiped at her eyes. "Eveningstar, I will miss you."

"Oh don't worry, Professor," I replied. "I expect I'll be around. But now, I've got to go." I threw my arms around her. "You can't know how much you've taught me, especially since I didn't think anyone could."

"Well, Evie," she straightened herself and rearranged her smart, gray suit jacket. "I am pleased to hear it. I'm sure your next phase will bring you many new challenges."

"You don't know the half of it," I answered. "I only hope I'm up to it."

"You'll knock 'em dead," she said.

"Thanks, Professor. That means a lot."

"Evie, you were wonderful." Joanna ran up and wrapped me in a tight hug. "Sorry to interrupt, Professor," she apologized. "I just couldn't help myself."

"I understand completely," the Professor replied. "I'll be off."

Everyone surrounded me with congratulations like in some musical Rocky remake. Before I knew it, it was time to head out.

Jo, Daniel, and I stood on the steps to nowhere outside Juilliard's main building. The city's night sounds rushed by us. I took both their hands in mine.

"Okay, I've got to go. But I'll be back before you can say, 'I love 80s movies,'" I promised myself as much as them.

"You sure will," Joanna squeezed my hand in sympathy. "And now, I'd better leave before I start blubbering. I know how much you hate that." She hugged me and left.

"You be good," Daniel admonished me.

"You'd better not tell me not to do anything you wouldn't do because, you know, that list would be pretty damn long."

"And I know you'd do them all anyway." He smiled at me, cupped my cheek with his hand and brought his lips to mine. "Now, go kick some Level 4 butt," he said.

I soared on a haze of lust. What can I say? He makes me squelchy. I opened my eyes, looked into his steady brown ones, and caressed his cheek. "Kickin' ass and takin' names. Yep, that's me. Okay, Daniel." I had stalled long enough. "I'll see you on the flip side."

I stepped back from him and into the shadows under the stairs to nowhere. I touched my wand and blipped up to my room in the Rose building. Another flick of my wand packed my clothes, sheet music, and keyboard. I floated everything up to hand height and grabbed it. I looked around the room one last time.

"Lots of memories," I sighed. I inscribed a sigil and opened a small portal to Core City. "Time to make new ones," I stepped through.

CHAPTER 2

My apartment in the heart of Core City looked the same as the last time I was home. My big, indulgent purple velvet couch sat diagonally to the two windows that met in the corner of the living room. My kitchen remained spotlessly clean and forever unused.

I started when distinct puttering noises emanated from the area roughly in the vicinity of my sink. A titter split the silence.

"Hark, who goes there?" I intoned. "Beware! For I am large and full of malice."

"Shh," came from within the kitchen. "She'll hear us."

I tiptoed to the kitchen doorway and flicked the light switch. Bright light bathed the room. The two candles that had stood lit in the center of the counter burst brightly and then flicked out as the two Fire Elemental Fairies who had been hiding inside them disappeared. After a few seconds, the white pillar candle relit. Torlyn Sunrider, Fire Elemental and dear friend, peeked out of the flame. Her younger sister Leili appeared in the other candle's glow. She had a hard time staying hidden within the flame and an even harder time suppressing her giggles. Leili had grabbed the unexamined life with gusto after last year's troubles had turned her into an actual firefly. The more wild the ride, the more outrageous the stunt, the more Leili wanted a piece of it. Fire Fairies. Go figure.

Elemental Fairies, Fire Fairies and Water Fairies, are actually made of the stuff. Sure, they can walk and talk, but their essence is the Element they're made of, if you see what I mean. So, Leili was always going to be creative, fiery, passionate, and sometimes destructive. Luckily, she had Torlyn to help keep her on the straight and relatively narrow. At least, I hoped she would.

While I waxed philosophical on Elemental Fairies and their role in the universe, a small puddle had formed on the blue pearl granite countertop.

"Tsk," I tutted as I reached for a hand towel. "How did that spill get there? I'd better clean that up."

The titters now reached gargantuan guffaw proportions as Ashlyn vainly tried to hush her sister. "Fiora," Ashlyn stage whispered. "You'll give it all away."

"What! Who is that?" I searched the room and rolled the towel up into a makeshift weapon.

"Evie," Fiora lifted her watery face out of the puddle. A young water fairy, she looked like flowing water that was contained in some kind of invisible person suit. Water moved through her and formed her, from her small dolphin-like tail to the tips of her ears. See, Water Elemental fairies are just that. They are water come to life.

"Evie," she repeated. "It's us."

"Aaaahhh," I mock screamed and put my considerable pipes into my shriek. I jumped back and clutched my hands in front of my chest.

"Fiora, you scared me!" I panted. I smacked my palms to my cheeks in surprise. "What could you possibly be doing here? Tonight? When you know that I have to get up early to start my Level 4 Training?" I stood ramrod straight at this last bit and lifted my nose as high in the air as my five feet two inches would let me. "You know I must be adequately prepared and well-rested in order to fully absorb the wisdom they will impart to me." The Chief's florid tones were easy to mimic and Fiora and Leili rolled in fits of giggles. "Ah, to heck with it," I abandoned the charade. "Let's drink!"

"Yes!" Torlyn sprung out of her candle flame, waved a hand, and lit every candle in the place.

"Finally, she's speaking sense," Clementine Robinbutter appeared in the kitchen doorway. A small, lean, cooking machine, she had cut her long curling strawberry blond hair into a smart bob and her green eyes shone with mischief.

She waved her silver spoon shaped wand in the direction of the counter, and a veritable feast appeared. A giant, purple Orroyo nut held small chocolate mousse cups on its many petals. The petal above each mousse dropped gold-colored sugar dust onto each cup. It would add the flavor the eater most wanted to taste. A rainbow of fruit from the farthest reaches of our land floated above a small waterfall of caramel. To eat, we'd need to pluck a fruit bit, dunk into the caramel and get it into our mouths before the cloud creating the rainbow moved over us and soaked us. Not that the Water Fairies would mind, but I didn't relish being sopping wet when I tried to get my drunk butt to bed sometime tonight.

Other mouthwatering dishes sat along the counter. One giant Tully's sub held court on the oak table that sat tucked in the corner of the kitchen. Clementine grabbed the sub, popped some plates into her other hand, and moved into the living room.

"Hurry up," she called from the other room. "It's going to get cold."

My smile faded. I missed Jo. And Daniel.

I moved to the cabinet and removed a small, turquoise saucer. I filled it with cream and healthy dollop of Amaretto and set it in front of the smaller fairies. The two younger Elementals fell on the concoction.

Torlyn Sunrider and Ashlyn Brookbearer, their older sisters, perched at the edge of the counter and mirrored each other's crossed arms and raised eyebrows.

Guilt sat on my face like too much blush, and I turned away from their knowing looks.

"What?" I turned back after I had reassembled my features into a too-wide grin.

"Evie," Torlyn floated up to my eye level. "They're going to be fine. He's going to be fine."

"I know," I sniffled. Yes! Me! I actually sniffled! "But, after last year, you can't blame me if I worry about them a little."

"No one's blaming you," Ashlyn shook her water head. "But the Magistrate has taken precautions. Nothing like that will ever happen again. And besides, Joanna is doing really well."

"True," I sniffed again and then raised my head. "True. I'm going to see to it."

"Uh oh," Torlyn said. "She's got a plan."

"Yep. I do. I'm just going to postpone Level 4 training for another year and head back to New York. It's just another year. I'm sure the Chief will understand … "

"Yeah, right," Clementine walked back into the kitchen. "Because they hand out Level 4 promotions every other day. Evie, you're already behind all the other trainees. You should stay here and complete your Level 4s. Then you'll be better able to protect them both, right?"

"I guess you're right," I conceded, still unhappy.

"Good," she handed me a shot glass full of a turquoise liquid. Veins of a more viscous, silvery liquid ran through the drink.

"Seriously?" I accepted the glass and raised my eyebrows. "You think I need a shot of 'Calm-the-Fek-Down' juice?"

"Don't you," Clementine shot back. "You are obviously tweaked and stressed."

"Look," I argued. "If I want to postpone my training for a year, it's my business."

Clementine skewered me with her green eyes. "No, it's not. You might think so, but it is really isn't. A lot of us have a lot invested in you getting properly trained. So you'd better just go and do it."

"What the hell are you talking about?" I shouted.

"I'm talking about Creative Fae getting promoted," she yelled. "Do you realize how long it's been since anyone who is musical or artistic in any way has been promoted to Level 4? It's been practically forever. The last time was before Mozart was born."

"What?" I gasped. "No it wasn't. Why it's only been … um … er." I quieted and thought about it. Shit! She was right. The last few hundred years had been focused on the more industry-oriented Fairy Godparents. There were few artistic FGs at the highest levels. Most were administrators and thinkers. Few were the creative and chaotic types, and even fewer were as messy as me.

I collapsed on my couch and stared out the window.

"So, what do you want me to do about it?" I grumped.

Clementine sat beside me and faced me. "Get trained," she said. "Get trained and show them that an Artistic Godparent can do great things as well as an Industrious Godparent." She slanted her eyes at me. "You don't want Parsnipa to get ahead of you, do you?"

"What!" I sprang up. "What are you talking about?"

"Oh, didn't you know?"

"Know what?" I ground out.

"Well," Clementine drew the words out. "You took off so quickly for your year off, and you were so busy during those first few months of wild monkey sex with Daniel that you likely never got the news. Parsnipa was promoted to Level 4 almost eleven months ago."

"No way!" I cried. "They would never." Parsnipa Roadspinner, bane to good times everywhere, had been a thorn in my side for the last two hundred years. She was starched, ramrod straight, and a major pain in my butt. I had beat her for Joanna's guardianship in the Pangenicum, but just barely.

"They would and they did," Clementine continued. "It seems she was so upset that you got promoted, and she raged so much about it that it tipped the scales of Complex Emotions and unlocked that achievement. That was the last thing she needed to be promoted, so they gave it to her. She's been off on her vacation, but I hear she came back early."

"So, that means … "

" … That she will be in class with you tomorrow?" Clementine finished my sentence. "Yes, it does. And that means that you'd better be there, and you'd better kick her ass all over that Training Stadium."

"When did you become so uppity?"

"I had an excellent teacher," she smiled and laid her hand on my shoulder. "Seriously, Evie. Much as I hate to say it, you really do have a responsibility to do this."

I was curious about something. "How did you figure it out? About the Industry Fae versus the Creative Fae, I mean?" I asked.

Clementine cocked her head and thought for a moment. "I guess I have a lot of time to think. You spend a lot of time waiting when you cook. You wait for cakes to rise. You wait for sauces to soak in all the herby goodness. And I've been spending my free time thinking. Reading and thinking."

"You'll have to show me what you've read," I stated.

"Sure," she replied. "The next time you have a break, we'll sit down, and I'll show you what I've got."

"That's settled then," I turned to the other Fae in the room. "Sorry, y'all," I said.

"We get it, Evie." Torlyn replied. Ashlyn nodded her watery head. Fiora was busy swimming in the punch bowl full of glowing Star Fruit and had ignored the exchange. Leili focused on my face.

"You'll need to kick ass, and make it count, Evie," she stated.

I raised my glass of CTFD. "To kicking ass and making it count," I shouted.

"Remember to stir it counter-clockwise before you drink or you'll be awake, pissed, and berserk for the next six weeks," Clementine admonished me.

"And we don't want that," I answered. I stirred the glass counter-clockwise. The silver liquid spread out into the turquoise and swirled into a shimmering waterfall of what looked like tiny fluid Native American rings.

"No, we don't," Clementine agreed as we all drank.

"Unless we do," Leili murmured. She retreated to her candle. "Unless we do."

CHAPTER 3

I managed to be vertical and conscious ten minutes before class. I stood at the door of the training colosseum and gathered my bits and pieces.

"Might as well get to it," I cleared the last of the cobwebs and pushed through the door. The door smacked me on the butt as it slammed shut.

Crap! This did not bode well.

Thwack! Thunk! Zweeoot! The sounds of sparring wands zinged throughout the cavernous room. Tall brick walls showed the black and jagged scars from deflected fire bolts. Some were probably bolts that had missed their mark as many FGs had no aptitude for the rough stuff until they were trained. But some trainees took to battle magic like sailors to sirens once they got the hang of it. Deflecting a bolt coming at you is as important as knowing how and when to fire. But, in the moment, often it's blind luck.

Five trainees squatted, floated, or stood among various structures, armaments, pieces of equipment, and sofas in the center of the round hall. Two students I had never met trained at the equipment. Floating spherical targets appeared and disappeared around them at random intervals. Sometimes they appeared solid, sometimes they were liquid, and at other times they reflected the room. It looked like whoever didn't get shot by the other combatant and hit one of those suckers would win each round.

One of the spheres snuck behind a combatant and sprayed orange goo down the back of her shirt.

"Argggh! I'm on fire!" She sprang from behind a worn, antique dresser and pawed at her back. Her opponent zapped her square in the chest with a violet colored light bolt.

"Point to Parsifal Ribbonthrasher," the tall redhead strode across the floor, her long, sinewy arms propelling her forward and her red braid swinging behind. No, wait. Wisteria didn't so much move as prowl. One minute you thought she was in front of you and coming right at you. The next she had snuck behind you and dropped you on your ass in the dirt.

"Halt!" Her voice carried over the din of moving machines and rolling air currents.

In her black army pants and tank top, she looked like a badass paratrooper who had just parachuted into the enemy camp in the middle of the jungle. A cheetah sidekick would complete the picture.

She stopped in front of the poor trainee who was still trying to douse the metaphoric flames licking at her backside.

"Be still!" Wisteria said.

The trainee came to a standstill.

"Do you know what you did wrong?" Wisteria demanded. "Do you know how you screwed up and just got everyone around you killed?"

"I ... I," the trainee stammered and shrank from the Mistress of Battle Magic. Now, here's the thing. It's not like this she was some sort of newbie Level One or even Level Two. She had been promoted to Level 4. So, she knew something about something. But better and stronger trainees than her had withered under the steely glance of the Predator. Yep, that's what we'd called Wisteria in the Academy. If you didn't know her, you had heard of her. If you did know her, you spent a hell of a lot of time cursing the day you had met.

"I ... I what?" Wisteria demanded. "I ... I am an idiot? I ... I can't focus? I ... I'm dead? Yes, you are. All three," she jeered. "If you can't accept your situation and maintain focus, you will die." She crossed her hands in front of her chiseled abs and stared down at her victim. "If you can't survive a little hot pepper, how the hell are you going to survive a real burning?" She closed her right fist and pumped it once. Her fingers flew open and a jet of red gold flame jetted out of her hand.

"Come on, Adelheid," she goaded. She wielded the flame before her.

Adelheid shrank back. As Wisteria advanced, she backed up further. Her wand fell to the floor. Her eyes shot back and forth around the gym. She felt behind her and connected with the arm of someone standing behind a pillar. Adelheid pulled on the arm.

"Oh no, Godmother Bierfarthing." The would-be rescuer tore out of Adelheid's grasp. "I will not get involved. It is your responsibility to fight your own battles."

Crap! I'd know that peevish voice anywhere. Parsnipa Roadspinner! For a minute, I'd forgotten that she would be here. The other two trainees stood statue still and avoided Adelheid's panicked eyes like vampires avoid sunlight.

I narrowed my eyes and studied Adelheid. She was slight. Her shining blond hair sat atop her head in a braided bun and her cornflower blue eyes screamed terror.

"Entschuldigung," Adelheid excused herself in her native German. "I did try, Godmother Flamethrower. Entschuldigung," her tears flowed.

Adelheid Bierfarthing. I remembered her. She loved nothing more than a good beer and a wood burning stove to drink it around. She had achieved Level Four status decades ago by helping topple some wall somewhere. But she hadn't been able to graduate to Level Four Active Duty because Battle Magics stymied her like the proverbial Gordian Knot.

"Excuses don't mean squat," Wisteria advanced on her. She drew back her arm, and the flame retreated into her hand. The Flame Thrower, her signature move, and we all knew it -

that is, all of us except Adelheid. She made the fatal mistake of thinking Wisteria meant to show her any kind of mercy.

I put my bag on the floor. My wand appeared in my hand.

I maneuvered around the obstacles in the room and flanked Wisteria.

The flame in her hand strengthened. It sat in her hand like a tiny, vengeful sun. While she talked, she tossed it into the air and tested its weight.

"What would you do if you had been protecting a charge?" She sneered.

"I ... I," Adelheid stammered.

"You will never learn," Wisteria shook her head. "And that means you'll graduate when Hell freezes over. And I can't have that."

Wisteria closed her hand. The flame extinguished. We all breathed a sigh of relief. She snapped her fingers and the flame reignited. She pitched it at Adelheid's head. It sizzled over our heads in a shallow arch straight towards Adelheid.

When Hell freezes over.

"Hey!" I shouted. I threw everything I had into that thought. My wand took my thoughts and made them real. It shot out a stream of ice. The fireball and ice shards exploded against one another in midair. The resulting rainstorm gushed down on us. It soaked the entire room in a single second.

"What the Hell!" Wisteria whirled around. Her lips thinned into a tight, white line. She leaned back and flared her nostrils like a puma scenting prey. Her fingers opened and closed as she prepped another fireball.

I managed to stand my ground, and I credit myself with appearing not to cower. In the moment though, I was grateful I hadn't peed my pants.

"Well, well," she advanced on me.

"Eveningstar Songbottom. They'd told me you had been promoted, but I didn't believe it for a second."

"Believe it." Did my voice just quake?

As she moved toward me, I retreated, but I tried to do it casual-like. I wasn't afraid of her. No sir. I was just getting the lay of the land.

I raised my wand and moved into the center of the huge gymnasium. Why had I not noticed before that it was huge and practically empty? It provided almost no cover. I had nowhere to run or hide. In fact, the few pieces of equipment in the place could prove to be better weapons than protection if Wisteria decided to pick one of them up and hurl it at me a la Darth Vader at the end of Empire Strikes Back. Shit! Now that I had thought of that possibility, every box, block, column, and pillar transformed into a deadly projectile.

"Look, Wisteria," I raised my hands and lowered my wand simultaneously. "This doesn't have to get uncomfortable."

"Oh doesn't it," her lips creased in what could pass for a smile on a beautiful demon. She wove around me in the back and forth movement of a martial arts Master. Her totem animal was the cheetah for a reason. She raised her wand and flicked it in my direction.

"Ouch," the scarlet bolt seared my butt. I rubbed my ass and turned my body to match her as she prowled around me. I bent my knees and tried to make myself a smaller target. She blasted two bolts: one high, one low. I threw myself out of their path and rolled to standing behind a scarred armoire. I bent in half and peeked out from behind it. Dammit! Where was she? Another bolt blazed by me from behind. I whirled. I drew my wand, but I was too slow and way too late.

With blinding speed, she rolled and came up in a crouch. Her wand spat out a length of rope. One end twined around my feet, tightened, and strung me up. The other attached itself to the ceiling.

"Crap!" I swung like the timer in a grandfather clock. Somehow, I held on to my wand.

Wisteria straightened. "If any of you helps her break the spell, you will answer to me." She gave a curt nod. "Class dismissed."

They all filed out before the Amazon from Hell. Adelheid looked at me with watery eyes. I shook my head and silently encouraged her to go. When it was just Wisteria and I left in the room, she flipped off the lights and walked out the door. She stopped one of the massive doors with only her foot and looked up at me in the darkness.

"Have a nice day, Songbottom," she called up to me. "Tomorrow, we get to work."

As my body stopped swinging, I put my wand away. Wisteria held a grudge. If I moved from this spot, it was going to be a lot worse than if I stayed here and took my medicine. The next twenty-four hours would be spent hanging upside down. I could be making fondue with Daniel, but no, I'd decided to come back here and complete my training. What an idiot!

"Crap!" I yelled again. It was going to be a long night.

CHAPTER 4

DANIEL

Daniel Evershed sprawled on the threadbare couch that served as his dining room, living room, and bed. He glanced around the tiny basement apartment that held everything he owned. The bathroom contained his dark room and was fully outfitted to print any black and white photo. Like every other Photography Master's graduate of NYU, he had multiple digital cameras or DSLRs at his disposal. But he loved film more. He considered his best shots ones that he had taken his trusty Canon AE-1 Program.

The candle on the coffee table lit by itself. The warm glow suffused the small room. A tiny, fiery face peered out at him from within the fire.

"Good morning Torlyn," he called. The Fire Fairy's entrances and exits via candle flame no longer surprised him although the first time she had appeared by stepping out of a candle flame he had dropped an entire pot of spaghetti.

Torlyn stepped out of the candle and formed into herself.

"Hi Daniel," she said. She watched him with glowing, hawk-like eyes but remained silent.

"Oh!" Daniel realized what was happening. "Torlyn, did Evie ask you to check in on me?"

"Well," she hesitated and retreated toward the candle flame.

"It's okay," he encouraged her. "You can tell me."

"Yes," she nodded. "She is worried about how things are going to go if she isn't here."

"And she asked you to look in on me." He smiled. "She and you are very sweet. As you can see, I'm fine. You don't really need to waste your time babysitting me." Daniel stood and moved toward the bathroom. "You know, I was taking pretty good care of myself before I met her. Really, you don't need to look in on me."

"But, that was before …"

"Before Zeke," Daniel finished for her. "Yes, I know."

"And, Evie just wants to be sure that he isn't going to try anything."

Daniel moved over to the table and crouched down next to her. "Torlyn, I'm fine. Don't I look fine?"

"Yes," she hesitated again.

"I'm just going on a job interview today, and then I'll be coming straight home," he tried not to smile at the bizarre picture he must be making right now. He was crouching next to a little female made of fire as he tried to convince her not to watch over him while she tried to do a favor for his Fairy Godmother girlfriend.

"Seriously, Torlyn," he said. "I'm going to be okay."

"If you're sure," she sounded dubious.

"He's sure," Leili had popped in through the same candle. She floated on lazy air currents.

"He's a big boy," she continued. "He can take care of himself."

"Thanks, Leili," Daniel smiled pleased that someone believed he could fend for himself. "Okay, now I really need to go or I'm going to be late." He looked around the cramped apartment. "Feel free to hang out as long as you like, but please douse the candle when you go."

He grabbed his canvas camera bag and his portfolio and left the apartment.

A fast subway ride brought him to Times Square and the offices of NewsBlitz.biz. A small, start-up news website, they specialized in New York City life, politics, and economics.

Daniel rode the small, rickety elevator to the eighth floor. The red door at the end of the hall held a small blue sign with the NewsBlitz.Biz logo emblazoned on it.

He pushed open the door and entered.

"I don't care what he said," a man yelled. "I think they got that contract illegally. Find out. Seriously. I'm not running word one until I have proof."

Daniel stood in the doorway to the one-room newsroom. Three desks sat in the cramped room. Two held a few papers, the day's New York Times, and laptop computers. The tall, muscular man who was yelling paced a figure eight around them. "Get it done," he gesticulated. He pushed the End button on his phone and dropped it on his desk.

Daniel took the opportunity to enter the room.

"Hi, you must be Tom St. James?" He moved forward and extended his hand. "I'm Daniel Evershed."

"What do you want?" St. James glanced him over and continued pressing buttons on his phone.

"We had an interview at noon today, for the photojournalist position." Daniel moved further into the room. He placed his portfolio on the empty one of the three cramped desks.

"Oh, sorry. Tom St. James." He shook Daniel's outstretched hand. His phone chirped, and he read the incoming text. "Hang on a minute," he shot off a rapid-fire response and stored the phone in his pants pocket. "So, what are we talking about here?" Another text beeped. This time he ignored it. His blue eyes focused on Daniel.

"An interview. My interview, for the photojournalist position."

"Oh yeah, right. Right. So, let's see your stuff." Tom rushed to the empty desk and opened the portfolio. He flipped through the pages of black and white images. He stopped at an arresting image of a woman who sat in a chair on the corner of Nassau and Wall Streets, near the entrance of the New York Stock Exchange. Her face was set in serene repose. Her clothes, although tattered, were clean. In her lap, a sign read, "For today, let what you already have be enough." The Stock Exchange loomed behind her.

"This one," Tom said. "This one is good. When did you take this? What did you use? What equipment? What F-Stop?" He scattershot the questions at Daniel.

"Last May, Canon AE-1 Program, no tripod, freehand, F-stop 32."

"Did you get her permission to use her image?"

"Yes."

"Let's see the photographic release form," Tom said.

"Turn the page," Daniel answered. On the following page, the woman's scrawling signature appeared on a form titled "Video and Photographic Release."

"Good." Tom nodded and perused the portfolio. He stopped at another image of a neighborhood basketball game. Two players were jumping for an errant ball. One's elbow was connecting solidly with the other's face. On the facing page, the same two players shook hands.

"What about these two?"

"Two weeks ago, the same Canon camera, freehand, F-stop 32. Shutter speed 1/250th of a second."

"Good thing it was a bright day," Tom commented.

"You know cameras?" Daniel asked.

"You'll find I know a little bit about everything but a lot about nothing. Now, tell me about this one," they continued in this vein throughout most of the rest of the portfolio. Tom asked probing questions. No detail was too small for debate or discussion.

They took a break after an hour.

Tom sat on the desk and propped himself up on his straight arms.

"So, Daniel, why do you want to work here? And don't give me the 'I believe in what you're doing' crap. Tell me the truth."

"I love taking pictures. I love this city. I want to use what I can do to make a difference," Daniel stated.

"Seriously? That's your answer?" Tom laughed. He stopped, looked at Daniel again, and guffawed.

"It's the truth." Daniel settled in to wait out the laughing fit.

After a minute, the giggles faded, and Tom stilled.

"Wait, you're serious," his voice quieted.

"I am."

Tom opened the portfolio and gazed at the first image for a long time. He nodded his head once and hopped off the desk. He sped over to the small coffeemaker on top of the filing cabinet and poured himself a drink. He downed it in one gulp.

"Man, that coffee sucks, but the caffeine does the job. Want some? Never mind. No one should have to suffer that sludge." Tom's words rushed over each other like a waterfall after heavy rains.

"Okay, so, here's what I'm going to need from you," he continued. "I need someone who will be everywhere at once. I need someone who can go to all parts of this city and capture the rough, the tumble, the news. Make it timely. Make it good, and make it real, and we'll be good." He poured more sludge and downed it. "You'll sit there," he pointed to the empty desk. "Are you going to need a computer?"

Dazed, Daniel nodded his assent.

"Good. Okay. I'll take care of that." Tom pressed a button on his phone. "Tell Phil we need a new computer. Mac okay with you?" He shrugged his head in Daniel's direction.

"Mac's fine." Daniel replied.

"Great. Okay," he spoke into the phone again. "Make it a Mac. Set it up and get in here by tomorrow. Oh and we'll need a printer and a scanner dedicated to him." He hung up the phone.

"So, wait," Daniel cleared his throat. "Does this mean I have the job?"

Tom opened his brown eyes wide. He stared at Daniel. "Did I forget to say that? I thought I said that."

"No," Daniel supplied. "You hadn't said that."

Tom dropped in his chair, leaned back, and stared up.

Daniel followed his eyes and saw the huge Goodnight and Good Luck movie poster that took up most of the ceiling. David Straitharian's cloaked black and white face gazed down at him.

"All the news that's fit to print and then some," Tom said by way of explanation. "He helps me think. Do you like Scotch?" He swerved onto a new topic of conversation.

"Depends on the company," Daniel hesitated. He remembered all too well the last time he had drunk Scotch. Zeke had almost killed him that night.

"Great. Come with me to my father's place tonight. He's having a wine and scotch tasting followed by a billiard tournament. It'll be a great place to make some contacts."

"Okay, where is it?" Daniel asked.

"Oh, it's at 235 West 57th." Tom said. He raced toward the door.

"If you get there before I do, just ask the doorman for the St. James Liquor party. He'll let you in.

Daniel stopped short at the elevator as the information sank in.

"Wait a minute," he said. "Your father is Mitchell St. James of St. James Liquors?"

"The very same," Tom answered.

"So, you're Tommy St. James," Daniel put two and two together. St. James's Liquors was the biggest Scotch and Whiskey distributor in the world. Mitchell St. James had built the company from nothing and still ruled it with an iron fist. Tommy St. James had been a fixture on the New York party scene for the previous fifteen years. Then, suddenly, a few years ago, he had left the scene completely. No one had heard from him since.

"So, if you don't mind my asking," Daniel said. "Why are you doing news? I don't mean to be crass, but it's not like you need to work."

"Actually, I do need to work," Tom's eyes hooded. "People like me especially need to work."

"If you don't mind my asking," Daniel repeated himself. "What happened?"

"Maybe someday I'll tell you."

"All right," Daniel backed off. Then, another thought struck him. "So, how did I get the job?"

Tom stopped in mid-stride. "It looks like you've always had the job. We just didn't know it yet." Then, he laughed and pushed Daniel out the door ahead of him. "Now, let's go get all pretty for the cameras."

"Pretty for the cameras?" Daniel stammered.

"Sure! Do you think this is just a party?" Tom laughed. "Oh no. We're going to get ourselves a marketing blitz. And if everyone thinks you're my new boyfriend, so much the better."

"What are you talking about?" Daniel asked.

Tom had started down the stairs to the street. He looked at Daniel behind him as he explained. "Look, you know who my father is. And you know we have a lot of money. And I've spent more than my share. So, everyone expects me to keep right on doing that. But, I've got a little surprise in store them."

"And that is?"

"You're going to think it's stupid but it's all about Goodnight and Good Luck. I saw that movie. I saw how all they wanted was the truth and I got it, you know? I got that the truth is all that matters. So now, I want to find and spread the truth."

"That's great," Daniel said. "But what does that have to do with getting pretty for the cameras?"

"They all think that I'm just a big party animal who likes pretty boys. And they're mostly right." Tom chewed on his lower lip and then smiled. "I do like pretty boys, but that's no longer the only thing I like. There will be a lot of power players there tonight. And, if they think we're just a couple of idiots who couldn't find their dicks with both hands, then, we'll be able to get in there and get the news."

They reached the front door of the building and exited. Daniel paused just outside the building and gazed along 48th street to the West Side Highway. Too much of his life had been spent hiding truths for the last year. He was in love with a Fairy for Pete's sake. And his mom had been hinting that it was time to meet her. Could he seek the truth in others while he couldn't be entirely truthful himself?

"Okay," he decided. "I want to go get some shots down in Chelsea on the way home, but I'll try to figure out a way to get pretty for the cameras."

Tom gave him a long, measured look. "Wow. You have no idea how pretty you already are, do you?"

"Um."

Tom barked a sharp, bright laugh. "Your girlfriend is one lucky lady."

Daniel stumbled and pushed his glasses back up his nose. "She is lucky, but it's got nothing to do with me. And I'm not sure I could ever call her a lady and get away with it."

Tom laughed again. "Oh, this one I'd like to meet."

"Wait, how did you know I have a girlfriend?"

"Are you serious?" Tom asked. He peered at Daniel. "Have you seen you? No, obviously you haven't," he answered his own question. "Fantastic!" He grinned. "Simply fantastic!"

He hooked his arm through Daniel's and they turned east toward the center of the Theater District. Tom studied him again. "Hell," he said. "You can come as you are, Daniel. Now, I need a drink."

Daniel slowed and thought about the easiest way to say what he needed to say. "Isn't it a little early?"

Tom barked out a laugh. "I meant coffee. Honey, I've had access to all the liquor I could ever want since I've been five years old. I haven't touched the stuff in years."

"Sorry," Daniel said.

"It's okay. Everyone else thinks I'm a drunk, why shouldn't you? But that's the way I like it."

"Why is that," Daniel asked.

"Because if they think I'm drunk, they aren't so careful about what they say around me. Oh and by the way, when we are around my family tonight, you'll want to call me Tommy. None of them know I go by Tom now. And you won't be 'in' unless you know to call me Tommy."

"How long has it been," Daniel asked.

"About two years," Tommy replied.

"All right, Tommy, I'll be there." Daniel grinned.

"Oh, baby," Tommy said. "They aren't going to know what hit them. I'll meet you at the front of the building at nine."

The Holy Apostles Soup Kitchen sat at the edge of the Projects in Chelsea. Situated at the corner of West 28th Street and 9th Avenue, it was the largest food outreach program in the city. Men and women roamed the grounds. A few worked in the small but vibrant community garden that sat in one of the recesses of the building. The vegetables and herbs grew, somehow, despite the shade. Daniel studied the garden. Tiny lights winked in and out and about the workers. Daniel smiled and moved closer to a concentration of the lights. A woman wearing a "Feed the World" t-shirt knelt at a corner of the garden. She added a small amount of rich, dark compost in a circle around each of the new shoots of some sort of leafy green lettuce and patted down the new soil. As she turned away to reach for a tall, metal watering can, several of the lights burrowed into the compost and down into the loamy soil. The soil shifted as if a whole bunch of worms had suddenly decided to aerate that one plot of land. The tinkling sound of giggling emanated from the soil.

Daniel crouched a few feet away from the woman and what he felt certain were Seed Fairies.

"Excuse me," he called. "What plants are those?"

"Kale," the woman answered. She pushed her curly, gray hair out of her eyes. She turned back toward the shoots of green and gave them a thorough watering.

"Would you mind if I snapped a few shots of you working?" Daniel asked.

"What for?" the woman inquired.

"I work for News Blitz. We're doing a story on the two New Yorks."

"Just two," she laughed. "I'd say there are more like 186 of them."

"True," he answered. "But I'm focusing on just two."

"So, which one is this?"

"I'd say this is the one where people need help and other people help them," Daniel replied.

She laughed again. "You're a charmer."

"Thanks," he smiled. "So, can I snap a few shots?"

"Sure, as long as I can keep working. I have to spread compost on this whole corner before I'm done for the day."

"Does it help with the growing process?"

"It's been a miracle," she answered. "Ever since we started using it, the plants have been growing, well, like weeds."

Since he knew what to listen for, Daniel heard the high titters coming from the soil. Laughing, the Seed Fairies burrowed to the next patch of vegetables to give them their blessings and encourage them to grow. To regular people, they appeared like dandelion fuzz floating on the breeze. To Daniel, they glowed with that inner magical flame of all fairies.

"We have a lot of people to feed every day," she continued. "So, it's great the plants seem to be doing okay with so little sun. We're very lucky." She shaded her eyes and looked up at the sliver of blue sky visible between buildings.

"Yes, I'm sure that's it," Daniel agreed. He snapped photos of her working. A tiny, reddish brown Seed Fairy landed on her right shoulder and waved at him. The viewfinder of his camera reflected her glow and made her look like a bit of fuzz caught on the t-shirt.

Probably all to the good, Daniel thought as he thanked the gardener, took back her signed release form, and left the garden plot. It was good that the Fairies were helping with the garden but staying unobtrusive. Good compost made for a better explanation than Seed Fairies cajoling the seeds to sprout and the plants to grow.

He moved back into the front of the building and entered through the large archway. Volunteers carried pots of food that would be doled out to hundreds. Some carried trays laden with silverware and dishes.

Many people being served held plates that contained a wholesome dinner. A few had already moved outside to sit at the four tables that dotted the sidewalk at the front of the building. Daniel took thirty or forty shots of the last of the cooking preparations and exited the building. This old building that fed so many was the perfect foreground, but the conspicuous consumption of the rest of the city was needed to bring up the rear.

Daniel angled his body in an attempt to capture the right shot. He adjusted the F-Stop and shutter speed to select different effects. He wanted to give the photograph just the right touch of gravity and hope. If he stood at the corner where the sign for the soup kitchen remained visible, he would also capture the grandeur of Madison Square Garden looming in the background.

He focused on the corner of the building with its sign announcing free food. A tall, lean man shambled into focus through his viewfinder. The man moved past him. He held a full tray that contained a plate of food, a cup, and silverware. Daniel snapped a quick series of shots. He looked at the small screen and nodded to himself in satisfaction.

"It'll work better if you stand across the street," the man's melodious voice carried.

"I'm sorry?" Daniel lowered his camera. He approached the man. He topped six feet, wearing tattered but clean jeans and a t-shirt. Fish netting covered his torso and wrapped around him like he had been snared in it and never extricated himself.. His hair stood out in shocks of gray from under his knit cap.

"You're standing a bit too close to get the full effect of the garden," he said. He sat at one of the small tables near the entrance, lay a paper napkin on his lap, and dug into his dinner.

"How could you tell that was what I was going for?" Daniel moved over to the table.

"I used to dabble in photography. It's been a while, though."

"May I sit?" Daniel motioned to the empty chair on the opposite side of the round table.

"Sure," the man replied. "My friend Robbie won't be coming here for dinner tonight so I'm on my own for now."

"Did you shoot in the city?" Daniel sat.

"Sometimes. Mostly, I shot when I traveled."

"Where did you go?" Daniel removed a small notebook and pen from his pocket. He motioned with them to the man in silent question.

"All over when they needed me to go," the man said. He changed the subject. "Are you working for the Apostles? And if so, do you by any chance have a French language Bible in there?"

"I don't work for them," Daniel responded. "I'm a photojournalist, and I'm here working on a story. Why do you want a French language Bible?"

"I think my French is getting rusty," the man replied. "And I wanted to practice up a little. Or Russian. If there's a Russian language Bible, I could use that too."

"I speak a little French. Would you like to practice with me?" Daniel said a silent prayer that he had chosen French in high school. He knew no Russian, but he might be able to keep up with his rudimentary French

"Oui," the man answered. "Je m'appelle Josiah. Comment vous appelez-vous?"

"Daniel." The two conversed in French for several minutes.

Josiah finished his meal and stood. Daniel accompanied him inside where he deposited his dishes into waiting tray holders. Uncertain how to ask the question, Daniel hesitated. They stepped outside the building and into the twilit air. Josiah leaned against the wall and looked up. Daniel mimicked him.

"Josiah, if you don't mind my asking, what happened? I mean you speak all these languages so ...." Daniel drifted to a stop.

"So how did I wind up on the street?" Josiah asked.

"Yes."

Josiah settled deeper against the wall. He closed his red-rimmed eyes.

"I used to have a house on the upper West Side. I used to have a wife. Somewhere, I have two kids, a boy and a girl. I haven't seen them for a long time. Probably never will again."

"Why not?" Daniel asked.

Josiah opened his eyes and gazed at Daniel. He withdrew a dingy flask from his pants pocket. He took a long draught, secured the cap back on the bottle, and returned it to his pocket.

"They didn't want anything to do with me after a while. It started small, but it got bigger. A lot bigger," Josiah said. "See, I used to be an interpreter at the United Nations. I was one of the people who had to say it right when the politicians were haggling about this or that. When those people start yelling and screaming at one another, things can get pretty heated." He paused and closed his eyes again. "Let's just say, it's a lot of pressure."

"So you drank," Daniel made it a statement.

"So I drank."

"Did you ever try AA or anything like that?"

"Sure, I even got my 90-day coin one time. I remember my wife was so proud that day. But on day 93, I fell off the wagon, and I never managed to get back on." Josiah rubbed at his eyes. "Not even Sandra could keep me honest. I loved my family, but I love the bottle more."

"Would you mind? Would it be okay if I tell your story? I'll change the names and some of the details." Daniel asked.

"Sure, but it's not very interesting," Josiah said.

"There you're wrong," Daniel scribbled "But I love the bottle more," into his notebook. He nodded to himself again and placed notebook and pen back in his pocket. "It's compelling. You're just a couple of miles from where you used to live and work and have a family. And the bottle put you here."

"Yeah, but I chose it. I know it, and I'm all right with it."

"Would you mind if I took some shots of you in front of the Kitchen?" Daniel held up his camera.

"No, I don't mind," Josiah answered.

"Actually, can we go into the garden?" An idea struck Daniel. Josiah and the garden would be a perfect combination. He hoped the Seed Fairies would come out and add their special brand of light to the shots. And Daniel was willing to bet that once the Seed Fairies got wind of Josiah, they would add him to their list of "Help to Grow" as well.

"Sure," Josiah answered. "I've got to take care of something first. A tremor passed through him as he reached for his flask. He swallowed deep.

"Addiction sucks," Daniel murmured.

"It sure does," Josiah agreed. He wiped at his mouth with the back of his hand. "Hey," he smiled, "there's your headline."

Daniel left the Soup Kitchen and made his way towards home. A small but bright light winked in and out of windows and streetlights just at the edge of his vision.

After a block and a half, Daniel stopped in mid-step.

"Torlyn," he called. "I'm fine. Really." Then, a thought struck him. "But, can I ask you question?"

Torlyn appeared in one of the diamond-shaped street lamps that dotted the edge of Chelsea. Her flame face morphed in and out as the electricity from the bulb coursed in and through her.

"What's up?" she asked.

"How would I find out who the Fairy Godparent is for a specific person?"

"Why do you need to know?"

"I met a man tonight. He's gotten a bad shake. He's an alcoholic, and he lost his wife, his family, his career, everything. And, well, I was wondering if there's anything his Godparent could do for him."

"What makes you think they haven't?" Torlyn grew bigger. She now took up the entire space of the interior of the lamp.

"If they had, he wouldn't be in such bad shape." Daniel replied.

"That's not how it works, Daniel." Torlyn answered. She sat on the current of electricity. "Everything is about choices," she said. "If you choose to drink, or do drugs, or run your car off a bridge, it's your choice. And you'll have to live with the consequences of that choice. A Godparent can't change that for you. They can't make you choose not to self-destruct. All they can do is offer help and nudges back in the right direction. But if your right direction is the bottle, or the pill, or the needle, then that's the choice and that's what they'll work with."

"But, he had a good life. Isn't it possible that his Godparent could help him get it back?"

"Look," Torlyn said. "I could probably figure out who it is, and I might be able to arrange a conversation. But before I do that, was this man unhappy?"

"What?" Daniel's mouth dropped open in shock. "What do you mean 'was he unhappy?' Of course he was unhappy."

"Really? Are you sure? Think about it. Did he look unhappy? Was he upset or sad or distressed?"

Daniel closed his eyes and remembered. Josiah smiled. He had friends. He seemed at peace with his circumstances, with his life. "He said, 'I loved my wife, but I love the bottle more.' Oh man! No, he wasn't unhappy. How is that possible?"

"Choices, Daniel." Torlyn smiled and her flame body flared brighter. "It's all about choices."

"Thanks, Torlyn," Daniel nodded. They made their goodbyes, and he headed towards home to prepare for the evening.

The St. James apartment sat in one of the older and more genteel buildings along the park. The facade boasted real marble and a doorman whose face lit up when Tommy and Daniel approached.

"Mister Tommy," the elderly gentleman cried. "It's a pleasure to see you. It has been a while."

"How are you, Mr. Caruthers?" Tommy smiled and handed the older man a package wrapped in brown paper.

"You shouldn't have, Mister Tommy, but I'm glad you did," the old man chuckled.

"Zabar's saves this provolone just for you, Mr. Caruthers," Tommy replied. He turned to Daniel. "This is my new friend, Daniel."

The three men exchanged pleasantries for a moment longer, then the younger men entered the building. The opulent furnishings in the lobby were dominated by a great couch in rich burgundy leather and a five-foot tall orchid plant in bold, brash yellows and burgundies. Gold filigree covered every available surface and the spotless carpet sank beneath their feet.

"Wow," Daniel breathed.

"You ain't seen nothin' yet," Tommy said. As they approached the elevator in the back of the lobby, he stopped Daniel. "Okay, now let's go over it again."

"We are not telling them we are dating," Daniel repeated the story they had rehearsed at the cafe. "We are just letting them think it. And if anyone asks, we met at the party of a mutual friend."

"And, I'll need you to pay attention to who talks to whom. Once we know all the players, we'll know better how to proceed."

Daniel narrowed his eyes in concentration. "But, this is your dad, right? What do you think is going on?"

Tommy paused. "He might be my father, but that doesn't mean he isn't a bastard, you know what I mean?"

"I do," Daniel exhaled a long, careful sigh.

The elevator pinged the seventh floor.

"Okay, baby," Tommy winked at him. "Show time!"

The two men entered the apartment. Immediately, a servant with a tray provided each with a shot glass full of amber whisky. St. James's Distributors offered the best whisky, whiskey, and spirits from anywhere in the world to anywhere in the world, and the release of the latest thirty-year, single-malt had drawn a sizable crowd of many of the city's wealthy and powerful.

Daniel sniffed the potent liquor. Nausea roiled through his belly as vicious memories of Zeke's attack gripped him.

"Damn!" he swore softly. He put down the glass on the nearest tray.

"Are you okay," Tommy hooked an arm through his. "You look a little green."

"I have some bad memories of whisky," Daniel whispered.

"Like a bad tequila incident," Tommy teased. His knowing grin transformed into a sympathetic smile. "Oh sweetie," he rubbed Daniel's back. "You really mean it, don't you? Let's get you a seat and some water."

"Tommy," the husky voice cooed at them from one of the side rooms in the spacious dwelling. "You brought home a pretty one, tonight." An impossibly tall and long-legged brunette stood artfully framed in the doorway.

"Hello, Nadia," Tommy replied. "My sister," he murmured to Daniel. "Be careful. She's pretty much a viper with an expense account."

Tommy led Daniel into the side room. It revealed overstuffed chairs, walls lined with bookshelves, and a full size fireplace. Daniel collapsed into one of the brown leather chairs.

"Take off your shoes," Tommy suggested. Wiggle your toes in the rug. It will help with the nausea."

"Seriously?" Daniel did as instructed. He burrowed his toes in the plush rug, and the knot in his belly eased. "Wow," he breathed. "Thanks."

"Old family secret," Nadia said. "Many St. James' have needed to cure a violent hangover quickly. Somehow, it does the trick."

"Who's here?" Tommy asked his younger sister.

"Oh, you know, no one important." Nadia walked over to Daniel's chair and stood behind him.

"Really?"

"No one as important as your new sweetie," she stressed the last word.

"So, who is here?" Tommy asked again.

"The mayor, a couple of senators, some Fortune 500 types with their wives in tow. Boring." Nadia glided over to another of the brown leather chairs and sat. She crossed one tapered leg over another and studied the two men.

"Are you still playing at being a newspaper man?" She grinned.

"Are you still playing at being a human being?" He responded.

"So," Daniel cleared his throat. Two pairs of identical blue eyes turned towards him. "What are we going to do?"

"Are you feeling better?" Tommy asked.

Daniel nodded.

"Then, we are going to go out there and meet and greet and see who is doing what to whom and how. If we can get a story or a lead out of the evening, I will consider it a big success."

"Of course," Nadia said. "You wouldn't consider spending time with any of us a success."

"Sorry, Darling," Tommy stood and pressed a kiss to his sister's forehead. "Duty calls."

"Yeah, well, when duty calls, I let it go to voicemail," she replied with a flick of her hand.

"No doubt." Tom laughed. "And that's why I love you."

"Back atcha, big brother."

"Come on, Daniel." Tommy beckoned. "I'll introduce you to the key players."

They walked into the main living room. Many of the city's leaders sat on the numerous chairs and sofas strategically placed along the bare marble floor. A few chose tidbits at a long table that held a variety of cheeses, squares of dark chocolate, and various black and hearty breads. A large bar dominated the entire left end of the room. Floor to ceiling windows along one entire length of the living room provided a view of Central Park.

"Okay," Tommy put his mouth close to Daniel's ear and whispered. "In case you don't recognize him, the man over by the bar, that's Mayor Tyson. Let's see what he's up to."

"Mr. Mayor," Tommy called to the short, muscular man. "It's a pleasure to see you again."

"Tommy," the Mayor's lips parted in a thin smile. His bald pate shone darkly against the crisp white of his shirt. "How's the news business?"

"Oh you know," Tommy exchanged his empty shot glass for a full one from a passing waiter's tray. "We're always looking for trouble," he toasted the Mayor.

Tyson laughed. "I guess as long as you make sure that trouble doesn't find you, you'll do all right."

"My thoughts exactly," Tommy grabbed Daniel's hand and pulled him into the conversation.

"Have you met my new friend, Daniel?" He continued to hold Daniel's hand. "Daniel, this is Mayor Tyson, King of the best city on the planet."

"It's an honor, sir," Daniel shook the Mayor's hand. Despite the warm night, the Mayor's hand felt ice cold.

"So, Daniel, what do you do?" The Mayor asked.

"I'm a photographer."

"Where has your work been shown?"

"Oh, um … "

"He is so new and hot, he is just on the verge of taking off," Tommy filled in smoothly.

"Good luck, boys." The Mayor raised his glass to an acquaintance and moved away.

"That went well," Tommy said. He placed his shot glass on a passing waiter's tray and replaced it with another empty one.

"What went well?" Daniel asked.

"We needed the Mayor to see you but not think you were a threat. Worked great! Now, let's go see those Senators. After that, we'll be ready to take on the Chief."

"The Chief?"

"My father," Tommy answered. "That's what he's called."

"Is that because he is the CEO of the company?"

"Nope. He's been called that since he was a little kid. Apparently, one time, playing Cowboys and Indians, he caught one of the cowboys and actually partially scalped him."

"What?"

"Yeah, he's a prize, my old man. He's a real prize."

Tommy removed two triangular martini glasses from a tray and handed one to Daniel.

"Drink this," he advised. "If you don't have at least a little liquor on your breath, you'll arouse their suspicions." He put his arm around Daniel's shoulders, and the two men leaned close to one another.

"But you don't drink anymore," Daniel protested softly. "How do you do it?"

"Me?" Tommy barked out a laugh as he dipped a finger into the glass. He rimmed his lips with the clear liquid. His tongued darted out and caught the vodka. Tommy closed his eyes for a moment and let out a quiet sigh. He dipped his finger into the glass again and then ran it along the column of his throat. "I use it as cologne," he finished.

"Tommy," a voice boomed from the corner of the room. Mitchell St. James lifted one great arm and beckoned them to him.

Tommy slipped his arm into the crook of Daniel's. He slid into the lurching glide of the always-drunk, and the two men approached the elder St. James.

"Hello Father," Tommy's slurred speech augmented his lurching motions. "How are you?"

"I'm well," Mitchell St. James focused his lizard-like eyes onto Daniel.

"So, you're Tommy's new boy," St. James stated. He raked his eyes up and down Daniel's lanky frame. "You're not terribly butch, are you? Tommy tends to like them a little bigger and more macho."

Daniel started. Only Tommy's arm firmly holding his kept him from jumping back in surprise.

"It's okay, baby," Tommy crooned and stroked a lingering hand down Daniel's arm. "Daddy likes to push my boyfriends' buttons just to see what makes them tick." He faced his father. "No, he isn't terribly butch. But he's got it where it counts. Don't you, baby?" He dropped his gaze to Daniel's crotch and caressed a hand across his buttocks.

"Don't answer that, Daniel." Nadia had entered the room. "It'll only make this more tedious." She maneuvered herself next to her father and took his arm in imitation of the manner in which Tommy and Daniel faced him. "You see, Daddy's always had a little trouble accepting Tommy's proclivities."

"I do not," he smiled at her, but his eyes remained fixed on Daniel. "Tell me something about yourself, Daniel. Other than that you like to suck my son's dick."

Daniel's eyes widened in shock. Then, he smiled. He held the older man's eyes and snuggled deeper into Tommy's embrace.

Mitchell averted his gaze first.

"I like all manner of things," Daniel answered. "I do like Tommy." He drew his martini glass in a circle in the air. "I like a good whiskey."

"Then, what are you doing with a martini?" Mitchell asked.

"It was what you were serving," came the smooth reply.

"Let's see what we can do about that." Mitchell said. He nodded to one of the many white-shirted, black-aproned waiters who hovered throughout the room.

"Bring us a bottle of the fifty-year-old in my study," he said. Without waiting for a reply or acknowledgement, he turned back to Daniel and Tommy.

"You're going to have to join us, Tommy," he said.

"Oh, no." Daniel answered for him. "I'm afraid I rather like Tommy sober or close to sober. He is much more attentive that way."

"Heh, I can see who wears the pants in this relationship," Mitchell laughed.

"I'd say we trade off," affection infused Daniel's words with a soft glow. While on the inside, he stood quaking that at any second their charade would be exposed, he found reserves of courage and of all things acting chops and pressed his advantage with Tommy's father. "It's less boring," he continued.

The waiter reappeared with a silver tray that held a bottle of St. James's signature fifty-year-old whiskey and four squat crystal tumblers.

"Pour," Mitchell commanded.

The waiter dispensed the amber liquid into glasses and held the tray in front of them. Mitchell, Nadia, and Daniel each took a tumbler.

"Tommy?" Mitchell made the question a command.

Tommy reached for the glass. Daniel shook his head sharply.

"I told you I want you sober tonight. I meant it," Daniel placed a firm hand on his arm.

Tommy started and stilled. The two men looked at each other for an instant. Tommy dropped his arm. He smiled his private thanks to Daniel.

"Bring him some water, please," Daniel said to the waiter.

The waiter nodded and hurried to comply.

"So, not drinking tonight." Mitchell stated.

"He's had enough," Daniel spoke for Tommy. He hoped Tommy would understand his actions. If his father kept watching him like a hawk, Tommy might have to follow through and drink.

"Well, well," Mitchell studied Daniel for a moment with raised brows. He turned to Tommy. "Looks like you might have finally found yourself a real man," he said.

"Looks like I might have at that," Tommy smiled.

CHAPTER 5

JOANNA

Joanna bent over the shabby couch and snapped shut the case of her beloved violin. She faced the strapping man who stood behind her.

"Believe me, Shane," she implored. "It's not like I have any feelings for Marcus or anything. I mean, he cheated on me and then tried to make me feel like I was the one who had done something wrong. I'd just like to make sure he can't do any more damage."

"Joanna, it'll be okay. He can't hurt you anymore." He took hold of her hands.

"No, but he could hurt someone else," she fumed. "And if he does anything even slightly Twinkie-like, I'll...."

Shane laughed. "I don't know what that means, but I'm sure it isn't good."

"That's what Evie named him last year, after he played 'hide the Twinkie ... ' never mind." She rushed on. "The point is we're going to be teaching kids, for Pete's sake. And if they do well at the Academy, they'll get to go to Vienna and play there. And if he messes with their chances, he'll pay. Big time!"

"If anyone can keep him on the straight and narrow, it's Joanna Brennan." Shane caressed her cheek with the tips of his guitar-roughened fingers.

She softened at his touch and tilted her face for a tender kiss. What started as comfort rapidly became richer and more intimate. His arms wrapped around her, and she moaned against his mouth. Her fingers twined in his dark blond hair as she pulled him closer. She melded herself against him. This time it was he who moaned low and deep. He spanned her waist with his hands and lifted her off her feet. Holding her, he walked the few feet to the door and held her against it as he ravaged her mouth. One hand held her up and against him, the other hand roamed over her body, and he cupped her breast in his hand. While he nibbled on her full lower lip, he pulled at her peaked nipple. She cried out and urged him closer. He kissed along her jaw until his lips hovered over her sensitive ear. She shuddered against him.

"So," he whispered. "Are you still thinking about the Twinkie?"

"Twinkie, who?" Joanna managed. Her breath ran ragged in her lungs.

"Good," Shane smiled, pressed against her one last time and then lowered her to the floor. "Now, go to it, my sweetheart. You'll be grand."

She wobbled away from him and picked up her violin case. At the door, she turned back towards him. A smile bloomed on her face.

"I see what you did there, Shane McDuggan. Well done, you." She ran back to him and touched his lips lightly. "And thanks."

"Hey," he smiled. "All I did was kiss my lady."

"That's not all you did, and you know it. Thank you, again." She turned and left the room.

Shane's eyes narrowed to slits as he gazed at the closed door. "But that's not all I'm going to do," he said. "Not by a long shot."

THE PIANO'S KEY

Joanna entered the Public School 165 gym to utter chaos. Students ran around the room and called random words to each other when they reached a particular spot in the gym. Several tables held violin cases in black and blue canvas. A group of music stands stood grouped together in the center of the room. A row of folded chairs rested against one of the walls. A slight, gray-haired woman stood over one of the tables and searched through a brimming full padded briefcase.

"Hello," Joanna called out.

The woman jerked her head up. She picked up a clipboard in one hand and a stack of papers in the other.

"So glad you're here." She juggled each expertly as she walked towards Joanna and held out a hand. "I'm Marjorie Majors. I'm one of the people handling the Academy's logistics. Welcome to Academy Violin Section 7."

"I'm Joanna Brennan. I'm happy to be here." Joanna answered. She looked around at the throng of kids. "So, these are the students?"

"They are, and they look like a wild bunch. You're going to have your work cut out for you, but I'm sure you'll do great."

"Wait. What do you mean I'm going to have my work cut for me?" Joanna narrowed her eyes as the inference sank in. "I'm supposed to be co-teaching this with two other people."

Marjorie smiled winningly. "I'm afraid there's been a bit of a mix-up. Instead of three instructors for this group, we have one. And you're it."

"But, I don't know how to teach. I can play, but I've never taught anyone."

"That's okay." Marjorie replied. "They've never had anyone try to teach them music before anyway, so you'll all learn together. Look," her voice became quiet and persuasive. "These kids have had almost no training. But you have a gift, and I know you can inspire them to love the instrument as much as we do. After all, it's the violin. How can we help but love it?"

"But if I mess it up," Joanna protested. "They won't learn enough to go to Vienna."

"Get as far as you can," Marjorie said. "I'm sure you'll be terrific, Joanna, and someday, they'll thank you for it."

She handed Joanna the clipboard and several packets of paper. "This is your admin clipboard and the information packet on each student as well as the sheet music. You will want to have them learn the first three pieces as soon as possible."

Marjorie rushed back to the stage and grabbed her briefcase, a laptop, and a third bag. She hauled each onto her shoulders and walked toward the exit.

"Marjorie," Joanna followed her in shock. "Where are you going?"

Marjorie turned around and studied the younger woman. "I have to drop off the piano packets at the school's choir room and then another six schools to visit within the hour," she answered.

"But, what do I do, now?" Joanna asked.

"Get them in their seats and start, I'd guess. Now, I've got to get to the choir room. The piano students are there. Luckily, there are fewer of them."

"How many?"

"Three, I think," she replied. "If they are anything like this group, you and the piano instructor will get to commiserate back at Juilliard. But, I'm sure it will all go very well."

A pit of anxiety sprang up in Joanna's stomach.

"If I might ask. Who is teaching the piano students at this school?"

"Um, let me see," Marjorie shuffled through her bag until she came up with another clipboard.

"The piano instructor is Marcus Shepherd."

"Crap!" Joanna cried.

"What's wrong?" Marjorie turned toward her. "Is there a problem between you two?"

"Nothing," Joanna stammered. "He's my … he's my ex-boyfriend."

"I'm sorry," Marjorie laid a sympathetic hand on Joanna's arm. "As much as possible, we tried to put instructors from the same schools together so that you would have someone you could talk to and rely on," she said. "I had no idea …"

"No, of course, you wouldn't," Joanna rushed to alleviate her regret. "I'm sure it will be fine," she straightened her shoulders and narrowed her eyes in determination. "In fact, I know it will be."

"Well," Marjorie checked her watch. "I have to run. You'll break for lunch at noon and then start again at one pm. Two fifteen minute breaks are built into the morning and afternoon so they will hopefully have sufficient time to work off some of this energy." She gave Joanna the rest of the details and departed.

Joanna took a moment to study the students. She noted the dynamics of which side seemed to be winning the impromptu game of War. One tall girl rallied her troops and led them with a combination of inspiration and example. Her cocoa-colored limbs blurred as she maneuvered through the maze of the tables and chairs.

"Hey, watch out," she cried to one of her compatriots. The boy twisted his body to the side and evaded the arms of his opponent. He ran up next to the tall girl and they traded an intricate hand shake in camaraderie. After the short interchange, she pointed off to the left, whispered an instruction in his ear, and he flew off toward the far side of the gym.

She's the leader, Joanna thought. If I can get her, I'll get them all. She watched and followed the flow of the girl's movements. She ran, dodged, and engaged with her opponents with an ease that illustrated her sense of motion and rhythm. Joanna walked over the table and placed her violin case on it. She removed the instrument and its bow and tuned it. She turned toward the fray and studied the leader of the pack again. Joanna noted the rhythm and flow, the melody of her motions. She improvised a driving tune that matched the girl's movements. With every duck or dodge, the melody dipped. With every whirl, the melody twirled with her.

The notes poured out of the violin. Sometimes fierce, sometimes lightning quick, the music and Joanna's inherent magic called to the girl. After a few minutes, her movements aligned themselves with the melody. No longer leading the creation of the melody, she began to move in time with it. The movement and the music coalesced into a perfect harmony of sound and motion. Joanna slowed down the music and urged the girl to turn towards her with note, line, and tune. She suspended one note as if over a precipice. The girl stopped. She closed her eyes and stood statue still until there was nothing left but sound and silence.

The echo of the last note hung in the air. Joanna improvised a hot groove. She infused the heat and pleasure of the tropics and the urgency of the hard staccato beats that so heavily influenced the rap and hip hop movements. The bow jumped and scraped across the strings in heartbeat licks. Through Joanna's magic, the student's heartbeat linked with the tattoo Joanna beat on the low G string of the violin.

She stared at Joanna with wide eyes as she held one last frenzied note and finished the lick with a flourish.

The girl shook her head and approached Joanna.

"How did you do that?" She breathed.

"Oh this?" Joanna motioned with the violin. "That was improvisation."

"It was really good," the girl reached out a hand toward the violin but then pulled back.

"You can touch it," Joanna said. She held the violin out to her. "Go ahead and pluck a string." She demonstrated by pulling her fingernail against the string.

The girl smiled and shook her head. "Yeah, but that's a long way from what you just did."

"True," Joanna agreed. "But that doesn't mean that you can't do it, too."

"Right," the girl scoffed. "Sure, I'll just get right on that."

"No, really." Joanna tucked her violin under her arm and moved over to the table that held the violin cases.

"Go ahead and open that," she indicated a case. As the girl unzipped the blue case, Joanna asked her name.

"Veronica."

"Okay, Veronica, let's talk about the violin." Joanna looked around at the rest of the class. "You all want to see this, too?" She asked.

The other kids looked at Veronica. At her small nod, they approached the table.

"This is a violin," Joanna explained. She held her bow aloft for them to see." And this is a bow. And these," she stroked her thumb across the bow's hair. "They come from horse's tails."

"What?" One of the kids laughed. "For real?"

"It's true. And when you draw the horsehair across these strings, that creates a vibration and that's how you get sound on the violin." She placed her violin in the appropriate position and drew a quick melody on it.

"Okay, Veronica," she said. "Now, let's try your violin."

"My violin?" Veronica asked. She took out the violin and mimicked the way Joanna was holding hers.

"Yep. It's yours for the duration of the class. And if you decide to keep playing afterward, you will get to keep it," Joanna decided she would figure out a way to buy these instruments for her students.

"That goes for all of you," she continued. "If you want to keep playing after this summer, I will make sure you can."

The rest of the students crowded around the table and each chose an instrument.

Joanna smiled at the collected group. "Okay," she said." We've got a lot to do, but I think we are going to be incredible. "Are you ready?"

As one, the students nodded their assent.

"Then let's get started!"

CHAPTER 6

EVIE

It's a good thing I don't get seasick. If I did, my twenty-four hours of upside down time would have been far more miserable. As it was, it wasn't so bad.

"Crap!" I cried as Torlyn drew into an inside straight on the River.

"I don't know where that eight of hearts came from," I grumbled. "But I suspect it wasn't the card that was supposed to come up last."

"Don't do the crime if you can't do the time," Torlyn crowed as she gathered her chips. The chips weren't real chips, of course. They were made of colored lights.

The loud screech of the back door screamed into the room. I started, and my eyes shot toward the back of the library.

"Uh oh," Torlyn gathered everything into her bag. "Looks like the Big Bad is back. I'd better jet."

"Yeah," I grumbled again. "It's not like you're afraid of her."

"No," the Fire Fairy paused. Her flame face blazed brighter for an instant. "She belongs to the Fire. So, I don't have anything to fear from her."

"Exactly." My consternation had started my rope swinging again. Wisteria's Element was Fire. Torlyn was a Fire Fairy. Everybody knew if you pissed off the Embodiment of the Element you'd chosen, you would have trouble. "So, it's not like you've got anything to worry about."

"True," Torlyn agreed. "But you're my friend, and she knows it. If I piss her off enough, she might take it out on you." She eyed my current suspended predicament. "Know what I mean? Then again," she murmured. "I might be able to send a little message of my own."

The tak tak of Wisteria's boots grew louder.

Torlyn stilled and blazed brightly in the middle of the room. Wisteria entered and halted in mid-stride.

"Greetings, Honored One," She inclined her head to her Elemental.

"And to you," Torlyn nodded at her Adept.

"In what manner may I serve you?" Wisteria eyed me and circled under us as she talked.

"In none," Torlyn glided closer to me. "I was just visiting with my friend," she emphasized the last word. I bit back a giggle.

Wisteria nodded. I couldn't tell for sure, but I hoped that she'd gotten the message. She glanced sideways at me and her eyes narrowed.

"I did not know you were such good friends with Songwith Evie," she spit out my given name.

"For quite some time," Torlyn replied. She blazed brighter. "In fact, you might have heard that she saved my sister's life last year."

"I would not agree," Wisteria said. "In fact, I'd say she almost screwed it up completely, and it was her Charge, Joanna Brennan, who saved the day."

"You weren't there," Torlyn looked down her nose at Wisteria. "Trust me when I tell you that she saved Leili's life. And even before then, Evie was special to me."

Wisteria closed her eyes and took a deep breath. When she opened them, her eyes glowed an angry green.

"Very well," Wisteria said. "I will treat her with the respect accorded to one who is a friend of the Fire Elementals."

"See that you do," Torlyn began to fade.

"Wait, Torlyn," panic laced my voice. "Can't you stay for a bit? Like for the next two years?" I pleaded.

"You'll be fine, Evie." her voice faded as she disappeared.

Crap!

Wisteria looked around the big gymnasium. She nodded and turned to me.

"So, Songbottom," she sneered. "Can't fight your own battles?"

"Wait, what?" I twisted my body and swung my arms until I rotated around to face her. "I did no such thing."

"Oh sure, so why was she here when I came in, and why did she feel the need to let me know to treat you like you're a mewling infant?" She waved a hand, and the rope holding me disintegrated. I careened toward the floor.

"Shit!" I sent a panicked thought to my wand. A shower of sparks flew of out my bag and a bean bag formed below me.

"Woof!" The breath knocked out of me as I slammed into the bag. Tiny, Styrofoam pills exploded out of the bag's creases and floated to the ground.

"Get up," Wisteria barked.

"Give me a minute," I gasped. "Can't breathe." My head lay twisted at an unnatural angle. I was lying on my back, but my face pressed into the brown vinyl of the bean bag.

"Do you think I give a crap?" She loomed over me. "Will your charges care if you can't help them because you a have stitch in your side? Get up," she yelled.

"Fine," I wheezed and straightened. The world righted itself, but lights winked at the periphery of my vision. I tilted my head from side to side. Semi-automatic rifle shots accompanied each motion.

"If this is all it takes to get you too pooped to party," Wisteria's lips parted in the thinnest of smiles, "We're going to have to break you ... in."

"Break me ... in?" I rasped. "What does that mean?"

"It means you're going to be pretty busy over the next few months," she held my gaze with intense green eyes. "In fact, I think we're going to schedule a few one-on-one sessions."

"One-on-one sessions?" I squeaked. Wisteria was going to rake me over the coals. Literally. After all, she was a Fire Adept. If anyone could get permission to rake someone over coals, it would be a Fire Adept. Shit! Fire hurts!

"Didn't you notice no one else is here?" She advanced on me. "Are you that clueless?"

"I'm not clueless." I defended my cluelessness as best I could.

"Right, fine," she nodded and crouched. "Defend!"

A glowing, red fireball streaked toward my aching head. I threw myself to the ground. It singed one of the pillars.

"That's one," Wisteria said.

"One, what?" I asked. I pulled myself to my wobbly feet.

"One damage hit," she bit out. "You will be fined for that."

"I'll be fined?" I cried. "You did it. You flung that thing at me. I was just defending myself."

"No," her voice took on a creepy, calm tone. "You weren't defending yourself. You were throwing yourself to the ground to protect your own body with no regard to who or what else might be hurt by your actions."

"My actions?" I stopped and stared at her. "But," I sputtered. "I didn't do anything."

"Exactly! You did nothing. As a Level Four, you are required to do something, anything, everything, to minimize harm. Got it?"

"So wait," I moved sideways and did my best to put bars, beams, and pillars between us. "You're telling me that not only do I have to not get hit, but I also have to make sure that nothing else gets hit?"

"Now you're getting it." In a split second she towered over me. She lay her big, long palm on my head and patted me like I was a dog who had just peed on command.

"Good. Very good." She reinforced my internal analogy. "There might be hope for you yet," she continued. I brightened at the compliment and stood a little straighter. Maybe I wouldn't be a complete failure at this Battle Magic stuff.

"I doubt it, but there might be," Wisteria dashed my hopes with her words.

"Some of these will be harmless discharges of magic," she continued. "Some will be the real deal. And you are going to have to figure out which they are, which to defend against, and which take on the chin." She shook her head slightly and parted her lips in her patented, predatory smile.

"Defend!"

Crap!

I ran for my bag. I reached it. I stuffed my arms in to grab my wand. A hissing seared nearby. I lifted my head. A livid orange fireball smacked me in the face.

"Ow!" I cried. I held my hands to my bleeding nose.

"I told you to defend," Wisteria sidled up to me. She lifted my head and turned it left and right.

Tears streamed down my face as much from humiliation as from pain. I hate having my ass handed to me, and it had been twice in two days.

"You're going to be fine," she stated.

"I know," I mumbled. "I'm not stupid."

"Could have fooled me," she replied. She waved her fingers in front of my face. The pain all but disappeared. My vision cleared. I felt better than I had in days.

"Why did you do that?" I put my fingers to my newly healed nose.

"Because I can't have you injured if we're going to get any work done," she answered. She waved her fingers and disappeared.

"But that was the last freebie," she called from across the gym. "If you need healing again, you'll either pay me, or you'll have to do it yourself."

"Pay you?" FGs didn't charge anyone for healing. We were required to help, if we could. "Pay you?" Shocked, I shot to standing. Another fireball hit me squarely in the chest. I flew back against the nearest pillar. I bounced and sprawled on the bean bag.

"Honestly, Songbottom," Wisteria sighed. "Don't you know anything about keeping your head in the game? Keep moving. Make yourself as small a target as possible. And try not to keep getting your ass kicked, ok?"

She disappeared and reappeared twenty feet away. This time she held her custom-made flamethrower. She pointed the business end at me. "Now, concentrate," she flipped the safety switch. "And defend!"

CHAPTER 7

JOANNA

"So, Veronica what did you think?" Joanna stacked the violins on the large cart the school had provided.

Veronica sheltered her instrument back in its case and closed the locks. She turned to Joanna and smiled.

"It was all right," she admitted. "I didn't think I'd like it, but it was all right."

"And this was just the first lesson," Joanna said. "You didn't get to do much but bow across the strings. We'll do a lot more in the next few classes. Before you know it, you'll be playing concertos."

"Right," Veronica smiled. "Sure, whatever you say."

"No, I'm serious," Joanna gazed into her eyes. "You can do it. I know you can."

The door to the gym screeched open.

"Ronnie," the young man stood in the doorway. "We've got to go."

"Hey Tariq," Veronica called. "How did you do?" She turned to Joanna. "He's in the piano group."

"I was in the piano group," Tariq said. "I'm getting kicked out." He sauntered into the room. "The teacher didn't want me in … " he paused. His eyes traveled to Joanna.

"She's okay," Veronica said.

"Yeah, whatever. It's no big deal. I've got other things to do anyway." Tariq walked over to the cart of instruments. He fingered a case for a second and snatched his hand back.

"Why would they kick you out of the program?" Joanna asked.

"Because, he can't read music and probably not anything else." The tall, lean owner of the bored voice posed in the doorway.

"Marcus," Joanna faced him. "How shocking that you weren't encouraging."

"I'm here to teach them piano," Marcus pointed a long, elegant finger at Tariq. "They were supposed to be taught how to read music before this class. If they can't read music, I don't have to teach them and neither do you. Those are the rules."

"There are other ways to learn," Joanna turned to Tariq. "You don't have to know how to read music. And you don't even have to play classical music. Trust me. I know. Do you want to maybe learn how to play the violin? I'd be happy to take you into my class."

Tariq gazed at her through narrowed eyes. He backed away from the cart of instruments.

"Like I said, it's no big deal," he moved toward the doorway and sidestepped Marcus.

"But you love to play," Veronica called after him.

"Not enough to put up with this shit," he answered. "Look, you coming, or not? I've got to pick up Calvin at the 95th Street Drop Center."

"Calvin's his little brother," Veronica explained. "Is it all right if I go?"

"Of course. Go ahead," Joanna answered. "I'll see you tomorrow."

Joanna held her temper until she heard the faint boom of a closing door. She skewered Marcus with a look.

"Why did you have to be such a jackass?" She fumed. "You could have helped him learn."

Marcus raised a black eyebrow and crossed his arms. "I suppose I could have, but that would have short-changed the two others who know how to read."

"You just don't want to put in any extra effort," she accused.

"Why should I?" He smiled. "We get to go to Vienna regardless, so why not do as little work as I have to? Besides, we can only take the top two anyway. Might was well cull the herd early."

"You're impossible!" She fumed.

"No, just efficient," he answered. He moved closer. He stroked one finger down her arm. "There was a time you liked my efficiency."

"Yes, well that was a long time ago," she kept her voice steady. "And you're not being efficient. You're just being an asshole." She surprised herself with her choice of words.

"Well, well, Joanna," he raised his eyebrows. "Looks like you've been keeping some interesting company. That bitch Evie's been rubbing off on you."

"You just think she's a bitch because she beat you in the Tripplehorn Competition." Joanna replied. "She won fair and square, and she'll do it again. Anytime you go up against her, you'll lose."

"Maybe," he drawled. "But it doesn't matter. I've got more important things to do." He walked toward the doorway of the gym. "It's going to be fun working together," he emphasized 'working' and made it sound lascivious. "And it'll be even more fun when we're in Europe together."

"We won't be together," Joanna rolled her eyes. "We'll just be in the same place at the same time. Your days of being anywhere with me are long gone."

"Why don't we see about that?" His eyes roved down the length of her body. The breath stilled in her lungs. He smiled, turned, and left without another word.

"I have a boyfriend. I love Shane" she whispered weakly to the empty room.

She locked the instruments in their closet. She closed her eyes and heard the long, slow notes the kids had played. Languid strokes of the bow produced the most beautiful sound. If the students learned that, she was certain she could train their ears to help them learn where their fingers needed to be placed in order to play on pitch and with the right rhythms.

Veronica showed great potential. It's too bad Tariq isn't a violinist, Joanna thought. I'd be happy to work with him. She clenched her fists at her sides. While she might have to share the school with Marcus, she refused to let him ruin either her or her students' experience.

"He's not worth it," she said aloud. "Get a grip, Joanna, and do better tomorrow."

EVIE

I ducked out of the path of another red fire bolt. The red ones hurt the most. That is, until that old softie decided to change things up and makes the red ones Red Herrings and turns the calm yellow ones into something that would have given Dante nightmares.

"Shit!" A red one scorched my left shoulder. I spun around from the impact. I crouched and whimpered.

"If you keep whining like a baby who's lost her binky, you're going to keep telegraphing your location." Wisteria called from across the gym. Maybe she was getting tired of target practice. Maybe she was ready to call it a day. Maybe some of the other students would show up and divide her focus away from me for a millisecond.

"It's a good thing I dismissed the other students for the day. You're going to need a lot more work to catch up to everyone else." She sounded farther away this time. Thank goodness.

"Ow!" I cried out. The heat from this zinger seared the top of my head. I crawled away on all fours. Every couple of steps, she knocked me over. I pushed myself upright and limped away from her.

"You really suck at this, don't you?" she goaded.

"I was good enough to beat a Bane at his own game," I panted.

"Zeke Dunne? He's a terrible example. First of all, he can't fight. Still, he ought to have been able to dispatch you and your boy toy pretty easily."

"You leave Daniel out of this!" I rocketed up. My wand shot a searing blue flame straight at her head.

She deflected it and boomeranged it back at me. I ducked at the last second. It blasted the pillar above my head.

"Now, you've got your head in the game," she remarked. "Good. You're going to need it."

She waved a hand. The columns and furniture scooted toward the walls. I threw my body out of the way of a pillar as it swung past me toward the corner of the gym. I rolled to standing and looked around the now bare gym. I faced her across a space of thirty feet.

"Nothing to hide behind anymore," Wisteria called. "Now you'll have to defend yourself or stop me."

"Isn't this a little advanced for the first day?" I panted.

"You used battle magic against a Bane. So, you're more advanced than some of my other students." Her grin was pure evil. "But from here on in, you'll have to defend yourself against me. And me?" She advanced. "I'm a little tougher to beat than some Bane."

After Wisteria finished with me, I shuffled out of the gym. I had almost enough strength to float my bag along. After a few feet, it fell to the ground and dragged itself behind me. A mewling sound escaped my lips. Every part of me had been pummeled or singed or both, and I had to do it again tomorrow morning.

I was too pooped to conjure myself back to my place. I made it to the bus stop, fell into a heap on the bench, and waited. My lids drooped closed.

"Level Four Godmother, Songbottom, Eveningstar. You have arrived at your destination." The whine of the drone bus driver permeated the haze inside my head. I opened bleary eyes and looked into the bright blue LEDs of the driver.

"I'm home, huh."

"You have arrived at your destination," the Drone replied and blinked its azure eyes at me in agreement.

I pulled myself to standing, groping my way along the aisle and managed not to fall onto the street as I exited.

In the morning, I dragged myself to the Healer's Pavilion. Every bone, heck every hair that hadn't been singed off, hurt like the Dickens. I leaned against the door and whimpered.

Head Healer Nightingale, or, the Doc, as everyone called her, turned her considerable girth in my direction. She moved with grace on little tiny feet. She wore silent, pink ballet slippers under her crisp white smock and tall, conical Healer's Hat. The pink was the only acknowledgement that any other color of the rainbow existed as every other single thing in the Pavilion was white or some shade of white.

"Godmother Songbottom, welcome," she exuded warmth. Muscles I hadn't been aware of being stiff, relaxed. The sunburnt feeling all along my skin eased.

"Healer Nightingale," I acknowledged her rank. I touched my palms over my heart and bowed. "Please, call me Evie."

"Very well, Evie," she said. "We have a lot to do so let's get started." She backed up a pace and clucked her tongue three times. "I can see Wisteria paid extra attention to you," she said. "Did you have a private lesson?"

"I did," I answered. "Does she do that a lot?"

"No," Doc waved her hands in a complicated pattern over my head. My pain eased until I felt nothing but acute hunger. "But sometimes, we see a fair number of you Level Fours who need more healing than usual."

"She hung me up, literally." I shrugged. I closed my fingers into loose fists to test their status. I could lose the use of my feet and still survive. But if something permanent happened to my fingers or arms and I couldn't play piano, again, I would not survive.

"Are you hungry yet?" Doc asked.

"Like crazy," I replied as my stomach growled.

"Normal after a healing," she motioned for me to follow her to the far end of the pavilion. Several white tables with white cloths sat in a semi-circle at the outer edge. Small, rounded chairs were set around each table.

"Sit," she invited me. I sat and within seconds a server produced a white plate on which lay several bananas, a bunch of blueberries, and a huge slice of pineapple. "You will need these to promote healing," she said. "The bananas will help your muscles, the pineapple will help your bones, and the blueberries will promote purification. It's your own energy that heals you, you know. So, you'll want to eat all of this to help you finish healing yourself."

"Wait, what do you mean, 'it's my own energy that heals me?' I saw you doing some mystical hokey pokey above my head. And when you were done, I felt better. Tons better. How was that me healing myself?"

She paused, closed her eyes, and mumbled something under her breath. I could have sworn it was something like, "Shit, don't they teach these Godparents any-freakin'-thing?" But I was sure that could not be it. Healers don't cuss like sailors, generally speaking. And Doc struck me as one who would look down her generous nose at anyone who did. So I was certain I had misheard her. But then, what did I know? I dated Zeke once upon a time.

"Your energy heals you, Evie," she said slowly. "You did it. You allowed it. All I did was to open the doorway so you could tap into the universal healing energy that surrounds us all and use it to make yourself better."

"But if I'm using universal energy to heal myself, how am I using my own?" I was confused.

"Nothing works in a vacuum," she answered. "If you move a single muscle, you are using energy. When you are injured or hurt, it takes even more energy from within you to fix what's wrong with you. And you want to get as much help as possible, so that's why you want to tap into the Universal energy field instead of just using your own. As for the fruit, it will help you replenish the energy you used to do it. I don't know what we'd do without these little miracles." She held up a single blueberry and then popped it in her mouth. "And besides, they're just delicious."

She motioned to the plate, once again. "Now, go ahead and finish your repast. We have a lot of work to do."

We started with wilted plants. I held my wand in front of me and stood before a leggy sweet basil plant. It had sat without water for a few days too many. Its tasty leaves had curled and begun to turn that gray brown they get right before they fall off.

"Concentrate, Evie," Doc admonished me. Why was everyone always telling me to concentrate? It's not like I had a serious problem with ADD. I mean, I was sometimes a little distractible, but really, who wasn't. I remembered this one time …

"Evie!"

The plant I had working on had drooped over the edge pot and looked like it was begging for mercy.

"Oops, sorry, Doc," I refocused my intention to my wand and asked it to send healing energy to the basil plant. A small cone of wet heat formed around the plant. The soil in the pot darkened as it moistened. The basil leaves began to uncurl and a few even turned a bright green, again.

"I'm doing it," I spun in a little victory dance. With my motion, the moisture from my wand swung around the room. As it suffused the air in the pavilion, the tiny water droplets combined with one another until they became big, huge drops. And since gravity works in its own particular fashion no matter where you are, they rained down on the entire pavilion and soaked everyone and everything.

"Sorry. My bad," my nervous laugh shook my wand and more precipitation dropped onto the already saturated room.

"Evie," Doc closed her eyes and took a deep breath. She remained still and silent.

I gazed down and then grimaced and raised my eyes to look at her. Her eyes opened wide, and she smiled.

"Okay. Now, I know how we will need to do this." She waved her hand in a complicated sigil in the air and the basil plant stood upright. Its leaves shone new and verdant. She waved her hand in another sigil and the room dried. "Next time," she said. "You will need to clean this up yourself."

"Of course, Doc," I gazed down at my shoes.

"But for now," she continued. "For now, we will step back a ways and work on your concentration.

"Josephus," she said to one of the other Healers in the room. "We're going to need to get the kittens."

The older Healer glided toward us and shot me a look through narrowed eyes.

"Is it as bad as all that?" He asked.

"Well," she replied. "This is certainly going to prove a challenge. So, we might as well start at square one."

"Very well," he replied. He moved toward one of the many doors in the round room.

"And Josephus," Doc called after him. "The puppies. Bring the puppies, too."

"What are we going to do with kittens and puppies?" I asked.

"You'll see," her lips parted in a mysterious smile.

Crap!

CHAPTER 8

ZEKE

The offices of Helping Hand were located on the upper West Side, near Columbus Circle. The suite on the fiftieth floor of the building bulged with leather furniture and dark, hardwood desks, credenzas and other accoutrements. A tall silver and lead clock dominated the main room. The Helping Hand logo of a large, silver hand reaching down to a small bronze one took up an entire wall.

Zeke Dunne strode along the hallway toward his office, which sat at the far end of the entryway to the suite. His secretary's desk sat as a barrier between his office and the outside world.

"Melissa," he barked at the immaculately dressed woman behind the desk.

"Yes, Mr. Dunne." She stood and straightened her tailored, gray Vera Wang suit.

"I need to call a Board Meeting. Make it for early next week."

"Yes, Mr. Dunne," she sat back down and began preparations to gather the entire Board of Directors.

Zeke paused at the doorway to his corner office. "And get me the Mayor."

"Yes, Mr. Dunne." Melissa seldom said anything else to him. He had hired her to be unobtrusive, gray, and effective. She was all three.

The phone that sat on his deep mahogany desk was ringing by the time he had walked into the room. He took no notice of the magnificent view of Central Park. He crossed the hardwood floor and picked up the phone.

"Mr. Mayor," he smiled. "How are you? How's the golf game?"

"Dunne, you are a bastard," the Mayor laughed. "I'm going to beat you next time and don't you forget it."

"I'm sure you will, sir," Zeke settled into his chair and kicked back. His eyes roved to the curly maple violin that sat in the glass case across from his desk. He stared at it in silence for a moment.

"But that's not why I'm calling you. We need to move up the timetable for the kick-off, and I wanted to make sure that would be something you and the Chief of Police would approve before I take action."

"It's not an easy thing to achieve," the Mayor's voice beat a staccato against his ear. "There are many young people who need to be introduced into the program. That will take time. We can't help them if we can't find them."

"True," Zeke agreed. "But sometimes, the perfect is the enemy of the good. If we wait until we have every single at-risk youth registered for the program, we might never get started with any of them."

"Ah, so better to have one or two and call it a day then to be patient and to do it right," the Mayor snorted.

"Sir, we started this initiative to help young people who otherwise have no choice. No chance." Zeke warmed to his topic. He relaxed into his patter with the certainty of a seasoned conman. "If we want to keep them off the streets, we need to register them for the program. Don't get me wrong. I want to find as many as we can, but we need to register at least some in order to make any progress at all. If we want this city clean and free of drugs, guns, and violence, then we need to start somewhere."

"And I'll bet you have the perfect place to start," the Mayor responded.

"It just so happens I do."

"Let's hear it."

"I say we should invest in the arts," Zeke said.

"The arts? We have plenty of arts programs in this city," the Mayor replied.

"Yes, but there's one particular program that we could fund that would provide a perfect partnership, a symbiosis, if you will. It's called the Academy, and it will provide us with unfettered access to some of the city's more at-risk young people."

The Mayor stayed silent for a few seconds.

Zeke opened a desk drawer and pulled out a small black box. He opened it and touched the contents while he uttered a silent incantation.

"All right, Dunne," the Mayor said. "I've trusted you this far, and you haven't steered any of this wrong yet."

"And I won't, sir," Zeke's voice oozed.

"I'm sure you won't. So, what will you need?"

"I think it would be great to have the database of all the kids involved. It's confidential, for legal reasons and because these students are all at risk, so I can't access the information without your involvement. Once we have that, we can identify their families and just exactly what it is they'll need to improve their situations. And then we can provide it."

"Fine, fine," the Mayor replied. "I'll have someone on my staff find it all out and get it to you within a few days."

"Excellent, sir. Thank you sir. I'll look for it then."

After a few of the required pleasantries, the Mayor hung up.

Zeke pushed the intercom button on his phone.

"Melissa," he said.

"Yes, Mr. Dunne."

"I'll need my car brought around. I'll be leaving for lunch and won't be returning until tomorrow."

"Yes, Mr. Dunne," she replied.

He terminated the connection, reached into his pocket and took out his phone. He dialed the number from memory.

"Yes?" the greeting was curt.

"We're on," Zeke said. "I ought to have the database of all the names within the next few days.

"Good. We'll need that data to go to the next phase."

"We'll be set soon," Zeke said.

"Good work, Dunne. I knew you had more to you than playing that fiddle."

"I do, sir," Zeke gazed at the glass case that held his instrument. He hoped his voice did not betray his longing.

"Keep up the good work, and you'll have it back soon enough," the man said.

"Yes, sir. I will."

"You screwed the pooch last year," he reminded Zeke. "And we don't reward failure."

"Yes, sir. I know. I won't fail again."

"See that you don't. I'd hate to have that little fiddle destroyed."

"I won't give you a reason. I promise."

"Of course, you won't boy," the man chuckled. "You might be many things, but you aren't stupid."

"No, I'm not." Zeke kept his voice level and obsequious. He had plans and none of them entailed pissing off one of the most powerful beings he had ever known.

"All right. Keep me posted on anything important." The connection ended.

Zeke closed the black box and replaced it in his desk drawer. He took a small cloth from the same drawer and cleaned his hands. He reclined back against his chair, gazed at his beloved violin, and smiled.

CHAPTER 9

JOANNA

Joanna was helping her students transform the cat yowling cacophony into music. Even if the player knew it inside and out, the violin could be one of the toughest instruments in the world to play.

Veronica had proven herself to be one of the best students of the few who came back after the first day. She exhibited focus, drive, and determination. She practiced with her eyes shut. Her body swayed with the bow strokes. Up and down, perpendicular across the strings she drew the long horse hair stick. She sped up the bow and screeched the next two notes. She pulled the bow away from the strings and grimaced.

"It's okay, Veronica," Joanna soothed. "It happens to every player."

"I've never heard it happen to you," Veronica responded.

"Believe me, it has. In fact, just last year, I was playing like I had never touched the violin before. I was trying to learn how to improvise instead of only playing what's written on the page, and I was rubbish at it. Complete rubbish. But after a while, I figured out how to play from both here and here," she pointed to her head and heart in rapid succession. "And that made all the difference."

"Sure, yeah, but you don't make it sound like someone is strangling a cat," Veronica grumbled.

"It was worse," Joanna laughed. "Anything I played sounded muted and deadened, like it had no color."

"So now we have to play in color?" One of the other two students spoke up.

"Yes, I think so Jamil." Joanna looked at each student in turn. She opened her case and extracted her violin and bow from it. She tightened the bow, put the violin under her chin and played through a quick and perfunctory version of the reel called, "Morning Dew."

"That went fast," Jamil said.

"Yes, it did." Joanna smiled. "But now take a listen to it." She played the tune again and infused it with a sense of fun and sparkle. The tune spirited them away into a daydream of a bright dawn, rustling leaves, and fairies dancing among dew drops.

"How did you do that?" Veronica breathed after Joanna ended the tune.

"Do what?" Joanna asked, her eyes open wide.

"I was. I mean, I saw." Veronica hesitated. "Did anybody else imagine the sunrise and really green trees?"

"Yeah," Jamil replied. "What's up with that?"

"These tunes are kind of special," Joanna smiled. "And if you play them from deep within your spirit, you'll take your audience on a journey too."

"Whatever," the bored voice broke the spell.

"Tariq," Veronica smiled. "Did you hear Joanna play?"

"Yeah," he replied. His eyes downcast, he loitered by the door to the gym. "That kind of music - not my thing."

"What kind of music do you like?" Joanna asked.

He stopped and thought for a moment.

"Jazz and Blues," he answered.

"Like who?"

"You know, Ellington, Oscar Peterson, Memphis Slim, Bud Powell."

"I've only heard of a couple of them," Joanna said.

"If you knew jazz or blues, you'd know all about them," he replied.

"Are they all piano players?" Joanna asked.

"Yeah."

An idea struck Joanna. "You know, I have a good friend you might want to talk to," she said. "She's out of town right now, but as soon as she gets back, I'm sure she'd love to talk piano with you."

"Whatever," he said again.

"No, really. Evie's great. As soon as she's back, I'm going to get the two of you together." She'll help him, Joanna thought. If anyone can reach him, she can.

"Well," Tariq's voice dripped. "Have her people call my people, and I'm sure we can set something up." He looked at Veronica. "Ronnie, you coming? I'm out."

Veronica nodded. She turned to Joanna.

"Are we finished for the day?"

"I guess so," Joanna answered. She studied Veronica's face. A thought struck her. "Veronica, I can get you home."

Veronica's smile failed to reach her eyes.

"White people don't go where we live. Ever." Tariq barked out a laugh. "Come on, Ronnie," he repeated.

"I've got to go," Veronica said.

"Okay," Joanna searched Veronica's eyes and saw fear. "But if you ever need anything, please, let me know. I'd like to help, if I can."

"I know," Veronica answered. "And you can't."

She gathered her things and left with Tariq.

Joanna turned to Jamil and Sandra, the other two students.

"Do you want to keep going or are we done for the day?" She asked.

"We're done," Jamil said. He stowed his violin back in its case and walked over to her.

"It was nice of you to try," he whispered. He and Sandra left together.

Joanna's eyes welled up with tears. She brushed at them with frustrated palms. She reached for her phone and dialed.

"Hello?"

"Daniel, Hi. It's Joanna."

"Hi Joanna," Daniel replied. "What's up?"

Joanna paused and breathed before she launched.

"I know you're working on the story about the two New Yorks," she said. "I think have a story for you. But I'm going to need your help."

DANIEL

Daniel hurried from the subway to Tom's Restaurant at 112th and Broadway. It had become famous for being featured in a television show a few years back, but people still went there for the food. He spotted Joanna sitting on one of the tall chrome and leather stools at the long, curved bar. Her honey colored hair sat in a neat ponytail. Her violin sat cradled between the stool and the bar.

"No, thank you," she said to the man who towered over her. "I don't need a drink, and I am waiting for someone."

"So, you can wait with me," the man kept trying.

Daniel approached the pair snagged the stool next to her.

"Well," he said. "You're done waiting anyway." He turned to the man and smiled. "Unless you want to buy both of us a drink."

"Freak," the man mumbled and turned away.

"Hey," Joanna said.

"Hey," he replied. "Are you okay?"

"Oh, I'm fine," she answered. "Sometimes, I need to remember to be more patient. That's all."

"Really? That's what you got out of that interaction?" Daniel laughed.

"Should I have gotten something else?" Joanna asked.

"He was coming on to you, and you didn't want him to, so...."

"He wasn't really coming on to me. He's just lonely," she looked in the man's direction. He was trying a line on another woman in the diner.

"And that's why he was coming on to you." Daniel laughed again. Even after what she had been through a year ago, Joanna still saw the best in people. They ordered coffees and faced each other over the hot brews.

"So, what's this big story you wanted to talk to me about?" Daniel asked.

Joanna sipped from her cup and blew her bangs from her eyes. With another deep exhalation she turned to face him.

"You know I'm working at the Academy, right?"

"Sure, the classical music thing. It sounds like a great project." Daniel replied.

"It is, but here's the thing," Joanna said. "Some of these students are coming from really dangerous parts of the city. And frankly, I'm scared for them."

She paused and took another swallow of coffee. "One girl," she continued. "Her name is Veronica. I don't know where in the city she lives, but it sounds tough. And her friend, Tariq, he basically warned me away from ever going anywhere near there."

"What did he say?" Daniel pulled out his notebook and jotted down notes.

"He said it's not a place white people ever go," tears welled up in Joanna's eyes.

"Jo," Daniel put a hand on her arm. "That's not really news, is it?" He kept his tone soothing. "Some places really aren't safe, for anyone."

"No, but they should be," her voice raised. "All these kids should be safe."

"And they're not," he finished for her.

She turned tear-stained eyes on him. "If there's something we can do about it, we've got to."

"Okay, you're right." Daniel made a few more quick notes. He stowed the notebook away. "Do you know where they live?"

"Somewhere way out North of here."

"If we can figure out where they live, maybe I can at least see what's making things so tough there."

"That would be great," Joanna sniffled and blew her nose into a napkin. "I'm sorry," she said. "I just really want them to be okay."

"Sure, I get it. Look, if you can find out where they live or at least their last names, I can take it from there." Daniel put some money down on the counter to pay for their coffees. They stood.

"I can give you Veronica's last name right now, and I know she goes to PS165-Z."

"165Z?" He asked. "Why the Z?"

"I think it has something to do with it being an annex of the Simon School, PS165. They have classes in trailers," Joanna said.

"That's a good start. I'll see what I can come up with at work."

"How are you liking it, by the way?" Joanna asked.

"It's certainly different," Daniel replied. "I went to my first whiskey tasting at the home of the owner of the St. James Distillery. And I think he owns much more than just that."

"Wow."

"Yeah, it turns out I work for his son, Tom. He's a character." Daniel said. "But, I like the work."

"Good."

Daniel saw Joanna to the Rose Building. He headed back to the NewsBlitz office where he busied himself at the computer. Tom's family's deep pockets had provided the finest in computer and other tech equipment. He had also invested in paid websites that only allowed access to private investigators.

"Okay," Daniel entered the username and password on the site's main page. "Let's see what's going on near PS165-Z."

The four trailers of PS165-Z sat tucked away near some of the warehouses by West Harlem Piers. The Piers had been turned into a park, but the surrounding buildings still told tales of shady deals from the drug import/export craze of the 1980s.

Daniel searched the CrimeScout.com website for recent news of criminal activity in the area near PS165-Z. In addition to breaking and entering reports, a few muggings, mostly of careless tourists, and one assault, he found a few rumors of rekindled drug activity.

He stopped and shook his head. "Great, Daniel," he muttered. "Now you're thinking that B&Es, muggings, and assaults are no big deal." But, the drug rumors might be worth pursuing. He typed in another search engine and looked up the address of the administrative trailer for PS165-Z. He also located the phone number and dialed it.

The phone rang multiple times before the school's voicemail encouraged him to leave a message.

"Hello," he said. "My name is Daniel Evershed, and I'm a reporter for NewsBlitz," Daniel explained the reasons for his call. He rattled off his number and requested a call back. He pocketed his phone and headed towards home.

Daniel arrived at the school the following afternoon right after the last class of the day had begun. Students scurried among the three trailers that stood parallel to one another like three large gray shoeboxes. A fourth trailer sat behind and perpendicular to them. A small, white sign near its door proclaimed "Main Office." He pushed open the door and entered.

Two women sat at two desks in the main quadrant of the trailer. Each held phone headsets to her ear and listened and gave rapid fire answers to whatever questions they heard.

"No, ma'am," one of the women said. "We can't let her back in school unless a parent or guardian accompanies her here for a conference." She listened for a moment. "Ma'am, I didn't make the rules, but I do know them. If you want her to be allowed back in the school after her suspension, she will need to come here with a parent or guardian and have a conference with Dr. Clifford. Yes, ma'am," she rolled her eyes, and her mouth moved in what appeared to be a silent prayer. "That would be fine, ma'am. I'm sure you will. Have a good day." Her low, musical voice punched out the last few words in a curt staccato.

With too much care, she placed the receiver back in its cradle. She pushed her chair away from her desk, stood up, and turned three clockwise circles. As she completed the last circle, she opened her brown eyes and saw Daniel.

"Oh! I didn't see you there. Sorry. My bad. Sometimes, I just need a minute." She smoothed her navy blue skirt over rounded hips and sat back down in her chair. "What can I do for you?"

Daniel glanced at the name plaque that sat at the front edge of her tidy desk.

"Good afternoon, Mrs. Sampson. I'm Daniel Evershed." He produced his press credentials and passed them to her. "I left a message yesterday about speaking with someone about a story I'm doing for News Blitz. Is this a good time?"

"Honey," she smiled and the southern tones in her accent shone through. "There's no such thing is a good time around here, but then again, there's no such thing as a bad time either. So, what do you need?"

"I'm working on a story about the dual nature of the city," he said. "Some have everything and others … ."

"Others go to school in trailers, if they go to school at all" she finished for him.

"Yes," he said.

"So what are you going to do about it?" she asked. She pushed her chair back from the desk and crossed her arms in front of her chest.

"I want to write about it."

The other woman in the room finished her phone conversation and turned her attention to them.

"Hasn't it been done before?" Her husky voice sounded like a razor being sharpened on a strop. "Look at the Occupy Movement. That's what they wanted to do, and it hasn't exactly made sweeping changes."

"True. Ms. … " Daniel glanced for a name plaque on her desk and saw the slot sitting empty.

"Jordan," she supplied.

"But, I've noticed that any time the story gets told, it turns either one or the other side off. I'm going to try to tell it differently." Daniel sat on the single metal chair in front of Mrs. Sampson's desk.

"How," Mrs. Sampson leaned forward.

"In pictures." I want to get incontrovertible proof that this duality exists. People discount what they read and what they hear all the time. It's harder to discount what they see with their own eyes."

"You're that sure of yourself, are you?" Jordan asked.

Daniel laughed. "Not at all. But it's what I've said I'll do. So, I'm going to do it." His determination hardened his voice and shone in his eyes.

"I've no doubt you will, but what do you want here?" Mrs. Sampson asked.

"I've heard rumors," he lowered his voice and leaned toward her in an innate gesture of trust. "I've heard stories that some of the kids who live in this area have been recruited into some dangerous activities."

"What kind of dangerous activities?" Mrs. Sampson asked.

"Transporting drugs," he answered.

"You think our kids are drug mules?" she narrowed her eyes.

"Honestly, I don't know. But I want to find out. And the thing is that if they are doing it, they are probably doing it for some pretty powerful and wealthy people. That's the duality."

Jordan stood and straightened her tan pencil skirt. She grabbed a tiny brown purse from a drawer in her metal desk. Far younger than Mrs. Sampson, she wore her long hair in thin, colorful braids that hung down her back. She walked to the door.

"Whatever," she stated. "It's not like it's going to make any kind of difference. I'm taking a cigarette break," she said to Mrs. Sampson. She left the trailer and slammed the door behind her.

"Did I say something to make her angry?" Daniel asked.

"No, sugar. She's just made that way," Mrs. Sampson replied. "Don't pay her any mind. She's good with the students, and that's all that matters."

"Now," she settled back in her chair. "Tell me more about these rumors. What do you know?"

"I'm afraid I don't know much. A friend who is working with some of your students heard some things that disturbed her. She asked me to look into it, because one of the students intimated that this area is far more dangerous than anyone might realize."

"Especially to the kids," Mrs. Sampson added.

"They are the most vulnerable," Dan agreed.

"So, who did the talking?"

"There is a girl named Veronica, and she has a friend named Tariq. My friend, Joanna, talked to them both, and neither of them feels safe around here," Daniel continued. "If it's possible, I'd like to talk to them."

"That won't be possible unless they have a parent or guardian present," Mrs. Sampson replied. "They would need to sign a waiver and give their permission for the children to be interviewed. Of course," she paused.

"What?"

"Tariq and his little brother have an unusual living situation," she said.

"Unusual?" Daniel prompted her.

"Their older brother has guardianship of both of them, but he's not much older than 18 himself." Her voice lowered as if she were talking to herself more than to Daniel. "I'm still not sure how that was accomplished, except that they don't have any other living relatives in the area."

"So, the brother is the one taking care of them?"

"When he's around. That's the sticking point, isn't it?" She rolled her chair over to the right side of her desk and tapped on the keyboard of her laptop.

"Yes, here it is," she said. "Tariq and his younger brother live with their older brother Jerome."

"Could I meet Tariq, do you think?"

Mrs. Sampson slid the laptop closed. "I don't think that's a good idea. I have no idea that Jerome would approve, and I would need his approval before I can give out any information like that on him."

"You're trying to protect him," Daniel tilted his head to the side. "I get that. Believe it or not, that's exactly what I want to do. If I can write the story, I might be able to help."

"Or, you cast a light on him and get him noticed, and around here, that's not necessarily a benefit." Mrs. Sampson stated. "I'm not sure there is anything more I can do for you, Mr. Evershed."

"That's okay, Mrs. Sampson. You've been a tremendous help." Daniel stood. He offered her his hand, and they shook. He paused at the doorway.

"If you don't mind my asking, why did you turn in a circle three times earlier?"

"Oh that?" Mrs. Sampson laughed. "That's just something my Grandmama taught me. I grew up in Louisiana, and when you needed to rid yourself of the negative, you had to do something positive. When I'd get upset, she'd get me up and we'd spin in circles until I felt all better. Oh, we'd spin and spin and the world would go all topsy-turvy." Her eyes misted with memory. "Nowadays, there's no room to spin and spin."

"Not in New York," Daniel said.

"But I still do a little something," she continued. "It can't hurt."

"No," Daniel agreed. He left the trailer and walked out into the sweltering afternoon.

Daniel paused outside the trailer, pulled out his phone, and dialed.

"Hey, Joanna," he said as she answered. "I struck out. So, I think I'm going to need to come sit in on one of your Academy classes. If he comes by to pick up Veronica again, I'll at least get to see him, and maybe he and I can talk."

Jordan stepped back into the trailer and sat at her desk.
"So, what did he want?" She motioned to the door.
"He wanted to get some information on some possible drug running activity going on in the neighborhood," Mrs. Sampson answered. "He thinks some of our kids are muling. Are they muling? Do you know anything about that?"
"How would I know?" Jordan huffed. She stood and slung her small bag back over her shoulder.
"Where are you going now?" Mrs. Sampson asked.
"Cigarette break."
"But you just had one," Mrs. Sampson pointed out.
"Whatever," Jordan pulled her phone out of her purse as she walked to the door. "I need another one."

Jordan stood in the shade of one of the lone maples that survived in the harsh environment of New York City. She dialed a number from memory.
"Yeah, it's me," she said as the phone was answered. "We might have a problem. There was a reporter at the school today. He's asking some questions."
"Who is he?" the man on the line asked.
"How the hell should I know?" She pouted. "Daniel somebody."
"Daniel Evershed?" he asked.
"Yeah, maybe. Whatever."
"Interesting," he replied. "You did well to let me know. Keep me posted if he shows up again."
"I don't think he will. Sampson wouldn't give him any information without a Guardian's permission, and we know no one is going to give that."
"True. That will have to be good enough for now. Well done."

THE PIANO'S KEY

"Whatever."

CHAPTER 10

EVIE

The fireball arched overhead. It soared towards the red and white circular target. At the last second, it careened away from the target and aimed straight towards a case of trophies against the far wall of the gymnasium. With a hiss, it scorched one Wisteria's Battle Magic Competition Trophies and knocked all the other ones to the floor.

"Seriously, Songbottom? You can't even get it in the same time zone as the target?" Wisteria strode over to the case that held her accomplishments. She waved her hand over the trophy. It levitated about five inches from its base. She walked towards me. It followed her like a floating puppy. She halted in front of me, gestured with a finger, and it dropped into my hands.

"Clean it," she barked. "And no magic."

"What?" I cried.

"A little time spent applying some elbow grease will do you good," she said. "You need to learn how to focus, or you'll never pass. And I want you to pass," she continued. "If you don't pass, I'll be stuck with you forever. You wouldn't want that, would you?"

"Oh, hell, no!" I said.

"Good." She nodded her head once. "Then, you'll clean this one, and you'll put all the others back exactly where they were before. Ah, ah, ah," she punctuated her words with a wagging finger. "No going back in time and no asking anyone else to help. Do it from memory, or figure out what the arrangement was. The key here, Songbottom, is focus. If you have it, you might survive. If you don't, you're toast. And more importantly so will your charges be."

She marched to the center of the room and stuck her hands on her narrow hips. "That goes for all of you," she yelled. "Anyone, and I mean anyone, who doesn't scare up some focus is going to fail. Am I making myself clear?"

"Yes," we chorused.

"I didn't hear you," she shouted.

"Yes," we yelled.

"Good. Be here by dawn tomorrow. Focus drills at sunrise. Dismissed," she snapped.

I set the heavy trophy down with a thud. Crap! My arms were killing me.

"Where do you think you're going, Songbottom?" Wisteria bit out.

"You said we were dismissed," I replied.

"You didn't think I meant you, did you?"

"Um, well, but I have to help Doc with the puppies." I had no better answer.

"I'm sure someone else can take over Puppy Patrol. You're on cleanup duty." She waved her hand over to the case. "I'd better see my face shining in them by morning," she sneered the misquote from one of the greatest movies ever made, The Princess Bride.

The rest of the class filed out of the room.

Wisteria sighed and walked back over to me.

"Songbottom, you got lucky last year. By all accounts, Dunne should have killed you. I wonder why he didn't," she mused. She stopped and her head turned toward me in a way that made me think, King Cobra. Her eyes bored into me.

"Why didn't he? Why didn't he kill you? He has the skills. He's more powerful than you are."

I stayed silent.

She bent down and studied my face.

"Tell me," she commanded.

"Well," I hedged. "We, um …." I extended the pause past the bounds of propriety. Heck, I extended it past the bounds of lunacy. "We used to date."

"You used to what?" She exploded. "Are you serious? You dated a Bane? Of all the idiotic things to do. Then again, if he dated you, he'd want to kill you for sure. So, why aren't you dead?"

"He wasn't a Bane when I dated him," I defended myself as best I could.

"Oh, so you turned him into one," she remarked.

"I did not!" Shock and outrage steamed out of me.

"He was seduced. By the dark si-."

"Tell me you weren't about to say he was seduced by the Dark Side," she laughed. "I love Star Wars as much as the next person, but really." Her guffaw rang out through the gym. After a few minutes, she calmed. She put a hand to her belly. "Oh man, Songbottom," she hiccupped. "You sure know how to pick 'em."

"Wait a minute," I retorted. "I picked Daniel."

"The jury's still out on that one," she stated and walked away from me.

"Hey," I caught up to her and grabbed her arm. She looked down at where I held her and slowly raised her eyes to mine. I removed my fingers from her rock hard bicep one at a time and moved a few steps back.

"What do you mean, 'the jury's still out on that one?'" I demanded.

"Nothing," she clammed up. "Just what I said. Nobody really knows him. And what I've noticed is that things and people that seem too good to be true, generally are."

"You're just jealous," I pouted.

"Jealous? Of you? Oh, boy do you have a lot to learn," she smiled.

"I know, and you're supposed to teach me," I had no idea why every single word that came out of my mouth sounded like I was a peevish five-year-old, but I was on a roll, and I was going with it. "So, get on with it, already," I goaded her. Why? I had no idea. Maybe I do have a death wish. "Teach me, O Great Flamethrower. Show me how it's done."

A tiny smile parted her lips. She flicked her fingers in my direction and my clothes transformed from cotton and silk into razors and lemon juice.

"Crap! What the hell!" I ripped them off.

"You'll have a lot worse if you go up against Banes without training, you idiot." She spat the words. "So get a grip. Stop thinking about your Boy Toy and clean up that trophy case."

She pivoted on her heel and marched out.

I grabbed my wand and transformed my clothes back into clothes and donned them again.

"What the hell's the matter with her?" I grumbled.

"She's just trying to prepare you," Torlyn appeared above my head. She crossed her flame arms in front of her chest and stared down at me.

"Prepare me for what?" I asked.

"For whatever's coming," she replied.

"Isn't that just dandy?" I hated the note of whining on my voice, but I ignored it. If I pretended I wasn't being a peevish brat, I could deny it to anyone who called me on it.

"Evie," Torlyn's voice held the wisdom of the ages. "You have to pay attention." Although she wasn't normally one to lord it over me, Torlyn was a lot older than, well, almost everyone. Fire was one of the original Elements, and she was made of fire. Some of the Elemental Fae, like Leili, came along later. They came along when various stars were born or went supernova or some other explosive fiery event. But Torlyn's parents were original, as in Big Bang original. And she wasn't born too many millions of years after that so she'd been around for pretty much forever.

"I'm trying, Torlyn." I prowled around the room. The more I thought about how she had been treating me, the more pissed I got. I swung around and faced Torlyn. "But she's such a … She's such a … ."

"Good instructor? Tough cookie? Hard-ass?" Torlyn supplied.

"All of the above," I replied.

"Count your lucky stars," Torlyn said. "You're going to need all three before we're done."

The clue phone finally rang loud enough for me to pick it up.

"Wait a minute, Torlyn. What do you know?" I narrowed my eyes up at her.

"I don't know a thing," she clammed up. "Just do your work."

"Fine!" I sulked. I grabbed my wand like I meant it. "Let's practice some dousing magic. How about you set up 'em and I'll knock 'em down?"

"Now you're talking," Torlyn rose towards the ceiling. She snapped her fingers and a hefty fireball coalesced in front of her. She snapped them again, and it careened toward my head.

"Yeow! How about a little warning, next time?"

"No one else will give you any. Why should I?"

"Good point." I raised my wand. "Again."

Three fireballs careened towards me.

I doused the first two. The third singed my eyebrows before I threw myself away from it.

"What am I? Luke Skywalker?" I rolled to standing.

"That would make me Darth Vader," Torlyn's flame face transformed into a fiery imitation of Darth Vader's black mask. The mask split into a hideous grin. "Round 2."

THE PIANO'S KEY

JOANNA

The students played through Twinkle Twinkle Little Star. The familiar tune sounded pure and true as the students held the last note. Joanna circled her arms and brought her thumbs and index fingers together in the universal sign for "Stop playing."

"Well done, you!" She applauded them. She turned to Veronica who had improvised a harmony line in the middle of the piece.

"And I loved that extra line you played, Veronica. I hope that you're proud of yourself for coming up with it."

"Really?" Veronica beamed. "Thank you."

A movement at the door drew everyone's attention. Tariq leaned against the door and studied the room. Veronica's smiled dimmed.

"Veronica did great, don't you think? They all did great," Joanna said.

"Yeah, whatever. It was all right." He shrugged.

"Could you do better?" Carlton, one of the other students, asked.

"Don't know. Don't care," Tariq answered.

"Sure, you could," he said. "Because you're so great at everything. Right?"

"I'm better than you are," Tariq moved into the room and clenched his fists.

Joanna eyed the two boys, stood, and approached them.

"He plays," Veronica moved between Tariq and the rest of the class. "But he needs a piano."

"Sure is lucky, there isn't one in here," Carlton smirked. "Or you'd have to show us just how great you play."

"Whatever," Tariq said. He turned to Veronica. "Let's go, Ronnie."

"You play piano?" Joanna interjected.

"What I do ain't none of your business," Tariq stormed out of the gym.

"Sorry, Joanna. He's just rude sometimes." Veronica packed her violin and hurried after him.

"No worries," Joanna called after her. She turned to the rest of the class. "You all are doing really well. I'll see you tomorrow."

As soon as the last student exited the room, she whipped out her mobile phone.

"Daniel, I'm sorry," she said. "They left a little early. I didn't get a chance to call you before now."

"It's okay, Jo," he answered. "I took a chance he'd show up today, and I waited outside the school. I'm actually walking a couple of blocks behind them both right now. I hope no one thinks I'm a stalker."

"I guess you have your press credentials with you if anyone questions you," Joanna said.

"Let's hope I don't need them. Uh oh, here we go. Gotta run. I'll let you know what I find out."

"You'd better," Joanna pressed the "End" key and finished the conversation.

"Damn!" Joanna swore. "I wish Evie were here. She'd know what to do." She paced the room a few times. On top of Tariq and Veronica, now she was worried about Daniel as well.

DANIEL

Daniel remained a short distance behind Tariq and Veronica. They walked uptown. The buildings morphed from the clean lines around the school and Columbia University to the rundown tenements in the surrounding neighborhoods. Ramshackle apartment buildings loomed high overhead.

Two men sat on the stoop of one of the buildings in the Projects.

"Yo, pretty mama," one rasped as he leaned towards the kids. "Come on up here and let me introduce myself."

"She's got somewhere to be," Tariq put a hand on Veronica's arm.

"She can get there late," the other man piped up.

"She's with me." He narrowed his eyes. "And she's going to stay with me."

"Why don't we see about that?" the first ground out.

"Yeah, why don't we?" Tariq said.

Daniel put his hands in his pockets and stood tall behind the kids. He stared at the two men until they noticed him. He removed the camera from the messenger bag and trained it on the foursome. He shook his head sharply at the two men. They both sat back down, and the kids walked past them. Daniel followed.

They approached a small, rundown building. A sign in front read "PS 326." Tariq jogged up to the opening door. He exchanged a few words with someone inside. Within a few minutes, a six-year-old boy exited. He took Tariq's hand. The two rejoined Veronica on the street.

The refuse from several days of non-attended garbage lay on the streets. Good thing, too, Daniel thought as he ducked behind a pile of trash bags at one point. Otherwise, they would see me for sure.

He was grateful he had his camera in a tattered messenger bag. His large camera bag would have drawn too much attention.

The young people crossed 137th street and turned left toward one of the more dilapidated buildings. Its twelve stories held many windows that were either broken or in disrepair.

Daniel withdrew his camera once again and focused it on the building's entrance. Veronica and the younger boy climbed the stairs. They turned and waited at the door. Tariq stood on the step closest to the street. The younger boy froze in place and stared into the sky. Veronica put a hand on his shoulder.

Daniel snapped a few quick shots. The three of them were family. And they were a family who suffered, especially Veronica. He zoomed in on her face. Were those tears? He strained to hear their conversation.

"Calvin, stop daydreaming," Tariq said to the little boy. "Go inside and check the mailbox."

"It's too high," the child replied.

"No it ain't," Tariq said. "Stand on your toes, and you'll reach it just fine. I'll be back before you know it. And Ronnie's gonna watch you and play with you until I'm home."

"Okay," Calvin said.

Veronica opened the door for him, and he entered the building. She gazed at Tariq with luminous eyes.

"I'm only going for an hour or two," Tariq said.

"That's plenty of time for shit to go wrong," she replied.

"Look, if you don't want to watch him, you don't have to. I'll figure out something else."

"Like what? You mean, you'll stay here? Great. Do that." Veronica opened the door again and motioned him inside.

"You know, I can't." Tariq called. He stepped on to the street. "So, you gonna watch him, or not?"

"You know I will," Veronica said.

"I'll be back."

"You better." She entered the building and disappeared from sight.

Tariq broke into a slow jog. Daniel followed at a discreet distance. Tariq wound through the streets towards the warehouses that still sat on the west side in the shadow of the Washington Bridge. He approached one of the smaller warehouses. It sat dark and abandoned. The large bay doors along the side stood locked with a rusted padlock. Tariq knocked on a small door to the left of the bay doors. Light streamed out as it opened. He slipped inside. As Daniel drew closer, he realized the windows had been painted with blackout paint. No one would be able to see inside unless he was allowed access.

"Shit!" Daniel swore. He hunkered down and held his camera ready for any opportunity to snap a shot or two the next time that door opened.

Within a few minutes, Tariq and five other young men of varying ages exited the warehouse. Three had the muscular blocky looks of football players. The others appeared to be in various stages of growing and filling out like any other teenaged boys. They moved so quickly Daniel got no glimpse of the building's interior. They each carried a black backpack.

"Yo man," one of the boys called to Tariq. "Don't be late again. He don't like it, and unless you want to be replaced …."

"I know," Tariq said. "I had to get my little brother from school."

"I don't care," came the answer. "And you know if I don't care, he won't."

"All right, man," Tariq said. "I get it. I won't be late again."

"Good. Okay. We meet back here in an hour and a half."

"But I have to get all the way downtown," Tariq said.

"Then, you'd better move your ass."

The boys scattered. Tariq sprinted towards the closest subway stop. Daniel hurried after him.

Tariq jogged the twelve blocks to nearest subway stop. He leapfrogged over the turnstile and avoided the fee. Daniel slowed to push his fare card through the slot and strained to keep his eyes on the swift teenager.

Daniel craned his neck over a number of people who waited at the station but could find no sight of him. Rush hour had arrived and New Yorkers were either headed home or to their evening shifts.

The train pulled into the station. The throng flowed into and out of the car as people changed places. As the doors closed, he caught sight of Tariq's blue jacket and black backpack.

"Stand clear of the doors," the mechanical subway voice announced. "The doors are closing." Daniel scampered onto the train as the doors rolled shut. He looked around the car and spotted Tariq leaning against the far wall at the other end of the car.

The train rolled downtown past the many stops on the upper west side. At the 23rd street and Seventh Avenue stop, Tariq darted off the train. Daniel followed. Tariq exited and headed west towards the Projects that populated Chelsea before its metamorphosis. Although the neighborhood had been revitalized in the nineties, much of its shady character remained. Tariq stopped at 23rd and 11th Avenue just before the neighborhood gave way to the warehouses and piers of the district. He jogged up the steps of one of the Georgian style houses along the block. Grateful that he brought along a telephoto lens, Daniel snapped a few shots of the space and Tariq from half a block away.

Tariq knocked several times. The open door revealed a tall, beefy man. He wore a side holster over his loose t-shirt. He motioned Tariq inside, and the door slammed shut.

Daniel crossed the street and approached the house. When he had achieved a good vantage point, he chose a building at random and mounted the steps. As he stepped onto the landing, the front door creaked open. An elderly, gray-haired woman exited. She lugged a rolling, metal grocery cart.

"Here," Daniel called to her. "Let me help you with that."

The woman's eyes narrowed in suspicion then widened in gratitude.

"Thanks, baby," she murmured in a soft southern accent. "Things are gettin' harder every day."

"You aren't from around here, are you?" Daniel asked as he carried her folding cart down the few short steps.

"No," she said. "My people hail from Georgia."

"What brought you here?"

"Fame. Fortune. Glory. The dream." She smiled.

"And did you get the dream?" He asked.

"You know when you get the dream, baby? You get the dream when it changes to something you can get." She leaned on her cart when he handed it to her.

"Baby, can you do me another little favor?" She said.

"Sure," he answered.

"My cane is still up there. Would you be a darlin' and bring it down to me?"

"Sure thing," he said.

He ran up the stairs and up to the glass-paned front door. He glanced across the street. Tariq and the man with the gun stood in front of a table. Daniel trained his camera on the window across the street. He zoomed his telephoto in through the opposite window. Tariq opened the black backpack. It contained several sealed, plastic packages of what looked white powder and one package of a blue powder.

The man nodded. He moved out of view and returned seconds later with a similar black backpack. He unzipped it and showed Tariq its contents. Bundled stacks of money lay inside. Tariq removed two random stacks. He flipped through them. He removed a pen from his pocket, took another random stack, and marked three random bills from all three stacks. He, too, nodded. He returned the bills to the backpack and zipped it up. He hefted it and left the table. Within a second, the door opened and Tariq exited still carrying the new backpack. He jogged back east down 23rd street.

"Shit!" Daniel searched the foyer for the cane. He grabbed it from right by the door and hurried down the front steps. He handed it to her.

"What took you so long, baby?" The woman's eyes narrowed in suspicion again.

"I couldn't find it. I guess I'm a tall guy, and it's a short cane," Daniel explained lamely.

"You are a tall drink of water," she smiled at him. "What's your name, baby?"

"Daniel Evershed," he replied. "What's yours?"

"Letitia Darling," she said. She straightened her short frame, cocked a hip, and shot him a searing, flirtatious glance with her caramel-brown eyes.

For an instant, he saw her in her prime. Shapely legs, killer curves, and a smile that could stop a truck flashed through his mind. She must have been something in her day, he thought. Even now, she possessed a vibrant beauty.

"That would have been a great stage name," he said as he left her.

"Oh, it was baby. It was."

Daniel jogged back towards the subway stop. He hoped Tariq was heading back uptown and had no other stops to make. If he had deviated from the path back to the train, Daniel had lost him.

Letitia rolled her cart along 23rd Street. The man with the gun exited his house. He crossed the street to her.

"Hey, pretty lady," he stopped in front her.

"What do you want?" She stopped her forward shuffle. She stared at him with slitted brown eyes. A wave of cold, clammy air passed through him.

He jerked back in reaction. "Just need a question answered. That's all."

"So ask it," she resumed walking.

"Who was that guy you were talking to?"

"No one. An admirer."

"Yeah, right." He smirked.

She turned suddenly icy blue eyes on him, and his blood chilled.

"He was an admirer. Nothing more."

"Was that a camera he had strapped around his neck?"

"It wasn't his neck I was looking at," she purred. With a flash of her once again brown eyes, she sashayed away.

"Um, uh, okay," he choked out. Against all reason, his heart beat a hasty tattoo in his chest.

He gazed after her for long moments. He shook his head and took a cellphone out of his pocket.

"Boss, it's me." he said into the phone. "I think we might have problem. There was a guy hanging near the house when the kid came by." He paused for a moment. "Yeah, I know. But, he had a camera."

Silence lengthened on the other end of the line. Then, the voice became terse. "What did he look like?"

"I don't know," he replied. "Tall, skinny, dark haired. Glasses."

"All right. I'll take care of it."

"You don't want me to do it?"

"No. Leave him to me."

Daniel jerked to a stop a few yards from Tariq as he ran down the subway steps to the platform. Again, he leapfrogged past the turnstile and headed towards the uptown 1 train.

Daniel pushed his way past the crowd leaving the station. He zigged and zagged to the platform. The odor of stale underground air permeated the place. A rat crossed the tracks and expertly avoided the third rail. Everyone settled in for the few minute wait until the next train arrived. Daniel removed his phone and dialed.

"Tommy," he whispered. "It's Daniel."

"I know it's you, darling," Tommy replied.

"I'm onto something."

"You want to get on something?" Tommy said. "Come on over. I'll give you something to get on."

Daniel paused and looked at the phone for a second. "Tommy, you're not making any sense."

"What else is new, baby?" Daniel heard laughter in the background. Understanding dawned.

"You're not alone, are you?" If Tommy wasn't alone, he was not free to talk, particularly if any members of his family were nearby

"Not even a little, but I am lonely." Tommy purred. "Why don't you come on by later tonight, and we can do something about that."

"How about seven?" Daniel asked.

"Done. I'll see you then, lover."

Daniel clicked off just as the train approached the station. Everyone boarded and squashed together. Daniel shimmied his way to the wall. He stowed his camera and kept a discreet eye on Tariq. The kid tried to appear nonchalant, but he kept a tight grip on the backpack.

After the train had passed through almost the entire island of Manhattan, Tariq exited where he had first boarded the subway. Daniel followed some distance behind.

Tariq entered the warehouse. A few minutes later, he reappeared and jogged away.

Daniel missed another chance of photographing the inside of the building. The door slid open and closed so fluidly it seemed nothing else lay behind it. The interior of the warehouse appeared to be gray.

"I'm just going to have to sneak in," Daniel said aloud. But how?

He noted the address, took one last shot of the front of the space, and headed back downtown.

He unlocked the doors to the NewsBlitz office and entered. Tommy rested his feet on his desk. The pristine creases in his pants remained somehow intact. His long, lanky frame looked relaxed. His eyes were closed.

"Hey," Daniel said. He lay his backpack down on his own desk and dropped into his chair.

"Tommy," he called louder.

Tommy's eyes popped open. He removed tiny ear buds from his ears and pressed a button on a small black box attached to them. He pressed another button on it, and it shut off.

"What are you doing?" Daniel asked.

"Oh, I, ah, sort of bugged my father's office," Tommy answered.

"You did what?" Daniel sat forward in his seat. "Why?"

"Would you believe me if I said, 'I don't know?'"

"I guess."

"Look," Tommy leaned forward "I've got a feeling. That's the best I can do. Every time I spend any time with my father, I feel like he's doing something shitty and getting away with it. I mean he's always a smug bastard, but he's been even more smug than usual. And I want to know what's going on."

"So you bugged his office," Daniel said. He pulled his camera out of his bag, removed its SD card, and inserted it into his laptop. He copied the card's contents onto the hard drive.

"Yep. That's where I was earlier when you called," Tommy said. "Sorry about all the 'lover' stuff," Tommy said. "I was trying to avoid having to have a drink, and I thought if I dialed the 'gay' up to eleven I'd give him something else to think about."

"And did you?"

"Yeah," he answered. "Believe me," he said, his eyes glassy. "I wanted it. Hell, I always want it. And acting like I'm drunk while I'm completely sober really sucks."

"But you gave it up." Daniel supplied.

"I gave it up," Tommy agreed.

"You ever worry about what will happen if you do have another drink. For real?" Daniel asked.

"Every fucking day," Tommy shook his head. "Every fucking day." He dropped his feet off the desk. "Now, why don't you tell me what got you all hot and bothered earlier? 'Cause I know it wasn't me."

Daniel scrolled through the shots he had taken while tailing Tariq.

"Take a look at these," he said. He brought the laptop to Tommy's desk.

Tommy watched the play of photos of Tariq, the warehouse, and the backpack exchange.

"Who's the kid?" Tommy asked.

"He's a friend of a friend, sort of."

"If he's a friend of a friend," Tommy said. "You'd better get him out of there and now. You know what that blue powder is?"

"No," Daniel replied.

"It's called, 'Heaven,' and it is really bad shit."

"How do you know what it's called?" Daniel asked.

Tommy laughed. "Who do you think gets all the designer stuff first?"

Daniel thought for a moment. Then, the light dawned. "Oh, you mean you."

"And those like me," Tommy said. "There's nothing that comes through this city that we don't see first."

"Do you know where we could get some?"

Tommy face fell. "I do."

"Where?"

"My sister."

He flipped his own phone out of his pocket. "If anyone knows where to get some 'Heaven,' it'll be her."

"Hey, baby," he said into the phone. "I need to ask you something. Hit me back. If not, I'll see you tonight." He disconnected and faced Daniel.

"Looks like we're going back to my father's place this evening."

"Why?"

"Because if she doesn't call back soon, she'll be there by nine pm."

"How do you know?" Daniel asked.

"Tonight's allowance night."

"You still get allowance?"

"Every week." Tommy swung his arms open. "What do you think pays for all this? It certainly isn't our subscribers."

"Why not?" Daniel sat forward and gazed at his friend.

"Because we don't charge. It's the news. It should be free."

"Sounds good to me," Daniel agreed. He reached into his desk, pulled open a zippered bag, and placed his SD card into it. He inserted a new one into his camera. As he looked up, he noticed a small photograph on Tommy's desk. The woman in it stunned him. Her long, blond hair coiled on top of her head in an artful up-do. Her pale, yellow gown accented her creamy skin. A single emerald stone nestled between her breasts. It reflected the dark, green fire of her eyes. She faced the camera with a mischievous grin on her full lips.

"Wow!" Daniel exclaimed. "Who is she?"

"That's my mother," Tommy answered.

"She's gorgeous," Daniel said.

"She was."

Daniel paused in his admiration of her perfect face.

"Was?" He asked it gently.

"She died shortly after Nadia was born."

"I'm sorry," Daniel said.

"Thanks. To be honest, I don't really remember her very well. I do remember she was always laughing, and no one could flirt like she could. My father utilized her charms to build his business more than once."

"What does that mean?"

"She was the kind of woman who could charm the light from the sun if she wanted to. Everybody loved her."

"If you don't mind my asking, how did she die?"

"Heart attack."

"That seems awfully young for a heart attack."

"I know, but apparently, she had a rotten valve or something. When they did the autopsy, they found that her heart had exploded. My father was in Scotland on a buying trip, and the servants were off for the night."

"Where were you?"

"I was already at boarding school. Nadia was alone in the house with her until the housekeeper came to work the next morning." He shuddered. "I'm glad she doesn't remember any of that." He furrowed his brow and doodled on the legal pad on his desk. He ended the doodle with a violent spiral scrawl.

"Are you all right?" Daniel asked.

"I'm fine," Tommy sighed. Tears glistened in his eyes. "It's just that whenever I think about it, I remember that she was really athletic, you know? She rode horses. She played a mean game of tennis, and she'd played varsity volleyball in college. I can't imagine that someone wouldn't have noticed she had a bad heart. But the house was locked. No one came in. The alarm never went off. None of the cameras showed anything was wrong. She just died." He slumped in his chair and dropped his head in his hands.

Daniel put his arm around Tommy while he cried. For a few minutes, all was silence except Tommy's quiet sobs. Finally, he took a tremulous breath and gazed at Daniel.

"Thanks." He quirked one side of his mouth into a lopsided smile.

"No problem." Daniel handed Tommy a tissue. "I lost my dad a long time ago."

"How did he die?" Tommy asked.

"He didn't, as far as I know." Daniel answered. "One day, he just disappeared. He went to work, and we never saw him again."

"Well, aren't we a couple of orphans?" Tommy gave a watery smile.

"Yeah," Daniel smiled in return. Once he was sure Tommy was back on an even keel, Daniel rolled his chair back to his desk and finished prepping his camera equipment.

"Tommy," Daniel changed the subject. "Do you need me to go to your father's place tonight?"

"No," Tommy replied.

"Good," Daniel answered. "I think I'm going to go back to that warehouse." He stored his camera in its bag, stood, and placed the strap over his shoulder.

Tommy's phone announced an incoming text. He flipped it open.

"Actually, I think you might need to postpone that a bit." Tommy called to him.

"Why is that?" Daniel paused at the door.

"Your presence has been requested tonight as well."

"For what?"

"Hell if I know," Tommy stood, pocketed his phone and moved towards the door.

"Maybe my father wants another look at my Boy Toy." He tweaked Daniel's cheek.

Daniel laughed and opened the door for his faux boyfriend.

"More than likely, he just wants to be sure I'm not spending too much money on you," Tommy said. "I have a history of doing that."

"You spent too much money on your boyfriends?"

"You could say that."

The two men jogged down the five stories to the ground floor.

"What's too much?"

"Let's just say one of them cost me in the six figures."

"No shit." Daniel stopped short.

"Oh, there was plenty of shit," Tommy snorted. "Most of it went up Justin's nose. And the rest of it hit the fan when Daddy Dearest found out."

"What happened then?"

"Let's just say it'll be a long while before Justin makes his way back to New York."

"Where is he now?"

"I have no idea. Last I heard, he was somewhere in the southernmost tip of Chile. Herding goats."

"Are you serious?"

"I might as well be."

Tommy sobered. "After my father found out about Justin and me and the cocaine, I never saw him again. One second he was in my room, and the next second three men came, marched him out, and he was gone."

"How old were you?" Daniel put a hand on Tommy's arm. They stepped out of the cool hallway and into the stifling heat of the city.

"I was sixteen. Justin was fifteen."

"And no one ever saw him again?"

"Him or his family," Tommy said. "I got one postcard from Chile. He said his father had gotten transferred there. He said he was fine, and that he'd write more soon." He stared into space for a moment. The cars, buses, and cabs crawled past them in the permanent twilight under the skyscrapers of the East Side.

"And he never wrote?" Daniel prompted.

"No."

"Hmm, I had no idea being your boyfriend was going to have such intrigue."

"Yeah, intrigue." Tommy smiled. "With luck, a boring evening with my father asking you questions about your family is the worst it will be. Me? I'm going to be pretending to be drunk off my ass. That ought to be fun."

"Can't you just stay sober?"

"And get the third degree? No thanks. No," he continued. "I'll be 'drinking' shots tonight and celebrating my anniversary.

You see, eleven years ago tonight is when Justin got removed. And that was the night I took my last drink and snorted my last line." He laughed, but his eyes looked anguished.

"You really loved him, didn't you?"

"I did. Do." Tommy replied. He stood stock still, shook his head, and grinned. "But enough about me. What about you? When are you going to check out the warehouse? I want to come too."

"You should," Daniel said. He gazed at Tommy's chic clothing. "You might want to dress down a bit, though. It isn't exactly an haute couture kind of neighborhood."

"I can dress down with the best of them," Tommy pouted. "Just wait and see."

"Looking forward to it," Daniel laughed.

They stopped at the front of the opulent building where St. James made his home. Tommy exchanged pleasantries with the door man, and they entered. He placed a black card into the slot by the button marked P for penthouse. The elevator whisked them to the top floor. A discreet ding announced their arrival.

Tommy transformed from an earnest young man into a foppish drunk in the blink of an eye. He draped an arm of Daniel's shoulder.

"Show time," he winked.

CHAPTER 11

EVIE

Six of us sat at various lab tables in Healing class. The square, windowless room held floor to ceiling shelves on three walls. Each shelf had jars and boxes of herbs and other accoutrements of the healing trade. On our tables, we faced an array of jars, bottles, and bags of herbs, minerals, vitamins, and several fluids I couldn't bear to name. I shuddered at one jar that held a viscous jumble of gels of various putrid colors. I had no idea what it was, and I was in no hurry to identify it. Some things are better left a mystery.

"Five minutes," the Doc called to us.

Crap! How the hell was I going to finish it in five minutes? I was going to need more like five hours to get this thing right. If I added the next set of ingredients right, the heart palpitation-healing potion should turn a shade of golden yellow, at least that's what the instructions said. I grabbed the pipette and dropped three dollops of liquefied bergamot root into my pot.

The stupid potion turned puce. It bubbled over the edge of the beaker, burped at me, and inched towards the edge of the black-topped lab table.

"Okay, that's just gross." I grimaced.

"Godmother Songbottom," the Doc approached my table. "The potion was supposed to turn a golden color at this stage."

"I know. I know," I yanked at my hair with both hands. "I tried to put it only three. I promise."

"I'm afraid you must have added too much Bergamot. The recipe calls for only two and two-thirds dollops," The Doc said not unkindly.

"Two and two-thirds?" I yelped. "How the heck am I supposed to figure out what two-thirds of a dollop is anyway? I'm no good at this," I continued. "That's why I hate to cook, too. I never know how to decipher the darned directions. What the heck is a dollop and how on all the worlds do you whisk?" I ranted. "And I don't see why I need to do this anyway when I can use this." I reached into my messenger bag and retrieved my wand. It glinted and reflected little rainbows onto the bottles on the walls.

"One good crack and they won't know what hit 'em." I brandished my wand to punctuate each word.

"Wands aren't always appropriate, and they don't always work," the Doc said. She drew a symbol in the air in front of my wand. Its light winked out, and it drooped.

"What would you do now?" she asked. She folded her arms and waited.

"Um," I frowned at my wand. Normally, it looked like a conductor's baton. Right now, it looked like someone had cooked noodles, thrown one against the wall to check its consistency and left it stuck where it landed.

"Here," she said. "Let's make things a little more interesting." She drew a fingernail across her forearm. A line of blood spurted from the wound.

"I'm here. I'm bleeding. And your wand won't work," her voice remained calm. "What are you going to do?"

"Um," I repeated. I swallowed hard and searched the room for anything I could use to staunch the shower of her blood. It dribbled onto the floor and pooled there. My breath rasped in and out of my lungs.

"Crap! Please don't do this." I threw my wand onto the lab table and rushed to the paper towel dispenser on the wall. I kept myself from sprinting out of the classroom all together and grabbed a bunch of paper towels. I returned to the Doc and wrapped her entire forearm in the paper.

"Okay," I panted. "Point made. I need to work on this more, and I will." I averted my eyes from the blood seeping through the paper. "Please, just stop the bleeding," I pleaded.

She inclined her head. She whispered something I couldn't hear, and the bleeding stopped. The paper towels disappeared. Her arm looked good as new. Not even a scar marred the perfectly smooth surface of her skin.

I stared into her eyes.

"However you did that," I breathed. "That's shit I need to learn."

"Yes," she said. "You do. You won't pass or graduate without that knowledge." She shook her head. "You've got a lot of work to do. I'd suggest you stay here and keep practicing, but you look too much like the puce of your potion. So, go. Come back tomorrow and try again."

I nodded and shuffled out the door.

"Evie," she called me back.

"Yeah?" My voice sounded morose even to me.

"Don't forget your wand." She floated it to me.

"Traitor," I mouthed at it. Wands were supposed to be unique and loyal only to their wielders. Heh, some loyalty. Then again, the Doc had access to magics I hadn't even dreamed of. She was a Level 5. Instead of retiring or moving into Politics or joining the Tribunal, she had decided to stay on as the Healing Instructor. So, she had it goin' on, but that didn't stop me from being bitter. I shook my wand. "You're supposed to serve me and not her."

It remained silent, but its spark returned.

"That's right," I continued. "You'd better work." But I knew I was only blowing smoke. Wands could be persnickety. I had always been able to count on my wand, and this new development didn't bode well.

"Crap!" I needed a drink.

The Any Port(al) in a Storm Tavern, or the Storm, as we called it, welcomed me with open arms. Not really. Tonight, the arms that sat discreetly at its sides were folded in an unwelcoming posture. Something you don't read in the bar's promo material is that the squat, wide building had at one time been some sort of Old Being. Not unlike the Time Keepers, it had evolved into a more sedate force on the planes of existence. The Time Keepers had at one point been the most powerful beings anywhere. They had moved stuff around through time and place and space to make things run more smoothly. They say an enclave of them even helped set off the big Universal Expansion an instant after whatever Bang started this whole place. But that was shrouded in the mists of time. Get it? Yeah, I didn't think it was that funny either.

On some levels, Time Keepers made the Universe go 'round. Without them, we would be lost. What's funny? It turns out alcohol does pretty much the same thing. No matter where you go in the known universe, someone, somewhere has figured out good ol' fermentation and the trick for turning fruits, grains, and veggies into wine, beer, and liquor. So, the beings who first discovered stuff like Whiskey and Krazhat'ka and made it happen in this solar system ended up literally housing some of the greatest bars on this or any planet. Did it squick me out a little to know that any time I sit inside the Storm to have a whiskey that I'm reclining against somebody's rib bone? Yeah, a little. But mostly, I just wanted me some Johnny Walker Gold. The rest was just details.

Tonight, the walls of the Tavern echoed the purple and melon twilight outdoors. Several of my colleagues reclined or played games at the various tables and booths strewn about the place. The long, oak bar sat almost empty. My favorite bottle of Johnnie Walker Gold sat high on a shelf above the rest of the many liquors that beckoned and glittered like a Siren with a sequin habit.

I had been nursing that bottle for close to fifty years. They distilled only 150 bottles of this nectar. While I would have liked to make it last, I wasn't much for patience or will power. Margaretha, the bar's current owner, took pity on me. She had never let me have more than a thimble-full at any one time.

Mar nodded at me while she finished someone's piña colada. What I loved about Mar? She didn't waste time with mixers. If you wanted a piña colada, you'd be getting one with fab Jamaican rum and fresh pineapple and coconut from a cracked coconut. Mar drove a screwdriver into a coconut and created a funnel for the milk. She upended the coconut over the colada glass and poured that sweet stuff into it. She added a pinch of fresh coconut on top. She launched the entire drink towards the back of the bar. It floated on the air currents until it landed on the table of the person who had ordered it.

"Neat trick," I said. I launched my small frame onto one of the tall barstools.

Mar spared me a half smile.

"Which part?" she asked. She waved her hand and the coconut split in half. She sliced the tender succulent flesh apart and placed the dish on the bar before me.

"The floating Colada," I replied. I stuffed a hefty slice of coconut into my mouth. Everything stopped while I savored the exquisite and unique flavor.

"What'll it be?" Mar asked.

I eyed the bottle of Johnnie Walker.

"I think I deserve a little of the good stuff," I replied.

"What's going on? Wisteria giving you a rough time?"

"When doesn't she?" The melodrama dripped from my sigh. "No, this time it's the Doc."

"You pissed off the Doc? How the hell did you do that? She has the patience of Job, for real, because you know, she's related to him."

"I know. I know. Really? She's related to Job? What else do you know?" I forgot all about my drama. No one knew much about the Doc, and if they did, they never spilled. Mar was older than I was by a good bit. She knew stuff.

"How about that drink?" Mar changed the subject. She reached up and cradled my Johnnie Walker Gold in her arms.

"Want some?" she asked.

"What do you think?" I salivated just looking at the inky black bottle.

"I'll have some too, since you're pouring. I'm thirsty." Wisteria swung one impossibly long leg over the barstool next to mine and rested her sinewy arms on the bar.

"Of course," Mar eyed me into silence even as I opened my mouth to tell Wisteria where to put her thirst. Mar poured a generous two fingers into a glass and placed it in front of the redheaded devil in black fatigues. She poured a half a thimbleful and placed that glass in front of me. Her narrowed gaze dared me to speak and for once I kept silent. The more Wisteria liked me the safer I'd be. Of course, she didn't necessarily know that bottle was mine. I eyed my measly drink as I tried to figure out how to drop that tidbit into the conversation.

"You've certainly been nursing that bottle for long enough, Evie. It's good to see it being sampled." Mar took pity on me and said it for me. She took a clean towel off a rack and polished glasses in the overhead hanging shelves.

"This is your bottle?" Wisteria raised an eyebrow at me.

"Yeah," I replied. "I've been taking my time with it and saving it for special occasions."

"How long has it been?"

"About fifty years."

"It's still mostly full." Wisteria eyed the bottle.

"What can I say?" I replied. "There haven't been too many special occasions in the last few decades."

She lifted the glass in silent toast and put her lips to the rim. She closed her eyes and sampled the tiniest bit of the whiskey on her lips.

"Mmm," she breathed. "Excellent."

"It certainly is," Mar smiled. "And it's good to share with friends."

"As long as we're all drinking, why don't you have some too?" I hoped I'd kept the whine out of my voice, but Mar's gaze told me she'd caught my petulant tone and didn't approve.

"If I weren't on duty, I would have some." She pointed those admonishing chocolate brown eyes in my direction.

"Don't worry, Songbottom," Wisteria laughed. "We'll leave you some."

"Oh, I'm not worried. I'm sure I can find more, somewhere. After all, they made a whole 150 bottles of it," I grumbled.

"That's the spirit." She thumped the table and laughed again. Mar joined her.

I couldn't help feeling like they were enjoying some secret little joke, and I was the punch line.

"So what's got you down, Songbottom?" Wisteria put her glass down and Mar topped it back up with the Johnnie Walker. "It can't be my class. You've been doing much better since your little night of a thousand swings."

"It's not your class. It's Healing and Potions." I swirled the liquid in my glass. The light golden color of the whiskey was the color my potion was supposed to have turned. Instead, it had become like something out of Vomit Encyclopedia with the color and consistency to match. Damn. I was never going to learn that stuff.

"Healing and Potions are important," Wisteria's sharp voice snapped me back to the present. "Don't screw around with that stuff, Songbottom. Learn it and don't screw it up."

She and Mar exchanged a brief glance and then each looked pointedly away.

"I won't!" I slapped the bar.

"Good. See that you don't," her clear green eyes bored into me.

Damn. Why was everyone so interested in how well I was doing in school? It's not like they were my parents or anything.

I had another eight months of this crap to go. I'd learn it by then. I was almost sure I would. Wouldn't I? I looked from Mar to Wisteria and back to Mar. They went about their cleaning and drinking business and ignored me as I studied them. They had access to knowledge and techniques that were way above my pay grade. So, if they wanted to keep something from me, there was pretty much no way I could get it out of them. Unless … unless, I got them drunk. Really drunk.

"Hey Mar," I called to her. "How about another round?"

Mar popped the cork again and poured each of us another glass.

"What time do you get off?" I asked her.

"In about five minutes." Mar answered.

"So, seriously, why don't you join us and have a drink?"

"I thought you were saving the bottle for a special occasion." She shook her dreads out of the way and reached for another dram glass.

"No reason today can't be a special occasion," I reached for my glass, and they reached for theirs.

"Cheers!" We clinked glasses and drank. I barely sipped mine but encouraged them to finish theirs. If they got ripped enough, maybe they would let something slip. They were acting strangely and I'd bet it had something to do with me.

What did they know that I didn't? I was going to have to find out.

CHAPTER 12

DANIEL

Tommy and Daniel stood in front of St. James in his palatial apartment.

"I didn't ask last time. What do you do, Daniel?" Mitchell downed his whiskey and placed the tumbler on a nearby table. A waiter removed the glass and placed another in his hand.

"I work with Tommy," Daniel answered. "I'm a photographer."

"A photo-journalist," Tommy added.

"You don't say," Mitchell stepped closer. He towered over both men, even though Daniel topped six feet by a good couple of inches. "Working on any hot leads?"

"Actually, I am." Daniel replied. "But, it's in the nascent stage. It'll be a while before I have anything concrete."

"Surely, you can tell me something," Mitchell coaxed. Bright lights appeared in his eyes. He stared into Daniel's.

Daniel jerked stock still. His eyes glazed. Some part of him fluttered in confusion but was soon silenced under the older man's relentless gaze.

"It's about a new designer drug," the words spilled from his mouth. "It's called …."

"Now, Daddy," Nadia interjected. "You can't monopolize these boys all evening. I want to have a little time with them too." She inserted herself between Tommy and Daniel and hooked her hands into the crooks of their arms.

Mitchell stared at the three of them. He bobbed his head in a curt nod. "Go ahead. But, you," he turned to Daniel. "I'm going to want to speak to you, again."

"I'll be looking forward to it," Daniel mumbled.

Nadia tugged on their arms and pulled them out onto the balcony. Daniel sagged against her and Tommy sprinted around to his other side. They manhandled him to a corner of the balcony. He collapsed against the red and blue granite stones that made up the walls and gulped great breaths of air. The lights of 57th and Central Park West winked and dodged below them. The trees of the Park calmed him in the encroaching darkness.

When he felt back to himself, he cleared his throat.

"What the hell was that?" He rasped.

"The Old Man's Whammy," Tommy said.

"We never could lie to him," Nadia added. "Even if you tried, he'd always get it out of you." She shivered.

Daniel rubbed his temples to alleviate the headache that had sprung up. What had St. James done to him? Certainly, he wasn't an average human. He closed his eyes and wished he could ask Evie about what had just happened. She would know or she would have gone on one of her trips back to her world and found out. He squared his shoulders in determination. She wasn't available. Besides, he didn't want to always rely on her to help him. This was something he needed to do.

"Was it like hypnosis or something?" Daniel asked them.

"Honestly? We don't know," Nadia said. "If you make the mistake of looking at him, you end up spilling your guts."

"Shit, Daniel," Tommy swore softly. "I should have warned you about those eyes of his before."

"Yeah, you should have," Nadia said. She gulped down the rest of her whiskey. "I need more. I'll be right back." She moved inside.

"But how come he hasn't figured out that you don't really drink anymore?" Daniel asked.

"That's easy," Tommy said. "I haven't looked him in the eye for over ten years. So, how are you feeling? Back to normal?"

"Getting there," Daniel replied. "Actually, I'd better get going. I was going to try and get closer to that warehouse tonight. There's got to be a way to get a look inside."

"Yeah, well, I'm going with you. And don't bother arguing. You look like hell."

"Okay, okay, you win," Daniel pushed off from the wall. "Let's go get your allowance and then head uptown."

"It sounds dirty when you say it," Tommy mused. "I wonder if there's a way for me to pay for NewsBlitz on my own."

"We could take on subscribers or ads," Daniel suggested.

"Yeah, maybe." He said. "But right now, it's time to pay the piper and get my paycheck. Do you feel up to going back into the fray?"

"Sure." Daniel ran his fingers through his hair and straightened his clothing.

Tommy checked the time on his phone. "He'll be in the study writing checks by now."

They walked inside past the French doors and back into the hubbub of the party. Tommy beelined for his father's study; the door sat tucked into the far corner of the large penthouse.

His father sat at a large mahogany desk at the far end of the study. An open ledger sat in front of him. He wrote out a check, tore it out and laid it aside. He proceeded to the next check and repeated the process.

A large bay window framed the views of twilight in the city. One wall displayed books on a variety of subjects. The opposite wall was a study in nooks and crannies. Two narrow doors sat recessed and almost hidden among the odd angles of the wall.

Nadia reclined in a chair in front of the bookshelves. One long, graceful leg was thrown over the arm of the chair. She tapped her ankle in rhythm to the swirling of the martini glass she held.

"Come on, Daddy," she slurred. "It's only for a month. And you're always telling me to get involved and do things."

"Going to Hawaii for a month to lie on a beach isn't getting involved," Mitchell replied.

"True, but it is doing things," she said. "And I'll be helping the ecotourism trade by being there. I mean you know wherever I go reporters are going to follow, and I'll be sure to recycle while I'm there so they write about it and encourage other people to do it too," she laughed.

"Okay, Pet," he smiled. "You win. But you can't go until after the summer is over. I need you here through the season."

"What? Why, Daddy?" she pouted.

"We have the Fourth of July gala for one thing, and there will be various events at the Hamptons house. I need you here to hostess. But you can go right after Labor Day and stay for two months."

"Oh yay," she sprang out of the chair and ran to give him a hug. She grabbed the check he had just written, folded it, and tucked into a pocket.

"And how about you, Tommy," Mitchell addressed the men waiting in the doorway. They entered the spacious room and stopped near the desk. The bright rays of the sunset gilded the room in golds and reds.

"Oh, I don't need to go anywhere," Tommy answered.

"No, you just need your allowance," the sneer came through in Mitchell's voice.

"For now, yes," Tommy admitted. "But Daniel and I have been brainstorming on how we might make NewsBlitz generate a little more revenue."

"Sounds great to me. You'll have to get me your business and marketing plans," Mitchell said. "I'll be happy to look at them and give you some feedback." He turned his mesmerizing eyes on Daniel. "Looks like you're a good influence on my boy."

"Thank you. We're going to try hard to make NewsBlitz succeed," Daniel looked a good few inches above the other man's head as he replied.

"This has gotten a lot less interesting," Nadia cornered the desk and moved towards the doorway.

"Tommy, I got your text," she stopped at the door. "What did you want to talk to me about?"

"Oh, yeah," he said. "We wanted to ask you some questions. Dad?" He turned to his father and looked discreetly at the checkbook.

"Yes, but I have some things I want ask you about," the older man replied. "Stay!"

Tommy froze in place. He barely turned his head and said, "Daniel, why don't you go hang out with Nadia. I'll catch up with you in a few."

Daniel nodded and followed the beautiful brunette out of the room.

Nadia reached for a drink from a passing waiter. She studied Daniel over the rim of her Martini glass.

"You might as well ask me your questions," she said. "It's going to be a while before they're done."

"How do you know?"

"When he says, 'Stay!' like that, it's going to be a marathon session. Either you've done something right, and he wants to grill you on what you're going to do next, or you've done something wrong and then you have to justify your existence. Either way, it tends to take a while. So," she swung her ice blue eyes in his direction. "What was it you wanted to ask me?"

"Um," he looked into her heart-shaped face and narrowed down to her pouting lips. A sizzle pulsed in his blood. His breathing came in small pants.

"Wait a minute," she hissed. "I know that reaction. I've seen that reaction from guys since I was thirteen. You're not gay!"

"No," he swallowed and stepped back a pace. "I'm not."

"But then why the pretense?" She moved closer to him.

He closed his eyes and braced himself for the reaction to spring up again. When it didn't, he risked opening them again. He wasn't the type of guy to fool around with women he barely knew and he would never dream of cheating on Evie, but Nadia's appeal was undeniable. He wondered whether this was her version of the captivating power her father possessed.

"Tommy thought things would go easier with your father if he thought Tommy and I were involved."

"But you're not," she smiled and slew him.

"Yes, um, but, um," he stammered. "I'm involved with someone."

"She's not here, though, is she?" Nadia draped herself on him. For a long moment, he couldn't breathe. He tore himself away and put distance between them.

"I had questions."

"You did," she agreed and sidled close again. "But do you even remember what they are?"

"Do me a favor, Nadia," he closed his eyes and tried to not inhale her scent. "Tamp whatever that is down, would you? I can't think straight when you do that."

"Do what?" she purred.

He waved his hand in a circle. "That, you," he indicated. "Turn it off."

"Okay," she pouted. She exhaled and the room dimmed a little.

Daniel's breathing returned to some semblance of normal.

"What is that?" He managed to control the urge to paw at her like a tomcat.

"You mean my charm?" Her smile was rueful.

"Yes, but it's way more than that. I mean, you're absolutely beautiful, but there's more to it than that."

"Don't know," she shrugged her shoulders and gave him fantasies of trailing his lips down their tender planes. He closed his eyes.

"It's been this way forever," she spoke matter-of-factly. "I don't remember a time when men and women didn't react to me like they're the cats and I'm the catnip. But, what did you want to ask me?"

"Yes," he got back to business. "Tommy and I wanted to ask you about Heaven?"

"Well, Daniel," she enunciated each word as if she was speaking to a small child. "Heaven is a place where good little girls and boys go if they do all their chores and eat all their spinach."

He smiled.

"That Heaven, I've heard of," he said. "I'm talking about the blue Heaven."

Her eyes darkened to a shade that almost matched the blue powder he asked about.

"Why do you want to know about it?" Suspicion colored her voice.

"I saw something today. I followed a lead and saw an exchange of blue powder for what looked like a lot of money."

"How much powder?" Nadia asked. Her skin was bathed in a sheen of sweat.

"A sandwich bag's worth along with several of white powder."

"In the city?"

"Yes."

"Shit!" She grabbed his arm and pulled him out onto a dark corner of the balcony. "Look, Daniel. I get that you and Tommy think you're some sort of newsmen, but this stuff isn't something to screw around with."

"What can you tell me about it?"

"Not much. I know it's addictive." She wrung her hands.

"Have you tried it?"

She gazed out onto the summer evening for a long moment.

"Once. I had three crystals dissolved in a glass of water." She closed her eyes. "It was perfection. Take every good thing that's ever happened to you and multiply it by a million. All the joy, all the love, unbelievable mind-blowing sex - all of them rolled into one fantastic high."

"Where did you get it?" Daniel asked.

"I have a friend who gets the latest designer stuff," she replied.

"So, it's not out on the open market yet?"

"From what I understand, it's still experimental. But it was an unforgettable high," Nadia shivered. She ran a shaking hand through her fall of hair. "Whew, I need another drink. Or some great sex. And since you aren't biting, I guess a drink it will be."

"Thanks for talking to me, Nadia."

"It was my pleasure," she replied. "And don't worry," she continued. "I'll keep your and Tommy's secret. He's not the only one who doesn't look Daddy in the eyes." She left the balcony.

Daniel gazed out over the city. He gave a sharp nod, tightened his grip on his messenger bag, and let himself out of the apartment.

"Time to get a look inside the warehouse," he said aloud as the elevator bore him to the ground level.

Mitchell sat across the desk from his son. Tommy faced him with glazed eyes and a slackened jaw. His hands drooped over the arms of the black leather chair.

"And that's it?" Mitchell asked.

"That's it," Tommy said.

"Very well, Tommy. You may go."

Tommy rose from his chair and shuffled to the door.

"Tommy," Mitchell called him back. He dropped a folded check into Tommy's outstretched hand and dismissed him.

"Did you get all that?" Mitchell asked after Tommy had exited the room.

The tall man stepped into the room from one of the recessed cubbyholes.

"I did."

"You will take care of this," Mitchell made it a command.

"I will," the man replied. He moved to the desk and stood in front of his boss and mentor.

"Don't screw up again," Mitchell motioned his dismissal.

"I won't," his silver eyes flashed with anger.

"Good," Mitchell lifted a tumbler to his lips.

"Will Tommy be a problem? He was going to go too."

"Don't you worry about Tommy. Tommy won't be anywhere near there tonight. You're dismissed," he continued.

Once Mitchell was alone, he leaned back in his chair and contemplated the near future. If all went as planned, and it would, a number of nagging little problems would be well resolved. He lifted his tumbler in silent salute to the heavens. And smiled.

CHAPTER 13

TARIQ

Tariq jerked awake by the sound of his work mobile phone.

"What you want?" He mumbled.

"Get your ass out of bed and get to the warehouse," the voice on the other end of the line commanded. "I have work for you all."

"It's after midnight," Tariq glanced at the time. "I can't leave my little brother."

"You want to keep working for me, you'll be here inside of twenty minutes." The phone clicked off.

"Shit!" Tariq swore. He pulled on clothes and grabbed his phone and black backpack. He checked on Calvin and found him sleeping. Since their grandmother had passed away, Tariq had done everything he could to keep Calvin with him. The foster care system would likely split them up. He would do anything to ensure that didn't happen.

"I'll be back, little brother," he whispered and eased out the door. Once outside, he grabbed a deep, shaky breath. He had no idea what kind of work needed to be done after midnight on Tuesday, but it couldn't be good. He took off towards the warehouse at a loping, easy jog.

EVIE

The evening was in full swing at the Storm Tavern, which was to say that punches were about to be swung.

"I don't care what you say," I yelled. "There was no way Boitano should have beaten Orser."

"You don't know what the hell you're talking about," Wisteria drew herself up to her full, imposing height. "Boitano deserved it. He won it. It's over. Deal with it."

"Ach!" I pulled at my hair. Sure Boitano had been great, but I had a soft spot for Orser and Wisteria was sticking sharp, pointy sticks into every soft spot I had. "If you had a brain in your head, you'd know that Orser was the better skater and the better artist. I mean sure Boitano was an incredible athlete and he had those thighs ...."

We both sighed as we recalled Brian Boitano's physique.

" ... But still, he was never the artist Orser was."

"Boitano was the better skater. He won. He should have won, and I'll buy a round for anyone who agrees with me!"

"What? That's ridiculous," I cried. "Just because you bribe a bar full of drunks into agreeing with you doesn't make you right. In fact, it makes you desperate for someone to think you know what the hell you're talking about!"

"If you two don't chill out, I'm going to send you both packing." Mar refereed.

"But Mar ... "

"Don't 'But Mar' me," she said. "This is my place, and if you don't tone it down, I'm going to ban you for a year."

"You wouldn't!" Wisteria and I exclaimed in unison. We might not agree about whether or not water was wet, but we both knew which side our bread was buttered on.

"Separate corners," she pointed her index fingers to either side of the bar's length.

"Fine," I huffed. I snagged my whiskey off the bar and retreated to the end of the long, wooden expanse. "But don't you give her any more of my whiskey."

Wisteria parted her lips in a feral grin. "If I wanted more, there'd be nothing you could do it about it."

Some wiser, chicken-shit part of me overrode the reckless, stupid part of me and shut my mouth. I put my lips to my glass and pretended to drink while I watched her out of the corner of my eye. We were heading for a showdown. I knew it. The trouble was that a showdown would mean a knockout within the first three seconds, and it wouldn't be her on the ground curled into the fetal position cursing the moment she'd been born. I only hoped I survived the encounter.

DANIEL

Daniel neared the deserted warehouse from across the street. It sat on the corner of the block. The front faced the park and the water. The George Washington Bridge shone in the distance.

Perfect! Daniel thought as he circled it. He looked for niches, windows, anything that he might pry open to gain access inside. There! Approximately seven feet off the ground, a small window sat cracked open.

Daniel found an old wooden crate a few feet away and placed it below the window. He scrabbled up the wall and clung by his fingertips. He held himself up with one hand and braced his feet against the wall while he pulled on the window. It opened with a small screech, and he slipped inside. He dropped to the floor with a small thump.

Other than the poor light that streamed in from the window, the interior sat in darkness. Daniel flipped on his small flashlight and surveyed his surroundings. He was in a small closet. Boxes of latex gloves, shower caps, and latex booties sat cramped into the small, square space. He pulled open the door and entered the belly of the long, rectangular building.

A lathe, a jigsaw, and a few other machine shop staples lay in various stages of disrepair. He shone his light on them and realized that although they appeared broken, they were clean and free of dust.

An adult sized work-out area took up an entire half of the room. Rings hung suspended from the ceiling. Monkey bars, balance beams, and punching bags were set up in a sort of obstacle course. He snapped a few shots of the equipment.

His weak light revealed an expanse of floor-to-ceiling white plastic curtains. He found a break in the curtains and slipped through them. Inside, several long, narrow tables stood in rows. One table contained vats of blue bricks made of a substance that looked halfway between a crystal and some sort of fudge. He wondered if that was Heaven in its raw form and gave that table a wide berth.

Another table held several mortar and pestles and cutting boards on which lay straight long cutting blades. A third table held row upon row of bottles with labels he could not pronounce. He snapped several pictures of the bottles and the vats of raw materials. The last table held seven plastic baggies full of the blue, powdery Heaven. Up close, he realized that it was not powder but rather uniformly sized crystals.

He poked one of the bags with his flashlight. It crinkled.

"So, it's more like a crystal than like fudge," Daniel murmured.

"Crystalline," a voice corrected him.

The lights in the warehouse blazed on.

"Shit!" Daniel whispered.

He sprinted to the edge of the curtains and pushed his way through them. Seven young men surrounded him in a semi-circle. They ranged in age fourteen to nineteen. The three largest, who looked like they would one day succeed as professional football players, held pipes and wrenches. One held a hammer. The others stood with bare hands balled into fists. The last, and youngest, stared at him with huge, terrified eyes.

"Look," Daniel raised his hands in supplication. "I don't want any trouble."

"Seems like you found some," the voice said again. Soft footsteps sounded along the cement of the warehouse floor.

"Stupid of you not to think it was too easy to get in here, don't you think?" The man walked out of the shadows of the Clean Room curtains and stood before him.

"You!" Daniel cried out.

Zeke waved his hand, and Daniel stood rooted to the spot.

"Me," Zeke smiled as he moved forward. "Last time we saw each other, you didn't look so alive," he said. "Let's see if we can't try for an encore." He nodded to the three largest young men.

"Do your thing," he said.

Daniel stood frozen as the largest of them swung his arm. The wrench whistled towards him. All but one of the others brandished their weapons. They beat him with feet and fists and steel. He fell and bled.

ZEKE

"Don't kill him," Zeke admonished them. "But you can damage him all you like."

For a few moments, the only sounds in the room were the strikes and thuds of a savage beating. A silence descended. A sob tore from Tariq's throat and shattered the stillness. The rest stood mute.

"Nice," Zeke approved the tableau. Daniel's blood coated the warehouse floor. His face was almost unrecognizable. He was broken. Zeke smiled again. He had heeded Evie's warning. He had not killed him or hurt him. He had not touched her little Boy Toy at all. So, any spells she had put on Daniel to make sure Zeke didn't injure him would not be triggered.

"I noticed you weren't as enthusiastic as your friends," Zeke trained his silver eyes on Tariq.

"He didn't do nothing, man," Tariq shook his head.

"You have a job to do," his voice hardened. "So get to it."

"No," Tariq backed away

Zeke dragged him up by his shirt. "Unless you want the same thing to happen to you, or better yet to your little brother …."

Tariq nodded. He approached Daniel and kicked him in the stomach.

"Again," Zeke said.

Tariq nodded and shuddered. He reared back and swung his foot at Daniel's head.

"Put your back into it," Zeke encouraged him.

Tariq kicked at Daniel again and again until with a last cry, he threw himself away.

"Good," Zeke nodded. He gestured to another man who had entered the main room. "We just need to do one more thing," he said. "Nero," he nodded to the man. "Give him some."

"What?" the man asked. "Why?"

"He was so curious about it, give him a dose," Zeke said. "In fact, give him five doses."

"But that's fifteen crystals," Nero objected. "If we give him more than ten at once, he'll lose his mind."

"We'll treat it like a science experiment. We've been wanting to see what would happen if someone takes that many all at once. Now, we'll know. Besides, we'll want to make sure he doesn't remember anything."

"If he survives," Nero said.

"Oh, he'll survive," Zeke said. "I'll make sure of that. He might be a vegetable, but he'll survive." He turned to Nero. "Dose him, and then clean the space. We're moving downtown."

"You heard the man," Nero barked at the young men. "Move!"

Nero took a chemical spoon from one of the tables and carefully ladled fifteen Heaven crystals onto it. Kneeling before Daniel, he pressed open his bleeding lips then poured the crystals down his throat.

"Shit!" Nero cried. He scrabbled away from him.

Daniel's body convulsed and bowed. He screamed in unconscious agony. Broken bones slammed and scraped together.

"What the fuck did you do?" Nero stared wide-eyed at Zeke.

"I was told not to kill him," Zeke said. "I wasn't told not to hurt him."

"Who told you that?" Nero panted.

"An old friend," Zeke answered. He closed his eyes for a moment. He stood statue still. After a time, he opened his eyes and glanced at Daniel. "And now, we'll see what we'll see."

EVIE

I nursed yet another drink. I was shit-faced. I knew it, and I didn't care.

"Mar, I want another," I called to her.

She ignored me. She is so good at that.

"Margaretha Swanglider, I want a drink. Right freakin' now!" I shouted. And the world exploded.

Screams. Blood. Pain. My screams. My blood. My pain. A thousand flaming arrows slashed through me. I writhed on a floor littered with broken glass and fire.

I screamed and screamed, and the sound clanged inside my skull. I knew the shame of pleading into the darkness.

From a distance, the rush of sound slammed into me.

"Evie, Evie. Can you hear me?"

"Evie, what happened?"

"Evie, look at me. Focus on me," the harsh voice commanded. "Don't you dare check out on me." A sharp slap rocked me.

"Come, on, Songbottom," a second slap echoed the first. The sting helped me claw my way back.

I sprawled on the floor of the Storm. Dozens of worried faces surrounded me. Wisteria's concerned mug floated upside down in front of me.

"What the hell?" I managed.

"You lost it and fell off the stool," her upside down head explained. I realized my head was being held steady in her lap. No way I was going to stay there. I tried to push myself up and collapsed against her when a wave of nausea grabbed me, and I threw up everything I'd ingested in the last three days.

Searing pain slammed into my belly. I was being punched by something, but I didn't know what. Each hit rocked me to the edges of consciousness until the last one when everything dimmed, and I dropped into the black.

TOMMY

Tommy ran towards Daniel's body. He slipped on the blood and slammed to the floor in front of him.

"Oh my God, oh my God. Shit! Daniel, can you hear me?" Tommy placed two frantic fingers along Daniel's throat. He sobbed as the flutter of Daniel's weak pulse played along his fingers. With blood-slicked hands, Tommy withdrew his phone and called the police.

"I need help. My friend, he's been hurt." He paused. "No, I don't know what happened. He's bleeding. He's not conscious. He's still alive, but I don't know for how long. Send an ambulance. Right fucking now."

"Don't die, Daniel," he whispered. He sat next to his friend and waited.

Tommy held one of Daniel's hands in his own. Tears streamed down his cheeks.

"You need to let us do our work." The paramedic tried to push Tommy out of the way.

"I'm not going anywhere," Tommy caressed Daniel's hand. "What the hell were you thinking?" And "Oh, my God. Please, be alive," fought over each other as Tommy cried. He pressed his palms together, put his fingers to his lips, and prayed.

The paramedics strapped wires and cables and suction cups to him. They put a tube down his throat and bandages around the worst of his bleeding cuts and wounds. Tommy rushed with them as they placed him on a stretcher and loaded him into the ambulance.

"You can't come with us unless you're family," the paramedic said.

"Like hell I can't," Tommy bellowed. "He's my partner, and I'm coming! Now get the hell out of my way." He bullied his way into the back of the ambulance.

"I'm so sorry, Daniel. I did this. This is my fault. I should've never let you come here alone. Why did I?" Tommy furrowed his brow as he tried to remember.

EVIE

I careened back to consciousness. Pain lanced through me. Tears streamed down my face.

Strong arms held me and rocked me.

"It's okay. You're okay."

"Oh Mar," I whispered. "I don't know what happened."

"We'll figure it out," the voice didn't have Mar's comforting and charming southern accent. In fact, the arms that held me weren't Mar's more full and motherly ones. They were whipcord thin and comprised of sinew and muscle.

I pushed against the broad expanse of shoulder as I opened my eyes and looked in Wisteria's turbulent green ones.

"What the hell!" I croaked.

"You fell. I caught you. Who knew you were such a fragile little baby?" Wisteria joked, but her eyes looked concerned.

"Thanks, but I'm fine," I managed.

"Are you, now?" She released me. I fell over.

"Damn!" I whistled through my teeth.

"What happened?" I asked.

Mar came over and crouched beside me while her ever-present sponges cleaned my mess.

"I don't know, babe," she answered. "You screamed bloody murder and fell over. Can you check your wards and protections and get some kind of trace?"

I nodded. I closed my eyes and sought out my various loved ones who weren't currently in front of me. My parents were fine. My sister was as okay as she was ever going to be. Joanna was great. Daniel was ... I sent my awareness across space and dimensions towards Daniel. He was not there.

"What the fuck!" I furrowed my brow and doubled my concentration. Where was he?

"What's going on?" Mar and Wisteria asked in unison.

"Daniel's gone!"

"He can't be gone," Mar said.

"I know, but I can't feel him. I should be able to feel him, right?"

"Well," she paused for a minute. "You are connected. You love each other. Of course you should be able to feel him."

I fought to my feet and nodded in gratitude to Wisteria who still had a hold of me. I swayed but managed to remain standing.

"I'm going to go find him." I reached for my wand and started the spell that would take me to him. "Wait a minute. If I can't feel him, how am going to find him?" I looked from Mar to Wisteria.

"Don't look at me," Wisteria put her hands in the air. "I'm not a seer. I'm a doer."

I looked back at Mar. After a pause, she nodded.

"Okay, but only for you." She reached under the bar and brought out a big, cast iron pot. She poured water into it and spoke words in a language I had never heard and would never learn. Her voice took on a singsong quality.

"Fah-ha-Jey, Lan-ha-Jey, tareah ya'h el ruo eeyah," Mar waved her hands over the water. Gray smoke appeared in the center of the pot. It swirled like cream in coffee. The patterns folded and melded into one another. The water stretched the dimensions of the pot. Lights, shapes that vaguely looked like humans, and distorted machines appeared at the edges. They melted into each other until they snapped into focus.

The image bounced and vibrated. We were looking into a moving car, an ambulance. A man lay prone on a stretcher, bandaged and still bleeding, wearing an oxygen mask. A man sat on a bench next to him holding his hand.

"I'm so sorry, Daniel. I did this. This is my fault. I should've never let you come here alone. Why did I?"

The bar tilted sideways. I fell. Someone caught me.

"That's, Daniel," I moaned. The world blurred as pain engulfed me. He was hurt, bleeding, and I was drinking and having pissing contests with Wisteria.

"No!" I shot to standing. My wand appeared in my hand.

"This stops now," I ground out.

"What are you going to do?" Wisteria grabbed my arm. I shrugged her off.

"It seems to me the best way to take care of this is to make sure it never happened. I'm going to go see Morrick."

"The Time Keepers won't change this. You know they won't." Mar stood before me. "I know, better than most of us, what it's like to want to go back and change time. And you know you can't."

"Look, I know about Amelia," I callously referred to the famed pilot Amelia Earhart–Mar's charge and her greatest failure. In my defense, I was way beyond thinking straight. "I know you would have gone back and changed things if you could. Which one of us wouldn't go back and fix things with a charge? But Daniel is my ... I love him," I finished.

"Just because Amelia was never my girlfriend doesn't mean I didn't love her." Her love burned through her and buffeted me.

"Mar," I said quietly. "I didn't know."

"It's okay. Back then, in the human world, no one did. If you did, you kept quiet."

We stood silently for a moment.

"Look," she said. "Going in wand blazing isn't going to solve this. You don't know enough yet. Stay here. Learn from Wisteria. You're going to need every bit of juice you can get to see this through."

"Why do I get the feeling you know a lot more than you're telling me."

Her eyes darkened. "I don't," she said. "I just know that every one of us eventually goes through the ringer and if this is your turn, then you need to prepare, and not just your battle magics but also your healing and your compassion. That's what he's going to need."

"Screw that," I shouted.

"They won't do it," Mar whispered. "I know. I tried. You won't get Them to change time for you. For Daniel."

"Oh yeah? Watch me." I flicked my wand and disappeared.

I skidded to a stop in front of the giant oak doors of The Palace of Time.

"Morrick! Morrick!" I pounded on the doors. "Let me in! I need to talk to You! Morrick!" I screamed. "Please, let me in," my voice hushed to a whisper. I leaned my head on the expanse of oak.

"Shit!" They weren't going to answer.

The big doorknob screeched, and the door creaked open.

Morrick, Itself, stood in the doorway.

"Oh thank goodness," I breathed. "I know the last time I was here it wasn't a good reason to bend time, but this time I have an excellent reason, a real reason. You have to help me."

Morrick contemplated me. I had sense enough to stand still with It despite my yen to grab It by what passes for Its shoulders and shake some sense into It.

"You speak of the human, Daniel Evershed," It rumbled.

"Yes, and you need to help him," I said. "I can't have him be hurt." I paced a frustrated circle. "I just can't have it, so you need to fix it."

"We cannot," Morrick replied.

"What do you mean, 'We cannot?'" I exclaimed. "You're the Time Keepers for Pete's sake. You're the only ones who can!"

"This was not an accident. This was not a due to a magical incident going wrong. This was purposeful and human-caused. Therefore, We cannot be involved."

"But you have to," I cried. I straightened. "You owe me one, Morrick." I pointed out to It.

"Yes, and someday, somewhen, you will be able to collect, and I will be able to repay you." It waved Its giant tree-like arm. "For this, I give you the gift of time to determine what it will take to help him and to heal him. Good luck, Evie. I wish I could help, but this was decided long ago." Morrick stepped back inside and shut the door in my face.

"I can't believe none of you will fix this. Just wait if You ever need anything from me again, Morrick!" Daniel was hurt. I hadn't been able to prevent it. But I was sure as shit going to fix it. My tirade slowed as an idea formed.

"Okay, Morrick," I ground out. "I'll take all the time in the world, and I'm going to fix Daniel. Then, I'm going to find who did this, and I'm going to grind them into such a fine powder, they won't even be good for flowing through an hourglass."

I hopped onto the nearest Ley Line and made my way back to the Storm Tavern.

I barged into the bar and ran up to Mar.

"So, I know what I need to do." I panted.

"And what is that?" She paused her work, faced me, and crossed her arms in front of her chest.

"I'm heading back to New York," I stated.

"You can't do that," Wisteria approached us. "You aren't done with your studies, and right now any magic you do will go off half-cocked."

"Whatever," I stomped about the bar. "Better that than standing around and doing squat. In fact, anything is better than sitting in a classroom and learning how to make stupid freakin' po-!"

"Evie," Mar stopped my rant with a gentle hand on my arm. "Be smart about this. You don't have enough knowledge to fix this yet. Finish up your learning and then go."

"And let him keep suffering? I don't think so."

"What if you could help him heal?" Mar asked.

"You have my attention," I paused in mid-step.

She moved over to the bar. She grabbed a big hunk of fluorite, one of the more fragile crystals in the known universe, and closed her eyes.

Within seconds, a lavender-scented breeze blew out of nowhere. My hair waved with it, and my eyes stung a little.

"What is it, Margaretha?" The Doc stood before us buck naked except for a bright orange shower cap. She held a cake of lavender soap in one hand and a washcloth in the other. I averted my eyes, but she appeared impervious to the staring or the shock on our faces.

"Oh, get over yourselves," she scolded us. "It's not like you wear clothes in the shower."

"True enough, Florence," Mar said. "And you've still got it," she nodded at the 800-plus year-old woman before her.

"Clean living," the Doc answered. "Now what's so important you needed to interrupt my evening cleansing routine?"

We all sobered.

"It's my boyfriend, my human boyfriend," I answered as Mar's excellent logic finally permeated my addled brain. "He needs your help."

"What happened?" In an instant, she wore her Healer's robe and was all business.

"He's been hurt," I started. The tears welled up, and I stopped.

"He is in a hospital in New York after taking a savage beating. We don't know how bad it is, but it looks terrible." Mar continued for me. I sent her a grateful glance.

"Let me see," the Doc said. Mar waved her over to the cast iron makeshift cauldron. She gazed into it. After a moment, she nodded her head, produced a small notebook from her robe, and made a few notations.

"I don't normally get involved in fixing specific humans. We are not allowed to interfere with their healing process or their medical practices," she said. "But there's something unusual about what is happening with him. At the least, I can see what I can do to alleviate his pain. After that ...." she trailed off.

"After that, what?" I asked.

"Honestly, Eveningstar, I am not certain," she answered. "I don't want to make hasty judgments or diagnoses." She stowed her notebook in her robes.

"Margaretha, where is he?"

"I'll send you the exact location," Mar said.

"Very well," the Doc replied. "I will need a few items from my lab. And then, Eveningstar," she pointed at me with her pen. "You and I will go together. You will not approach him alone. Is that clear?"

"Yes, Doc. I won't approach him alone," I looked down.

"Eveningstar," the Doc's tone made me raise my eyes.

"Yes, Doc?"

"Uncross your fingers behind your back and say that again."

"Yes, Doc," I uncrossed my fingers. "I won't approach him alone."

"Wisteria," the Doc called to her.

"Yes, Doc?" she replied.

"We will need you to accompany us," she said.

"But I have classes to teach," Wisteria sputtered.

"You also have assistants. Get them to cover for you," the Doc said. "Something is going on, and we are going to need a tactician. You will serve in that capacity."

"Yes, Doc," Wisteria acquiesced.

The Doc closed her eyes for a second.

"We leave in thirty minutes," she opened them and looked at each of us in turn. "Go prepare." She nodded her head at Mar and disappeared.

Wisteria stomped back to the bar, downed her drink, glared at me, and also disappeared.

I leaned against the bar and looked at Mar with interest.

"Not that I'm not glad that we're going to be doing something, but what the hell just happened?" I asked.

"What do you mean?"

"First you know the Doc's first name. And you used it. Second, Wisteria didn't use it 'cause nobody ever does. Third, the Doc had the gonads to tell Wisteria what to do, and she hupped to it. What's up with all that? Why is the Doc such a big deal? She's just a healer."

"Evie," Mar raised her eyes to the heavens for a moment and then turned to me. "Healers are the most important of us all. When we need them, no one else will do. Right?"

I flashed on Daniel. He was bruised and bleeding and unconscious.

"Right," I agreed and swiped at my face with rough hands.

"So, I'd suggest you head over to your place and pack for New York."

"Yeah," I said. I had some plans on that score. I'd leave the healing to the Doc. I sucked at it anyway. Me? I was going to find out who did this to him, and then I would make them pay. I rushed towards the front door.

"Evie, don't do anything stupid," Mar called after me.

"Who, me?" I replied. I blazed home on a streak of livid, red energy.

Mar shook her head.

"Too late," she said. "This is going to be bad." She strode over to the cauldron and tapped it twice with her right hand." A face appeared in the murky water.

"Hey," Mar looked down into the cauldron. "We need to talk. It's important."

The sharp knocks on my door broke my concentration.

"What!" I called through the door.

The Doc appeared in the middle of my living room holding a small black case and a walking stick. She wore scrubs and had a stethoscope around her neck.

"It helps to look the part," she explained.

"Right," I agreed. "Fewer questions that way."

I grabbed my own small, black duffel and slung my messenger bag over my head. My wand, human ID, and some

American money all sat in the bag. Anything else I needed, I'd have to manifest.

We hopped the Ley Lines and landed in a supply closet at Mt. Sinai.

"You go first," I nudged the Doc. "I'm not quite presentable."

She looked me up and down, shrugged, and exited the closet.

I produced a mirror, opened a box of tissues and rubbed at my face to remove the tear stains. I figured it would be better to seem ruddy and weather-beaten rather than like I'd been bawling my eyes out.

I caught up to the Doc who stood at a crossroads of two long hallways. She consulted a chart she had in her hands. An orderly passed by us wheeling a cart full of instruments.

"Orderly," she called.

"Yes, Doctor," he stopped in his tracks.

"I need East Wing, room 405," she said.

"Right down this hall, and it'll be the third door on your right."

"Thank you," she said. "And get some sleep. You could use it. I know your newborn is keeping you up, but you need to be fresh to do your work, and you deserve to sleep. Here," she reached into her bag and pulled out a picture of a smiling three-toed sloth. "Put this over her bed. She'll sleep, well, like a baby."

"Yes, Doctor," he took the picture with a funny look on his face. "Thank you, Doctor."

"You know, Doc, I don't think that's how most doctors give medical advice or prescriptions in New York City Hospitals," I said.

"Most doctors aren't me," she strode past me towards Daniel's room.

"True that," I hurried to follow her.

We found room 405 and entered. The room held two beds and two tall but narrow tables next to each bed. One bed sat empty. Daniel lay in the other. He was covered in white sheets and had a breathing tube down his throat. The whoo-swish of the respirator and beep-beep of the heart monitor sounded through the room.

His bruised and bloodied face lay in stark relief to the white of his pillow. Raw scrapes scoured his cheeks. The large gash on his forehead had been stitched and bandaged with gauze. Bruises covered every other exposed part of him. My gorge reared up. I backpedaled until I smacked into the light blue wall at the other end of the room. I swallowed hard and tried again. I got a few feet away and froze in place. My eyes remained locked on his battered face.

"Shit!" I whispered. "He looks so bad. Is he as bad as he looks?" I set my bag on the table by his bed side and knocked his phone and wallet off it. I restored them both and stepped back.

"He's not great," the Doc was all business. She moved to the foot of the bed and perused the chart that hung off the metal footboard.

"Hmm," she flipped a page. "Ruptured spleen, collapsed lung, contusions, bruises, and internal bleeding." She turned to me. "I've seen worse."

"Yes, but have you healed worse?"

"Evie," she snapped. "Get over yourself and get over here. I'm going to need your help."

"That's some bedside manner you've got there, Doc," I whimpered.

"You don't need my bedside manner," she replied. "He does." She placed Daniel's chart back on the its hook and moved to the far side of his bed. "As for you, I've learned that sweet words and niceties mean about as much to you as a gnat to a Triceratops. You don't notice them, and if you do, you don't respect them."

"True that, too." I steeled myself and neared the bed.

"Stand on the other side of the bed opposite me," she directed. "Do you know how to do 'Illusio' spells?"

I nodded.

"Good. Set one up while I do my own diagnostics." She placed her hands a few inches above Daniel's body and closed her eyes. A hum buzzed around her and Daniel as she moved her hands to the top of his head and then worked her way down his entire body. She paused over his chest and belly, then, continued on until she again stopped at his left knee. Once she had finished the trip across the landscape of his physical form, the buzzing ceased. She opened her eyes and stared blankly for a moment.

"How is he?" I shifted from foot to foot.

"The chart is mostly right," she said.

"But?" I restrained myself from screaming.

"There's something else going on," she murmured. "I can't put my finger on it, but something else is wrong."

"Can you fix it?"

"I don't know," she answered. "I'm not exactly sure what it is." She cocked her head to the side as if she was listening to something. She closed her eyes. I froze in place and waited. After a few minutes, she shook her head again.

"I can't pinpoint what I'm sensing," she admitted. "But, I can at least fix what I can fix." She looked around us and then stared at me.

"Eveningstar, The 'Illusio' spell, please."

"Oh crap!" I cried. I grabbed my bag off the table by Daniel's bed. I removed my wand from it and wove a quick spell. Anyone walking past the room or even into the room would now see nothing but the two of us standing near his bed. Anything else that might happen would go unnoticed.

"Okay, Doc, done," I said.

"Someday soon, Eveningstar, you will need to learn how to do that without using your wand as a focusing tool," she admonished me. "You won't always have it, you know."

"Yeah, I know," I agreed. "But today is not that day, so I'm not going to worry about it."

She shook her head at me for the umpteenth time and got to work.

The light around them brightened and formed into an egg shape. And it felt good. So good. Every muscle in my body relaxed. I lounged against the edge of the bed and tried my damnedest to stay awake and aware. But really, all I wanted to do was curl up, relax, and have a long, restorative nap. And I never nap!

The air inside the Egg swirled with ribbons of light. All colors of the rainbow and a few human eyes couldn't see spiraled and flowed. Daniel's body vibrated. He looked less substantial. I could swear I saw the bottom sheet of the bed through his body.

As the Doc waved her hands over his face, his bruises faded and disappeared. The swelling on underneath his bandages receded, and the bandages hung on him limply.

Within a few minutes, he gagged and coughed. His body bowed. The Doc nodded once and took hold of the long corrugated breathing tube with one hand. She pressed on his shoulder with the other hand, and he calmed. Then, she slid the tube out of his throat so he could breathe on his own. He settled.

"Whoa," I breathed.

"'Whoa' is right," A familiar voice murmured beside me. Torlyn hovered next to my left ear.

"Hey Darling," I whispered. "Thanks for coming, but how did you know we were here?"

"Are you kidding? Everyone knows you're here. There's an 'Evie' beacon all over this hospital. I just happened to be the first to get here."

"Hey, are Fire Fairies allowed in hospitals with all the oxygen and all the machines and stuff?"

She drew herself up to her full minuscule height of about five inches.

"Songbottom," she ground out. "I know how to control my flames. No spark goes where I don't choose it to go."

"Good to know," I said. "And sorry. I'm not exactly myself right now."

"What happened?" she asked.

"I don't know," I said. "But I aim to find out. As soon as he wakes up, he'll tell me and then I'm going to kick some ass. Want to come?"

Torlyn looked at Daniel for a few long seconds. He looked better. The swelling and bruising were all but gone. But he was still hooked up to a number of machines.

"Do you even have to ask?" She said.

"I didn't think so, but I wanted to make sure," I replied.

"Yeah, Evie," she said. Her entire body blazed like a tiny sun. Then, she cooled her jets and returned back just a bright candle level of flaming. "We'll figure out who did this, and we'll make them pay."

Fire Fairies aren't like the more reason-oriented Air Fairies, and they're definitely not like the more peaceful and Zen-like Earth fairies. Fire fairies are more, "Blast first and ask questions way later." And Torlyn? She had a temper. Even if she didn't feel she owed me for helping her sister Leili regain her own form after she had been transformed into a firefly last year, she was always up for a little rumble.

"You know, you don't owe me anything, Torlyn," I remarked.

"That's where you're wrong," she said. "But that's not why I'm doing this."

"Why are you doing it? I asked.

"He told me he didn't me need me to look for out him, but I should have been there."

"This isn't your fault," I cried.

"Maybe not, but as soon as we find who did this, there's going to be some payback."

The egg around the Doc and Daniel dissipated. She heaved a huge breath and finally lowered her hands.

"Doctor, how is he?" A no-nonsense voice behind us asked.

Torlyn and I whirled around. The Illusio spell still held for the most part, so luckily the short woman couldn't see Torlyn. I hoped she hadn't seen the last vestiges of the egg as it disappeared. She moved past us and over to Daniel. She gripped his hand and waited.

"Physically, he's going to be okay," the Doc answered. "His bruises and contusions are healing nicely. The internal damage wasn't nearly as extensive as previously thought. However, I can't speak to his state of mind, or his state of being." A world of meaning shone in her eyes as she looked at me for that last part.

"So, what are you saying?" I asked. There might have been a world of meaning shining in her eyes, but I was more dense than most on my best days. Today couldn't even be counted as a mediocre one.

"And who are you?" The woman looked me up and down. Her chocolate brown eyes held a trace of suspicion and her lips pressed together in a scowl.

"I'm Evie," I answered her.

She smiled and her face transformed her into a handsome woman. She ran her fingers through her short gray hair and walked towards me. She took my hands and stared into my eyes.

"Evie!" She exclaimed. "Finally! I'm just sorry it's under these circumstances. I've been after Daniel to bring you to Baltimore to introduce you, but he's been claiming 'too busy' for months now."

"Oh, my stars," I cried. "You're Daniel's Mom! I'm Evie," I repeated.

"Yes, I know. You already said that." She smiled again. "I'm Nancy Evershed." She extended a hand. "It's good to finally meet you."

"It's really nice to meet you," How lame could I be! What I really wanted to say was, "Don't you worry, Mrs. Evershed. I'm going to figure who did this and turn them into pulverized dog shit." But instead, I was limited to platitudes and niceties. I hate platitudes and niceties.

"So now, the question is what we're going to do about this." She was all business. "Doctor," she continued. "What does he need, and how do we get it for him?"

"I'm afraid we won't know all those answers for a while yet," the Doc admitted. "As I said, physically, he is well on the mend."

"And otherwise?" Nancy Evershed gripped Daniel's hand more tightly. She suffered no fools. That much was obvious.

"We'll just have to see. We won't know for a ... "

Daniel stirred. He sighed. His eyelids fluttered and opened.

"Danny," his mother smiled at him. "Welcome back to the land of the living."

"You had us really worried, Daniel." I peeked around Daniel's mother.

He closed his eyes and swallowed. He winced. He curled into himself and tried to swallow again.

"Water," he croaked.

"The discomfort you feel is from the intubation tube," the Doc supplied. "That bruised and sore feeling will go away in a little bit." She muttered something the rest of us couldn't hear. Daniel relaxed back against the pillows.

I poured water from a pitcher into a plastic cup that sat on the dresser against the wall. I held it for him while he sipped through the long red straw.

"Thank you," he spoke louder and more clearly. The Doc had worked her magic yet again. He looked at all three of us in turn. He squinted at us and shook his head. He rubbed his eyes and gazed at each of us again.

"I don't mean to be rude," he began. "But do I know you?"

"What?" I cried. "You don't know us?" I realized I was being Captain Obvious, but I was beyond caring.

"Evie," the Doc put a steadying hand on my shoulder and made a quick motion with her other hand. Daniel and his mother froze in space. For the moment, they couldn't see or hear a thing. "You will need to calm yourself." She kept her hand on my shoulder, as much to reassure me as to shut me up, of that I was sure.

"But," I sputtered.

"But nothing," she murmured. "We knew this might happen. We knew there was a danger something might happen."

"We knew? We knew he wouldn't remember me? When did we know that?" My voice pitched towards the hysterical. "You might have known that. I didn't know a freakin' thing," I bellowed.

"Hush, child," she tutted at me. I heaved a huge breath and by some miracle calmed down. She stood over him, closed her eyes, and waved her hands over his head. She moved them to his heart, and then down to his belly.

"What are you doing?" I interrupted her.

"Scanning him."

"And?"

"And I can't sense him."

"What do you mean you can't sense him? He's right there."

"I know he's right there, Evie. But while he is there, part of him isn't. His memory appears just gone. There's no 'he' in him right now," She stepped back towards me.

"Whatever is wrong, fix him." I demanded.

"That's not something I can do," she replied. "Memory is a funny thing. Everyone's works differently. That's why we can't just fix it. I can mend a broken bone, because I can sense the bone, the marrow, the calcium. It is there for me to work with. But I can't fix his memories. I can't spin them out of thin air. I can't mend something that, for the moment, isn't there. His will come back, in time. Likely."

"And if it doesn't?" I stepped towards him and stroked the hair off his face. I placed my lips on his forehead.

"Let's cross that bridge later, Evie. Now come back here so we don't surprise them by being in different places when they come back."

I crossed over to her and lay her hand back on my shoulder so we recreated where we had been before she froze them.

"Now remember, stay calm," she admonished me.

"Right, I'll try," I said.

She waved her hand and everyone came back to the here and now.

"No, I don't know you. Should I?" Daniel continued as if he had not been frozen in time and space for five minutes.

The Doc approached him. "Do you know where you are?"

He looked around the room.

"I'm in the hospital. Why am I here?"

"You had an accident." The Doc spoke to him but silenced me with a warning glance. "You had some head trauma, and it seems to have affected your memory."

"I'm Evie," I plowed into the fray. The Doc once again put a restraining hand on my shoulder.

"Evie, why don't we let Mrs. Evershed go first?" She admonished me for the umpteenth time in the last fifteen minutes.

I blushed deep scarlet and shut my mouth.

"Of course," I said.

"I'm Nancy Evershed. I'm your mother." Her no nonsense tones gentled a little.

He stared at her for a long moment.

"I'm sorry. You don't look familiar," he finally said.

"That's okay," she replied. "You don't look much like me anyway. You're the spitting image of your father when he was your age."

My ears perked up at that. Daniel had mentioned his mother often over the last year, but he would never talk about his dad.

Daniel looked around the room.

"What do you need, Daniel?" I asked him.

"Daniel? Is that my name?"

"Yes," Nancy answered. "Your name is Daniel Armstrong Evershed."

"Armstrong? Seriously?" He attempted a smile.

"It's a family name," Nancy's stern tones were back in business.

"It's good to know someone in the family has a sense of humor," he said.

They fell into an awkward silence that I rushed to fill.

"I'm Evie," I said again.

"You already said that," Daniel replied.

"You might have forgotten," I huffed. Then, I deflated. "Sorry," I explained. "I'm not great in delicate situations."

"Ya think?" A floating voice above me said for my ears alone. I spied Torlyn still hanging on a stray sunbeam and gave her the evil eye.

"It's okay," Daniel continued. "So, we know you're Evie. Now, how do we know each other?"

"Um, we're um." For what might be the first time in my overly verbose life, words failed me.

"She's your girlfriend, Daniel." Nancy came to my rescue. I'm not sure how often it has happened, but I was betting it wasn't a common occurrence to have your mother introduce you to your girlfriend. And since I still sometimes had trouble actually uttering the words that I was someone's girlfriend, I was doubly grateful that someone else had identified our relationship so succinctly.

"Yes," I sighed in gratitude. "I'm your girlfriend. We've been seeing each other for a little over a year."

"And what do you do?" He asked politely.

Again, words, those traitorous buggers, failed me. The remembering Daniel knew what I really did for a living, but this Daniel had no clue. And besides this wasn't the time to talk about it.

"I've been finishing up some training to come back here and do something." I hesitated over that last part because I wasn't exactly sure what the Tribunal had up their sleeves for me. Whatever it was, I was going to make sure it would keep me near Daniel from now on. "And I'm a musician," I sounded lame even to my own ears.

"What kind of music?" Daniel asked.

Holy crap! On the inside, I grabbed both sides of my head and yanked. I ran around and set a bunch of stuff on fire. I found whoever did this to him and turned them into ground chuck. On the outside, I answered his questions.

"Mostly classical piano lately, but I play pretty much anything I can," I stayed as polite as Daniel even though I really just wanted to climb on top of him and do all sorts of outrageous things to him until he couldn't help but remember me. I'm not trying to toot my own horn, but we had some serious fireworks in that department.

"I'd like to hear you play sometime," he said.

"That would be great. In the meantime, what are we going to do?" I tugged on the sides of my hair.

Daniel smiled at me.

"Do you remember me doing this?" I asked. Hope sprang from me and danced in the room on shining crystals of the air currents.

"No," his reply came slowly. "But it feels somehow …." He sagged against the pillows as if even that little bit of effort had cost him.

"It's okay, Daniel." The Doc spoke up. "You don't have to do any more now. It will come back, in time. And you'll have all the help you need and then some," her eyes twinkled as she nodded towards me.

"Absolutely," I vowed as a plan took shape inside my head. "I won't leave your side until you're all better." I reached into my bag and brought out my wand. I whispered a few words and cast a "Fool-Me-Once" spell. The spell was only useful the first time someone met you. I would get Nancy to agree with my plan before she knew me better.

"I know you left a bunch of stuff undone in Baltimore, right?"

She nodded her reply.

"So, I'm sure you want to get back to things, right?"

She nodded again.

"Evie," The Doc's one-word warning bounced off me. I knew what I was doing, I prayed.

"So, why don't you head home and we'll keep you updated every step of the way."

She nodded a third time.

"You seem like you are in excellent hands, Daniel." She moved towards him mechanically. She lay a hand on his forehead and then leaned down and kissed his cheek.

"I'll only be a phone call away," she said. She paused at the door.

"I wish we had met under different circumstances, Evie. But I am pleased to have met you at last. Take care of him," These last words were said without any trace of the "Fool-Me-Once" spell's tranced out intonation. Her love for her son would break through even the most powerful of spells. That was good to know.

"I promise you, Nancy. I will be here for him every step of the way." I walked to the door and took her hands in mine. "He's going to be fine. Better than fine," I promised her.

She stared into my eyes, nodded one last time, and left the room.

"Torlyn," I whispered. "Can you make sure she gets home okay?"

"Will do," came the reply. The room darkened a smidgen as the Fire Fairy left.

"So, what now?" Daniel asked.

"You're going to need to rest," the Doc answered.

"I'm not hurt or anything else," he said. "So, do I need to be in the hospital? I think I'd like to go home. Shit!" He threw his head back against the pillow. "I don't even know where 'home' is. How's that for messed up?"

"I can take you home," I pounced on this. I had been wondering how to get him out of the hospital in order to put my plan into motion, and he'd handed me the perfect reason. He wanted to leave.

"Okay," I moved to the small closet and removed his clothes. I gasped. Dried blood and grime covered almost every inch of his shirt and pants. I dropped the shirt and transported some of his clothes from his place into my hands. I faced the outside of the room and pasted a bright smile on my face. I would not cry, I swore to myself. I would obliterate whoever did this damage to him. I would drink their blood. I would dance on their graves. But I would not cry.

"Right," I said. "Let's get you dressed." I walked over to his bed and tugged at the sheets.

"Hey, wait a minute." He pulled the sheets back up to his chin. We had a brief tug-of-war over them.

"Look, Evie. I think I'd like to get dressed on my own, if you don't mind," he said.

"I do mind. I've seen you naked lots of times!"

"Yes, but I don't remember that!" He yelled. He stilled and studied me. "In fact," he spoke slowly. "The only proof I have that we even know each other is that you told me we do."

"For Pete's sake," I cried. "Your mom knew me."

"No, she didn't." He pulled away from me. "She just met you. She said so. So, you could be anyone." Suspicion danced in his eyes.

"Bother!" I exclaimed. My eyes fell on his phone that still lay on the table.

"I'm in your phone," I cried.

"What?"

"I'm in your phone. You can call me," I repeated.

Daniel opened his phone and clicked through to his favorites. He pressed the screen. My phone chirped the opening strains of Bach's Cantata and Fugue in D Minor.

"See? I told you," I crowed. Just to drive the point home, I answered.

"Go for Evie."

That strange little echo that happens when you are in the same room as the person you're talking with sounded through his phone as my voice bounced up to the satellite and then came in on his receiver a quarter of a second after I said the words.

"Okay, so we know each other," he sounded mollified.

"Yes, we do," I agreed.

"You are my 'In case of emergency' person. Am I yours?"

"What?" I raised my eyes to the ceiling. We were about to get into dangerous territory.

"Am I your 'In case of emergency' person?" he repeated.

"No," I admitted. I crossed my fingers behind my back because I could tell the lies were about to gush from my lips.

"Why not?"

"Because, if there is an emergency, chances are I'll be able to help you out of most any jam." I treaded lightly and hoped he wouldn't notice the obvious.

"But if you have an emergency, I'd be of little use?" Daniel mused.

Damn. His head injury hadn't slowed him down any.

"No, not really." I hedged. "Don't get me wrong. You are a great guy, but if we get into a 'damsel in distress' situation, I'm not the one who's going to be the damsel."

"Evie," the Doc cautioned me with a word.

"What?" I turned to her. "I'm just being honest."

"Sometimes, brutal honesty isn't the best way to proceed," she shook her head slightly.

"No, I'd rather she were honest," Daniel said. "That way, we'll know where we stand."

The Doc nodded once and retreated to the other side of the small room. She stood with her back to us and looked out the small window into the gathering darkness.

"So, if you wouldn't be the damsel, that means I would be," Daniel continued.

"That's how it's been," a part of me knew I was about to take a long leap off a short pier, but I couldn't stop myself. "But it hasn't always been your fault." I paused and thought for a second. "In fact, usually, things have gotten sketchy because you know me."

"Does that mean what happened to me is because of you?" He sat up in his bed.

"No," I held my hand up. "Scout's honor, or whatever they say. This time, it wasn't because of me. But, I wasn't fast enough to help you."

"It seems to me like it's high time I figured out how to help myself," he mused.

"But I want to help you." I got as close to pleading with him as my pride would allow.

"Yeah, but like you said, you won't always be there." His eyes were eloquent.

"No, I won't." I admitted.

"And often, the reason things get bad is because of you, or so you said."

"Yeah. I'd have to say that's true." His logic was dawning on me, but I was still swimming in murky seas. Yet I had to agree. His life was more dangerous with me in it.

"So in order to stay safe, it's better for me to take care of myself."

I nodded.

"And not be with you."

"No, no freakin' way," I cried. "I'm responsible for you, and I'm not letting you out of my sight until you're better!"

"That's not your call, Evie. I'm responsible for myself." I'd never heard him sound stern before. I hated it.

I looked anywhere but him. If his next words were going to be what I thought they were going to be, I would implode.

"I don't want to see you for a while," he said.

"What?" My eyes flew to his face.

"I need to figure things out, and I need to do that on my own."

"So, what, you're breaking up with me?" I swiped at the tears that were threatening to overflow.

"Evie, as far as I know, we're not really together, are we? I don't remember you," he whispered.

"But I remember you," I took his stiff fingers into my hands. "I love you. We love each other."

"I don't know that. I don't feel it. In here." He punched at his heart with his fist. "Can you understand that?"

I nodded. I didn't trust my voice. I backed away from the bed toward the door. If I could have backed out of the hospital, the city, the country, and the planet, I would have done it. I crashed into a wall of muscle.

"Ow!" we yelled together.

I whirled around and stumbled. The tall, muscle-bound guy with the impeccable taste in clothes caught me, picked me up with two hands and left me standing.

"Who are you?" I demanded.

"Daniel! You look so much better." He maneuvered around me and rushed towards Daniel's bed. He looked Daniel over. "I'm so glad you're okay. I'm so sorry. I wanted to come with you. I still can't believe you went in by yourself."

"Went in where? What are you talking about? Who are you?" Daniel's questions came rapid fire.

The man skidded to a halt. He cocked his head to one side. He looked at me and then at the Doc.

"What's going on here?" He asked.

"First, who are you?" I stood at my tallest and stared up at the gorgeous man in front of me.

"I'm Tom St. James." He replied. "I'm Daniel's boss and friend."

"Boss? You got a job?" I smiled at Daniel.

"I guess I did." He closed his eyes and leaned back against the pillow.

"What do you mean, you guess?" Tom asked.

"Daniel has had a head injury." The Doc turned from the window and came back towards us. "He is having some memory issues."

"In other words, I don't remember anything."

"Holy shit!" Tom cried. He wrung his hands. "So you don't know where you were or what happened?"

"No," Daniel answered. "Do you know?"

"Honey, do I have a lot to fill you in on!" Tom sat on the edge of Daniel's bed.

Daniel shook his head. "I need you to wait a minute. Evie, Doctor," he looked at each of us in turn. "If you don't mind, I'd like some privacy."

"Certainly," the Doc replied. She strode to the door. "Evie," she prodded me.

"Right," I said. I turned back to Daniel.

"Can we talk soon?" I asked. I looked a couple of inches over his head. I couldn't meet his eyes. If I did, I'd lose it all over the place.

He shook his head.

"I think I need some time to figure things out, Evie. It's all just too much." He took a deep breath. "First, let me figure out what happened. And then …."

"And then?"

"And then if my memory returns, I'll know how to proceed. And I'll get in touch with you. After all, you're my 'in case of emergency' contact. I'll know how to find you. Can you understand?" His voice took on gentle tones.

My eyes widened in shock. He was letting me down easy. He was dumping me.

"Wow," I murmured. "You're dumping me. I wonder who's going to win the office pool on that one?"

"What?" He asked.

"Nothing. Let's just say my coworkers haven't exactly been supportive of our relationship. There's been a pool going for some time now about how long we would last and who would dump whom." I turned the door knob. "Now, I guess we know."

I marked a last subtle protection sigil in the air in his direction.

"Daniel, if you need me, come find me," I said.

"I will," he answered. "I promise."

I closed the door behind me. I stalked the hallway. A tiger in a cage had nothing on me.

"What the hell!" I exploded. "We need to figure out how to fix this. If we don't fix this and fix it soon, he's going to get hurt even worse because even though he doesn't remember any of the bad bugaboos that go bump in the night, they all remember him. And then when you add whoever it was who just beat the crap out of him and this is going to really suck and then I… we have to figure out … "

"Evie, breathe," the Doc interrupted my tirade.

"What?" I paused mid-step.

"You aren't breathing. And you won't help anything if you pass out."

"Look," I yelled at her and raised the eyebrows of a couple of passing nurses. "I need to make sure he is going to be okay. And then I need to figure out a way to get him his memory back, and then I need to figure out how to get him back to normal, because I need him to...." Tears flowed down my cheeks. I turned my face to the wall.

"How about you just need him?" The Doc was all kindness. "It's okay to just need him."

"No, it's not," I sniffled. "If I just need him and don't protect him, all hell breaks loose. And now he doesn't even want to see me."

"Maybe that's not a bad thing, for now," the Doc said.

"How can you say that?"

"Maybe it's not a bad idea for him to learn some self-defense." Her eyes sparkled with an idea. "In fact, what if we made sure he got into an accelerated self-defense course taught by a teacher we know and trust?"

"Like who?" I asked.

"Like me," Wisteria had appeared beside me. I whirled. Damn, she was quiet. She carried a small, black duffel and wore her customary black fatigues and hiking boots. Her long red hair was pulled back in its ever-present braid.

"Can we arrange it?" The Doc asked.

"I don't see why not? We can offer it at the local Y and nudge him into taking some classes. And that way I can teach him some techniques and keep an eye on him while we figure out what the hell is going on."

Wisteria turned to me. "And you need to head back and complete your coursework. Marlon Bardot is taking over my classes until I can get back, and he'll do great by you."

"What the hell are you talking about?" I turned shocked eyes on her. "I'm not going anywhere."

"You can't be here," she towered over me. "You're not ready to be back here. Your battle magic is too wild and unpredictable. You'll likely kill yourself before you do any damage to anyone you're actually trying to hit."

"Too freakin' bad. I'm staying right here," I retorted. I crossed my arms over my chest. I wasn't leaving the city. No way. No how. I stared at each of them with a "Just try to make me leave" look in my eyes.

"Okay," the Doc said. "If that's the case, then we'll need to find something for you to do."

"Do?" I asked. All I planned to do was shadow Daniel and make sure he didn't get so much as a paper cut in the darkroom.

"Yes, 'do,'" Wisteria towered over me. "You're not exactly a lady of leisure, now are you? You're going to have to work."

"Work?" I swallowed hard. On top of everything else, I was going to have to get a job? Shit!

"You aren't a student anymore, Evie, and that means getting a job," the Doc's voice sounded soothing and gentle even though she was delivering crappy news. Somehow, I started feeling a little better. I could get a job. I could work. And make enough to pay for living in the city? Hah, not likely. I'd have to augment my pay with a little magic. Yeah, that'd work.

"That won't work," the low British tones of the Vice Tribunal Chief sounded right next to me. I shrieked and jumped a good six inches off the ground. "If you're going to live in the city, you will have to work to pay for your things just like everyone else." She continued as if she hadn't just stopped my heart five ways to Sunday.

"Where did you come from?" I gasped.

"The broom closet, where else?" She parted her lips into a feral grin. She'd been around long enough to have seen the witch trials of the fourteenth and fifteenth centuries. Rumor had it that she had even been undercover trying to help those imprisoned and had been accused of witchcraft herself. So, she didn't take kindly to anyone being hurt, abused, or falsely accused.

"How is Daniel?" She looked at the Doc. "Will he return to health?"

"He will," the Doc responded.

"Good, now let's figure out how we are going to resolve this situation." She moved down the hallway towards the lounge.

"Wait a minute," I caught up to her. We all entered the lounge. The Doc closed the door, said a couple of words, and the door transformed into a wall. For the next few minutes, everyone would pass by us and not know, remember, or care that the lounge was even there.

"How did you hear about all this so quickly? And how did you know that I'm going to stay in the city? And why is the Tribunal taking an interest in Daniel? What's going on?"

The Vice Chief sat in one of the orange-backed chairs around a small round coffee table. She didn't have to answer my questions. In fact, she could just tell me sit down and shut up and I'd have to do it most riki-tik or risk being kicked of out of the Fairy Godparent Guild.

She gazed up at me for a long moment. She gave one curt nod as if she had made some sort of decision. "I heard about this from Margaretha Swanglider. She informed me as soon as you left 'the Storm.' I knew you would want to stay in the city because we're a lot alike, you and I, and that's what I would do. The Tribunal is taking an interest because the stakes are higher than either you or Daniel, if you will pardon me for saying so. And as for what's going on, that is what we are going to determine over the course of the next few weeks. We have some idea, but we will need to flesh out the details." She nodded at me, again. "That is where you will come in." She turned to Wisteria. "And you."

"Me?" Wisteria asked. "Look, I'm always up for a little rough and tumble, but I'm mostly retired now."

"There's something brewing, and we need you, 'boots on the ground,'" the Vice Chief stated. "It might be nothing, but I would rather know." She pulled a sheaf of papers from her ever-present satchel. "Now, let's see how we're going to work this," she smoothed the papers out. "You, Wisteria, have already secured a position as the martial arts instructor at the Vanderbilt YMCA on East 47th. It is the closest to Daniel's work."

"What am I teaching?" Wisteria snapped to attention.

The Vice Chief consulted her papers. "Karate, Mixed Martial Arts, Street fighting, and Tai Chi." She read.

"Tai Chi?" Wisteria raised an eyebrow.

"Like everyone else, you could use some down time," the Vice Chief explained. "The relaxation techniques will be helpful to your students and to you."

"You do know it's the deadliest martial art if it's used that way, don't you?" Wisteria asked.

"We do, but we would prefer you focus on the more meditative aspects of it when you teach it to Daniel. Now, the MMA class? You can go ahead and teach him how to do battle."

"The Vanderbilt Y," Wisteria said. "I'd better go and take a look at their facilities and see what equipment might need supplementing."

The Vice Chief handed her the top three pages from her sheaf.

"The top one will be your credentials and the second two will yield all the other open doors you will need to protect those who need protection and teach those who need to learn.

"Vice Chief, Doc, Songbottom," she accepted the pages, folded them, and hid them in a pocket. "I'm out." She disappeared.

The Vice Chief smiled and turned to the Doc.

"Is there anything else you can do for Daniel or for any of the other patients at this hospital right now?"

The Doc, too, closed her eyes for a moment. Boy, I wish I could just close my eyes and get all the answers like they do. Whenever I close my eyes, I just start seeing visions of the next meal I'm going to crave. Maybe I should take a Tai Chi class or learn some other way of paying attention. They make it look easy. But, I know it's not.

The Doc smiled a tiny smile and shook her head.

"This is a good place, a healing place," she said. "For the moment, there is nothing I am needed to do. Daniel's physical injuries are almost completely healed. His memory is not my purview and besides, I have a feeling he will have more than his fair share of reminders of the life he was living." She raised her eyebrows in my direction.

"Very well, then." The Vice Chief made a mark on her sheaf of papers. You'll be needed in Core City to finish your term."

"What about her?" The Doc shrugged her head in my direction. "She doesn't have sufficient training yet."

"True, but she has plenty of the bull-headed in her, and that will carry her a long way." The Chief answered as if I wasn't there. Have I mentioned how much I hate it when people do that?

"But not in healing," the Doc said.

"No, not in healing," the Vice Chief agreed. "She'll have to make do with her other resources."

"Okay, you two do realize I'm right here, don't you?" I paced the lounge. "You're talking in riddles. What other resources do I have? How do I fix this? What do I do next?"

"You go to work," the Vice Chief said.

"Oh yeah, work," I parroted. I gazed at my boots. What kind of work did they have planned for me? I wasn't much good at anything except the piano and being a Godparent. And lately, that one hadn't been too necessary. Joanna had been my only charge for a while, and I was betting I'd lost my chops.

"You're going to be the new counselor/artistic director of the new 127th Street Youth Center."

"Me? A counselor? Have you lost every last marble?" Incredulity raised my voice to a shriek.

The Vice Chief consulted her papers. She penciled in a hash mark next to one of the lines.

"Are you grading me?" I asked.

"No, but we were expecting your protest, and you just made it. Everything is going according to plan."

Plan? What plan?

"Whose plan?"

"The Plan."

The answer did nothing to assuage the thousand butterflies that had just started a conga line in my belly. The truth was I didn't like kids. No, wait. That wasn't true. The real truth was kids terrified me. Every time I spent time with one, I was certain I would drop him on his head, or get distracted and she'd end up playing in traffic.

"I'm going to say it right now." I stood stock still. "I will suck at this. Please don't make me do it."

"It is already done," the Vice Chief made another hash mark on the page. "You start at the Center tomorrow. You will be responsible for working with the youth, getting them what they need to keep them in school, and providing them with as many resources as possible to help them thrive. You will also develop an arts program."

Arts program? I was terrible at art. I failed that "Draw a turkey by tracing your hand," thing in art class. I hadn't improved even a smidge in the intervening two-hundred years.

"Could I do a music program instead?" I asked.

"You could," she replied. "But you'll have to come up with the instruments, music, and other accoutrements on your own."

"Don't I get the standard expense account?" I asked.

"No, you will be working like everyone else. Besides, it would look suspicious if you were suddenly able to afford a lot of instruments. You are just out of Juilliard, remember and don't have any contacts."

"You're right!" I whirled with excitement and squeezed the Vice Chief in a bear hug. "I don't have any contacts in the real world. But I have contacts at Juilliard."

"So?" She asked.

"So, I can make that happen."

"Good. As I said, you start tomorrow." She turned to the Doc. "You're sure Daniel is fine."

"Physically, he'll soon be as good as new. Of that I'm sure," she answered. "So, his work with Wisteria should proceed without a glitch. I'd like to see him start with Tai Chi for its meditative aspects, but I imagine he will want to start with something a bit more hands-on."

"Wait a minute. How do you know Daniel will want to take Tai Chi or anything else for that matter?" I asked.

She closed her eyes for a moment.

"That is being taken care of right now."

DANIEL

Daniel watched Tom with hooded eyes while he paced the length of the small room.

"Look," Tom threw his hands up. "I don't know how to say it, so I'm just going to have to put it out there. This is all my fault," he drew his hands in a wide circle.

"What do you mean this is all your fault? How could this be your fault? Did you beat me up?"

"What? No, of course not," Tom said. "But you were on a story for the paper when it happened, and I'm your boss, so it is my fault."

"No, Tom," Daniel said. "If I was on a story, then I was doing my job. Whoever did this to me, this is their fault. Not yours." He could see that Tom remained unswayed.

Tom slumped into the chair by his bedside. He dropped his head in his hands.

"Jesus, Daniel," he mumbled. "You could have died."

"But I didn't." Daniel reminded him.

For a moment, the two men sat in silence.

"Tom," Daniel said. "Look at me."

Tom raised his tear-stained eyes.

"This is not your fault." Daniel said again. "Repeat after me, 'This is not my fault.'"

"This is not my fault," Tom parroted.

"Good," Daniel relaxed against his pillow. He thought for a moment.

"So, if I was on a story, what was I working on?"

"Oh no," Tom jumped out of his chair and resumed pacing. "You're not going to do any more work on that. It's over. It's done."

"Did I get the story?" Daniel asked. "Did we print it?"

"No." Tom answered.

"Then it's not done, is it? So, why don't you tell me what it is I was working on?" Daniel said.

"Because I don't want you to do anything more on it. It's too dangerous," Tom said.

Daniel lay back against the pillows and studied his boss. He realized he needed to trust someone. Tom might also be his friend, but the only thing he knew at all was that he worked for this guy. He looked deeply into Tom's eyes and found only worry.

"Look, Tom, if I'm going to figure out what happened to me, I'm going to have to finish the story." Daniel said. "And that means I'm going to need to know what it was I was working on."

"Okay," Tom relented. "There's this designer drug called Heaven, and it is dangerous stuff." He looked at his hands. "You were researching it. You found a warehouse. You showed me some pictures. It looks like they are using young kids as drug mules. And you were running down a lead. I was supposed to go with you, but I got detained. By the time I found you, you were already hurt." His voice caught on the last word. "Oh, Daniel. I thought you were dead when I first saw you. I never want to go through something like that again."

"Yeah, well, I'm kind of hoping I won't have to go through it again either," Daniel's smile was rueful. "So let's make a deal," Daniel said. "You don't do anything stupid and dangerous, and I won't do anything stupid and dangerous." He stuck out his hand and the two men shook on it.

"So, what's next?" Tom said.

"Next, I need to get out of here." Daniel motioned to the clothes Evie had dropped on the other bed.

"Would you mind passing me my clothes?"

Tom obliged and did not turn around when Daniel removed his hospital gown. Daniel raised his eyebrows in question. "Are we good enough friends for you to watch me change? Do we play sports together or something?"

"Honey, believe me. It's nothing I haven't seen before and plenty of times." Tom chuckled. "And I've been in plenty of locker rooms but hardly ever to play sports."

"Oh," Daniel nodded. "Are you gay?"

"As the day is long," Tom replied.

"Got it," Daniel said. He finished dressing.

"I have to say," Tommy eyed Daniel as he deftly bent to tie his shoes. "You're doing so much better than I thought you would be by now. Daniel, you were really hurt. I was hoping you'd be conscious again sometime in the next week. But here you are ready to leave. Miraculous."

"I guess I must be a quick healer." Daniel murmured.

"That must be it."

They left the room together and checked him out of the hospital.

"Where do you want to go?" Tommy asked.

"First, I want to go home, shower, and eat." Daniel stopped short. "Where do I live?" He reached into his pockets and produced a wallet and a set of keys. He flipped open the wallet. "Hey, I live in the Village," Daniel said. "Good to know. I'm going to assume I have a camera there."

"Yeah, you must have a spare. Your camera wasn't at the warehouse when I found you. I'm guessing whoever beat you up took it."

"Probably," Daniel winced. "It's so strange to think about getting the crap beat out of me but not remembering any of it."

"And you look amazing compared to how I expected you to look. Seriously, Daniel, they messed you up."

"Yeah, I get that." Daniel stopped in the middle of the sidewalk. "And I need to do something about it."

"What do you mean?" Tom asked. He hailed a passing cab, and the two entered it.

Daniel gave the cabby his home address and then turned back to Tom.

"I mean I need to get some self-defense training. I need to learn how to protect myself."

"You could buy a gun," Tom suggested.

"No, I won't do that. But I need to do something."

Tom closed his eyes for a moment and lay his head against the back of the seat.

"Hey, I just remembered." He focused on Daniel. "There's a new martial arts training curriculum at the YMCA near the office. They are going to be teaching Mixed Martial Arts, Karate, Tai Chi, all that sort of stuff. Maybe you can sign up for classes there."

"That might be just the thing. I'll look into it," Daniel said. "At any rate, I want to be able to protect myself better than I did."

The cab crawled downtown during the tail end of rush hour.

"It would have been faster to walk," Tom muttered.

"Yeah, but I'm not quite ready for five-mile walk," Daniel said. "You don't have to come with me," he continued. "I'm sure I can find my way down to the Village."

"Oh no," Tom replied. "You're stuck with me. And then after you've had your shower and grabbed your gear, we need to go to my father's house."

"Why?"

"He wants to see us."

"Does he know what happened to me?"

"I assume so," Tom said. "He seems to know everything that happens in this city."

The cab stopped in front of the Greenwich Village brownstone Daniel called home. It looked unfamiliar to him.

"I can't possibly live here," Daniel said. "There's no way I could afford this, right?"

"Right," Tom laughed. "I certainly don't pay you that much."

They exited the cab and tried to unlock the front door. The key failed to open the lock.

"Maybe you live in the basement," Tom suggested.

"Now, that's more like it," Daniel said. They moved around to the door partially hidden by a postage stamp sized garden. Daniel fit the key in and turned it. They entered his tiny English Basement efficiency.

Daniel studied the space. He appreciated the well-organized nature of whoever had laid out the small space.

"Good to know I'm efficient," he said.

"So what are you going to need?"

"First, a shower. Then, clean clothes. And then my camera."

"You shower. I'll get the clothes and then we'll look for the camera," Tom suggested. "And then, let's go see my father and find out what the heck he wants."

Daniel moved into the bathroom and found that the shower held photographic trays. An ancient photo enlarger sat in the sink. He rearranged the various pieces of equipment, stripped, and turned on the water.

"By the way, when we're around my family, you call me Tommy," Tom called from the living room. "And another thing? You're my boyfriend."

Daniel's eyes opened wide. He pushed his head out of the bathroom. "What? I'm your boyfriend? Tommy, I don't know how to say this, but I don't think I'm gay. I mean I lost my memory and all, but when I got a good look at Evie, I have to admit I thought she was hot."

"You're supposed to think she's hot. She's your girlfriend."

"Huh, she is my girlfriend. I'll have to think about that," Daniel mused. He turned curious eyes to Tommy. "But then how am I your boyfriend?"

"It's a long story. I'll explain on the way. But you're going to want to be sure you can play that off. We don't want my father to catch us in a lie." A faraway look came into his eyes. He looked frightened. "Daniel, we never want that to happen."

CHAPTER 14

EVIE

Okay. I had a job even though I was going to suck at it. Now, I needed to find a place to live. On impulse, I headed to Jo's at Juilliard. She was good at this sort of planning thing.

Jo opened the door and enveloped me in a giant hug.
"Oh Evie," she cried. "I'm so sorry about Daniel and so glad he is going to be okay."
"Wow, news travels fast," I said. "How did you hear about it?"
"Torlyn swung by and let me know." She pulled me onto the threadbare couch that occupied most of the space in the little main room of the suite. "Tell me everything!" She demanded.
I filled her in on the latest drama.
"Holy Shit!" Joanna swore. "Are you okay?" She calmed down in a heartbeat as only she could. "How are you handling him not remembering you?"
"About how you'd expect," I jumped up and paced the small room. "I've dropped out of school. I'm not finishing Battle Magic or Healing Magic because I'm going to stay here

and be ready if anyone else tries anything with Daniel. And I'm going to have a job." I plopped back on the couch.

"Job? You already have a job," Jo was ever-reasonable.

"I do, but it's not like you need me anymore and they haven't given me any other charges so for now, I'm good to go. Yeah, believe it or not, I'm going to work at a youth center. I'm going to start a music program there too. I just need to round up the instruments."

"You can't conjure them up?" Jo waved an imaginary magic wand in the air.

"No," I answered. "They all have to come from somewhere, and my expense account has gone the way of the do-do. I didn't expect reaching Level 4 to be quite so expensive." I said.

"But that's not the part I'm worried about," I jumped back up and resumed my pacing. "I'm going to have to work with kids. Jo," I turned to her. "I have a confession to make. I don't really like kids."

"But I'm sure you're really good with them," Jo's face screwed up in thought. "Actually," she said. "I don't ever remember you having much to do with kids."

"Because they terrify me." I admitted.

"You're going to do fine. I know you. You'll figure it out. You always do."

"Here's hoping." I waved an imaginary tumbler of whiskey at the heavens. "Now, I just have to find a place to live, and I'm good to go. But really, where the heck am I going to be able to live on no money? It's not like a youth center is going to pay New York City apartment wages, and I'm sure it will be weeks before I see my first check." I hung my head.

"Wait!" Jo's eyes lit up, and I immediately felt better. She's like that. When she's happy, the rest of us tiptoe through the tulips.

"I have the perfect solution," she cried. "You should stay here."

"Um, Jo, I graduated. I can't just stay at the school."

"What if you could? Okay, look, here's my idea." Her words tumbled out. "I'm going to be gone in a few days. We're flying out with the students on Friday. So, the room will be empty. And what if you were to take over working with the students who can't go?"

"What do you mean?"

"Well," now it was her turn to pace. "We can only take the top two students from each group. So, a bunch of the students who have been working really hard will just have to stop playing. But what if instead they kept playing with you? At the youth center?"

"That's not a bad idea." I sprang up and grabbed her hands. "Jo, you're a genius!"

"A Real Genius," she called back our old joke and one of my favorite movies. "Let's go see Professor Weingart. Maybe you can use some of the instruments we won't be using after we leave. It's perfect!"

We grabbed our various bags and left the room.

"Evie, it is lovely to see you again so soon," the Professor sat at her desk and looked, as always, perfectly coiffed. "But what brings you back here?"

"Professor," I started. "We have an idea." I pitched the plan to her.

She sat back and interlaced her fingers.

"This idea has possibilities. I was not pleased with the idea of simply abandoning the students who tried and practiced but who were not chosen to travel to Europe. This could be the ideal solution." She gazed at me with speculative eyes. "I believe you would excel at helping some of these more at-risk students, Evie. Yes! We will make this happen." She slapped her hands on her oak desk.

"And can I stay in my old room?" I raised hopeful eyes to her. "It would make my life so much easier, and I could hit the ground running because I wouldn't have to waste time on an apartment hunt."

"But you will have another job," she pointed out. "How will you reconcile all your duties?"

"Part of my duties will be to start a music program at the Youth Center," I answered. "This will pet two cats with the same hand, because I'll combine working with the kids at the Center with the kids from Washington Heights who aren't going to travel with Joanna."

"The Youth Center is up on 127 Street, and the school I am teaching in is on 125th," Jo supplied. "So, I'd bet a lot of the same kids will be the targeted audience. In fact," she warmed to her topic. "I can take Evie with me to rehearsal tomorrow, and she can introduce herself to the students and do a little promo to them about the Center."

I threw her a "Thanks for the extra work, I didn't need any sleep tonight anyway," sideways glance, but I had to agree it was a great idea.

"Okay," I agreed. "I'm still not sure how on all the worlds I'll be able to teach anyone anything, but I will try."

"Done and Done!" The Professor smiled. "Let's do this!"

"This place is a dump!" I announced as we entered the so-called music room at the 127th Street Youth Center. The large, square room held broken chairs, toppled tables, and enough grit and grime to fill a 1940s detective novel. Four crates sat around an old cable wheel in a makeshift configuration of table and chairs. The cable wheel held an ashtray and a few soft drink cups. The detritus from many fast food meals festooned the area.

Three windows along one wall opened toward the front of the Center. Muck, dust, and dirt obscured the outside. Although it was early evening and the sun still shone brightly, the room sat in shadows.

"Nothing a little elbow grease won't solve," the Professor said. She carried two violins in their cases on straps on her shoulders. She held a bucket and various cleaning supplies in her hands.

"We're never going to clean this up before next week, much less tomorrow," I grumped. There are a few things I hate. One of the biggest is cleaning, anything ever, by hand. With the Professor here, I wouldn't be able to work any cleaning spells. I'd have to actually scrub something. Ewww.

"This isn't a music room. This is a room where music goes to die."

"Evie," Joanna the Reasonable put a hand on my arm. "We'll do the best we can and get as far as we can. Besides," she smiled at me in sympathy. "The room isn't what's bothering you. And the cure for that is some good old fashioned motion." She laid the instruments she carried in a corner by the windows and looked around.

"Look," she pointed to the opposite corner. A dilapidated piano sat tucked against two walls. Dusty canvas partially covered it, but the wood that was visible was a dark rosewood.

I pulled the canvas off the upright grand. I was betting there were more than a few broken strings inside her. The keys had yellowed with age and the wood stain had worn away in large patches, but she had promise. I could work with this.

The Professor walked over to the instrument. She laid her hand on the keys and played a light arpeggio. Several notes in the chord didn't sound as the strings were indeed broken or just missing, but the rest of the notes rang pleasing and warm. The tinkling of the highest few notes tickled our ears.

"Well, well," she said. "A Baldwin." She leaned down and examined the keys. "This is circa 1926 - the height of the roaring 20s." She ran a hand along the top. "I'd wager she has some stories to tell," the Professor mused.

"Ooh, I'll bet it was a piano in a Speak Easy," Joanna cried. "How wonderful!"

I closed my eyes and scanned the instrument. I grinned. I knew this piano. Heck, I'd played this piano. In the 1920s, she had been the player piano at El Fey Club, Larry Fay's speakeasy. Larry ran whiskey from Canada to New York and used the club to unload and house the liquor. The place had been a Hell's Kitchen staple, and I'd visited more than once.

It's now a place called the Perfect Pint, and I'd been there more than once, too. Of course, I almost always headed to Tully's after he opened his pub, but sometimes, you needed a quick dram, you know?

"I'd love to know the piano's history," Joanna continued. "Do you think there's a way to trace that?"

"Regardless of where this baby comes from, I'm thinking we'll need to restore her to her former splendor." I met Joanna's eyes and promised her the story at a later time.

"In the meantime," the Professor smiled at us. "I'd say we have some cleaning to do."

I surveyed the muck, grime, and trash that lay heaped all over the room. Several large piles of plywood and long two-by-fours lay strewn about.

"You're not kidding, Professor. This is going to take some serious elbow grease. Why don't you go pick up some cleaning supplies?" I nudged her towards the door. "Joanna and I will get started on getting some this trash out of the room."

"I can help with that, you know." She glanced at us over the rims of her small glasses.

"We know you can. But Evie and I can get started moving the big stuff, but we can't clean the windows or other surfaces without at least some rags and such. If you wouldn't mind doing that, it would be terrific." Joanna's smile worked its magic. The Professor nodded and left.

"Thanks for helping her leave, love." I rubbed my hands together and dug my wand out of my black messenger bag. "Now, I can make all this crap disappear without breaking a sweat."

Joanna eyed me doubtfully. "Aren't you going to have to explain where it went?"

Sometimes, Jo is just too darned logical.

"Okay, I'll just make it change locations from here to the dumpster."

"Hopefully, it's already closed so no one suddenly sees it appear there," she supplied.

I made a sigil in the air with my wand, and outside a small breeze knocked the dumpster's top closed. We got to work. Before long the room sparkled. Some of it was real sparkles since I couldn't help myself and added a bit of pixie dust into the three coats of fresh white paint I had given the walls. Iridescence was going to be the name of the game here at Evie's House of Music. Besides, the pixies weren't going to miss it.

I stepped to one corner of the room and admired my handiwork.

"Not such a dump anymore," I said.

"It looks great," Jo agreed. She finished wiping down one of the three tables that still stood. They were old. The wood was cracked in spots, but they were sturdy oak. They would do very well.

We loaded the instruments onto the tables: woodwinds on one, strings on another, and percussion on the third. All told, we had collected three violins, two flutes, a French horn, one djembe hand drum, and a bunch of eggs, tambourines, and claves. We could make quite an orchestra with this motley crew, especially once I restored the upright grand. I turned my attention to the Baldwin. An old dame, she had a few rough spots and wrinkles. But, I was betting that once I got her back on her feet, she would sing like nobody's business.

"So, is it going to take a big spell to restore her?" Joanna approached the piano.

"A spell?" Shocked raised my voice an octave. "Oh no! No, this grand lady needs to be restored by hand." I approached the instrument and touched the yellowed keys with reverence. The Baldwin was made with resin keys not ivory, for which I was grateful. As far as I was concerned, the only place ivory belonged was on either side of an elephant's trunk. Still, I would have to locate a source for it. That might mean a trip to the Baldwin factory.

I rubbed my hands in anticipation. I'd have to set up a few alarms to remind me to head back to civilization because me in a piano factory was almost like me at the Jumping Cow when

Mama Brader rolled out new ice cream flavors. I could get lost for days, weeks, or months.

I retrieved a notebook from my bag and wrote out a list of supplies and materials I would need to bring the instrument back to her former splendor. Piano wire, more than a few mallets, shellac, a few pieces of rosewood to match up to the bites someone had taken out over the years - I would need them all.

"Okay, love." I turned to Joanna as I stowed the notebook back in my bag. "I need to go on a supply run to old the Baldwin factory in Trumann, Arkansas, and the abandoned one in Greenwood, Mississippi."

"But you start work tomorrow, and you were going to come by and meet the students." Jo protested.

"I'll make it back in time, Jo. Provided I set my alarms so I don't get lost in piano land, I'll be back before you know it," I promised. I raised my wand high. "Okay, you," I admonished it. "I know you like it when I lose my shit around all things music. But you've got to remind me that I need to come back. I start a new job at the Center tomorrow, and I can't be late."

My wand drooped at the suggestion that we were going to have to work a nine-to-five, but straightened up and flew right upon hearing that we would need to keep to a schedule. My wand often has a better handle than I do on the whole responsibility thing. It's been disappointed in my lack of time management skills more than once.

"Okay, sweetie," I enveloped Jo in a bear hug. "Back in a jiff."

I turned my head sideways, spied the nearest Ley Line and jumped.

CHAPTER 15

DANIEL

Daniel and Tommy arrived at St. James' penthouse in time for Evening Nightcap. A black-clad waiter ushered them into the long, rectangular room that served as Mitchell's home office and study.

"Come in, boys, come in," the elder St. James smiled broadly at the two younger men. "Good to see you again so soon, Daniel. I heard you ran into a bit of trouble. You don't look like you're much the worse for wear," he remarked.

"I guess I'm a quick healer," Daniel replied. He accepted a tumbler of whiskey from one of the ubiquitous waiters.

"All except your mind, eh Daniel?" St. James' smile failed to reach his eyes.

Tommy lowered his head in apology. "Sorry, sweetie. You probably wanted to be the one to share or not share that tidbit. But I tell my father everything."

"So, you heard I've lost my memory," Daniel said.

"And yet the rest of you looks hail and hearty," St. James raised his glass slightly. "I wonder why that is."

A noise from the back of the room interrupted them.

"Ah, there you are," St. James called to a tall man who had entered the room from one of its recessed doors.

His black hair was cropped close to his head and his face looked carved from stone. His bored, silver eyes assessed both younger men. His eyes widened for an instant when he looked at Daniel, but just as quickly the bored look returned to them. He turned to St. James and lowered his head a mere inch. He accepted a whiskey tumbler and came to a stop at the right edge of the big desk that dominated the room.

"Ezekiel, you remember my son, Tommy," St. James gestured to his son. "And this is his new boyfriend, Daniel Evershed."

"Boyfriend?" Ezekiel's brows arched.

"Yes," Tommy lied smoothly. "We've only been seeing each other for a little while."

"And now you'll get a chance to get fully reacquainted. It will be just like the first time all over again." St. James laughed.

Ezekiel looked at them each in turn.

"It's good to meet you, Daniel," Ezekiel stuck out his hand and Daniel clasped it. Ezekiel wrapped his long, tapered fingers around Daniel's and ground the bones of his hand together. The two men shook for longer than was necessary.

"Call me, Zeke," he continued as he released Daniel's hand. "I've always found Ezekiel so formal."

"Good to meet you, Zeke," Daniel put his aching hand in his pocket to hide its slight tremble.

"Let's have a toast," St. James commanded. "To your continued good health and recovery, Daniel."

"To your health," Zeke appraised Daniel over the rim of his tumbler and then downed the amber liquid.

"Zeke, have we met before?" Daniel asked. He could swear he had never seen the man before, but something about those silver eyes struck him.

"Not in this lifetime," Zeke answered. "But if you are going to be involved with Tommy, I'm sure we'll see each other again."

Daniel and Tommy made their apologies and left the apartment as quickly as they could.

"I'm still not back at top speed," Daniel said.

"Oh, I understand," St. James replied. "You need to get your rest. You could do it here. We have extra rooms," he suggested.

"I think Daniel would prefer his own bed," Tommy smiled. "And me in it," he continued and broadened his grin. He manhandled Daniel out of the apartment and out into the street.

"What was that all about?" Daniel asked.

"Zeke," came the terse reply.

"What about him?"

"You don't want to attract his attention."

"Why? Do I know him?"

"No," Tommy answered. "And like most things that have anything to do with my father, the less you know the better."

St. James and Zeke settled into the two leather chairs with their whiskey glasses.

"So, he doesn't remember you," St. James smiled. He motioned with his hand and a waiter brought him a box of cigars. He went through the lighting ritual and took a long drag. Unlike most, St. James inhaled deeply, closed his eyes, and reveled in the bolt of energy that shot through him. There was nothing like a good cigar.

"Apparently not," Zeke's eyes remained hooded.

"Good," St. James said. "That could prove useful. Get to know him a bit better."

"He might not remember me," Zeke responded. "But I could tell he sensed something about me."

"If you can't do it, get Jordan to do it. She's always good at that sort of thing."

"Will do." Zeke placed his tumbler on a tray on the side table and stood.

"And Ezekiel," the command was almost a whisper.

"Yes?"

"See that no one else comes to investigate our little venture."

"And if Daniel does?"

"Then, you will have to see to that too."

CHAPTER 16

EVIE

I made it back to the Youth Center with a little time to spare before I had to meet Jo at the school. I placed the hammers, string, and rosewood next to the piano in a neat pile. I glanced around one last time and took stock of the various instruments stacked about the room. Jo and the Professor had done a lovely job cleaning the windows, floor, and every other visible surface. I was a little sorry that I hadn't come back in time to help them white tornado the room, but let's face it, I pretty much suck at anything I don't like to do. And I hate cleaning with the white-hot passion of a thousand suns. If I could get my wand to do it, that was one thing, but if I had to put mop to floor? No. A thousand times no.

"Okay," I told my wand. "I can't delay this any longer. I have to go meet these kids." Crap! I was afraid. I wasn't kidding when I said I wasn't good with kids. It's a matter of fear. Either they're afraid of me, or I'm afraid of them. Usually, it's the latter. This was either going to rock or it would be the biggest disaster since they tried to remake Footloose.

I straightened already lined up instrument cases. I gave the walls a last once-over to ensure no paint dust would adhere to any of the instruments. I danced a little jig (and you know that's a ploy because I can't dance for beans). I procrastinated as much as I could without getting to the point that I would let Jo down, and then I hopped over to her school.

JOANNA

"As you all know, today is our last day all together," Joanna announced. She stood in the center of the semicircle of seats, stands, and students. They had all worked hard, and it pained her to know she could only take two of them with her to Europe.

"The Academy has made their choices, and your parents have already given their permission for you to fly to Europe. We will meet on Friday afternoon and head to John F. Kennedy Airport together." She looked at each of the students in turn and smiled. "You have all worked hard, and I'm so proud of you. I hope that you realize just how much you have achieved by learning how to play these instruments. I hope you will keep playing for the rest of your lives." She raised her hands in entreaty. "I wish we could take you all with us. Every one of you deserves to go."

A small sound at the door attracted her attention. Her face blossomed into a grin. Evie stood in the doorway. Her ever present black messenger bag lay at her hip. Her dark red hair was pulled into a high ponytail. Her blue eyes bore an expression made of equal parts mischief and apprehension. Joanna wasn't used to seeing Evie scared. Not that she should have been; she would rock this! And Joanna would enjoy watching Evie stretch for once. Evie had helped her so much. It would be great to see how much Evie grew through working with these kids.

"But I have a special surprise for those of you who will be staying here. You aren't done with music. Not even a little bit." She motioned for Evie to move further into the room. "I want to introduce you to my good friend, Evie. She's going to be starting a music program at the 127th Street Youth Center, and

I hope all of you will continue playing and studying with her for the rest of the summer and maybe beyond."

Evie sauntered into the room and assessed the group. Her smile broadened and her personal brand of charm and magic blazed to life.

"How's it going?" She asked and somehow that was all it took. She exchanged greetings or nods with everyone and sat at the back of the room.

The next few hours flew by while Joanna ran everyone through the pieces they would need to know for Europe. At the end of Bach's Brandenburg Number 3 Concerto, Joanna lowered her conductor's baton.

"We're going to stop a little bit early because Evie and I have a surprise for you. We were trying to figure out how to make sure you all could keep practicing after the Academy is over, and we think we've got it. We've gotten permission to store the instruments at the Youth Center. And that way you can come play them anytime you like." She paced the room and waved her hands as she talked.

"And we're going to walk over there right now and take the instruments with us so you can be sure where you put yours and then find it again. So let's pack everything up and we'll head over." A small movement from Veronica caught her attention.

"What is it, Veronica?" Joanna asked.

"If we're leaving right now, Tariq will miss us," she looked nervous.

"Oh, okay. He usually comes before class is over, so we can wait at least until then." They waited until the very end of class and Joanna turned apologetic eyes on Veronica.

"It's okay," Veronica seemed to read Joanna's mind. "He didn't pick me up this morning either."

Joanna nodded in understanding.

Everyone gathered their instruments, Joanna and Evie lugging the two cellos, and they all left the building.

"Good thing it's not that far," Evie blew her bangs off her forehead in the heat.

THE PIANO'S KEY

"I can only imagine what it must be like for people who play cello all the time," Joanna smiled in sympathy to all musicians everywhere.

"Yeah, it's not like I'll be lugging a piano anywhere anytime soon," Evie agreed.

"Tariq," Veronica called to Tariq as he and Calvin rounded the corner in front of them. "I thought you weren't coming."

"Nah, I was just running late," he smiled, but his eyes looked haunted.

"It's cool," Evie appraised him as she lowered the cello base to the ground. "Why don't you grab the cello from Joanna?"

"Who are you?" Suspicion raised Tariq's voice.

"This is Evie," Joanna answered. She had hoped Tariq would arrive before they left. She especially wanted Evie to meet him and take his measure. In her mind, Tariq acted tough, but he was still a child and with Calvin, he had undertaken a great deal of responsibility. When she had been his age, her biggest worry had been the fierce desire to play Carnegie Hall. She had a feeling his concerns ran much deeper. "She is my friend, and she's going to be starting a music program at the 127th Street Youth Center. We're going there now to drop off the instruments so everyone can keep playing even after the Academy Program is over. You should come with us."

"You're pretty. Pretty and shiny." Calvin said. He reached up and grasped Evie's hand.

"Shiny?" Joanna raised her eyebrows at her friend.

"He must see me like you used to," Evie replied soto voce.

"Thanks, sweetie," Evie held on to Calvin's hand and hoisted the cello against her side. Together they walked towards the Center. Tariq followed in their wake.

"Here we are," Joanna announced as they stood before the tall door that led to the music room. Evie opened the door with a flourish. The sparkling walls, clean floor, and array of instruments greeted them. Light shone in through the now-clean windows. Everyone except Tariq entered the room.

"Nice!" Veronica breathed. The others echoed her sentiments.

Tariq hesitated at the entrance.

"Do you want to come in, Tariq?" Joanna crooked her fingers in a "come in" gesture.

"Not a good idea," Tariq answered.

"To come into the room?" Confusion laced her voice.

"Naw," Tariq said. "It's not a good idea to have a music room here."

"The Youth Center has approved it so I don't see why it would be a problem." Joanna searched Tariq's face for answers.

"This is Darnell's place," was all he said.

"Darnell? Who's Darnell?" Joanna asked.

"You'll see."

Joanna tipped her head, shrugged, and went back to the others. Reluctance showing in every step, Tariq followed her.

"So anyway, for those of you who will stay here for the summer, you can come here and play whenever the Center is open. Right, Evie?"

"Absolutely," Ebullience broadened Evie's voice. She propped the cello against the wall and dug out the keys.

"You're welcome to come by any time. And we're going to hold classes of one sort or another. Some classical. Some traditional. Some improv. Some jazz." Tariq started at the mention of jazz but otherwise stood stock still. Joanna noted his interest and made a note to tell Evie at the earliest opportunity.

"I haven't figured out exactly how it will all happen yet," Evie continued. "But maybe you can help me fill in the blanks."

"What do you mean?" One of the students asked.

"I don't want to teach you stuff you don't want to learn. I figure we'll get more done if you are doing what makes you happy."

Silence answered her as the students absorbed what she said.

"This place is all right," Veronica admired as they entered the newly-cleaned-out music room. Everyone deposited their instruments on the tables that stood on the periphery. Several chairs and music stands made a semicircle in the middle of the room. A single black stand stood at the center point.

Joanna sauntered to Evie. "He's the student I wanted you to meet," she whispered. "I think he likes jazz."

Tariq rocketed towards the Baldwin piano. He put a hand on it and then jerked it back as if it had scalded him.

"What a piece of shit!" He circled around it.

"She needs a little help, but I wouldn't go trash talkin' her," Evie approached him.

He started. Guilt slashed across his eyes. "What, are you gonna give shit me about saying 'shit?'" He asked.

"Oh, I don't give a good damn what you say, man, I just don't want you to disrespect the instrument." Evie laid a hand on top of the piano. "She's been around a long time. I played her when she was at her peak, and let me tell you, she was something."

"Whatever," Tariq moved away from the Baldwin and prowled the rest of the room.

"I'm restoring her," Evie's voice carried to him. "You'll have to see her when she's back in top form. She plays like a dream."

"Right," he responded again.

"Some of the jazz greats have played her." Evie exuded nonchalance, but Joanna could tell she was warming to her subject. Nothing pleased Evie more than reminiscing about some of the great pianists regardless of the genres of music they played.

"Fats Waller, Willie 'The Lion' Smith, some of the greats have played out on her."

Tariq's steps slowed. He faced Evie.

"Yeah, I think even the Duke came downtown from the Cotton Club to play her a time or two."

"The Duke? Really?" He moved toward her then slowed. "How do you know? You weren't there."

"I'm older than I look," she grinned at him.

"Yeah, but you aren't that old," Tariq placed his hand on the back of the piano.

"You'd be surprised," she said. They shared a smile.

A commotion at the door to the music room got everyone's attention.

"What's up with this?" A tall, broad-shouldered man sauntered into the room. Three others followed on his heels. They all looked like football players who had just been on a bender. Big and brawny, they practically snarled as they surveyed the room. Joanna stepped towards them. The students were her responsibility, and she needed to ensure their safety first and foremost.

As the obvious leader approached, Joanna could see that although he was physically imposing, he was not as old as he had first appeared. In fact, he appeared almost her age.

"Excuse me, who are you?" Joanna asked.

"None of your business," he replied.

Joanna inclined her head as the answer dawned on her. "You must be Darnell."

"Yo Tariq, what up?" The leader was so big he dwarfed the rest of the room and its occupants. He strode towards Tariq and Evie.

"Yo Darnell," Tariq replied. He moved so he placed the piano between the two of them.

"What's going on here?" Darnell made the question sound like a threat.

"This is the new music room at the Center," Evie stepped in front of him. She gazed up at him and somehow made it seem like she was dwarfing him. Joanna took a second to marvel yet again at her friend's power and sense of self. Joanna shook her head ruefully. She herself had a long way to go before she reached that sort of self-confidence.

"This ain't no music room," Darnell growled. "This is my place. Nobody comes in here. Those are the rules. That's how things are done around here."

"It looks the rules have changed," Evie withdrew her wand from her messenger bag. To anyone who didn't know better, it looked like an ordinary music conductor's baton. Joanna knew better. Darnell didn't. Although she knew Evie could handle herself, Joanna worried at her bottom lip. They were also responsible for the students.

"And the stuff in here?" Darnell continued. "That was my stuff."

"Oh, so you were the one who left it such a mess." Evie nodded. "Well, we cleaned it up for you. If you want any of your stuff," she emphasized the last word. "You can find it out there. In the dumpster."

"What the hell, bitch!" Darnell and his goons lunged toward her like a regiment of muscle. Everyone else in the room made themselves as small as they could.

"Evie," Joanna cried out.

Evie slanted a gaze at her. And smiled.

EVIE

"Don't worry, Jo. I've got this," I smiled.

The four idiots advanced on me. I sighed. It wasn't the first time my size had lulled people into assuming I was unassuming. Idiots. But, I'd been needing to scratch an itch for a minute now so this was a good thing. Daniel had upset me more than I'd let on and these nincompoops would provide an appropriate distraction.

"Really, gentlemen," my voice could have been more snide, but I wasn't sure how. "You don't want to do this." I traced a small sigil in the air with my wand. Three of the hulks grabbed their crotches as if tiny mechanical crabs had just started nibbling on their unmentionables. Which they had. The crabs were in development at NASA for the next space mission to Venus. They would roam the surface, take microscopic soil samples, "taste" them to determine their composition and then put them back where they found them. So, they were useful for multiple functions, in addition to grabbing and pulling up tiny samples with their sharp little pincers. I was going to have to disinfect and replace them at NASA's Goddard Space Flight Center later, but for the moment they were perfect.

While the three goons yowled and howled and grabbed at themselves, I faced Darnell. He wasn't stupid. The instant the other three had been sidelined, he had stopped and retreated a couple of steps. He was big, but he was out of his depth, and somehow he seemed to know it. Good!

"What the fuck!" He yelled at his troops.

"My balls, man!" One of them whimpered. "They're on fire!"

"Make it stop," another cried as he fell to the floor writhing.

"I'd be happy to oblige," I said. "On one condition. You three will need to chill out, leave, and not bother this room or anyone who is in it, ever. And you don't come back unless you want to play music. Do we have a deal?"

"Okay!" One of them panted.

"Deal," pleaded another one.

The third one rocked and moaned while he cradled his privates.

That left Darnell. I turned my attention back to him. I traced another small sigil. His eyes teared up. His nose ran. The veins in his neck popped to the surface. He stood stock still, but his breath torpedoed in and out of his lungs. The world's hottest pepper, the Carolina Reaper, had just dissolved inside his mouth. I was sure he had no idea how it had gotten there, but he was doing his damnedest to show not even a hint of weakness.

Sweat poured off him. The shakes had started. He would soon lose his bowels. If I didn't time it just right, we'd have a serious mess to clean in just a few seconds. I waved my hand and the pepper disappeared.

His breath exploded out of him in a great whoosh. He collapsed onto one of the music chairs. It creaked under his great size.

"Water," he gasped.

"Actually, you need some sort of bread to soak up the oils." I reached into my bag and handed him a piece of the whitest and spongiest white bread I could conjure.

"Put it in your mouth and hold it on your tongue," I instructed him. He did as I said. I looked around at the rest of the idiots. Fear shone out of their eyes.

Once the red had receded from his eyes and his breathing had returned to a semblance of normal, I leaned down into his face.

"You're going to want to find a new place to hang out, Darnell," I murmured. "This one is no longer available. You will honor the same you deal your friends have agreed to. You don't come back here unless you want to play music. Do we understand each other?"

"We do." Hatred narrowed his eyes to slits and his voice to a husky whisper.

"Good," I stowed my wand in my bag. I stepped back from him and turned to the rest of the room. "These gentlemen were just leaving," I announced.

Darnell stood. "Get up!" He kicked the leg of one of his comrades. They rose from the ground and hunched protectively over their middles. All four shuffled towards the door. Darnell turned back in the doorway.

"Tariq, let's go!" he commanded.

Tariq stepped forward from around the piano. He looked at me and for an instant I saw terror in his eyes. He banked it and moved towards the exit. He turned back to Veronica who was holding Calvin in her arms.

"Can you watch him for me until I get back?" He asked.

"Yeah," she answered. "Just pick him up at my place later."

"Cool. Thanks," he said and walked out.

"Evie," Joanna came up to me and whispered. "He needs your help."

"How do you know that?"

"I just do," she replied.

I took her word for it.

"Hey Tariq," I called. I ran down the hall after him.

He turned back and looked at me with tormented eyes.

"You're welcome back anytime," I said. "I'm restoring the piano. Maybe when I'm done, I can teach you how to play a little."

"I don't think so," he replied.

"Why not? You might like playing."

"That's not something I need to learn," he fidgeted with his hands and hopped from one foot to the other.

"Yes, but it's something you might want to learn," I replied.

"Trust me," he looked at me with eloquent eyes. "There's nothing there I can learn from you. Now, I'm gone!" He ran out of the building.

"'There's nothing there I can learn from you,'" I repeated. "What the hell does that mean?"

I hurried back to the music room as I mulled it over. He seemed like a good kid. And he definitely took good care of his little brother. I smiled. Calvin was an angel. I paused in thought. Note to self: Check and make sure whether or not Calvin is part angel. Of course, if Calvin were part angel, that would make Tariq part angel too, and I just didn't see that happening.

"Oh well," I shrugged. Metaphysical questions weren't really my thing.

I headed back to the room and did a quick scan for any of them who might be lactose intolerant.

"Okay," I announced as I entered. "Who wants ice cream?"

Tariq caught up to Darnell and the others down the street from the Center.

"What you doing there?" Darnell asked.

"Nothing. I was just picking up Calvin and Veronica."

"Why didn't you call and tell me about the bullshit with my room?" Darnell growled.

"We just got there when you showed up," Tariq answered.

"Yeah, and you were too busy with Veronica to pay me any mind," Darnell nodded. "You trying to tap that ass, boy?"

"Naw, man, it's not even like that. She's just a friend," Tariq evaded the subject as best he could. The last thing he wanted was to give Darnell any reason to take an interest in Veronica.

"Oh, so what? You trying to make time with the shorty with the red hair? She out of your league." Darnell laughed then stopped. "I'm gonna need to teach that bitch a lesson. Who is she, anyway?"

"Her name is Evie, and she's going to be running a music program out of the Center," Tariq replied. "That's all I know."

"Go find out more and then tell me." Darnell cracked his knuckles and swore. "Damn, man! My hands are still sore from the other night when we gave that white boy his beating."

"I'm still sore too, man." One of the others piped up.

"Me, too," one of the others echoed.

"We're all sore, except you, Tariq," Darnell towered over him. "You barely touched him at all. I bet your hands aren't hurting even a little bit." He grabbed one of Tariq's hands and wrenched it.

Tariq gasped in pain, but otherwise stayed silent. He stood statue still. Any reaction now would spur Darnell on.

Darnell laughed and released him.

Tariq ignored the throbbing in his hand and let it fall to his side.

"So yeah, man. Go and see what she's up to and let me know. I'm going to make a little time with that Shorty. She's going to be sorry she messed with me."

"We're not gonna go back and mess up her room, are we?" Refrigerator-sized Wayne spoke up for the first time. Although he was huge, his voice quaked in fear.

"What, you stupid?" Darnell punched him in the arm. "That's trivial, man. We need to figure her shit out. Then, we hit her, and we hit her hard." He turned to Tariq.

"So you go on, little man. Go find her and see where she goes, who she knows, and where she hangs her hat. Then, hit me up."

"Look, man," Tariq said. "She's just doing her job, you know? She didn't know it was your place."

"Yeah, but when she found out, she didn't apologize, and she didn't leave. She disrespected me, and I can't tolerate that."

"Look man, it was bad enough beating up that guy. We can't do that to no girl. It ain't right." Tariq tried to keep the pleading note out of his voice. He hated hurting anyone, and Evie hadn't done anything but be nice to him and to Calvin. "Besides, she's working at the Youth Center. So, it's not like she's rich or anything." If he could make Darnell feel like Evie wasn't worth it, he might just leave her alone.

"Don't you worry about that," Darnell commanded. "You do what I told you and leave the thinking to me." He grabbed a fistful of Tariq's t-shirt and dragged him up off his feet. "You don't, and I might have to take a closer look at that Veronica girl or your little brother." He opened his fingers and Tariq fell to the ground. "You get your ass over there, and you report back to me. I'll take care of the rest."

CHAPTER 17

DANIEL

A windowless, rectangular room with worn wooden floors, the YMCA gym served as the basketball court, volleyball court, and martial arts studio. Long blue gymnastics mats had been placed along the floor's length. Before he entered the room, Daniel bowed. "You have to bow in to show your respect to the room," the woman at the front desk had instructed him. "I walked in without bowing and the instructor almost took my head off," she said. "You wouldn't think a woman so pretty could be so mean." Daniel had promised that he would bow, paid his dues for the class, and headed towards the gym.

As he entered the room he noted the variety of people. Some older, some younger, they had a common goal. For one reason or another, they had all decided to learn Street Fighting and Mixed Martial Arts.

Daniel found a patch of wall that did not have a piece of equipment and leaned against the wall of the dojo, as it was called. He studied the rest of the group. Of the four women and eight men in the room, only a few looked like they would be able to handle themselves in a tense situation.

One of the women separated herself from the crowd and came towards him. Tall and lithe, she moved like a cat. Her chocolate-colored skin and rows of tiny, colorful braids contrasted beautifully with the crisp, white gi she wore. Daniel smiled his approval at her beauty and at her approach. She leaned against the wall next to him.

"Quite the motley crew, aren't we?" She smiled. Her smile made her more stunning still. Daniel's hands itched for a camera. He wanted to photograph that sexy smile and the promise in her startling green eyes.

"Yeah," he agreed. "But it won't hurt any of us to learn something about how to defend ourselves."

"True," she nodded. "I'm Jordan." She extended her hand.

"Daniel," he clasped it with his hand, and they shook.

Jordan began a series of stretches against the wall that tightened her karate gi and tautened Daniel's belly muscles in response. Seriously, he thought, women who look like her should never be allowed to stretch like that in public. He did his best to look anywhere but at how her uniform highlighted her rounded behind as she put one foot on the wall, bent her knee, and leaned into the stretch.

"Aren't you going to warm up?" She asked.

"Oh, I'm warming up just fine, thank you." He answered and earned a throaty laugh from her.

"I'll take that as a compliment," she gazed at him with frank interest.

"You should."

"So, Daniel." She continued. "What do you do when you aren't learning how to defend yourself?"

Daniel hesitated. He knew what he did. He just couldn't remember ever having done it. Supposedly, he was a photographer, but he could not remember ever taking a single photograph. He hoped that he would somehow know what to do when the time came. He sighed and plunged in.

"I'm a photojournalist," he answered.

"How interesting! Are you working on anything right now?"

"Well ... " he uttered.

"Class," the tall redhead barked the single word and silenced him. The entire class snapped to attention. They lined up in a single line in front of her. Some adopted the 'at attention' stance of the military. They all froze in place. She appraised each person in the line with a critical eye.

"I'm Wisteria Flamethrower. You call me 'Sensei.' This is our dojo," she indicated the room with a long, elegant hand. "We train here. We do not eat here. We do not socialize here. We do not flirt here," her cold eyes fell on Daniel and Jordan. "When you walk in here, you honor the learning space, and you bow." She demonstrated proper bowing technique. "In this course, you will learn how to disarm attackers. Sempai," she shouted.

An athletic man in his mid-thirties ran to the doorway. He wore a gi that had seen many years of use but was still clean and pressed. His black belt had grayed with age. He put his heels together, faced his feet at a forty-five degree angle, placed his hands at his sides and bowed, and then entered the room. He ran up to the Sensei and bowed low at his waist. He kept his eyes slanted down and just slightly away from her.

"You will learn how to disable attackers." She gave a sharp nod. He lunged at her in a blinding fast attack. She pivoted to the side, enveloping his wrist in one of her hands. Then she gave what looked like a small flick of her hand and he flew about ten feet, somersaulted, and landed on his back. His momentum never stopped as he pulled his knees to his chest and launched himself back to standing. He ran back towards her, stopping a few feet short, and bowed once again. He faced the class and froze in place.

"You will learn the vulnerable spots on every body." Wisteria used her Sempai, or head student, as a teaching tool. She pointed to his eyes, throat, solar plexus, knees, and feet. "You will learn about the ones that few people know about, but they are ones that will disable a person within seconds." She pointed to the inside of his elbow, his liver, and the side of his hip and knee.

"You will learn how to capitalize on any error on the part of your opponent." She nodded once. The Sempai blazed into action. He kicked at the side of her knee. She turned into the kick and let her knee bend with the force he had exerted on it but still dropped to the floor.

He fell on top of her. He reached his forearm around her throat, grabbed it with his other hand, and squeezed. She put one of her hands over his forearm and tugged in an attempt to free herself. He held on and squeezed more. Her head bent at an unnatural angle. She labored to breathe. He kept up the pressure until she slumped against him and passed out. He dropped her to the floor and she sprawled in a heap. The next instant, she swung her leg in a vicious circle and clipped him in the forehead. He fell to the floor and lay still. She left him on the floor, kept her eyes on him, and spoke to the rest of the class.

"How did he screw up?" She asked the class.

"He didn't check that you had really passed out," Daniel spoke. "He trusted that what he thought was happening was actually what was happening."

Wisteria threw him a grim smile. "Exactly. Now," she continued, "He started pretty well. If he had connected, he would have dislocated my knee at the very least. But he trusted me, and that was his mistake. Don't ever trust your opponents to be honorable. If they were honorable, they wouldn't be trying to hurt you."

She leaned down and pressed a hand to her student's shoulder. She said something the rest could not hear. He nodded once and jumped back into a standing rest pose.

"In this class, you will learn how to stay alive. You will learn techniques on what to do when you are attacked with hands, knife, or gun. You will learn close-quarter combat. You will learn strategic thinking for situations that are dangerous but not imminent. This is an accelerated course. You will be here five nights a week for three hours a night. You will not miss a class, or you will be expelled. You will not be late. You will give no excuses because none will be accepted. Am I clear?"

"Yes, Sensei!" They responded as one.

A bare hint of a smile passed her lips. She gave a crisp, single nod. She moved to the far right of the room and took the measure of each person up close and personal.

"You are?" She inquired.

"Robert Marshall, Sensei!" The short, wiry man replied.

She shook his hand.

"Push-ups. Now! Until I tell you to stop," she commanded. He dropped onto his hands and toes in a military-style push-up position and began to count off each one.

She moved down the line of students. She paused at each one, shook his or her hand and then barked out an exercise for them to do.

She stood in front of Daniel. "You are?"

"Daniel Evershed, Sensei!" He called out. She grasped his hand in her rough grip. Funny, he thought. Her hands looked softer and more delicate from far away. His surprise transformed into shock as a buzzing sensation filled him. An electric shock coursed through him from head to toe until he felt like his entire body had fallen asleep and was going through the jolts of waking up. She released him, and he sagged for an instant. The next second a sort of white heat flowed through him. He straightened and rolled back his shoulders.

"Push-ups," Sensei commanded. "Until I tell you stop."

"Yes, Sensei," he replied. He dropped to the ground. He had no real knowledge of who he had been before he lost his memory. While he might have been athletic in some respects, he had no illusions about his lanky physique. He wasn't the type to drop and give anyone fifty, push-ups or otherwise. But right now, he felt strong. He felt certain. He pumped his arms, tightened his belly and continued to work.

At his side, Wisteria had reached Jordan. They clasped hands and just as quickly released them.

"What are you doing here? Didn't think you would need martial arts training," Wisteria murmured. "You look like you can handle yourself."

"I can handle myself, but a girl's gotta do what a girl's gotta do," Jordan replied.

Wisteria smiled.

"Pull-ups," she ground out. "Until I tell you to stop."

"Seriously?" Jordan's voice lowered to a whisper.

"Seriously, unless you want me to kick you out of class," Wisteria answered. "I'd be more than happy to do that."

"No Sensei," Jordan emphasized the title snidely. "Pull-ups it is." Jordan strode to the pull-bar suspended from the ceiling, and jumped up. She grasped the free-floating bar with both hands and began a rhythmic count of each pull-up as she completed it. She worked like a machine. Each pull-up was a piston pump executed with perfect precision. She released one of her hands and continued to do the pull-ups one-handed. She looked down at Daniel and winked.

Wow! Daniel thought. She's not even working hard.

"And this isn't the only time I have a lot of stamina," she said to him.

He started and shook his head. He respected self-confidence, but her confidence bordered on an arrogance that chilled him.

"Rei!" Wisteria shouted to them. "Stop what you're doing after the next ten count." She motioned to the mesh bags full of boxing gloves that sat to the side of the one of the mats. "Find a pair of gloves that fit and line up."

The students chose gloves. They lined up in front of her and stood at attention. She evaluated each one and finally nodded.

"Right, now let's talk self-defense. First, that's what this class is all about," she sped towards Daniel and punched him with a blinding fast right hook. He had no time to react. She had been a blur and appeared in front of him so suddenly that he rocked back on his heels at the contact. She pulled her punch at the instant and barely connected with his jaw.

"Be faster, think faster, Daniel," she admonished him. "You have to prepare for anything and react to it without thinking." She streaked to another student and feinted a jab towards his throat. "It needs to be in your muscle memory. Your reptilian brain needs to see the danger, prepare for it, and react to it before your conscious mind even has a clue as to what's happening." She blurred to each student at random as she talked. Sometimes, she punched. Sometimes, she kicked. Sometimes, she swept legs and they landed on the soft mats. Other times, she grappled them into an inescapable choke hold.

One by one they started sensing where she would be and one by one their reaction times quickened. Jordan was the only student who seemed to have no trouble meeting Wisteria's attacks with solid defenses.

The rest of the class whizzed by as they went through warm-ups, exercises, and the three punching styles they would learn the first few weeks. At the end of class, they swept off, folded, and stacked the mats in a corner of the room.

"Rei!" The Sensei shouted a last time. By now each student had figured out that meant "Attention and line up." She paced the line like a drill sergeant. "You weren't bad for a first day. Tonight, soak in Epsom salts because you don't want to be sore. Tomorrow, we get started. Dismissed!"

The students bowed to her, and she returned the mark of respect. They dispersed.

Jordan matched steps with Daniel.

"Do you want to go grab a drink?" She asked.

"Um," he hesitated with his reply. He had no reason to distrust her. She seemed straightforward. She was certainly gorgeous, and she had made her interest in him plain. He would have had to have been deaf, dumb, and blind, as well as an amnesiac not to notice that. Still, some intuition held him back.

"Mr. Evershed, a word!" Wisteria's voice cut through the distance.

He had no idea why the sensei would want to speak with him, but he sent a grateful thought in her direction nonetheless.

"Yes, Sensei," he called. He turned to Jordan. "Thanks for the invitation, but go ahead without me."

"Tomorrow, then." She made it a statement.

"Yeah, maybe," he answered. He walked back towards the center of the gym.

The Sensei stood in front of the stacked mats as he approached. She held a clipboard and pen in her hands.

"Yes, Sensei," he stood in front of her and bowed.

"Mr. Evershed, why are you taking the course?" She asked without preamble.

"I need to learn how to defend myself." He replied as truthfully as he knew how.

"You need to learn? Not you want to learn? Clear-cut distinction."

"Yes."

She gazed at him with unblinking eyes. He returned her assessment and found no artifice. That pleased him.

Despite the fact that he didn't know her, he trusted her. She was brusque and straightforward. He respected that now more than ever. He wanted no bullshit. Either things would be aboveboard, or they wouldn't be at all.

"Why is it a need? What happened?"

"I was attacked, and left for dead, and I don't want to ever feel that helpless again," he replied. He paused. He had not said this to anyone yet; if he said it now it would somehow be more concrete, more real. He inhaled and plunged in. "When I regained consciousness, I couldn't remember anything. I have amnesia."

She gave a brief nod and returned to her task of placing the training gloves into bags. He was grateful for the lack of sympathy. He was unsure how he would have reacted if she had turned solicitous.

THE PIANO'S KEY

"Memory asserts itself. It tends to come back," she finally spoke. "And if it doesn't, then you let go of your attachment to the old life and make a new one."

"Easier said than done," he shrugged.

"No," she stared at him. "Not the right attitude. Have you heard that saying, 'Argue for your limitations and they're yours?'"

"No, but it's a good one," Daniel said. He grabbed one of the bags and finished replacing the smaller sized boxing gloves as they talked.

"So, there's your answer." She gave the barest hint of a smile. "And you want to learn how to trounce all comers."

"No, I want to know that the next time something like this happens, if it does, that I'll know what to do."

"You have amnesia." Wisteria pulled no punches. "How do you know that you didn't know what to do before?"

"Look at me," Daniel pointed to his lean frame. "Do I look like a fighter?"

She faced him fully. "Do I?" She asked.

"You look like you could handle yourself in any situation." He appraised the lean physique, the whipcord musculature, and the 'take no prisoners' set to her eyes. "I need to know I can do that as much as I need to know how to do it. Does that make any sense?"

"More than you know," she said. "Much of what I teach is in the mind. We have to break some ingrained patterns. Then we have to fill our heads with the knowledge and give our bodies practice in repetition so they start following what our minds direct them to do." She smiled for real this time. "Good thing your head's mostly empty right now. You won't have so much unlearning to do.

"Okay," she slapped her hands together. "Let's get started then."

"What, now?" He asked.

"Can you think of a better time?" She hefted two of the mats, unfolded them, and returned them to the floor. Together, they unfurled and laid out the entire mat setup.

"Look," she continued. "I could see you weren't here just to get in shape or learn a little light self-defense. Every time I teach, I take on a student to train even harder than in the accelerated course. My Sempai tonight has only been studying with me for four months. He's coming along," she said. Her eyes clouded. "I had a student in my last class who was gifted. I worked her hard. I could have trained her to be a great fighter. She has tremendous power but not one iota of patience. And then she did something stupid and left before she had had a chance to complete her training. So now, I am looking for another First Student. If you want it, the slot's yours."

In answer, he walked to the edge of the mats and bowed.

"Good," she nodded. She bowed and stepped onto the mats. "Defend," she cried and torpedoed towards him.

He sidestepped in a perfect copy of her earlier demonstration at the beginning of class. He reached for her hand to pivot and flick his wrist. She turned the tables, grabbed his reaching hand and sent him flying to the mat.

He sprawled and tried to regain his breath.

"First thing's first," she stood over him. "Let's teach you how to fall."

"I know how to fall," Daniel replied. "Obviously, I can at least do that," he pointed to himself.

"And that's where you're wrong," she extended a hand and hefted him to standing as if he weighed no more than ten pounds. How did she do that?

"Falling isn't just about hitting the ground," she instructed. "Falling is one of the best defensive moves in all martial arts. And sometimes..," she took hold of his gi, tugged at him, and folded herself to the ground. She landed easily. He flew across the mats once again.

"Ow!" He landed hard on his shoulder.

"Let me see," she leaned towards him. She touched her hands to his shoulder, pressed in two spots, and the pain dissipated.

"How did you do that?" Awe hushed his voice.

"Field Med Tech," she replied. "Stand up!" She pulled him back to standing.

"Lesson Number One," she said. "When you fall, don't fall."

"Don't fall?" He parroted.

"Exactly. Don't just fall. Fold. Let your body fold to the ground and then you can redirect every bit of the force of your fall away from you."

She demonstrated a back fall to him in slow motion. She stood with her feet hip-width apart. All at once her upper body rounded forward while her knees bent and her butt folded towards the floor. As she neared the floor, her arms raised to shoulder height. She didn't so much fall as she collapsed and rolled onto the mat. When her back glided onto the floor, she threw both arms to her sides and slapped the mats. The sharp staccato of the slaps echoed through the gym.

In an instant, she tucked her feet under her, flipped, and kipped back to a standing position.

"Now you try it."

Together, they worked on his back fall. For the next two hours, he rounded, rolled, and folded onto the mats. He repeated the pattern until he was able to fall backwards at will and without any fear.

"It's strange," he panted. "I don't feel afraid of falling."

"Why's that strange?" She asked.

"Because I don't know if I am, or rather was, afraid of falling? What if I'm doing something that I'm deathly afraid of, but I don't even know?"

"Now isn't that you arguing for your limitation?" Wisteria rushed him, and he fell backwards and away from her such that she didn't lay a hand on him.

"Good," she nodded. "Now, let's do Lessons Number 1.25 and 1.5 and 1.75. You need to learn how to fall to either side and eventually forward."

They practiced side falls for another hour until they felt natural to him.

He had no idea if he was even at all athletic, but this felt right and good and almost easy. There was a flow to his movements that felt natural.

Her punch came at his face lightning fast. He stepped back and away from her, changed the weight distribution between his feet and rolled in a perfect side fall.

"Good," she gave a curt nod, which for her seemed like the extreme of high praise.

His grin was feral.

"Now, here's Lesson Number Two," her grin was just as feral. "Never just fall. Always try to take 'em with you. That's when the fun really begins."

"Oh, I really need to learn how to do that," he stated.

"And you will. But first you're going to practice a whole lot of Lesson Number One."

CHAPTER 18

EVIE

Tariq caught up with us as we descended into the subway. The kids had unanimously voted for ice cream, and there was only one place to take them - The Jumping Cow. I led the way, and Joanna brought up the rear to make sure no one lagged behind.

"Hey, where you all going?" Tariq called out.

"Evie is taking us for ice cream," Veronica replied. She dug her subway fare card out of her backpack and slid it through. He followed her, but he neatly jumped over the rail.

I met his eyes. For an instant, his face registered, "Shit, I'm busted." Instead, I raised my eyebrows, and then I couldn't help it. I nodded my approval. I was sure money was in short supply for him and Calvin. Besides, Tariq was still a small kid. He took up hardly any space on one of those trains.

He slid me a quick grin, and we shared a moment of perfect understanding as I helped Calvin through the turnstile in front of me.

Jo was the last to join us, and we headed toward the trains. A few stops later, and we exited at 87th and Amsterdam - the home of the Jumping Cow. The mural on the window had been amended. In addition to the depiction of the old nursery rhyme where a cup and spoon ran off together (in this case they were sneaking towards a bowl of ice cream) and a beautiful art nouveau cow jumped over a succulent-looking moon, mountains of seasonal fruits like strawberries and blueberries now festooned the outer edges. A waterfall of caramel fell into a lake in which chocolate-covered pretzels floated. A volcano at the top erupted chocolate chips and dollops of whipped cream.

The Cow, as regulars call it, is a New York institution. It was started by the hippie children of some very wealthy New Yorkers. The kids wanted to run an establishment that catered to all, provided delicious ice cream in an almost infinite variety, and did it all as cruelty-free as possible. In other words, when the cows at the upstate farm gave milk, ice cream was made and the storefront was open twenty hours a day. When the cows decided they'd had enough manhandling, the store closed.

Luckily, the cows had been frisky recently. It looked like there had been plenty of milk, and the place was doing a bustling business. We pushed into the shop. The kids stared at the incredible array of ice creams and toppings.

"Welcome to the Jumping Cow," a familiar voice said to the patron next in line. "Now, what is your favorite flavor: sweet, salty, bitter, or sour?"

The kids watched as Jonas, the owners' son, talked the customers through a complicated set of questions to determine the perfect ice cream dish that would give them what they needed right now. As he looked up for the next in line he noticed his wide eyed audience with me in the middle.

"Mama," Jonas called to the back. "Evie and Joanna are here."

Within seconds, Rose "Mama" Brader emerged from the back of the shop. Her long blond braid had a little gray in it, but otherwise, she, as always, looked the same.

"Eveningstar!" She came around the long expanse of freezers and enveloped me in a giant hug.

"Eveningstar?" A couple of the students snickered.

"Yeah," I smiled. "Why do you think I go by Evie?" I didn't hate my name ... anymore.

My parents had wanted a dulcet kewpie doll who would love beauty, harmony, and all things girlie, which is why they'd named me after the goddess Venus, the Eveningstar. What they got was me, and we still didn't agree on anything except that I did like harmony. But it was the musical kind and not the 'everybody be nice to each other' kind.

Mama Brader held me at arm's length. Even though I had a good couple of hundred years on her, I still called her and thought of her as, 'Mama.'

"How are you, child?" She asked.

"I'm fine. I'm great!" I replied.

"Great you might you be, but you aren't fine," she tsked at me. "But we'll soon fix that." She started to lead me towards the freezers and opened her mouth to start the question and answer that would lead me to my path through the delectable road of ice cream when I interrupted.

"Actually, I'd like to introduce you to my students," I tugged her towards them.

"Your students?" She raised her eyebrows in question.

"Yep! I'm the new music program coordinator at the 127th Street Youth Center."

Mama laughed and clapped her hands together in delight. "How perfect!" She exclaimed. She leaned into me and kissed both my cheeks. "I could not have asked for a better role for you," she whispered in my ear. "This is your path."

"You think?"

"I do," she nodded and turned towards the rest of our little group. She greeted Joanna with another huge hug, and then she turned to the students.

"I'm Mama Brader," she introduced herself. "Who here is interested in some ice cream?"

A chorus of "I am" and "Yes" and "Me, me" rang out.

"Let's make that happen," she cried. She ushered the kids into line, and Jonas began the question and answer game.

"Mama," I took her aside. "Can you pay attention to that kid, please?" I indicated Tariq with a nod of my head. "Joanna thinks he needs something special, and I don't see it."

"No, Evie, not yet," she replied. "But you will."

"I just don't know what I'm doing with kids this young," I whined and got those raised eyebrows in response for my trouble. "It was easier with Joanna," I plowed on. "She was older. I knew more about what she was going through. I could help her out."

"Yes, but you were more her friend than anything else and that was the right thing, but it wasn't what Godparents are really supposed to do," Mama pointed out.

Startled, I gaped at her. I had no idea how Mama Brader got her information, but I'd hoped that I'd at least been more inconspicuous than broadcasting my FG job and status to anyone and everyone.

"Don't worry, Evie," she continued as if she had read my mind. "Your secret is safe with me. But," she gazed at the group of students. "These kids don't need a girlfriend." She stared hard into my eyes. "They need a guardian, especially Tariq."

Had I mentioned his name? No, I had not. I added that little tidbit to the long list of mysteries about Rose "Mama" Brader. I'd likely never know how she knew what she knew. But, damn! I was glad she knew it. I studied him. He was texting someone. How did he afford a mobile phone, I wondered. Then the thought dissipated. Everyone had a phone nowadays. I was surprised Calvin hadn't pulled one out and started playing a video game on it.

"Okay, I'll be their guardian," my voice hitched. I'd have to guard these kids. Crap! I prayed I was up to the task.

"Thank you, Evie," Calvin approached us holding his bowl of chocolate chip ice cream with hot fudge, whipped cream, nuts, and a big, fat cherry on top. Huh! He got a perfectly normal ice cream. This kid had no real issues or troubles he was trying to handle. I gazed at Tariq with respect. He was making Calvin's life as normal as possible. At fourteen years old, he was already an adult with adult responsibilities. And he was handling them beautifully, if Calvin was any indication.

Tariq turned away from the ice cream station. He held a bowl full of bittersweet chocolate and French vanilla ice cream. Rich, blood-red real cherry syrup flowed down the ice cream in fine rivulets. Shards of dark chocolate ice cream protruded from the vanilla ice cream like stiletto knives. I shuddered.

"Mom," Jonas called to her, and she left me. They held a whispered conversation. She patted his shoulder, smiled at him, and he left the station for the back room. A few seconds later, another server took his place.

Mama returned to me.

"Jonas needed a break," she explained. "Tariq's needs were," she paused, "A challenge."

"A challenge?"

"Yes. Be there for him and whatever you do, do not give up on him. Ever!" I'd never heard Mama be stern before.

"I won't," I promised.

"Good," she relaxed. She left me to serve the rest of the group.

I watched Tariq as I ate my usual Mother's Milk ice cream bowl. He was going to need me, and I was going to have to put on my big girl underpants and be there for him.

"Okay," I saluted him with my bowl from across the shop. "I'll be there for you."

"Be there for who?" Joanna sat down next to me and dove into her bowl of dark chocolate with real vanilla syrup with star fruit, watermelon, and hazelnut toppings.

"Tariq," I replied around a mouthful of ice cream.

"Yeah," she nodded. "There's something about him. I can't my finger on it, but it's there."

"Both you and Mama have said it, so it must be true. I don't need anymore than that. I'll take care of it," I promised again.

"Good," she relaxed and dug into the bowl for another delectable mouthful of ice cream. "I wish I was going to be here to help you," she murmured.

"You've got your own thing," I said. "And you'll have your hands full with those two in Europe."

"Not to mention Marcus," she sighed.

"Marcus? What about Marcus?" Curiosity piqued, I sat up and took notice.

"Didn't I mention it? They placed us together as co-chaperones and co-leaders of our group. He will work with the pianists, and I will work with the string players."

"Holy hell!" I cried. "How are you about it? Are you okay? Does Shane know?"

"Shane knows he's going to Europe but not that we'll be working together," she answered. "It's not a big deal," she put a hand on my arm. "Evie, I've got this. If I could give a Ramrock the business, I can certainly handle the Twinkie." She referred to her ex-boyfriend by the name I had given him last year when he had cheated on her with her roommate Chloe. It turned out it hadn't been Chloe's fault because that jackass Zeke had spelled her into it, but still, that incident started a chain of events that almost ended the world.

"Okay, if you say so," doubt peppered my voice.

"I do say so. I'll be fine." She set her jaw. "If Marcus tries anything, I'll kick his butt."

"You go, girl!" I crowed. I loved Joanna the hearts and flowers girl, but I realized I loved this badass version just a little bit more. A weight I didn't know I'd been carrying lifted off me. I sighed. Okay, that was one less thing to worry about. Now, I just had to deal with Tariq and the rest of the kids. I could do it, couldn't I?

CHAPTER 19

DANIEL

Wisteria threw a killer right hook at his jaw. He ducked and grabbed her passing arm. He stepped forward, shifted his weight, and allowed her own forward motion to snap her arm up behind her back. He held her with almost no effort until she tapped out by lightly hitting his arm with her open palm. He released her immediately and stepped back into ready stance.

"Nice!" She complimented him. From her, that one word was the highest praise he had heard her give anyone. They had been working together after class for the last few nights. He still wasn't sure why she had decided to teach him privately, but he wasn't about to argue with his good fortune.

"Watch your weight shift so you don't telegraph your plan too early," Wisteria said. "Not everyone will sense it, but those who do will drop you." She motioned for a repeat of the same attack and response. As he shifted his weight, she offset hers and suddenly she had reversed his defense on him. She pivoted on her back foot, pressed her hand to his hand as he held her other arm and allowed his arm to twist around and behind him. She stepped forward and lifted her energy and weight up as she released his arm, and he somersaulted forward as he flew seven feet in the air to land in a heap on the mats.

"If I had held on just a little bit longer to your arm, it would have slipped the socket and you would have been heading the hospital right now," she admonished him.

"And speaking of heading," he bowed to her. "I need to leave a little early tonight."

"Oh?"

"I have to go to work," Daniel said.

"Lots of photojournalism to do in the City That Never Sleeps," sarcasm dripped from Wisteria's voice.

"I'm going to go to the place where I was attacked and see if I can figure out why."

They worked as a unit to pick up, fold, and stack the mats.

"I don't suppose you'll listen when I say you don't yet know enough to protect yourself from an actual attack," Wisteria said.

"It's something I have to do," Daniel stated as he hefted his camera bag from the corner of the gym.

She inclined her head in a curt nod.

"Thank you, Sensei. I'll see you tomorrow." He bowed to her and left the Y.

Two transfers brought him to the western-most edge of the Washington Heights neighborhood. He found the warehouse with no problem. It stood dark and foreboding. He studied it under the cover of the late night sky. He spied a loose brick a few feet from the entrance, grabbed it, and sent it flying through one of the windows. He climbed in and shone a flashlight around the cavernous and completely empty space.

"Shit!" he swore softly. Whatever had been here before, whatever he had seen that had led to his attack, it was now all gone. He snapped a few shots for reference and headed back towards the window. He exited the way he had entered. He jumped the few feet to the sidewalk and straightened.

"Freeze! Put your hands where I can see them," the command came from behind.

"Shit!" Daniel said again as he raised his hands and turned towards the police officer who had a gun trained on his midsection.

"Officer, I can explain," Daniel began.

"And you'll get your chance," the cop snatched one of Daniel's hands and swung it behind his back. He cuffed it and repeated the process with his other hand.

"You have the right to remain silent," he recited Daniel's Miranda rights.

"I know my rights, Officer," Daniel said. "I wasn't doing anything illegal."

"So breaking into a warehouse isn't illegal, now?" The cop laughed.

"I'm a reporter on a story." Daniel explained.

"What were you after?"

"Something illegal was going on here, and I was investigating what it could be."

"How do you know something illegal was going on?" The officer marched him towards a waiting squad car. He cupped Daniel's head and handled him into the back seat.

"I can't tell you." Daniel sat forward to both protect his hands and balance the camera that was still slung over his neck.

"Protecting a source?"

"No." Daniel answered simply. He had no real proof anything had happened in the warehouse except that he was found there after his beating. "But I know something illegal was happening here."

"You can tell all that to the judge. Lucky for you, night court is still in session."

"It was either the cops or the coroner," Tommy said later as Daniel walked out of lock-up.

"Thanks for bailing me out," Daniel said.

"You're not a real investigative reporter until you've been arrested a time or two." Tommy smiled. "So, I guess you broke your reporter cherry. Good for you! I hope it was worth it."

"It wasn't," Daniel stated. "The place was empty. Whatever was going on there, it's all gone now."

"I wish I'd paid attention when I was in there with you. But, I'll be honest. The only thing I could see then was some white plastic curtains, you, and a huge pool of blood." Tommy shuddered.

Daniel stowed his wallet and keys in his pockets. He bent over his camera bag and breathed a sigh of relief that neither the camera nor the film appeared disturbed. He took a couple of experimental shots with the ancient Canon AE-1 Program. He'd drop it off in the morning at the one place in the city that still developed film. Likely, the film would lead nowhere.

The two men left the police station and headed back downtown. They arrived at the NewsBlitz office and sat with chairs facing each other.

"Damn!" Daniel swore. He jumped up and paced the small room. "How the hell am I ever going to figure this out?" He pounded on his desk.

"Easy there, Tiger," Tommy raised his hands in entreaty. "You'll figure it out. We'll figure it out."

"How? I can't remember anything. I don't know anything. I can't fix anything." Daniel paused in mid-step and attempted one of the breathing exercises Sensei had taught him in their after-hours sessions. Within seconds, he gave up.

"How the hell am I supposed to do this?" He shouted. He pounded on his own head with his fist. "It's locked in here, but I can't access any of it. It's like it's all just gone. And I don't know if I'm ever going to get any of it back. What do I do if I never remember?"

"You make a new life, with new memories," Tommy answered. "Sometimes, the memories are so bad that it's better not to have them."

"I can't live like that!" Daniel grabbed his camera bag and headed out the door.

"Where are you going?" Tommy called after him.

"I don't know. I just need some time to think." Daniel answered and left.

EVIE

Bach's Cantata and Fugue in D Minor interrupted my dream of swimming with dolphins near the Marianna's Trench.

"What?" I mumbled.

"Evie, it's Rose Brader."

"Mama?" I snapped awake. "What's wrong? Are you okay? Thomas and Jonas?" I asked about her husband and son. "What happened?"

"Somebody destroyed 'The Cow,'" she stated quietly. "They came in and well, they just destroyed it. I thought I should call you."

"Give me a minute, and I'm there," I said. I grabbed my wand and within seconds I entered what was left of one of my favorite places in the universe. The freezers were pulled apart. Someone had taken a dump in several of the ice cream tubs. Broken glasses, tubs, cups, and dishes littered the floor. Light fixtures had been torn down from the ceiling, and black spray paint covered the beautiful mural on the front windows. Almost nothing remained solid and standing except the walls.

"Mama, no," I surveyed the carnage. It would take months to rebuild. I touched my wand and began an incantation to find those responsible and ground them into dust.

"Evie," Mama held her hands out to me. I grabbed them. "It will be okay," she said.

"Don't do anything," she indicated my wand with her chin. "Vengeance isn't what's called for here."

"Oh, what is called for?" Livid tears streaked my face.

"Understanding," she answered.

"Understanding? Understanding?" I shrieked. "I don't think so. I'm going to find whoever did this and make them pay."

"Holy shit!" Tariq stood at the remnants of the front door. He covered the top of his head with arms. His eyes rounded in fear, as I rushed towards him.

"What are you doing here?" I demanded.

"Uh, um," he stammered. Unshed tears pooled in his eyes. He rubbed at his eyes and faced me.

I studied him with narrowed eyes. He knew something about this.

"Tariq, tell me right now. What do you know about this?"

"I don't," he swallowed, hard. "I don't know anything." The lie dripped from his lips and lay flat and obvious before us.

"This is going to need to be fixed, Tariq. And you know who did it so you'd better tell me right now." I yelled.

"It's okay, Tariq," Mama inserted herself between us. "I'm sure you don't know a thing about this."

"Mama, how can you say that?" I cried. "Of course he knows. He's just lying!" I was behaving like a complete shit, and I knew it. I heaved a breath.

"Come on, Tariq," I tried my damnedest to wheedle or wrest the answer from him. "You can tell me. You won't get in trouble. I promise."

"Yeah, right," he answered.

"I'm sure you're in a tight spot here," I coaxed. "You do know what happened don't you? But you can't tell me."

He stayed silent. He looked at me with eloquent eyes as if he was trying to tell me something I was too stupid to understand.

"Man, your life must be tough keeping all these secrets," my better judgment fled and hid. Here I was yelling at a scared kid. Should I know better? Yep. Did I know better? Nope.

"You don't know shit about my life!" He screamed. He took off down the street.

"Shit! Shit, shit, shit, shit, shit!" This time I covered my head with my hands.

"Eveningstar!" Mama's shocked voice cut through my pity party.

"I know, Mama, I know." I hung my head. "I'll go find him and see if I can fix this."

She shook her head. "He won't listen to you now. Give him some time, and you'll get your chance to make this right."

Shame overwhelmed me. How could I have yelled at a frightened child? Some Level 4 Fairy Godmother I was turning out to be. Tears flowed down my face.

"Can I at least help you clean this place up?"

"No, you need to go. Go get your head on straight. In cases like these, I find it's best to do like Vizzini. Go back to the beginning," Mama's kind voice made me feel even worse.

"Yes, Mama."

I left "The Cow," in far more capable hands than my own. I needed to get my shit together. It couldn't get much more screwed up than it already was, but if I didn't do something soon, I might just see the worst it could get.

What the hell had I been thinking? I pulled my hair with both hands. I was the lowest of the low. I was the stuff Low wouldn't scrape off its heels. Even Parsnipa wouldn't yell at a scared kid. Mama was right. I needed to get my head on straight. Tomorrow, I'd find Tariq and see if I could mend fences. But tonight, I'd better figure out my crazy insides, or I'd be no good to anyone.

I shuffled east towards the park. I walked in at 85th Street and made my way south past the Mariner's Gate playground. From the second I entered the park, the city's night noises receded. Something about all those trees created a buffering hush inside one of the biggest parks on Earth. The park never closes, but at this late hour everything sat deserted.

I wound my way through the paths until I stood in front of the Falconer statue. It depicts a person in Elizabethan dress with a falcon. I sighed. This statue represented yet another of my failures. When someone vandalized it and stole the falcon back in the '50s, I'd been unable to catch the culprits and retrieve the falcon. And when it was returned to the park, I had nothing to do with fixing it. I'd been less than useless even though I'd been assigned to fix it up. I swiped at the tears that threatened to overflow and allowed myself one sniffle.

"Okay," I muttered to myself. "If you're going to fix any of this mess, you'd better get over yourself."

I stared up at the statue. If it could be restored and come back better than ever, dammit, I could too. I checked in with my wand and found it droopy. It resembled an undercooked noodle. I sighed again. Great! When I was shooting "in the pocket," my wand was straight as an arrow and helped me work my magic like a great conductor wielded her baton. When I was down in the dumps, my wand reflected that state of mind and right now, it was dangerously close to flaccid territory.

"No!" I shouted. I marched away from the Falconer and headed south towards the Heckscher softball fields. I picked up my pace until I was running full tilt. The few lights on in the middle of the fields streaked by me as I raced through the park. My feet pounded on grass or pavement. I paid no attention to my destination or my surroundings. I flew through the night.

I finally stopped just past the softball fields. My breaths came in quick, harsh gasps as I looked around. Although my heart pounded, I grinned. I was close to the swing sets at the Heckscher Playground. These were the best swings in the park, maybe the entire State of New York. Daniel and I had our first non-date here. My grin faded. I had tried hard to keep my despairing thoughts of him at bay. Every time they had threatened to float up into my consciousness, I'd squashed them back down. But sure enough, they had leaked out elsewhere.

I strode to the swing set, sat down, and kicked my legs out. I pumped until I arched almost 180 degrees. My head was easily level with the top bar, and I laughed.

"What the hell!" Daniel walked out of the dark towards me.

"Daniel?" I shook my head to clear it. Did I conjure him? I shook my head again. No, my wand was not in any shape to do anything of the sort. So, where did he come from?

"Evie? Holy shit! I didn't expect anyone else to be here."

"Where did you come from?" I parroted my thoughts.

"I came from work. Wait, where did you come from?"

"I came from the Jumping Cow."

"Why did you come here?" We both asked in unison.

"I needed to get my head on straight," we both replied together again.

We laughed and then quieted.

"Would you care to join me?" I motioned with my hand to the other swing.

"Yeah, I would," he sighed. He mounted the swing and we pumped our legs in rhythm until we both arched above the top bar. In a sad deja vu of the last time we came here together, he stole glances at me while we swung.

"So, I know why I need to get my head on straight. I don't remember anything," he said after a while. "Why do you need to do yours?"

I mentally picked up and discarded a bunch of possible answers. This Daniel had no idea I was an FG, and I couldn't tell him. So, I settled on, "The Cow got trashed tonight. Somebody destroyed the entire place. It's going to take a miracle to fix it. But that's not the worst of it," I continued. "The cherry on top is that I yelled at a kid."

"Why did you do that?"

I stopped my swing with my feet as I thought about the answer.

"He knew something about who trashed the Jumping Cow tonight, and he wasn't talking."

"Oh," he thought for a moment. "So, you yelled at him to get him to tell you."

"Not my finest hour, I know." I tugged at my hair and got up to pace around the swings.

"But you were trying to help," he pointed out.

I paused mid-stride and gazed at him. Why is it was always those around me and never me who had the reasonable gene? I had overreacted but my heart had been in the right place. With luck, I'd be able to square things with Tariq and also figure out who had trashed The Cow. Although, knowing Tariq knew something about it clarified who had probably done the deed. Duh!

"Thanks, Daniel. I think I know what to do next. Now what about you? What brings you to the park at night?" I asked.

He straightened. "I needed to be out in the open after a night in jail."

"You were in jail?" I exploded. "Are you okay? What happened?"

"I'm trying to figure out what happened to me," he explained. "So, I went back to the warehouse where I was attacked."

"Wait," a red haze descended on my vision. "So, you went back to where you got hurt? Where you could have been hurt again? How could you do something so dangerous and stupid?"

"You don't get to tell me what to do." He stiffened.

"I'm not trying to tell you what to do, you idiot." I marched up close to him. I poked him in the chest to emphasize my words. "I'm trying to make sure you stay alive!"

He grabbed my fingers mid-poke and enclosed them with his hand. He laid my palm against his chest and the staccato rhythm of his heart tattooed against me. He snaked his other hand to the back of my neck and coiled it in my hair. He pulled until I lifted my face. His brown eyes shone with fire and fury. He lowered his head until his mouth was millimeters from mine.

My breath stopped in my lungs. I waited.

He dragged me to him and claimed my mouth with his own. He pushed through the barriers and kissed me deeply. He left my hand pressed between us and used his other hand on me. He cupped my breast with his palm and teased my already taut nipple between his thumb and forefinger. A moan escaped me, and he smiled against my lips as his tongue fought with mine. He pressed his palms to my butt and lifted me and I wrapped my legs around him. He buried his lips against my throat and used his teeth on me, his scruff scraping along the sensitive skin. I groaned again and held him more tightly with my legs. His power drugged me. I arched my hips into him and he groaned in response.

He carried me into the trees that surrounded the playground, backed me up against a tall oak, and held me there with one hand. He looked at me for long seconds as if searching for something. Then, he gave one curt nod. He lowered me to my feet and knelt before me. He unfastened my belt, unzipped my pants, and slid them off me. He slid a finger inside the black silk of my underwear and traced the inside of the band. His nail scraped lightly against the sensitive skin there and I cried out.

"You like that, do you?" He repeated the motion, and I moaned again.

"Tell me," he ground out. "Tell me you like it."

"I like it," I gasped. "Do it again."

His smile was feral. He stood as he twisted his hand inside my panties and slid it down until he cupped me. I rocked against his fingers, but he pulled them away. I sobbed in disappointment.

"No," I whimpered.

"No, what?" He whispered.

"Don't stop."

"Tell me," he said again. "Tell me you like it."

"I do. I like it. Don't stop." I arched my hips towards him as I spread my legs. He plunged his fingers into me. He pushed into me until I thought I would burst from the pressure and the pleasure. He stroked me again and again. His fingers brushed at my secret places. The scents of sex and night-blooming jasmine mingled. I was rising. The pressure built within me. I was almost there. And then he pulled out of me and left me gasping.

"No, not quite yet, Evie." He whispered in my ear. "We have a ways to go before I'm ready to let fly." He pulled back and stared down at me.

He lifted his fingers to his lips. He looked into my eyes as he tasted each one.

"Mmm, you taste good." His voice had gotten low and husky. He ran his eyes along my body.

"I want to see more of you. Take off your shirt." He murmured.

I looked at him. He was as familiar to me as my own hands, but he was also a stranger. This stranger pulled at something inside me. He touched something dark, something dangerous.

I watched his eyes as I slowly unbuttoned my shirt. One button after the other revealed my skin. He watched each inch like it was a revelation. His hands convulsed as if he was barely holding himself back.

"Stop!" He commanded again.

I stopped in mid-motion with the shirt half on me.

He lowered his lips to the hollow between my breasts. He moaned.

"Damn, you're so beautiful."

My heart beat a trip hammer against his mouth. He pushed my flimsy bra off my breast and captured my nipple with his teeth. I held his head with my hands and moaned. His tongue slid over and around me.

He trailed kisses down my belly until his hot breath fanned against my core. He slid my panties off me and hauled my legs onto his shoulders. He plunged his tongue inside me, and I convulsed around him. He set up a drumming rhythm with his tongue as his fingers played inside me.

My moans became cries as he pounded into me with tongue and teeth and hands. He released me, and I sagged against the tree. He lifted me off the ground until our faces were even.

"I want you," his voice was ragged.

"I want you, too."

"I don't have protection. You need to know that. And I don't know what this means, and you need to know that too."

"Have you, have you been with anyone else since you lost your memory?" I closed my eyes and waited for his answer.

"No."

"Then, do it," I threw every caution to the four winds. I'd figure it out later. Right now, if I didn't have him inside me, I would implode.

He took a second to rid himself of his own pants. He leaned me against the tree. I curled my legs around him. He slid all the way into me. I opened my legs and took him in further. I reached for more of him with hips and arms and lips. My center wove around him and squeezed and held him. For a long moment, we froze. And then, he moved in me.

DANIEL

Home. She felt like home. Shit! Daniel thought even as he tucked his hips and entered her more deeply. He pressed himself against the length of her body to hold her against the tree. His hands molded her breasts and traveled down the curve of her waist. He cupped her hips and pulled her closer until he could no longer tell where he ended and she began. He tasted her lips and the column of her throat. The curve of her shoulder enflamed him. His body remembered her even if he didn't. His breath heaved in his lungs as he slammed into her. He sped up until he heard her whimper with the need to release the pent up pressure. Then, he slowed. He propped her up with his hands and pulled out until he had almost slipped free of her heat and then drove into her again. He went blind with need and speed and sensation. Again, he tortured them both. Again, he almost withdrew and then sheathed himself in her dewy skin. She screamed his name as her muscles tightened around him like a scorching fist. Now, she held him to her. When he tried to pull out again, she clamped around him and drove her hips against him again and again. Her name ripped from his lips in ragged gasps.

"Yes," she sobbed. "Yes, in me. With me. Yes, Daniel, yes." She closed around him and flew.

With a last drive, he came and emptied himself into her. His hips pistoned against her. The silent night was slashed with their cries. He held her tightly against him. Their sweat poured off them to the earth below. His breath caught in his lungs as pain overwhelmed him.

A bright blue light pierced his blindness. He screamed in agony and collapsed to the ground. He protected his head with his arms, but this came from within as the memory bulldozed back into his consciousness.

A flame, cobalt and flying. It careened over his head. He was no longer in Central Park. He lay in a dingy alley. Barely alive, barley breathing, he was helpless. Evie stood over him. She held a short stick. With it, she shot violent flashes of blue flame at someone across the alley. The flames obscured his face from Daniel. She wounded him. He fell. She hurt him and relished it.

She dropped her stick and cradled his head in her lap.

"Oh god! You're alive!" Evie stroked his cheek. She looked up from him towards the far end of the alley. "You went too far this time," she said to someone. "If I see you again, I will kill you."

The memory dissipated. Evie crouched over him. Her bare skin glistened in the darkness.

"Daniel? Are you okay? Daniel, talk to me." She touched him with a shaky hand.

"What?" He swallowed convulsively. "What the hell was that?" He pushed to sitting and shrank away from her.

"What happened? What did you see?" She reached out towards him but then dropped her hand.

"I saw something. I remembered something. You were fighting with someone I couldn't see. There was blue flame. What the hell was that?" His tone accused her. "What did you do? Who are you? What are you?"

"I'm," she paused and heaved a breath. "There's no way to say it but to say it. You know how there are stories about mythical creatures like mermaids and nymphs and fairies? Well, they're not so mythical. In fact, most of them exist. See, I'm a fairy."

"What? What the hell does that mean? You mean you're not human?"

"That's what you said last time I told you," she wiped at her face with her hands.

"Last time you told me?" He tried to process and failed. He stared at her open-mouthed. "You mean I knew that you're …."

"A fairy," she supplied.

" … Before I lost my memory."

"Yes, you did. And you were okay with it."

"I'm not okay with it now," he shouted. He lay still for a moment and looked inward. As bizarre as it sounded, for some reason, he believed her. Somehow, she wasn't human, and he just could not deal with that right now, maybe not ever.

He cradled his burning head in his hands and laughed.

"Of course," he muttered. "Of course, the woman I just had sex with against a tree isn't human. Why should that surprise me?"

He rose from the ground and got dressed. He refused to look at her. If he looked at her one of two things would happen. Either he would kiss her or strangle her and neither seemed like the appropriate option right now.

"Look Evie," he said as he buttoned his shirt. "I don't know what the hell is going on or who the hell you think you are, but I want you to stay away from me."

"But, I need to protect you, at least until you regain your memory," she argued.

"I don't need your sort of protection. I want you to leave me alone. I mean it," his eyes were deadly serious. "Whatever this is, I don't want it. So stay away from me."

She nodded.

He stood above her suddenly uncertain. Despite how much he wished to be away from this craziness, he could not leave a woman alone in Central Park in the dark.

"You don't have to see me home, Daniel." She read his mind. "I can make my own way."

"If you're sure," he said.

"I'm sure."

"Okay," he turned to leave.

"Daniel?"

"Yes?" He faced her one last time.

"Stay safe."

He closed his eyes against the lovely, weeping, and oh so beautiful woman in front him. Whatever this had been, it was no longer.

"You, too," he said and left her.

EVIE

I watched Daniel walk away. I cast an invisibility bubble around myself. This time when the tears fell, I let them do their thing. This Daniel didn't know me, and he didn't love me. I couldn't do anything to protect him. Wisteria would have to take on that task, and if I could trust anyone to be too bull-headed to fail, it would be her. So, for now, Daniel was in the best possible hands.

"The worst is not so long as we can say, 'this is the worst.'" Edgar said in "King Lear." I finally figured out the meaning. Just when I thought it couldn't get any worse, the bottom bottomed out yet again. I guessed as long as I was alive, it could and likely would always get worse. I wept until the sobs subsided. Afterward, I felt cleansed. In all my three-hundred and six years, I had never understood how a good cry could really clean you out. Now, I knew. And what was more, I knew what I had to do.

"Enough!" I clenched my hands into fists. If I couldn't fix Daniel, I had plenty of other items on my to-do list. If I wasn't going to have the love of my life in my life, I would be damn sure I excelled at my job.

I stood, dressed, and grabbed my bag. I dug out my wand.

"Time to get to work."

CHAPTER 20

ZEKE

Zeke sighed as he supervised the construction of the new lab. Several workmen hung the ever-present white, plastic sheeting along the ceiling of the secondary production area. It would trail to the floor and be held in place by magnets. The production area on the other side of the warehouse had already been completed. The tables, balances, and mixing bins were sterilized and ready to produce Heaven in quantity. The latest batch had just been processed. All it needed was testing and analysis, and then they could release it to their sellers.

"St. James will be here soon," he announced. "Make sure they're hung and done perfectly before he gets here."

"Yes, Mr. Dunne," the workmen answered in unison. They redoubled their efforts.

Zeke nodded and turned away.

"Shit!" He whispered hoarsely. How had he fallen to the point where he was dealing drugs? No, he wasn't even the one dealing them; he was supervising. He spent his time going over tally sheets and itemized lists of quantities, distribution statistics, and efficacy.

"Well, my boy," St. James appeared at his side, "If you hadn't fucked up so monumentally, you wouldn't be in this position." Zeke carefully didn't react to either the surprise of St. James' sudden appearance or the intrusion of having his mind read again.

"Mr. St. James, welcome to the new space," Zeke replied smoothly. "We are ready for the taste test," he continued.

"Excellent! Let me get my little guinea pig." He pulled his mobile phone out of his pocket and made a call. "Bring her in," he said.

Within a few minutes, Nadia shuffled into the room. Two men flanked her on either side. She looked straight ahead and did not acknowledge anyone else in the room. She stumbled, and one of the men caught her. She did not thank him.

Her eyes focused on St. James.

"Daddy," she murmured.

"Hello, Pet," he smiled. "Sit her down," he instructed the men with her. They led her to a nearby chair. The chair had belts at the foot and hand rests. They strapped her into it.

"Daddy?" She looked at St. James with questioning eyes.

"It's okay, Pet," he said. "I just need to be sure you won't hurt yourself."

"I won't," she appealed to him. "I promise."

"I know, you'll try," he replied. He motioned to Zeke. "Let's make this quick. I have an appointment at six."

Zeke spooned five crystals of Heaven into an eight ounce glass of water. The water turned a vivid royal blue. He stirred the two until the water had become clear again.

He knelt before Nadia and held the glass to her lips.

"Drink it," he instructed her.

She drank the entire contents of the glass and slouched into the chair. Her head lolled to the side, and her eyes closed to slits.

"Monitor her," St. James instructed the two men. "I'll need to know what she sees, hears, and says."

"Yes, sir," one replied.

"Zeke," St. James commanded. Zeke followed him to a small office located at the rear of the warehouse. The office sat in disarray. A whiteboard took up an entire wall, the computer had not been connected to the internet, and boxes of paper still festooned the floor. Zeke had not expected their sudden move.

"See to it this place is cleaned up," St. James sniffed in distain.

"Yes, sir," Zeke replied.

St. James sat in the room's single chair.

"I noticed the liquid still turned blue," St. James began without preamble. "You will fix that by the deadline."

"Yes, sir," Zeke repeated.

"Have I misplaced my confidence in you, Zeke?" He asked. "I vouched for you when others would have abjured you. You would have been a man without a country, as it were. And none of us wants that. I'm sure you've heard how bad things can get if you're a former Bane, and I know you won't want to get empirical evidence of it." St. James stated.

"No sir, I won't. I'll make it happen. I have vowed it. I won't let you down." Zeke hated sounding like a sniveling lackey, but that was his role until he could change it. So, he got down on his metaphorical knees and licked St. James' boots.

"We'll have everything ready to go by the deadline. We'll even run a smaller test before," Zeke promised. "That way we can take care of any issues before the main event."

"Yes, you will," St. James replied. "My guinea pig out there certainly can't be the only test subject. She's far too special to give us unbiased data."

"She's your daughter sir. Of course she's special." Zeke lowered his head obsequiously.

"She might be mine."

Zeke's eyes snapped to St. James' face at his slight emphasis on 'might.' Was there a chance Nadia wasn't his daughter? If that was the case, Zeke might be able to use that to his advantage. He filed the information away.

St. James kicked his feet forward, resting them on his heels. "But she's not Bane material," he continued. "She got some of the allure but little of the will to succeed." He sighed. "Neither of my children inherited the required tenacity. Too much of their mother's sensibilities."

St. James' phone rang. "Yes!" He barked into it.

"Sorry to interrupt sir," one of Nadia's caretakers spoke. "I think you need to see this."

"What is it?" St. James snapped.

"She's lucid."

"So soon?"

"Yes sir," he replied. "Please come sir. She's starting to ask questions."

"Fine." He punched the End call on his screen and stood.

"Come!" He motioned to Zeke. The two men exited the office and approached the center of the space.

"Daddy," Nadia called to him with a smile. She strained towards him and lifted her cheek. Her bonds still held her.

"Hello, Pet," he replied. He leaned towards her and scrutinized her eyes. She relaxed against the back of the chair

"How is she?" He asked her handlers.

"I'm fine, Daddy, but I'm bored. I want to go out tonight." She pouted. "But I'm out of money. Could I have an advance on my allowance? Please?"

"Certainly, you can," he said. "But first, we need to finish up this little task. And then, I'll take you to eat and you can get anything you like at Bergdorff's.

"Thank you, Daddy!" Nadia clapped her hands together.

Everyone else in the room froze. Her hands had been bound to the chair just a few moments before. Zeke steepled his fingers in front of his mouth. He had been certain she was bound when they had returned to the room.

"Did you release her?" St. James made the question a threat.

"No," the replied in unison.

All four men studied her for a minute.

"Pet, I'm going to need you to sit very still for me," St. James knelt before her again. "We just need to take a little tiny pin prick of a sample of your blood, and then we can go eat. He motioned to Nadia's handlers. They raced to comply.

Nadia sat still while they drew blood, dressed the puncture, and returned her to rights. She smiled at her father.

"Can we go now, Daddy?"

"Yes, Pet," he answered.

She stood. Zeke stared at her feet. He was certain they too had been bound to the chair.

"Go out to the car," St. James instructed her. "Tell Alphonse we are dining at Morimoto's before we go to Bergdorf's."

Nadia walked out with her handlers trailing behind her.

"What just happened?" St. James demanded.

"I don't know, sir." Zeke answered. He did not bother to add that he had been with St. James and so knew everything that he did.

"Find out." St. James loomed over Zeke's own tall frame. "She didn't just remove her bonds," he muttered. "They disappeared."

"Yes," Zeke said.

"She only got some of the charisma and beauty of the Banes," St. James continued. "The human genes were too powerful so she got no other abilities. Damn humans," he swore and retreated from Zeke for an instant. He prowled the perimeter of the room. He shook himself like a dog clearing snow off his coat. "Regardless, she should not have been able to disintegrate her cuffs. Find out how she did it. Test her blood," he pointed to the three vials that sat on the table. "If it's not some latent Bane ability that is just now manifesting, then it's the drug that made it possible."

"Bane abilities don't appear so long after puberty," Zeke agreed. "She would have shown some talent for it earlier. Could she have signed an Accord?"

"No, they would have had to recruit her, and they wouldn't do that without my permission!" St. James said. "She doesn't know anything about the Order so it must be the drug! Figure it out Dunne," he instructed. "Test this batch and then destroy the rest of it. Heaven is only supposed to make them think they are having the life of their dreams and getting whatever they want. It's certainly not supposed to actually give it to them. We can't have humans running around who can manifest whatever they want to manifest!"

"No, sir." Zeke replied.

"Good. Then, test it and destroy the rest of this entire batch." St. James moved toward the exit.

"This will set us back a few days or even weeks, sir." Zeke called after him.

"I know." St. James replied from the doorway. "That might be even better. If it's not the summer solstice, it will be July 4th." He smiled. "That's somehow more fitting."

Alone in the lab, Zeke studied the vat of sparkling blue crystals. He donned a mask and gloves. He removed several sample jars from the sterilizing oven that sat in the corner. He filled them with Heaven, labeled them for testing, and placed them in storage. Then, he removed two more jars, filled them, and placed them in the pockets of his coat. His reasons for his actions remained unclear even to him. But he was a Bane, and he lived by his instincts and drives. He nodded in satisfaction and lit a match. This batch had not yet been aerosolized. It would not yet be potent in airborne form.

The batch of Heaven whooshed and crackled as the fire caught. The drug hissed and spit like a snake as it burned and dissipated. Plumes of silver smoke curled towards the ceiling.

Lost in thought, Zeke watched the smoke strike the ceiling in a shower of sparks. The barest trickle of a plan formed.

CHAPTER 21

JOANNA

Joanna paired and discarded the clothes in her meager wardrobe. Her bed sat littered with skirts, jeans, blouses, and other accoutrement. The open suitcase at the edge of the bed sat empty.

"I just don't know what to take," she fumed.

"Wear whatever you want," Evie lounged on the one bare corner of the bed. "Just remember that they are going to be interested in how you teach, not what you wear."

Joanna shot a rueful glance at her friend.

"Evie, you are gorgeous. You can wear a potato sack and a ratty t-shirt and pull it off," she dropped another blouse into the "Might take it" pile. The three piles so far were "Might take it," "Won't take it," and "Can't possibly take it." She was just not a fashionista. She had spent her life and energy devoted to playing the violin. Things like fashion had never been a blip on her radar. Now, she was going to Europe's more opulent and cultural centers, and she was terrified she would look like a country bumpkin.

Evie threw her head back and laughed.

"You just have no idea how stunning you are, do you?" She reached for her phone. "Should we call Shane and ask him?"

"No!" Joanna cried. "I mean, um, he's working, and I wouldn't want to interrupt him."

Evie's eyes narrowed.

"What's going on with you two? Trouble in Irish Paradise?"

"No, I, honestly, I don't know." Joanna closed her eyes for a moment. "He's been acting a little strange," she said. "Ever since he found out Marcus was going to be my touring partner in Europe."

"He couldn't possibly be jealous of the Twinkie, could he?" Shock raised Evie's voice.

"I don't know," Joanna admitted.

"Wait a minute," Evie rolled to standing. "What's going on here? Does Shane have reason to be jealous?" She clasped Joanna's arms in her hands.

"No, not really," Joanna said. "I mean, that is, you know Evie, he was my first serious boyfriend. So, there's always going to be some connection."

"Holy crap!" Evie paced the tiny room. "You do remember what happened the last time you had anything to do that creep, right? The world? Almost ended?"

"I know," Joanna hastened to reassure her friend and fairy godmother. Evie so didn't look the part that sometimes Joanna forgot she had taken a vow to guide and protect her for the rest of her life. "And I'm fine. Really, I am. It's not like I'm going to get involved with him or anything. He is all sorts of wrong for me, and I know it." She grabbed Evie's hands with her own. "I'm fine. I just need to finish this my own way, you know?"

"No you don't. In fact, let me finish it for you," Evie clenched her hands into fists. "I know just what to do."

"No, Evie. Don't get involved," Joanna's voice was firm. She wasn't often firm with anyone or anything, but she felt strongly in this instance. "Marcus is my problem, and I'll deal with him."

"If you're sure, because I can totally disintegrate him," Evie said.

"I'm sure," Joanna said. "I'll take care of it."

She stepped away from her friend and returned to the mass of clothing on her bed. She chose several pieces and outfits at random, folded them, and placed them in the suitcase.

"Now, let's talk about you. How are you doing? With the Center? With Daniel?"

"Oh, um, fine." Evie turned away from her and gazed out the room's tiny window.

"You're not fine." Joanna said. "Spill."

"I wasn't going to tell you because it's all so screwed up, but I saw Daniel last night. We ran into each other at the swing sets in the park. And …."

"And?" Joanna prompted her.

"And one thing led to another, and we hooked up. Against a tree."

"Wait, you had sex? Against a tree?" Joanna squealed. She wasn't sure which shocked her more, the fact that they had sex or that they had done it against a tree in Central Park.

"Yes."

"How was it?"

"Oh, the sex was great! Really, some of the best sex we've ever had." Evie's eyes filled with tears.

"Oh, Evie," Joanna put her arms around her friend. "What happened?"

Evie sniffled and held on tightly.

"The during part was fantastic. I'll tell you, there are some things about the new Daniel that I kind of like. He was," she paused for a moment. "Powerful and confident. I'd guess that's the best way to describe it. He's never been a slouch in that department, but there was something different this time." She smiled and sniffed one right after the other.

"And after?" Joanna nudged her. She shoved her clothes over and sat down next to Evie.

"Right after, something happened. And he had a vision or some memory came back or something. If I'd been more in my own head, I would have tried mitigate what he saw somehow. But considering he'd just blown the top of my head off, I was in no shape to help him through whatever happened." She jumped up and paced around the bed. She tugged at her hair with both hands and sank back down.

"It's going to be okay, Evie." Joanna hugged her once more.

"I hope so, and it better happen soon because this sucks. Who knew being a Level 4 would suck so bad?"

"You just became a Level 4, and you'll persevere eventually. I just know you will." Joanna comforted her. "I wish I wasn't going away right now," she sighed. "I'd like to be here to help you through this whole thing."

"I'll be okay." Evie pulled back from her and smiled. "Besides, I'm going to have plenty to do with the Center and rebuilding the Jumping Cow."

Tears sprang to Joanna's eyes. "That's so terrible. How is Mama Brader taking it? Are there any clues as to who did it?"

"No, although, I think someone we both know knows more than he's telling."

"Who?" Joanna asked.

"Tariq. And I'm going to have to figure out what he knows and help put the Cow to rights and deal with the music program at the Center. That ought to keep me out of trouble," Evie rose from the bed and started folding random clothing. She put them in piles by theme as she talked. "Now that Darnell knows the music room is off limits unless he wants to come play music, things ought to calm down on that front." Then she stopped.

"Wait!" Evie knocked on her head with a closed fist. "Hello! McFly!" She emoted, a la the bully in a beloved 80's movie. "I can't believe I didn't figure it out sooner."

"Figure what out?" Joanna asked.

"What Tariq knows. It was Darnell. It had to be. Now, I just have to get Tariq to tell me what he knows. And once I do, I'll kick Darnell's ass into next week.

"Be careful with him, Evie," Joanna admonished.

"With Darnell? Please. He's no match for me."

"No, with Tariq. He is special, I think. He needs your help. Okay?"

"Okay," Evie promised.

"Evie," Joanna dodged around Evie to see behind her back. "Are your fingers crossed?" Fairies couldn't lie if asked a direct question unless they had their fingers crossed behind their backs. Evie had used that little technique to her advantage on more than one occasion.

"No, I'm not." Evie raised her hands in front of her. "But honestly, Jo. I'm not sure what I can do."

"He's a tough nut to crack, but I think he's hurting on the inside. And I think the same thing could be said about you." Joanna gentled her tone.

"Me? I'm a tough broad," Evie protested.

"Yes, you are." Joanna agreed. "But you're also hurting on the inside right now. If you could remember that with Tariq …."

"Okay, okay, you win. I'll look out for him and try to help him out. Not that I know where to find him or where he hangs out."

Joanna furrowed her brow. "The only time I've seen him is with Veronica, but she'll be leaving with me so I don't know." She brightened. "You know what Evie? I think you won't have to go to him. I think he'll come to you."

"What, is every single person I know some kind of psychic?" Evie cried.

"I'm not psychic. I just think Tariq needs music in his life. You didn't see him book towards that piano when he first entered the music room. I think that's your 'in.' Fix up the piano, and he'll show up. 'If you build it, he will come.'" Joanna pressed home her advantage by quoting another 80's movie. Evie could never resist those.

"Field of Dreams? Really? You're going to quote Field of Dreams to me?" Evie placed a last pair of slacks into the suitcase and shut it. "So, I get him hooked on the music room by fixing the piano. I can do that. I have all the materials. Now, if only had I the money for all the other things I need."

"Speaking of funding, I had an idea about that," Joanna picked up her violin case from the small desk that sat by the window. She put her arms through its arm loops and carried it on her back like a backpack. "What if you held a fundraiser for the music program?"

"You mean like a telethon?" Evie asked.

"No, it would be like a big dinner, and you could charge a bunch of money per person and that money could go to paying for all the stuff you need like instruments, lessons, equipment, desks. All that sort of stuff."

"That's not a bad idea," Evie said. "We could invite a bunch of the hoity toity Fae folks, but their form of legal tender tends to be a little different. So, how would we get big donor New Yorkers?"

"I say you ask the Professor about that. She knows everyone who's anyone in the music scene in this city."

"That's perfect! Jo, you're a genius." Evie snapped her fingers and the suitcase floated out behind them as they left the room.

"Good," Joanna grinned as much in pleasure at the floating suitcase as Evie's promise that she would try to help Tariq. After all this time, seeing magic still had not become commonplace. Although she was made mostly of magic, generally she just felt like a completely normal person. She herself had no control over magic or any magical powers at all. The only magical thing about her was the fact that magic didn't work on her. So, any time she witnessed it in action, it thrilled her.

Joanna grabbed her purse and backpack off the purple couch that served as the room biggest piece of furniture.

"Okay, I'm ready," she announced.

"Is Shane meeting us at the airport?"

"Yes. Tully needed him to finish his shift. Tully's enjoying semi-retirement, I think. But that means Shane has to take over more of the work."

"That's good," Evie smiled. "It'll keep him out of trouble while you're gone."

"What kind of trouble could he get into?" Joanna asked.

Evie broke into a fit of giggles. "You see, that's why I love you, Jo. You honestly don't have any idea what kind of trouble a guy like Shane could get into if left to his own devices."

They reached the airport without incident, although Joanna repeatedly checked her phone for texts or voicemails that would indicate a problem.

"I really would have rather picked them all up," she fretted.

"Yes, but then we'd need three cabs," Evie pointed out. "Besides, I'll bet everyone's parents will want to say goodbye in person."

"I guess," Joanna furrowed her brow.

"Jo," Evie grabbed her friend's arm as they walked into the terminal. "It's going to be okay." She paused. "Or, are you having a 'Joanna' feeling?"

"No." Joanna fumbled with her backpack to produce the ticket, her passport, and her ID. She stowed them in the pocket of her travel pouch.

"Joanna," Veronica called from the ticketing line. She waved them over.

"You're here," Joanna breathed a sigh of relief.

"Yeah, we're here." Veronica replied. "Do you want to take cuts?"

"No, I'll get in line last, I think." Students from other groups were trickling in as they stood near the long line. Again, her belly clenched. She checked her phone for the time and for any last-minute messages.

"Always the responsible one," Marcus had appeared at their sides. He carried a small black leather satchel and held a rolling matching leather suitcase at his feet.

"Hello, Marcus," Joanna aimed for nonchalant. She squared her shoulders and looked him in the eye.

"Twinkie," Evie gave him a curt nod.

"Joanna," Shane called from the entrance. He jogged over to them. Joanna smiled into his eyes as he approached. He was still the most strapping guy she had ever seen. His slightly too long blond hair fell in his blue eyes. She reached up and brushed it off his forehead as he leaned down for a kiss. He tugged her honey blond hair and hooked it behind her ear.

"Okay, everyone," Marcus shouted to assembled group. "You need your tickets and your passports. And keep your stuff with you, because I'm not your babysitter," he grumbled.

"You're going to be fine," Joanna smiled at the students. She explained the procedure for boarding and going through security to the students. She ushered them into the security line.

"Marcus," she said. "Why don't you take the front of the line and I'll bring up the rear?"

"You just want to watch me walk away," he smirked.

Joanna chose to ignore him.

Shane did not. He approached Marcus. Up close, Shane towered over him.

"Are you sure you want to be talking to the lady like that?" His voice was mild.

"What do you care?" Marcus huffed.

"I care a great deal, and so will you if you don't watch your mouth." Shane reached for the smaller man.

"Shane," Joanna stepped in between them and put a hand on Shane's chest. "Please ignore him. He's not important." She gazed into her boyfriend's eyes and silently begged him not to make a scene in front of the students.

"I know that, Joanna," he smiled. "But I won't have him speaking to you like that."

"They're only words," Joanna said. She leaned into him.

He lowered his head and brushed his lips against hers. A heat started low in her belly like it did whenever he kissed her like that. He tangled his hands in her hair and deepened the kiss.

"Ooh, Joanna," the students crowed and hooted at their display.

Joanna extricated herself from the embrace and patted her hair back in place. She would have preferred to pat down her bright red cheeks, but there was no way she was going to live down the embarrassment of having been so thoroughly kissed.

She couldn't help herself and snaked her arms around his waist.

She reached up and touched her lips to his.

"I'll miss you," she whispered.

"I'll miss you, too," he replied.

They held each other for a moment longer. Then, she moved over to Evie.

She wrapped her arms around her friend.

"I'm sorry I'm not going to be here for the rest of the summer," she said. "You have so much going on. Are you going to be okay?"

"Of course, I am," Evie cocked an eyebrow and grinned. It was only because Joanna knew her so well that she detected the note of uncertainty in Evie's voice.

"You're going to do great," Joanna whispered. "With the Center, the fundraiser, Daniel, everything - I just know it."

"Thanks, love," Evie said.

"I love you both," Joanna picked up her bag and moved towards the security line. After a few steps she whirled around and ran back to them. She reached into her bag and withdrew a bottle of water. "Could you take this? I can't take it with me in line."

"Sure," Evie smiled. "No problem."

"And you'll watch out for Tariq?"

"I promise," Evie laughed. "I'm on the job."

"Thanks, Evie. You're the best!

With one more quick hug for Shane she moved through the metal detector and entered the interior of the terminal. She would miss Evie and especially Shane, but this adventure would be marvelous. She hadn't wanted to show them how excited she was to fly out because she didn't want to hurt their feelings. She was going to spend time in the birthplace of much of the music she loved best. She couldn't wait!

CHAPTER 22

TARIQ

"Come on," Calvin pulled Tariq down the street.

"Where you wanna go?" Tariq laughed.

"I want to go see the shiny lady again. She's nice and pretty." Determination lent a dogged quality to his voice.

"You wanna go to the Center?" Tariq asked. Shit! He didn't want to go there. Evie already thought he knew more than he said about what happened at that ice cream store. He didn't want to give her any opportunity to ask him more questions about it.

"Yes!" Calvin stopped. His face slid from sly smile to hopeful pout back to sly smile as he looked up at him.

"She's pretty and shiny, and she has good cookies."

"You keep saying she's shiny. What do you mean?"

Calvin grabbed his hand and pulled him along again.

"You know, shiny, like the sparkles on Veronica's old dolls."

"Boy, you are a little crazy." Tariq shook his head but once again allowed himself to be dragged towards the 127th Street Youth Center. Eventually, someone would find out everything he'd done, but hopefully today would not be that day.

"I know," Calvin raised serious eyes to him. "But it's okay."

Tariq froze. Ever since he was born, people had said Calvin was special. Sometimes, they said he was crazy and a problem child. He had always tried to shield his little brother from the worst of what they said about him. He was sorry any of it had gotten through.

"Tariq," Calvin tugged on his hand. "It's okay," he repeated. "Now let's go."

They entered the Center. It was only marginally cooler than the heat of the New York afternoon but being indoors provided shade and that counted for a lot.

"Come on," Calvin dragged him along towards the music room. They stopped at the door.

"I'm sure it's locked," Tariq said.

"Not locked," Calvin insisted. "Try it."

Tariq pulled on the knob, and the door swung open.

"See?" Calvin ran inside, sat down at one of the big djembe drums and patted it with his small hands.

Tariq's eyes were glued to the piano. It drew him. His fingers trailed along the newly-lacquered wood as he circled the instrument. Calvin's staccato rhythm on the drum disappeared from his consciousness. He sat at the bench, opened the key cover, and ran his fingers feather-light over the keys. He spread his fingers and played an experimental chord on the old instrument.

He smiled.

Some of the notes were still not hammering. Perhaps certain strings were missing. But the piano had a warm yet clear sound in the notes that did play. Without thinking, he launched into a fiery rendition of the Duke's "Sophisticated Lady." He slid into "Take the A Train," and out of that, he flowed into "It Don't Mean a Thing."

He drew the last chord out into an arpeggio and swiped at his wet cheeks with his hands. He glanced over at Calvin and smiled. His little brother was lost in his own world as he tapped on the different parts of the drum.

Tariq shook his head and launched into another of Duke's most famous pieces, "Mood Indigo."

As always, the music took him, and he was lost in its grip.

SHANE

Shane and Evie stood together and watched Joanna, Marcus, and the students pass through the various checkpoints and head towards their gate. They watched until everyone had disappeared from view.

"I assume you're going to do something about him," Evie stuck her hands in her pants pockets and rocked back on her heels.

"I aim to," Shane replied. He folded his muscular arms in front of his chest and gazed down the hallway. He formulated a plan as he stood rooted to the spot. His lids lowered in concentration. He would need to find someone to help at Tully's, but he was damned if he was going let Jo be with that jackass in Europe all summer long.

"Good. Then, we understand each other," Evie said.

"Aye, that we do."

"Okay," Evie moved away from him. "I need to head back to the Center. Want to come with me and have a shorter ride back in to town?"

"Sure," he replied. "I still don't quite believe this mode of transportation you use," he said.

"It's okay. You don't need to believe it for it to work," Evie laughed.

Together, they moved towards the women's bathroom.

"The Ladies? Can we not use some other place?" Shane stuttered.

"Come on, you big strapping lad," Evie giggled. "I'll make sure it's empty."

They entered the bathroom. Evie removed her wand from her bag, inscribed a symbol with it and grabbed Shane's hand.

The bathroom faded from view around them and was replaced by intersecting blue-lit walkways. Many millions of them connected, disconnected, lay in concentric circles, and crossed one another all around them.

"The Ley Lines," Shane murmured as they stepped onto a small one. "Nope, still don't believe it."

They had taken no more than four steps when Evie nudged him off the path. They both jumped off the Line and another women's bathroom formed around them.

"So, tell me, Evie. Why the Ladies all the time? And do others like you use the men's rooms?"

"I'm sure they do," Evie answered. "I know I seldom have call to do that. But as for the reason I use the Ladies room? It's because no pays attention when you go in so when you come out of one, no one ever wonders whether you had been in there before. They just assume you were and they didn't see you enter."

"Logical," Shane nodded. They approached the music room. He grasped the knob to open the door.

EVIE

"Wait, stop," I commanded. I closed my eyes and melted into the soaring yet melancholy version of "Mood Indigo," that emanated from within. I cringed each time one of the necessary notes didn't sound. I had had no time to fix all the hammers that needed replacing. It's a crime that this player doesn't have a perfect instrument to play, I thought. Masterful and mesmerizing chased each other in my head to describe the playing. The sorrow shone through each chord like the first ray of sun on a rainy morning. It stunned me and left me breathless.

A "tap, tap, taptaptap" sounded from behind the door in rough accompaniment to the piano. It didn't accompany the masterful playing. Rather, its haphazard nature indicated someone who didn't give a fig about what else was happening and was just having great fun bangin' on a drum.

We entered the music room.

"What are you doing here?" I cried, surprised.

THE PIANO'S KEY

Tariq jumped away from the piano as if it had just zapped him.

"Nothing," he stammered. "I was just ... um ...." He fell silent.

"He was just playing," Calvin greeted me with a sunny smile. "Hi Shiny Lady."

"Hi yourself, youngling." I approached him. He lifted his arms in the international "Pick me up," gesture, and I hoisted him onto a hip. He wrapped his arms around my neck and settled in for a rest. This kid was something. I was honored that he had decided I was trustworthy. He must have sensed that I would protect him or die trying, because he fell asleep in the blink of an eye. His dead weight comforted me.

Tariq had watched our exchanged with his mouth wide open.

"It's okay," I assured him before he could object. "He'll always be fine with me." I never let my gaze waver to show him I meant business. See, when a Godparent promises you something, it will take a cataclysmic event to keep her from delivering.

"Okay," he nodded once.

"Now, to business," I moved towards the piano and motioned for him to approach. "Your playing, where did you learn?"

"I don't know," he evaded. He looked anywhere but at me. "My grandmother had a piano when I was a kid. And I used to play it sometimes."

I searched into him for a minute. Honestly, it's not something we're supposed to do. There are rules about how much we are allowed walk in and play around with people's heads. But I had a feeling this kid wasn't about to give me much of anything unless I pried it out of him with a metaphysical crowbar. Poor kid! He really didn't believe he was a kid anymore even though he was barely fourteen. This would bear further scrutiny.

"But you don't have one anymore?" I prodded.

"No, we had to sell it when she got sick."

"Ah," I said. I narrowed my eyes at him.

"What?" Suspicion leapt into his eyes as well.

"Nothing. You are a great player," I said. "Want to play some more?"

He moved towards the instrument and pulled up short.

"Nah, I've got to get Calvin home. Besides, music is for pussies."

"Excuse me?" I protested. "I'll have you know that some of the toughest people ever born were musicians. Music is your birthright," I continued. "And you'd better know that. It's in your bones. And with the way you played 'Mood Indigo, just now, it's in your blood too."

"Whatever," he waved a dismissive hand.

"Whatever?" I argued. I motioned to Shane. "He's a musician. Do you think he's a coward?"

Shane, bless his heart, stood to his full, impressive height. He bent his brawny arms and placed his fists on his hips. He towered the three of us and quirked his lips in a lopsided smile. He wouldn't hurt a flea, but he could look like every inch the 'Irish Tough' when it suited.

"No, he isn't a coward." Tariq trailed his eyes all the way up until he met Shane's.

"And he plays guitar like you've never heard," I wished I'd thought of adding a guitar into the mix here in the music room. I didn't own one and would have to purchase one. With luck, the fundraising idea would take hold and I would be able to purchase all the instruments I wanted.

"Thank you, Evie," Shane said. "Appreciate it."

"My pleasure," I smiled at him and then turned to Tariq. "Lots of musicians have shown incredible courage in their lives. Why, look at the Underground Railroad?" I exclaimed. "The people who travelled it were incredibly courageous, and they used songs and music to hide in plain sight while they travelled."

"What's this then?" Shane asked. He might have known about the stories of how slaves traveled the Railroad and used songs as code. He was likely helping me make a point.

"Well, Shane," I smiled at him. "Songs like 'Wade in the Water' and 'Ride the Chariot' were sung as codes to help people escape the South using the Underground Railroad. See, like 'Ride the Chariot' was a code to tell escaping slaves that they needed to be ready go and when and where they needed to be to catch a coach up north." I paced the small room with Calvin in my arms. "And a way of avoiding the slave owners' dogs was to wade through water to make it harder for the dogs to catch their scent. So, that song was sung to remind people to get into the water to avoid them."

"Whatever," Tariq sighed.

"Whatever?" I cried. "We've barely scratched the surface. You have no idea the miracles music has made." I sat down in front of the djembe drum. The djembe gave me an idea. It was probably a stupid idea. It was definitely a dangerous idea, but when has that ever stopped me? I threw all caution to every wind and plowed on.

"Music has helped people survive against all odds when they might have died otherwise. The slaves used it on the Underground Railroad but they also used it beforehand. It was their solace in unspeakable conditions."

"What the hell are you talking about?" Tariq rolled his eyes.

"I'll tell you. The slaves, people who survived unbearable torment, used music to survive."

"Yeah, right." He backed away from me. He moved around the piano and put distance between the two of us. "What's a white woman doing telling me about the music of the slaves? How could you possibly know?"

"I know," I said. "I just know." The air between us crackled. I was too young to do anything about the atrocities when they occurred, but by all the heavens, I would have changed things if I could.

I tightened my arms around Calvin, and he shifted.

Tariq took a deep breath and approached me. The look in his eyes said it all. I still held his little brother. He was going to get Calvin away from me and leave.

Calvin clasped his hands around my neck and held me more tightly.

"Evie," he whispered.

"Hold on a minute, sweetie." I said to him.

"He doesn't understand," he said. "You're going to have to show him."

Yep, I've come along way. I now had five-year-olds telling me how to do my job. And the kicker? He was right.

"You're right, Calvin." I smiled at him. He was headed for greatness. No doubt about that.

"Your brother's right," I spoke to Tariq. "I'm going to have to show you. You and me, we're going on a little trip."

"I'm not going anywhere with you," Tariq shouted. "Put my brother down. Now!"

He moved towards us. Calvin shook his head.

"Tariq," Calvin murmured. "It's okay."

"Calvin, come here," Tariq soothed his tones.

"No, Evie has something to show you and I think you need to go with her." Calvin's odd, wise eyes gazed from one to the other of us.

"I'm not going anywhere with her. This white bitch don't know a thing!" Tariq yelled.

"White?" I was incredulous. "That's the problem? You think I'm white?"

"Of course you're white," Tariq scoffed.

"She's not white, Tariq," Calvin said. "She's sort of all colors."

"What are you talking about, Calvin?" Tariq narrowed his gaze on his brother.

Calvin scrutinized my face. "You know. She's white and black and brown and blue and purple and yellow and pink and green. Mostly, she's sort of sparkly."

"No, Calvin," Tariq said. "She's white."

"No," Calvin insisted. "She's all sorts of colors. She's like a rainbow lady." He looked at me. "Show him."

"I don't want you to show me anything," Tariq asserted. "Just put him down, and we're leaving."

THE PIANO'S KEY

A low hum started buzzing in the room. The strings on the piano vibrated in sympathetic harmony. The lights flickered, once, twice, and then dimmed all together. Tariq took no notice. He stared at us with an unwavering intensity.

"In for a penny, in for a pound," I sighed.

I looked from Tariq to the piano and back again. "So, I'm going to tell you something that will probably freak you out. And I'm not supposed to tell you so that's going to get me a hefty fine, but we're not going to get anywhere until you know. So," I heaved sigh. "I guess I'm your fairy godmother."

"You're my what?" Tariq laughed.

"I'm your Fairy Godmother. I must be, or you wouldn't be such a pain in my ass. Normally, the Fairy Godparent Guild assigns us our charges, but I have a feeling you're a special case."

"I'm not a special anything," Tariq maneuvered around the room until he was within arm's reach.

"Calvin, come on," Tariq implored.

"No," Calvin said. "Not until Evie shows you."

"Shows me what?"

"This," I removed the dampening spell all fairies wore to cloak our appearance. The mask fell away. My true colors shone and yes, sparkled. Purples, magentas, vivid blues, yellows, reds - they all danced across my features. My face was still my face, but the colors looped and swirled.

Tariq's eyes opened saucer-wide.

"What the hell," he breathed.

"This is more what I really look like," I explained and tried hard to make it sound vaguely normal as the instruments all played themselves in a passable version of the "Star of Munster" Irish Reel. My wand danced in mid-air with glee as for a moment it was free to look like its actual glittery self instead of the conductor's baton it appeared to be whenever I spent time here. I sighed. So much for normal. "But generally, when we are hanging out here, on Earth, we want to blend in a little."

"And you're my what? My Fairy Godmother?" Tariq's legs wobbled, and he folded to the floor. He cradled his head in hands and fell silent.

Calvin tugged on my hair. "Are you my fairy godmother, too?" He asked.

"Baby, I don't think you need a fairy godmother." I smiled at him. "You've got it going on without any of my help. I'm still curious as to how you could see what I look like when I work pretty hard to keep it hidden."

"I don't know," he pondered. "How does anybody see anything?" He asked.

"See?" I grinned. "You don't need a fairy godmother. It looks to be like you could be a Fairy Godparent yourself. Or a tiny reincarnation of the Buddha. That's it. You're a Tiny Buddha." Calvin and I both giggled.

"You see all this?" Tariq asked Calvin.

"Yes."

"And you're okay with it?"

"Yep. It's Evie," Calvin said as if that explained everything.

I smiled my thanks to the kid. If Calvin hadn't been here to normalize this for Tariq, it might have gone a lot less smoothly. As it was, we weren't out of the woods yet.

The reel ended and the hum and harmonics spontaneously set up by the various instruments in the room had quieted to a dull roar. I dampened my glamour and returned to what I normally look like to the human world.

"So," I attempted to sound casual. "About that little trip …."

Tariq shot to standing.

"I'm not taking any sort of trip with you." He grabbed Calvin from my arms. "I have to take care of Calvin." His young man's voice was firm.

I approved, but that did not deter me from my mission.

"I know. Calvin is the priority. But so are you." I gentled my tone. I nodded my head in Shane's direction.

"Shane will watch him, won't you Shane?"

"I sure will," he nodded. Shane had seen my true face back in the winter during a drunken evening playing Truth or Dare. I thought I could hold my liquor, but even a Fairy can't hold a candle to a sufficiently motivated Irishman.

"Calvin and I will spend some time playing drums and then I'm thinking there might be some Mac and Cheese in our future." Shane stood and sobered.

"He'll be okay with me. I promise," Shane said. He walked to Tariq and stuck out his hand.

"Okay," Tariq clasped his outstretched hand.

"Excellent! Let's go." I cried. "But wait," I paused. "I just have to run to the restroom for a minute."

"Seriously?" Tariq rolled his eyes. "That's what Veronica does every time we are about to go anywhere. She always has to go right before we're ready to walk out the door."

"Yeah, well, that's just how it is. But where we're going, we aren't going to need any doors."

"What?"

"You'll see," I grabbed my messenger bag, snagged my wand out of midair, and jogged out into the hall. While we had been talking, a big part of me was concentrating on a plane that flew somewhere over the Atlantic Ocean. I needed to make sure that was going to go well, and I couldn't be there myself. I needed reinforcements.

I entered the Ladies room and looked under the stalls to make sure I had the place to myself. I waved the tip of my wand so it made a triangle with the tip pointing down. A blue light after-effect hovered in the air as the ancient symbol for the Water Element beckoned a couple of particular Elementals. I pulled out Joanna's water and stared at the bottle.

"Hey, Ashlynn, Fiora, can you drop by, please? I need to ask you a favor." I watched the bottle until two eyes and then four eyes blinked from within. I opened the bottle and poured the water on the floor. The Brookbearer sisters, Ashlynn and Fiora, formed and stepped out of the puddle.

"What's up, Evie?" Ashlynn, the older sister, asked.

"How would you feel about spending a little time in Europe? Specifically on the Danube?"

"Love that river," Ashlynn exclaimed. "Why? What's up?"

"Jo just got on a plane. She's headed to Vienna, Austria with a bunch of students." I hopped up and down in my impatience. "And the Twinkie is on that plane, too."

"Oh no. Is Joanna okay? What can we do? How do we take care of it?" Fiora shook her watery head. Droplets of water flung off her. She was the younger of the two and more prone to worry.

"We're on it, Evie." Ashlynn said. "We'll make sure he gets nowhere near her."

"Thanks, loves."

The Water Elementals rose on a humid air current, flowed into the sink, and disappeared.

I sighed in relief. It wasn't that I didn't trust Jo. She could take care of herself and had proven it when she dealt with the Ramrocks last year. But we all could use a little extra help every once in a while.

I returned to the music room. Shane and Calvin were taking turns banging the drum.

"Okay, let's go," I announced. Fear leapt into Tariq's eyes, but he banked it. "It's going to be okay, Tariq." I assured him.

He rose from the piano stool and walked past me towards the doorway.

"Where are you going?" I asked.

"I thought we were leaving." He angled his head at me.

"Oh, we're not going that way," I reached for his hand. "We're traveling a different way."

"Watch my little brother," Tariq gazed at Shane meaningfully.

"He'll be fine." Shane promised.

Tariq curled his fingers around mine.

"Ready?" I smiled at him.

"Okay." Uncertainty radiated off him in waves, but he stood his ground.

I inscribed the Traveler's sigil in the air with my wand and softened my focus until the room's walls dematerialized and the iridescent blue of the Ley Lines took their place.

"What the Hell!" he breathed. The Ley Lines' lattice-work stretched outward.

"See that wide Line over there?" I pointed to a Ley Line a few yards away from us.

"Yeah," he followed my finger.

"That's like a superhighway. It will take you from big place to big place. Each of these Lines represents a pathway. The broader Lines are like huge superhighways. So, walking on them will allow us to from big place to big place. And we'll be able to do it quickly."

"How quickly?" Tariq asked.

"We'll be able to cross a continent in a few minutes. Each of the smaller Lines off the main thoroughfares is a smaller destination." I pointed to a thinner Line. "So, if we wanted to go to South America, we'd hop on a major Line. Then, we would need a smaller Line to choose the country, say Argentina. An even smaller one would make it Buenos Aires. See what I mean?"

"Okay," Tariq squared his shoulders. "So where are we going?" He asked.

"Senegal."

"Senegal? Like in Africa?"

"Yep."

"No shit!" His eyes widened.

"None whatsoever." I grabbed his hand. "Are you ready?"

"No, but that don't change anything."

We left our entry point and made our way to a larger Line, no more than two feet wide.

"Okay, we've left Manhattan." I announced. From there, we walked a few yards until we stood at "V" crosspoint to two huge Lines that were as wide as New York City street. One angled off to our left, and the other angled to our right.

"What do we do now?" Tariq stilled.

"Well, the one on the left goes to Europe. And the one on the right goes to Africa."

"So, we go with the one on the right?"

I nodded. With a silent three-count we stepped onto the main Ley Line Thoroughfare. Despite looking like streams of light, the Lines felt solid under our feet, like shiny AstroTurf. We walked a few hundred yards until we came to another circular crossing station. The platform branched off into more than twenty smaller Lines. I gazed at each for a minute.

"It's this one," I pointed to one of the Lines on the left. We hopped off the main one and onto it. After a few more turns, we reached our destination. I inscribed another sigil in the air, and a palm tree materialized before us. The Line beneath our feet faded into a fine, white sand. A brilliant, lavender sky merged with dark, turquoise water to the horizon. Waves rolled to the shore and left their frothy white shadow as they receded into the deep. Tariq spun around a full three-sixty. The sun had just set.

"Welcome to Senegal," I said.

He ran to the edge of the ocean, bent down, and caught the waves in his hands.

"I've never been to the beach before," he cried.

"It looks like you like it."

"Yeah," he grinned. "I do."

"Good." I turned away from him and walked up the beach.

"Hey, Evie," he called. "Where are you going?"

"Oh, nowhere," I glanced back at him. "You wouldn't be interested."

"How do you know I wouldn't be interested?" He jogged up to me and paced me.

We moved towards a stand of palm trees that sat in front of a small cafe. The square, terra cotta building had windows on three sides. A large courtyard faced the shore. Umbrellas in hues of golds and reds dotted the courtyard and provided shade for several tables.

THE PIANO'S KEY

"Well, after what you said before about music being for pussies ..." I stretched out the last word as a "dun, pat, pat, pat, dun, pat, pat, pat" reached us on the slight breeze.

"Do you hear that?" I asked him.

"The drums?" he replied. "Sure, I hear them."

"You remember that sound, Tariq," I instructed him.

We entered the courtyard. Four men drummed on goblet-shaped djembes. The two younger drummers beat a steady rhythm while the two older drummers added other percussive lines. The oldest man added an intricate pattern to the already pounding rhythm.

The four wove rhythms around each other's patterns. At a sign from the oldest drummer, the others played the same pattern until, as one, they all hit one last blasting bass note.

"Bon," the oldest drummer grinned. The younger men high-fived each other and laughed.

As we approached, I tapped my wand and murmured a Universal Interpreter spell.

"Good evening," I said. To their ears, I had just uttered a perfect, "Bonsoir."

"Good evening," they replied.

"I am Evie. This is my friend, Tariq," I continued. "He's from the United States of America, and he has never heard authentic djembe drumming."

The men welcomed us and invited us to join them. Tariq took a chair close to them.

"The djembe is an ancient drum and a wise teacher," the Baba said. Tariq perched on the edge of his chair. His eyes grew round as the men discussed drumming and its history.

"The djembe has been part of our history for many thousands of years."

"Have they always been played the same way?" Tariq asked.

"As far back as any can remember," the teacher replied. "Do you want to learn a rhythm?"

"Sure," Tariq approached and stood at a respectful distance from the aged teacher.

"Look here," the Baba struck the drum dead center with his cupped palm. "This is the lowest and fullest sound the drum makes," the teacher said. "Try it."

Tariq cupped his hands and struck the drum in the center of its round head. Each 'dun' reverberated across the patio as he set up a pounding backbeat rhythm. The other drummers layered other, more driving rhythms over and on top of Tariq's bass tones. Tariq incorporated other strikes into his drumming pattern. The other drummers adapted and modified their rhythms to match his pace and style. After a few moments, the teacher raised his hands, and the drummers sounded the "pat tak pat tak" pattern that finished the session.

"Yes!" Tariq raised his hands in victory.

"Nice job, kid," I shouted, and we celebrated with a high five. I turned to the teacher. "Baba," I said. "Can you tell us about that first rhythm you were playing when we came up?"

"This one?" The Baba struck the same "dun, pat, pat, pat, dun, pat, pat, pat" pattern.

"That's the one," I agreed.

"This is one of our oldest rhythms," the Baba rested his wizened hands on the head. "At one time, it was the call for the young men to come to the aid of those who needed it."

"So the drummers were warriors?"

"Not all," he answered. "Some were healers. Some were hunters."

I glanced at Tariq. He hung on the Baba's every word.

"And now? What are the rhythms for now?"

"Now, they serve as reminders."

"Of what?" Tariq asked.

"Of what was before."

"Baba," Tariq stood before him. "Would you be willing to teach me that rhythm?"

The teacher eyed the young man with intent, dark eyes. He nodded.

"You know the bass sound," the Baba said. "Now I will show you the drum's other songs."

Tariq sounded each of the drum's three main tones. He played with a light, sensitive touch.

"Now, let us try the rhythm," the Baba demonstrated the complicated pattern. Tariq experimented with it and then slid into the rhythm with the certainty of a prodigy.

I raised my eyes to the sky. Hours had passed. I sighed.

"Much as I hate to say it," I broke into their excited discussion of the difference between percussive playing in piano versus drumming. "But, we have to be going."

"Do we have to, Evie?" Tariq looked at me with pleading eyes.

"You'll get to come back and visit," I promised. "But now, we've got to jet."

"Thank you, Baba." Tariq gave a slight bow and extended his right hand. They shook gravely and then grinned at one another like they were both fourteen years old.

We said our goodbyes and made our way to the cafe.

"Why are we going this way?" Tariq asked.

"A, I need some coffee," I answered. "And B, now that the beach is hoppin' with night owls we can't exactly disappear there."

"So how are we leaving?"

"You'll see."

"Na-uh, I'm not going in there," Tariq said as he faced our exit strategy. We had gotten a strong coffee to go and now stood in front of the ladies room door.

"What? Why not?"

"'Cause it's the girl's bathroom," he stated as if that explained everything.

"So, what?" I rolled my eyes to the heavens. He had just gone form musical genius to typical fourteen-year-old in the space of a few seconds.

"So, whatever! I'm not doing it. You come into the boys bathroom."

"Na-uh," I shook my head and grinned.

"So, I'm supposed to go into the girls' bathroom, but you won't go into the boys'?" Tariq accused.

"Okay," I begrudged him the win and gave him a huge wink. I covered my eyes with a hand and grabbed onto his arm with the other.

"Lead on," I cried.

He pushed open the door, and we entered the room. I held onto his arm and muttered the Traveler's Incantation. The room dissolved, and we stood back on the Ley Line.

"So, where to next?" He asked.

"We're heading back a little closer to home," I said.

We walked across the Atlantic Ocean in just a few hundred yards. The crossroads to head back to New York loomed to our right. I motioned Tariq towards the left to a smaller Line.

"We're not going back to New York?" He asked.

"Nope," I answered him. "We're going to the Caribbean."

"Why?"

"It's the next stop on the journey."

We walked towards one of the tiniest circular crossroads. I tugged on his arm.

"Sit," I invited him.

"We're not coming out?" Tariq folded to a cross-legged position next to me.

"This will be a shorter visit," I said. "And we're not going to visit so much as observe."

I made a curtain-opening motion with my hands. The Lines dissipated so we could see out. The breeze wafted a fruity aroma. Turquoise water lapped against the white sand of the shore.

"Now where are we?" Tariq asked.

"We're just outside of Santo Domingo, the capital of the Dominican Republic," I explained. I shifted over a few inches and the scene before us changed. We left the pristine waters of Boca Chica beach and viewed the city itself. I pointed to a building near the city center. The view refocused on a class in progress on the third floor.

THE PIANO'S KEY

Five boys and two girls sat in a semi-circle. They cradled drums between their bent knees. Their teacher sat in the center between them. He lifted his hands and struck the drum head.

"Bueno," the teacher said in Spanish. "We begin."

The youngsters struck a "dun, pat, pat, pat, dun, pat, pat, pat" rhythm on their drums.

"Sound familiar?" I asked.

"That sounds like the rhythm the Baba was playing." Tariq tapped the rhythm on his thighs.

"Can we go meet them?" he asked.

"Next time," I replied. "But for now, just hold on to that rhythm, okay?"

"Sure," he answered. "That's easy."

"Alright, then. Let's go." We backtracked until we came to the Continental Ley Line. This time, instead of going up to the right, we went down to the left.

"Where are we headed now?" Tariq asked.

"You'll see," I smiled.

As the room materialized around us, Tariq yelped. Two dummies dressed like pirates loomed overhead. A rainbow-colored, plastic macaw peered down at us. Fragrant jasmine festooned the oak credenza that held a steel sink. Strands of purple beads hung from the ceiling.

"Where are we?" Tariq breathed.

"We're in New Orleans," I answered.

"So, we're back in the US?" He asked.

"Sort of." We left the bathroom and entered the club. "I'd say this town is a land all its own."

"Welcome to Daniel Jack's," I encompassed the entire space with a wave of my hand.

He stared goggle-eyed at the thousands of blossoms that sat in pots all over the place. They might have appeared strewn about, but I knew the owner, and she was anything but haphazard.

"Delilah? Are you here?" I called. "Come on out and say, 'Hey!'"

One of the most beautiful women ever born strode into the room from a side door. Long curling black hair flying, she zoomed right past me and into the kitchen.

"I told you, Marcel," her voice purred from the back. "If the gumbo doesn't satisfy me, then you will serve nothing but cheese and bread tonight."

"But D," a voice mewled. "Nothing ever satisfies you."

"And don't you forget it," she replied. "Now, see there's enough pepper in this gumbo."

She glided back into the main space and swept past me again. She halted in front of Tariq.

"You a player?" She asked.

"Um, no," he stammered.

"Then what are you doing hanging with her?" She hitched her head towards me, and her black cat's eyes flashed in my direction. "She only hangs with players."

"Well, I'm not a player," Tariq kept his eyes on the floor. I didn't blame him. He wasn't the first to try to avoid looking at the goddess who stood before us. You spent too much time looking at Delilah, you were liable to forget food, water, or your reason for existence.

"But you are a musician," I said to him. I turned towards Delilah but kept my eyes averted off her face. Fairies aren't immune to her charms either. "He is a gifted pianist."

"Really," she waved a perfect hand towards the piano that sat in the window of the square room. Wide-eyed, Tariq trailed her across the expanse of bare floor. Some said she was goddess. Some said she was a voodoo priestess. Some said she was the devil herself. A few, very few, lucky souls knew for sure, but they weren't talking. Tariq slowed as we neared the piano, and I took pity on him.

"Actually, Delilah," I stepped in front of the piano. "I was hoping maybe you'd play a little for us. Something traditional."

"Cajun?" She raised an eyebrow.

"Older," I said.

Her eyes glowed in understanding. She steered away from the piano and moved behind the long mahogany bar that sat along one entire side of the room. She hefted a tattered guitar case onto the bar and flicked open the locks. She lifted a historic Gretsch Streamliner and strummed it with reverence.

"Some say that Robert Johnson played this baby," she whispered.

"Did he?" I asked.

"No," she answered.

"Would you know for sure?" I couldn't help myself. I tried to find out a little more information about her every time I saw her. Everyone knew the legend that Robert Johnson had sold his soul to the Devil in exchange for being able to play the way he had. Rumor had it Delilah had been there. Some said she had played a bigger part in the exchange than just as a bystander. She wasn't a Bane. But, as for what she actually was, that remained a mystery.

Her lips parted in a grin that must have helped the sun rise this morning. A warm river of joy flowed through me, and I glanced away.

"I might," she laughed. She hung the strap around her neck and strummed the guitar. Finding it in tune, she set up a rocking, choppy rhythm. She kept that up with her strumming hand as her left hand flew over the neck and evoked a melody that was at once mournful, bluesy, and fiery. Within a few seconds, we were clapping our hands in time to her playing.

"Sound familiar?" I whispered to him.

"What?" He whispered back. His eyes remained glued to the up and down strikes of her rhythm hand. Good, I thought. He would remember this.

With a final run of notes up the neck, Delilah finished on a couple staccato bursts.

We applauded.

"As always, D, you are amazing." I thanked her. "But now, we've got to run."

"You mean you aren't going to play something for me?" She indicated the piano again.

"Next time," I said. "We need to get back to get his brother ready for bed."

"All right," Delilah purred. "But you owe me a song, Eveningstar."

I stilled and nodded. If Delilah thought you owed her a debt, you paid it. I'd need to come back and play for her, if I knew what was good for me. We said our goodbyes.

"Okay," I said. "We have one more stop."

When we reached our destination, I opened the doorway. Two round, hammered copper sinks and a tall, ornate mirror greeted us. A mint plant in a terra-cotta pot sat on a cabinet.

"Not again," Tariq groaned. "Do we always have to come in and out in the bathroom?"

"Yes, we do." I answered. "It's the safest and easiest way. It's because-"

"I know, I know. No one ever pays attention to who's been in the bathroom. But I've got news for you, Evie. People will notice if a guy comes out of the ladies room. I promise you. They'll notice."

I rolled my eyes at him and waved him ahead of me. He pushed the door open and looked left and right before he slid out into the hallway.

The long hall opened into the main listening room. Small, round tables and rickety chairs dotted the space. The walls were constructed of bare, hard wood panels. A few signed photographs of some of the Blues' greatest artists hung along one wall. The bar took up the entire length of the other side of the room. No one except us and the wizened bartender were in residence. His white hair curled tightly to his mocha-colored skin. His shoulders stooped, but his hands raced as he lined beer glasses on the back counter. A tiny raised stage sat at one end of the bar. An even smaller upright, baby grand piano sat tucked away in the corner. Tariq lagged behind me and went to study the photos as I moved forward.

"Hey Earl," I greeted the man behind the bar.

He turned milky brown eyes on me, and his face split into a grin.

"Well, look at what the cat dragged in," he dried his hands on a towel hanging from his waist and made his way around the bar. He enveloped me in a giant hug. "Been a while," he said.

"Sure has," I answered. I turned to Tariq and motioned him forward.

"Earl, I would like to introduce you to Tariq. He's a player, and he's good."

"Tariq, I'd like to introduce you to Earl Tate, one of the best Blues players ever born."

"Now, don't you go saying all that," Earl demurred.

"I can if it's the truth," I arched my brows at him.

"Well, that's a fact," he smiled.

"See, Tariq, there's one thing that's not allowed in this place and that's lying. You lie in here, and you'll pay a price. Isn't that right, Earl?" I asked.

"Sure is," he answered.

"So, as I was saying, Earl is one of the best Blues players you'll ever know."

"Welcome to Club Indigo," Earl extended his hand, and Tariq took it.

"But, aren't you the bartender?" Tariq asked.

"I am, but that doesn't mean I can't also play now and again," Earl said.

I hooked my arm through Earl's and drew him towards the piano. Tariq trailed behind us.

"See, Earl owns this magical place," I said.

"Magical?" Tariq curled one corner of his mouth.

"It sure is." I said. "One of its greatest powers is that anyone who plays this stage sees their true path. And if it's the path of the musician, then the club itself tells everyone who can hear."

"How does it do that?"

"Notice how there aren't any speakers or monitors on the stage?" I asked.

"Yeah," he replied.

"Well, that's because the pros who play here don't need 'em." Earl sat at the piano and played a few chords to warm up. "What do you want me to play?" He asked me.

"Some of that good old time Chicago Blues," I answered.

"So that's where we are?" Tariq whispered to me and hushed as Earl played.

Earl set up a blues rhythm percussion line with his left hand and slid into a rumbling progression with his right hand. As he played, Tariq beat the rhythm on his thighs. Earl finished with a flash.

"Oh yeah," I breathed. "No one plays like you, Earl." I bowed my head. Sure I could play some classical and folk music, but the Blues? I'd never heard a player like Earl.

"Damn!" Tariq cried. "I never heard the piano played like that before."

"Like what?" Earl asked.

"Like it's a drum," Tariq placed a reverent hand on the top of the upright, baby grand.

"The piano is a miracle," Earl smiled at him. "It's a string instrument, and it's a percussion instrument. You want to play, son?" He scooted over and made room for Tariq.

"Yeah, I'll try." Tariq sat. He placed his fingers just above the keys and launched into a souped up version of "Honeysuckle Rose." His fingers flew the length of the keys but then migrated to the right in silent invitation to the master player at his side. Earl joined in and his rhythm complemented the Tariq's syncopations. They melted the old jazz standard into a bluesy, breezy lament and then whirled it up into frenzy of sound. They finished with a flourish.

"You know your stuff," Earl said. "Don't let anyone catch you saying you're not a player."

"Thank you," Tariq replied. They gazed at one another for a long moment.

"I hate to do this, but we've got to go," I stood.

"Come back," Earl invite us. "Someday, you'll play here," he said to Tariq.

My jaw dropped. Earl had never invited me to play here. I knew my stuff, but I wasn't a player like these two were. They were special. A blind man in the dark could see that.

"Thanks, man," Tariq extended his hand and they shook. We said our goodbyes and headed back towards the restrooms. Tariq rolled his eyes at the Ladies room door.

"Okay, okay," I opened the door to the Men's room. We hopped onto the Ley Lines.

"Hold on a sec. I have one more thing to show you." I said as he started walking back the way we had come. I pulled an mp3 player out of my bag and handed him the ear buds.

"I need you to listen to this," I said.

"Okay," he inserted the buds into his ears, and I pressed the Play button.

The unmistakable pattern of "doot, doot, doot, doot," echoed in the cavernous space. Tariq smiled and grooved a little as he listened.

"That's Michael Jackson," he removed the ear buds.

"Yep, That's 'Billie Jean'" I said.

"So, why did I need to listen to it?" He asked.

"Did you hear the rhythm of the song?"

"Sure," he beat the staccato rhythm on his thighs.

"Does it sound familiar?"

"It sounds like the rhythm the Baba played in Senegal," he cried, astonished.

"Yep, and doesn't it also sound like the song we heard in Santo Domingo?" I tapped that rhythm on my own thighs. He joined me.

"Yeah, it's the same," his eyes were bright.

"And what about the stuff Delilah played?" We tapped the identical rhythm again.

"And in Earl's playing! But how did that happen?" Tariq asked.

"And isn't that the question," I replied. "How do you think it happened? How did that same rhythm get from Africa to the Dominican Republic?"

"I dunno. I guess people must have brought it with them when they traveled."

"Who were those people?"

He froze. He raised his eyes to mine.

"Slaves," he said.

"Slaves," tears slid down my face in sorrow for all those who had suffered. "The people who were captured and taken from their homes to this part of the world on the Slave Routes brought their music with them. They suffered unbearably. Many died. But they kept their music alive. You can hear it in the music of the West Indies and in the Delta Blues of New Orleans, and even in the Chicago Blues Earl played. And it stayed alive all the way to Michael Jackson. And it will go on and on. That's how important music is to all of us, to history, to time itself."

"Wow!" he whispered.

"Yeah, wow," I continued. "They showed great courage in unbelievably hard situations. They were warriors and survivors. They were incredibly brave to play music and to keep it alive, no matter what. So I don't want to hear you say that music is for pussies ever again. Okay?"

"Okay," he breathed. He lowered his head, and we stood together in silence.

I swiped at my eyes to remove the twin streams of tears.

"We should head back," I said.

The girls' bathroom of the Youth Center materialized around us. Tariq stayed silent about my choice of egress location. I hoped it was because he had some things to think about. Making music wasn't for cowards, and he was a natural. I hoped he would grow into his potential and bring his incredible gift to the rest of the world. Ooh, that gave me an idea!

The sound of giggles and drumming floated towards us from the music room.

"What have we here?" I asked. Shane, Calvin, and Professor Weingart were banging out raucous rhythms and grinning like they were all six years old.

Tariq and I grabbed drums and joined them. For a few minutes, we made a joyful noise.

"What a delight," the Professor cried when we finished. "I can't recall the last time I had such fun." She shook Calvin's hand. "And you, young man, have a great gift for rhythm."

"Thank you, Professor Weingart," Calvin replied.

"Oh my stars," she cried. "Only my students call me that. Please call me, Edith."

Edith, huh? I wasn't sure I'd heard anyone call her that. Ever. She was always Professor Weingart or the Professor. Even the other professors at Juilliard called her, "Professor."

Tariq touched his little brother on the shoulder.

"How are you doing?" He asked.

"I'm good," Calvin answered.

"I'm well," Tariq corrected him automatically.

"Shane and me had fun," Calvin continued as if Tariq hadn't interrupted.

"Shane and I had fun," Tariq corrected him again.

"No you didn't, because you weren't here," Calvin giggled, and we all joined him.

"Not that I'm not happy to see you, Professor, but what are you doing here?" I asked.

"I came by to see your program," she replied. She looked around the room at the few ragged instruments I had been able to gather.

"It seems that you need some help outfitting this music program," she began.

"Don't I know it!" I sighed.

"Joanna mentioned her idea of holding a benefit for this music program." She continued.

"Yes, but I don't know the first thing about doing that," I moped.

"Eveningstar," she chided. "You surprise me. I've never known you to give up on anything. But, here, I'd suggest you might need a little help."

"Would you help me, Professor?" I raised my eyes to hers.

"Of course. This is an excellent cause, and I am sure we can rally many to it," she answered. She removed a small, filigreed notebook and matching pen out of her smart, gray bag. "Now, we will need a location, a caterer, volunteers, publicity, attendants, donors, and entertainment," she jotted.

"Speaking of entertainment, I have the perfect headliner," I said.

"Well, you are certainly gifted enough," the Professor looked up from her notebook.

"Oh no," I jumped up and walked over to the piano. I opened the key guard and ran my fingers along the keys. "I wasn't thinking of myself. I was thinking it should be a local. It should be one of the people who uses the Center."

"An excellent idea," she agreed. "Who did you have in mind?"

"I think Tariq should do it," I crooked my finger at him to join me at the piano bench.

"Oh no," he retreated. "No way. I'm not playing piano in front of anybody."

"Remember what you learned on our little excursion," I reminded him. "Music isn't for wussies. Professor," I turned to her. "You should hear him play. He's magnificent. Come on, Tariq," I hoped I didn't sound like I was goading him. But, if the Professor liked what he did, it would open a world of doors for him and not just because of the Benefit.

He glared at me with narrowed eyes. He was pissed, and I couldn't care less. I was gambling on his raw talent winning over the Professor.

He shuffled towards the piano and sat at the bench. He placed his hands on the keys and launched into fiery version of "It Don't Mean a Thing If It Ain't Got That Swing." He took us on a roller coaster ride through the peaks and valleys of the song. Shane, the Professor, and I all gaped. Calvin patted his thighs in time to the music. Tariq soared up the keyboard in an arpeggio that took our breath away and then rumbled down the bass line with a tip of the hat to "Take The A Train" at the very end. The kid loved his Duke Ellington. He rolled the song to a stop on a chord that had us up and cheering.

"Yeah, baby, yeah!" I shouted.

"Well done, you," Shane agreed.

The Professor gazed at Tariq. "You have a gift - one that should be nurtured," she praised.

"Thank you," Tariq replied.

"You're both special," she eyed them. "We're going to figure out how to help you."

I raised my hands in a subtle gesture of victory. I had hoped to get the Professor interested in Tariq's talent. But she looked like she was interested in both of them, and this might prove even better.

"And now, who's hungry?" the Professor asked.

"I am!" The boys shouted in unison.

"Pizza for everyone," she cried. "Put away the instruments, and we'll go."

The boys and Shane set about straightening the room. The Professor turned to me.

"You've convinced me, Evie," she said. "We will hold a benefit for this place, and I will figure out how to help these boys." She put a hand on my arm. "Do you know their situation?"

"Um, no." I was sure I looked guilty.

"Calvin told me their grandmother died months ago. Their brother Jerome left shortly before then. They have had no adult in their lives who could care for them long-term, until now."

"Oh, no, Professor. I'm no Mom," I backed away from her.

"Although I'm sure you care about them, you have other responsibilities. I was referring to myself."

"You?" I'd never thought of her as a motherly type, but that showed how little I knew.

"Yes, I've been thinking it's time I made some changes to give back a little for the blessings I've had. These two boys have given me the perfect opportunity. If they want me in their lives."

"How could they not, Professor?" I threw my arms around her.

"I hope you are correct, Evie," she smiled. "Shall we go eat?" She asked to a chorus, "Oh yeahs," from Shane and Tariq. They followed her towards the door.

I looked at Calvin. He stood frozen in place and stared towards the ceiling.

"Are you okay, sweetie?" I asked him.

"Yes. I'm okay." He answered. He shook his head and shrugged.

"Calvin, were you daydreaming again?" Tariq asked. "He does that all the time. Our grandma said he was thinking big thoughts," he explained. He took his brother's hand. "Come on, Calvin. We're having pizza. Edith said we could have any toppings we want."

Calvin's eyes lit up. He skipped to the door with Tariq.

"I want pineapple and strawberries on my pizza," he called to the Professor.

"Man, I don't think pizza is a dessert. You don't put strawberries on pizza."

"You might not, but I do," Calvin declared, and Tariq laughed.

"You got it, little brother." They left the room.

I looked at where Calvin had been staring. I saw nothing.

"Hey, wait for me," I yelled as I ran to catch up. "I want pizza too."

CHAPTER 23

DANIEL

The sidewalk retained the day's warmth. Waves of heat radiated off it as Daniel prowled through the Bronx neighborhood. He wore ratty jeans, an old t-shirt, and for once his ever-present camera was not with him. He ran his hands along the stubble on his cheeks and mussed up his hair. He approached the faded brick tenement building in the gathering darkness. The metal front door had once been a sign of security. It now stood open and unhinged. He found apartment 2G, turned the knob, and shuffled through.

"Who the hell are you? What you want?" The young man at the lab table pulled a gun out of his waistband and trained it on Daniel sideways. Daniel glanced at the gun and then ignored it. He looked past the man to the table. It contained three balances, numerous plastic bags, and large packets of a white powdery substance.

That's not Heaven, Daniel noted.

"Hey, man," Daniel slurred his words. He hoped he sounded vacant enough to pass for an addict. "Mario told me to come here."

"Mario told you?" The guy pulled a phone out of his pocket with his free hand.

"Yeah, man. He told me you had a way to get me a 'little slice of Heaven.'" He used the code word his contact had given him and prayed it was enough.

"So, if I call Mario, he gonna tell me he knows you?"

"Yeah, man."

"Call Mario," the man spoke into his smartphone. After a few rings, a rough voice came on the line.

"What you doing sending people to me?" The man said without preamble. He listened as the man on the other end spoke.

"You sure he ok?" He asked and listened again.

"All right." He hung up and lowered his gun.

"Why you didn't tell me you the one who fixed Mario's computer? He's been talking about that for days." He stashed his gun in waistband.

"I didn't think it was necessary," Daniel answered.

"Well, it was necessary, 'cause see, I need some help with my iPad," he pulled an iPad out of a backpack at his feet and held it out to Daniel.

"What's wrong with it?"

"If I knew that, man, I'd fix it my own self. I'd take it in, but it has some 'sensitive information' on it, and I don't need anyone else up in my business. You know what I mean?"

"Sure," Daniel sent a quick prayer that he would be able to fix the tablet. He pressed the button and turned it on. He handed it back as the password prompt appeared.

"Ah crap, man, I don't remember what it is now," the young man tried several combinations until one worked. He returned it to Daniel.

"So, everything comes up," Daniel examined the iPad's apps and everything looked normal.

"Yeah, man, but look at my iTunes app," the guy whined. "You press it, and the music doesn't come on. And I need my tunes, man."

Daniel tried the app and it froze in place. Pressing songs or any of the other active parts of the app produced no result. Daniel smiled. He had limited experience with iPads, but he knew how to fix this problem. He held the button combination that performed a hard reset on the iPad. The iPad dutifully shut down and restarted. After the password had been entered again, Daniel pressed iTunes and hit a random song. Pink Martini's, "Amado Mio," poured out of the speaker.

Daniel raised his eyebrows in question.

"Hey, man. Pink Martini is great!" the guy responded to the unspoken question. "Just listen to that piano. That Thomas Lauderdale can play!"

The piano. Something tickled the back of Daniel's mind. There was something about the piano. He shook his head to clear it and placed the fleeting thought aside. He would unpack it later. He listened to the song until it finished, and appreciated both the interplay of musicians and the singer's powerful yet lilting vocals.

"So, what you want?" the guy returned his iPad to his backpack and studied Daniel.

"I need some Heaven," Daniel replied.

"Naw, man. I ain't got any Heaven. I got blow and crank, but none of that blue shit," he said.

"When will you be getting some in?" Daniel asked.

"Rumor has it a big shipment will be coming in a couple of weeks," he said. He resumed stacking small plastic bags of cocaine while he talked. He paused and gazed at Daniel. "Why you so interested in that stuff? It's so new ain't nobody even tried it," he said.

"I have," Daniel said.

"Is it good shit?" he asked.

"It's like nothing you've ever experienced," Daniel couldn't bank the quake in his voice. They both paused for an instant and acknowledged Daniel's fear and addiction.

"I'm Teddy," the guy passed Daniel a card with his phone number. "Call me in two weeks, and we'll do business. And since you fixed my iTunes, I'll even give you a discount."

"Thanks, Teddy," Daniel pocketed the card and left the apartment. Once outside, he called Tommy.

"It's in two weeks, Tommy," he spoke into the phone. "The shipment will be here in two weeks."

"That doesn't give us a lot of time," Tommy said on the other end of the line.

"No, but it will have to be enough," Daniel answered. If what he had experienced was a tiny dosage, the possibility of a large supply of the drug filled him with dread.

"Are you coming back to the office?"

"Not yet," Daniel walked towards the subway stop. "I'm going to get a workout in before I come back." They said their goodbyes and ended the call.

Adrenaline coursed through his system. He needed to work some of it off, and the YMCA had a 24-hour a day policy for members.

He let himself into the building with a code and made his way towards the training room. He donned a pair of loaner gloves and worked the large hanging body bag. His punches echoed in the empty room. He jabbed, hooked, and crossed, up and down the bag. He had not yet learned any of the kicks that might work in a street fight, but Wisteria had promised to show him a couple the next time they had a private lesson. Sweat poured off him in rivulets. He paused and rubbed his eyes with his forearms to dry his face.

"Not bad," a voice behind him said. He whirled around and crouched into a ready stance.

"Not bad at all," Wisteria nodded once from the doorway and approached him. She wore black gloves and her customary black tank top and pants. Her fiery red hair was tamed in its usual long braid.

They moved to the boxing ring-size mat that covered the center of the floor. They both crouched in ready stance. At a signal from her, they sparred. For a while, the only sounds in the room were the soft squeaks of their footwork and his grunts when Wisteria landed one or other punch. With each increasing smack, his anger grew. He watched for an opening.

She gave him none. He rushed her with a fast punch. She ducked his right cross and came back with a jab to his jaw. His head rocked back. He shook it off and came at her with a flurry of punches to the body. She avoided most of his punches. She flashed out with one hand and dropped him. He sprawled on the mat and tried to calm the stars that floated at the edges of his vision.

"Don't lash out so quickly," she instructed him. "You reaction times are good, and you're an amazingly quick study, but you're fighting angry and fighting angry gets you killed." She extended her hand. He hooked a hand around her forearm and sprang back up.

"Again," he said.

"No, you're too pissed." Wisteria answered.

"I am pissed. I have a right to be pissed," Daniel prowled the mat like an angry leopard.

"That may be, but anger has no place in combat. Your mind has to be clean, peaceful. We've gone over this before. You have to stop and breathe." Wisteria stood still and closed her eyes.

"Breathe, my ass! Do you have any idea what's going on in this city?"

She didn't answer him for what seemed like a decade. Her breathing steady, she resembled a Botticelli statue more than a lethal martial arts expert.

"I do," she finally said. "And I understand your being angry, but acting out in that anger and aggression won't get you what you want."

"It might," Jordan entered the room. "It just might," she repeated.

"What are you doing here?" Wisteria snarled.

"You said the gym is open 24/7 to members so I came to train." She glanced from Wisteria to Daniel. "And if you don't want to spar with him, I will."

Wisteria pressed her lips together and gave a curt nod.

"Remember," she said to Daniel. "Don't fight pissed." She loosened the Velcro on her gloves and left the room.

"Ah, alone at last," Jordan grinned. As she stretched her arms behind and rolled her shoulders, her tight white body suit accentuated her every curve.

"Did you mean it when you said we could spar? I know you're a lot better than I am. I'm not sure I'll be able to give you a good workout." Daniel tried to keep his mind on his training.

Jordan trailed her eyes along his body. Her eyes slowed at his hips and then came to rest at his troubled brown eyes.

"Oh, I think you could give me a great workout," she purred. She donned her own crimson gloves and stood opposite him on the mat.

"Begin," she whispered.

He attacked with a few furious jabs. She deflected them. He grappled and attempted an uppercut combination. She evaded him.

"Come on, Daniel, is that all you've got?" she goaded.

He attacked with a hook and cross combination. She pivoted so he overbalanced and landed on the mat.

"Dammit!" He pounded the mat in frustration.

Jordan laughed and her high, pert breasts strained against her tight suit. His eyes traveled down her trim waist to her rounded hips and along her lean, fighter's legs. He crooked his lips in a lopsided grin. He swung out with a low roundhouse kick and knocked her feet out from under her. With a surprised yelp, she fell beside him. He rolled on top of her and pinned her arms above her head with his gloves. They lay intertwined. Her breasts pressed against his chest. He stared at her smiling mouth. Her laughter subsided as she lifted her head and bit his lower lip. He gasped in pain and surprise. She used her tongue to lick clean the drop of his blood on her lips. He lowered his head until he captured her tongue between his teeth. She moaned and moved underneath him. Her hips stroked up and met his hardness.

"You'd better get that thing out, or I'll do it for you," she whispered.

He smiled.

"You don't believe in taking your time?" He asked as he removed his gloves and shirt.

"Not about this," she panted. She lowered her hands began removing her own gloves.

"No," he commanded. "Leave them on."

She raised an eyebrow but complied.

He lowered his mouth to her breast and his teeth found her already taught nipple. He bit down, and she cried out. She tried to clasp him to her but her gloved hands slipped off his sweat-slick back.

"Don't move," his voice a harsh whisper he shoved her hands back above her head. With one rough motion, he tore her bodysuit and left her torso naked. He rolled the leggings down until she wore only her gloves and a necklace. Her mocha-colored skin glistened with sweat and lust. He raked his eyes along her length in appreciation.

"You are something," he cupped a full breast and rolled her nipple between his fingers.

She watched him with dark cat eyes. He settled himself on top of her.

"Spread your legs," he said. She obeyed.

"Lift your knees." Again, she obeyed.

He touched his lips to hers in a soft caress and then plunged himself all the way into her in long stroke.

"Oh," she moaned, low and long.

He gripped her hands above her head and moved inside her. She met his thrusts with her own. They mated in a fury of motion. His vision hazed as he pounded into her. Something felt off. He thought to stop, but his body had other plans. He worked in her until, with a hoarse scream, she wrapped her legs around him and flipped him over until he bucked under her. She rode him high and hard. He reared up and fastened his teeth on her throat. He grabbed her hair and pulled her back under him while his thrusts became deeper. She convulsed under him gripped him with her muscles as her orgasm echoed through the gym. He hardened even more as he approached his own peak. At the last minute he pulled out of her. His hoarse shouts joined hers as he jettisoned.

They quieted until the only sounds in the room were their harsh breaths.

"See?" She lifted a languid arm and ran it along his back. "I told you you could give me a good workout."

Daniel couldn't shake the feeling that he had just done something wrong. He shook his head to clear it.

"What's wrong, lover?" Jordan murmured. "You looked like you had fun. I know I did. So what's up?"

"Nothing," Daniel answered.

"Come on, you can tell me," she nudged him with an elbow.

"I was seeing someone and now I'm not, but …."

"But you feel like you were just unfaithful," Jordan smiled.

"Yeah, I guess I do." Daniel admitted.

"She's not here, and she never has to know about this, does she?" Jordan asked.

"No, I guess she doesn't."

"So, don't worry about it." Jordan said.

Daniel stood and gazed down at her.

"I'm sorry about your bodysuit," he said.

"I'm not." She lazily captured her lower lip between her teeth. "Why don't you get out of here?"

"I think we should clean up, don't you?"

"Oh, I'll take care of it," Jordan promised.

"If you're sure."

"I'm sure."

With one last look at her, Daniel left the room.

Waves of guilt assailed him as he changed into his street clothes. He didn't owe Evie anything he told himself. Hell, he couldn't even remember having dated her. "Shit!" He bit out as he slammed the locker door shut. It didn't matter. He still felt like he had just cheated on the woman he couldn't remember loving.

"How screwed up is that!" He pressed his forehead to the locker. There was nothing he could do about it now. It was done, and he had done it. He hoped that Evie never found out regardless of whether or not he ever regained his memory. They weren't dating. He hadn't cheated on her. But he couldn't shake the feeling that he had cheated and had screwed up something vital.

Jordan laughed as she rolled to standing. She opened her locket and bent to scoop Daniel's fluids into it.

"I don't think so," Wisteria had materialized at the door.

"Oh come on now," Jordan pouted as she straightened. "I screwed him so it's only fair that I get to keep the results."

"You and I both know how powerful sex magic can be," Wisteria circled Jordan.

"Yes, we do, and this is mine," Jordan claimed. She bent one more time to her task

"No, it's not," Wisteria parted her lips in a feral grin. "But you can try to leave with it. That would be fun."

Jordan lifted her Bane eyes and studied the warrior queen for a long moment.

"Fine. It doesn't matter. He had sex with me, and that's powerful enough." She straightened again and moved toward the locker room. A form-fitting, white tailored silk suit materialized on her as she moved. She stepped into a pair of gold and white Jimmy Choo's as she sauntered off the mat.

"And Jordan," Wisteria called after her. "I don't think it would be wise for you to either do that again or let Evie know it happened to begin with. She might be a newbie, but she has a lot of power. I don't think you want her good and pissed at you."

Jordan turned back and cocked her head.

"I thought you said never to fight angry," her smile was wicked.

"Just a word to the wise," Wisteria shrugged.

"Yeah, thanks." Hips swaying, Jordan left the gym.

"Crap!" Wisteria murmured. Evie wasn't her favorite person, but she hadn't deserved this. Daniel would likely feel terrible for having slept with Jordan when he regained his memory, but he had still done it. And at some point, the piper would demand his payment.

Wisteria sighed. She pulled the long, black-handled switchblade that was her wand out of her belt holster. She inscribed a sigil in the air over the detritus of Daniel and Jordan's activities. The mat dissolved and was replaced by a brand new one.

"Who would have thought I'd be reduced to cleaning up after other people's sex acts? How ironic," she murmured. Wisteria had taken a vow of celibacy hundreds of years before so this was a singular experience.

"A little crude but not in accurate," Margaretha appeared beside her. She put her arm around her friend's shoulder.

"What are you doing here?" Wisteria returned the one-armed hug and relaxed into her mentor's embrace.

Mar held her closer for an instant and then pulled away. She paced the length of the sparkling new mat.

"Apparently, things are about to heat up. I heard from Morrick," she referred to the ancient Time Keeper.

"Morrick? Why is It getting involved?"

"I don't know. It wouldn't tell me why. All It said was to get my butt to New York. So, here I am." Mar replied. "Whatever is going on, it's big. Morrick hasn't gotten involved in the affairs of humans for millennia. Even Evie couldn't get it to budge, and she is one of Its favorites."

"Shit!" Wisteria swore.

"No doubt." Margaretha agreed.

CHAPTER 24

ZEKE

Zeke had just returned to his office when Mitchell St. James strode in unannounced. The creases in the slacks of his impeccable Armani suit bent and straightened as he approached Zeke's desk.

"Mr. St. James! What can I do for you?" Zeke rocketed to standing.

"You can fill me in on where we stand." St. James towered over the younger man.

"Everything is on schedule," Zeke supplied. He walked around his desk and stood face-to-face with St. James.

"Have you fixed the drug's manifestation issue?" St. James asked.

"Yes, we have," Zeke answered. "The drug no longer manifests what the user craves. It just makes them think they are getting their hearts' desires."

"Will you need my guinea pig for another test?" St. James asked.

Zeke's stomach roiled at the callous way St. James referred to his daughter, but he kept his face neutral.

"We've tested it," Zeke assured him. "There should be no need of further tests on your daughter. Everything will be ready."

St. James loomed over Zeke. He stuck a pointed finger in Zeke's chest. A sizzling electric current emanated from his finger leaving Zeke's skin blistered where St. James touched him. He did not flinch.

"See that it is," St. James said. He removed his finger.

Zeke clenched his hands into fists to keep from rubbing his chest.

"I promise, Mr. St. James. All will go according to plan," Zeke placated the older man.

St. James stared into his eyes as if he searched for something. Zeke kept his eyes guileless and stared back. The silence lengthened until Zeke was certain a dropped pin would sound like a grenade. He remained still and quiet.

St. James barked out a laugh and dissipated the tension between them.

"Well done, boy," he clapped Zeke on the back and sent him lunging forward. "You might have some balls on you yet."

"Thank you, sir." Zeke put the obsequious smile into his eyes, and St. James bought it.

"Make sure we are set for the Saturday before July fourth." St. James commanded. "I have a gala to attend and that will give me perfect cover. None of this must ever be traced back to me or to us." He leaned down and drew his face close to Zeke's. "Am I clear?"

"Crystal clear, sir." Zeke said.

"Make sure that nothing gets left to chance," St. James said. "You know many were against you being trusted with such a complex campaign, but I vouched for you. I would hate to lose faith in you."

"No, sir. You won't have to sir." Zeke practically groveled.

After St. James left his office, Zeke walked to his glass-encased violin. He stroked the glass as softly as he would his lover's face. As a Bane, he had been required to give the Order everything. He had given them his biggest fears and his greatest loves. His love had been the music he coaxed from this one instrument. The punishment of seeing it but being unable to play it lashed him with exquisite pain. His fingers quivered with the desire to touch his instrument and then curled into impotent fists upon the glass. He gathered calm around him like a warm blanket. While he ached to play his violin, it was only his second love. His first love he had managed to keep from the Order. And until he was ready, he would remain vigilant.

He shut his eyes and pictured the bottles of Heaven he had purloined. They would remain hidden until he was able to use them. He imagined the power he would yield, and his body shimmered with an indigo light. If he did this right, St. James would soon be calling him sir, and he would have everything he wanted.

"Soon," he whispered to the empty space. "Soon."

He thought of Evie. She was the reason for all of this. Damn her.

The alarm he had placed on her, when she accessed magic, triggered again when she showed her true self to those boys. He scratched his head at her stupidity, but at least she was reliably stupid. She always thought with her heart and not her head and that would work to his advantage. He had hightailed it to the Youth Center. If nothing else, until he was ready, he would keep tabs on her.

He had followed her and Tariq across the ocean. He had watched them play and raised his eyebrows at the knowledge she imparted to him. She had some brass ones teaching a human about how much power music could give to the music maker. He had not realized she and Tariq were so chummy. That would help his ultimate plan.

When they returned to the music room at the Youth Center, he had stayed to watch. Cloaked from them, he had perched on a light fixture.

As they readied to leave, Tariq's brother had gazed up at him.

Evie approached the child.

"Are you okay, sweetie?" She asked him.

He answered in the affirmative, but when he nodded his eyes had met Zeke's.

After Calvin left, Evie stared at Zeke's location. His cloak held, and she saw nothing. She shrugged and hurried out of the room.

Zeke shook himself out of his reverie and smiled. It was good to know that he had even a little power left where she was concerned. And Tariq and Calvin would give him even more. He would need every advantage if his plan was going to work.

"It will work," he pounded on the unbreakable glass case that held his beloved violin. "It has to work."

DANIEL

"You did what?" Tommy reared back in his chair at the NewsBlitz office. He winged his arms back and forth until he righted himself.

Daniel sighed. He wasn't proud of what he had done. He would have talked to an old friend, but those were hard to come by right now since he had no idea who they were. Tommy had proven himself trustworthy more than once. Daniel had to trust someone, or he would implode.

"I had sex with Jordan, one of the women from the gym."

"Good for you," Tommy cried. "It was bound to happen sooner or later, and now it has." Tommy paused and cocked his head to the side. "Did you remember what to do?"

"What do you mean did I remember what to do? Of course I remembered what to do."

"Are you sure? I mean, did you ask her if she had a good time? Did she ask for your digits? Was she just being kind or were you really up to snuff?"

"She screamed when she came, so I guess I was." Daniel had the grace to blush.

"You are such a bad boy," Tommy crooked his finger. "It's even more surprising that anyone was willing to sleep with you in your tiny little place."

"We weren't there," Daniel's blush turned crimson. He sat in his chair and faced his friend.

"Oh?"

"We were at the YMCA."

Tommy toppled out of his chair and convulsed with laughter on the floor.

"Okay, okay, enough." Daniel dropped his head in his hands.

"Oh no. That's not nearly enough. I thought it was only people who play for my team who got it on at the Y-M-C-A." He mimed the letters with his arms in reference to the song.

"I guess they're not," Daniel smiled. His smile dimmed, and he quieted.

"So what's the problem?" Tommy asked.

"I keep feeling like I cheated." Daniel admitted.

"Wait a minute," Tommy rolled to standing in one fluid motion. He righted his chair and sat. "Are you talking about you and Evie? Look, sweetie. You're not dating her. Not to sound all blunt and everything but hell, you don't even remember her. So, how could you have cheated?"

"But if I did remember her, I would have been cheating." Daniel ran his fingers through his hair in frustration.

"Yes, but if you remembered her, you wouldn't have been with Jordan in the first place, so you wouldn't have been cheating that way either." Tommy pointed out.

"How do I know that?" Daniel yelled in exasperation. "How do I know the kind of person I was? I might have been a liar and a cheat and an asshole. I have no idea."

"Listen," Tommy put his hands on Daniel's shoulders and stared into his eyes. "I didn't know you all that long before you lost your memory, but you didn't strike me as a cheater or an asshole. Trust me, I have a good nose for those, and you aren't one. I think the fact that you're even worried about it, shows that you're no asshole."

Daniel smiled.

"And besides," Tommy continued. "There's no guarantee that you'll ever get your memory back so you might as well move on, you know?"

Daniel sobered.

"I'm sorry, man." Tommy said.

"No, you're right. I might never get it back," Daniel agreed. "So, I'd better just live the life I have now. To that end," he sat in his chair and swiveled it to face his computer. "Let's get back to work."

"What do we know?" Tommy angled down to see his monitor.

"There's going to be a big shipment of Heaven released on the streets in two weeks, according to my source." Daniel said.

"Do you trust your source," Tommy asked as he flipped his phone out of his pocket.

"As much as I can. At least, he had no particular reason to lie about it," Daniel answered.

"Good enough. So, if we can figure out exactly where and when, we can be there …."

"And stop it," Daniel finished.

Tommy glanced at him sharply. He dialed a number on his phone.

"Okay," he said as the phone rang. "You hit the streets, and I'll hit up my contacts, and we'll see what we can dig up."

"Done," Daniel stood, gathered his equipment and left the office. He would do whatever he could to stop a large-scale release of Heaven. He had tried to seem at peace with his situation to everyone around him, but he hated not knowing who he was. Of all people, he might have talked with Evie about it because he felt like he could trust her, but since he'd slept with Jordan even that avenue was cut off to him.

"Damn," he swore as he stepped into the lightening skies of a New York City dawn. "This is going to suck."

CHAPTER 25

EVIE

I lugged another box of crystal vase centerpieces inside and wiped the sweat from my eyes. I leaned against the 20 other boxes I had already loaded in and gazed at the chaos that was once the music room.

Looking cool and coifed as always, Professor Weingart entered the room carrying a huge bundle of silk ribbons. She set them down and surveyed the room.

"It looks like we have almost everything we need. We'll need to pick up the flowers the day of the gala, but the florist is right near the venue so that will work very well."

"Professor, how did you manage to book the Grand Ballroom at the Plaza for the gala?" I raised my brows in question.

Let's just say that the event Coordinator at the Plaza and I have a relationship. Her son may have had a private lesson or two in piano performance," she grinned.

"Does he want to go to Juilliard?" I asked.

"Oh no. David is a rock and roller all the way. In fact, Billy Joel is his hero. He is determined to take the rock music world by storm, and I helped him get started."

"You know rock music?" I gasped.

"Why yes, Evie. I am an aficionado of music of every sort."

"Of course you are," I grinned.

She opened one of the boxes and held the royal blue and gold ribbons up to it.

"Yes, this will do very well." She turned to me. "Although we were able to procure the room, they could not spare the food or decorations. Those we will need to see to ourselves."

"I don't know about you, but I'm no cook." I shook my head.

"And you will not have to be. Tully has graciously offered his and his staff's services for the event. They will close for the day and work the gala."

"That Tully," I grinned. "He's a peach."

She smiled in agreement and produced a small notebook from her gray bag. She flipped through a few pages.

"Now, then, about the guest list. I realize it is short notice, but it is the weekend before July 4th so everyone might still be in town." She wrote a few lines in the book. "And besides this is for an excellent cause, so I am certain we will get a good turnout. We will have the Carltons, the Winchesters, the De Felizes, the Solomons, and the Whittingtons, and all their entourages. We have yet to hear from the Hastings, the St. James family, the Northrups, and the Guitton families, but I'm sure they will reply in the affirmative. All in all, this thousand dollar a plate evening should net us a tidy sum for the Center."

"You are a miracle worker," I said. I carted the boxes to a corner of the room and stacked them. I was no interior decorator and my aesthetic ran to, "Don't live in a pig sty," but I could lug stuff around with the best of them.

"Evie, will you be inviting Daniel to the gala?" She asked it delicately.

THE PIANO'S KEY

I paused in my heavy lifting and leaned against the boxes once again.

"Honestly, Professor, I don't know." I knocked on my head with my fist. "Wait a minute, what the heck am I talking about? Of course, we should invite him. But ...." I stumbled to a stop.

"But you are concerned he won't come?"

"Yes, but I still think should invite him." I squared my shoulders.

"I definitely think you should invite me," a familiar voice announced from the doorway.

"Mar!" I ran to her and threw my arms around her. "What are you doing here?"

"I heard you needed a bartender for your shindig," Margaretha entered the room followed by Wisteria.

I pulled Mar over to the Professor and made the introductions.

"Mar is the best bartender on this or any planet," I stated.

Two of the most important women in my life exchanged pleasantries. The Professor turned to Wisteria and extended a hand.

"I'm Edith Weingart," she said.

"Wisteria Flamethrower," Wisteria introduced herself as the two shook hands.

"I'll be the bouncer," Wisteria offered.

"I'm not sure we will need a bouncer at the Plaza," the Professor said.

"You'd be surprised," Wisteria settled herself on one of the chairs. Although her lithe form appeared relaxed, she still resembled a cheetah about to strike.

"And if I may, you look more like someone who stepped out of a Pre-Raphaelite painting than you do a bouncer," the Professor said.

"Looks can be deceiving," came the reply.

A smile played along the Professor's lips. "I'm certain," she said. "Now," she clapped her hands. "We have a great deal of work to do to prepare, so let us begin."

Over the next two weeks, we all worked our tails off, perhaps no one more so than Tariq. Every time I turned around, he was in the music room practicing his pieces. More often than not, Calvin was seated on the floor nearby coloring, or rather re-coloring some superhero vanquishing villains. After the third day I found them waiting for me to open the room for them, I gave Tariq a key.

The morning before the gala, I entered the music room to a souped up version of, "Mood Indigo." Tariq's fingers flew over the keys as he coaxed blinding speed, syncopated nuance, and an intricate rhythm from the typically contemplative and melancholy piece. Then, just when I thought he could go no faster, he hit a dissonant, lifting chord and stilled. I raised to tiptoe as I waited with bated breath for his resolution. The echoes of the chord bounced around the room like after images of sun glare. He waited. My fingers itched to strike the next chord, but I remained frozen in place. This wasn't mine to complete. It was his. He left me hanging on the musical precipice for a good five seconds.

After an interminable wait, he touched the keys in a soothing and sad final chord. He played it without ornamentation as the culmination of a roller coaster ride through that well-known Duke Ellington song. A part of his genius lay in the fact that he knew none of the rules. I didn't think he would have cared about them if he had known them. But this way, his interpretations evolved from his imagination.

"Wow!" I breathed.

Tariq started and turned to me. A shy smile crossed his face, but he said nothing.

"That was fantastic." I walked to the piano. "I haven't heard you play 'Mood Indigo' like that before. Is this new?"

"Yeah," he answered. "I was playing around with it to see if it worked. I think it does. It's going to be my last song tomorrow night."

"You're going to blow them away!" I enthused.

"Where's Calvin?" I asked.

"He's with the Professor," Tariq answered. "She wanted to take us both to the High Line, but I wanted to practice. So they went by themselves."

"Are you okay with that?" I set my packages on one of the tables and sorted them as we talked.

"Yeah, of course." He closed the key guard and stood from the piano. He helped me stack the bidding cards for the silent auction we would be holding during the gala. Several people the Professor knew had donated items for the auction.

Tariq's mobile phone rang. He excused himself and took the call outside. For a couple of seconds, I tried not to eavesdrop, but I gave up the pretense of being virtuous and craned my neck and ears towards the door.

"No, sir," Tariq said. The couple of sentences were too muffled for me to hear. Then he said, "Yeah, I'll be there."

"I've got to take off, Evie." He returned to the room. "Sorry, I can't help anymore."

"It's all right," I answered. Truth was, his help was slowing me down. As soon as he left, my wand and I would finish both the sorting and the stacking of every single piece of paper in the room. I took a closer look at his face. Something felt off.

"Are you okay?" I asked him.

"I'm fine. I've just got some stuff to take care of," His eyes slid away from mine. He looked at a point past me as he answered. "I'll see you tomorrow." He said as he walked towards the door.

"You know if you need anything you can just ask me, right?" I tugged on his arm to turn him around.

"I know," he said. "But this is something I've got to do myself." He smiled at me and left.

I pursed my lips in thought. He was a genius in music. He was a fantastic older brother to Calvin. He was incredibly brave since the death of their grandmother. But he was a rotten liar.

My phone broke out with "Toccata and Fugue in D Minor."

"Go for Evie," I sang into it.

"Evie, it's Rose Brader," Mama Brader's voice came across the metaphorical line. "We seem to have run into a challenge. And I was hoping you could help."

"What's up, Mama?" I asked.

"It's the freezer space at the Plaza. It seems they have insufficient space for the desserts." Mama and her crew had donated their time and ice creams as the culinary piece de Resistance for tomorrow night. "We need to, er generate more space, just for the next twenty-four hours. If we can't do that, I'm afraid the ice cream will be useless. So, if you could help by increasing the storage space for a little while …."

Ah, I gave a great nod. Mama knew what I was or at least she knew that I was capable of 'generating' space. I'd always wondered. Now, I knew.

"Got it. I'll be right there," I grabbed my bag and headed out. I rushed for few things in this world. Mama Brader's ice cream? Yeah, saving it was a priority.

CHAPTER 26

TARIQ

Tariq entered the warehouse space through a small side door. He was happy that the Professor had been willing to look after Calvin while he ran his 'errand.' If she had been unwilling or unable, he would have had to skip the meeting because he would rather die than have Calvin anywhere near any of this.

He made his way into the main chamber of the warehouse. Several large jar-like containers sat on the two tables in the center of the space. Each was filled with the blue powdery substance known as Heaven. Tariq knew it was a drug of some sort, but he had not heard about what it did.

Darnell and the others were already present. Darnell lit up a cigarette and made smoke rings as he exhaled.

"Put that out," Zeke ordered as he appeared in the room.

Darnell complied and stuck his hand out.

"Hey man. How you doin'?" Zeke walked past him to take position in front of the tables that held the drug, and addressed them.

"As you can see, the supply has arrived," he stated. "You will each get a jar to disperse in your assigned locations.

Darnell, you will disperse it at Time's Square station. Johnny T, you will be at Time's Square above ground. Tariq, you will handle Grand Central Station." Zeke handed out the rest of the assignments. He opened his laptop, pressed a few keys and the architectural plans for the Time's Square subway station projected onto the wall of the warehouse.

"Now, we're going to go over these plans for each of the locations. Johnny T, you will have an easy task since you can be anywhere in Time's Square. The rest of you will need to memorize your set of plans and the instructions to get to your dispersal spot." Zeke pointed to the gym equipment. "We chose you for this because of your physical abilities, and you've all been training hard. You'll need that training in order to pull this off." He handed each young man a surgical mask and a single sheet of paper. "These are the steps to priming the Heaven. Once you're at your spot, you will follow these instructions exactly. If you do anything wrong or out of order, the drug will be neutralized and will be useless." He looked at each one in turn. "Trust me," he said. "You don't want to make that mistake. Our boss would not be pleased."

"How will we know if we did it exactly right?" Tariq asked.

"If the powder stays blue and falls to the ground, you did it wrong. If it becomes transparent, you did it right." Zeke answered. "Now," he continued. "Let's go over the steps to priming the drug." He took them through a series of physical steps and phrases they would need to say, drilling them until the actions were second nature.

"How we supposed to say this shit wearing these stupid masks?" Darnell pulled his surgical mask off and snapped its rubber band.

"You don't wear it, you'll be exposed to the Heaven," Zeke answered. "I don't care if you do that. Just don't do it until after you have completed all of the steps."

"Hey, getting exposed to a good new drug would be Ace," Darnell grinned.

Zeke narrowed his eyes and studied Darnell for a long moment. "Suit yourself," he murmured.

"Once you've dispersed the entire thing, leave and don't go back. And whatever you do, don't backtrack. You will also want to throw away your shoes and the mask without touching them, unless you're Darnell, who's an idiot." Zeke shrugged.

"Then, what?" Tariq asked.

"Then, nothing. Then, your job is done, and you will get paid," Zeke answered.

"So, we're just spreading the drug out for everyone to get high on?" Tariq asked. "That doesn't make any sense. Unless ... you want to get them hooked." Understanding lit Tariq's eyes.

"The first one's always free," Zeke's lips lengthened into a tight smile.

"So, when we doing this?" Darnell asked.

"Tomorrow night," Zeke replied.

"What? No, I can't," Tariq cried.

"You can't? What, you have some big plans?" Zeke raised his eyebrows.

"I do." Tariq shifted from foot to foot. "I have somewhere I got to be tomorrow night."

"What are you doing that's so important you'd risk not getting paid?" Zeke asked.

"I'm playing piano at a thing, at, um a gala." In that instant, Tariq would have dearly loved for the ground to crack open and swallow him whole.

"And you're playing at this gala tomorrow evening?" Zeke grinned. Then, he laughed. He laughed for what seemed like a long time. Tears streamed down his face as he sobered. "Just to make sure, where is this gala at which you are playing piano?" He made it sound snide.

"At the Plaza."

"Of course," Zeke nodded. "You definitely work in mysterious ways," he murmured to the ceiling.

"So, that's why I can't do this tomorrow."

"Then you don't need to get paid either."

"Fine." Tariq made up his mind. "Don't give me the money for tomorrow night, but give me what you owe for the last two runs I made for you."

"I'm not giving you shit." Zeke appeared in front of him and hoisted him up by his shirt. Tariq's feet dangled a few inches above the floor. "You're going to do this and do it for free." He dropped Tariq. He drew his phone out of a pocket and pressed it on.

"You have a cute little brother," he changed the subject.

"You leave Calvin alone, or I'll …." Tariq rushed towards Zeke.

"Or you'll what?" Zeke waved a hand and everyone else in the room froze in place. Tariq looked at the others for any sort of support, but they remained still and silent. Zeke approached Tariq. "You're going to do exactly what I say and do it perfectly or Calvin will disappear forever."

"What the hell are you talking about?" Fear colored Tariq's voice.

Zeke turned on his phone and showed Tariq a selfie of him and Calvin. They stood together in a darkened room.

"No, he's with the Professor." Tariq whispered.

"And she thinks she returned him to you earlier this evening," Zeke supplied. He opened a video file on his phone and held in front of Tariq's face.

In the video, Tariq saw Professor Weingart and Calvin at the door to the Youth Center as they were about to enter.

"Oh there you are, Tariq," she said towards the camera.

"Hi, Professor. Hi Calvin." Tariq's voice said.

"What the hell!" Tariq watched himself approach them in the video. "That's not me!" He shouted.

"Sure looks like you," Zeke said.

"We had a lovely time at the High Line," the Professor held a small paper bag out to Calvin. He took it, but stared open-mouthed at Tariq.

"Was it fun?" The on-camera Tariq asked.

"It was fun." Calvin answered.

"Well, Professor, Calvin and me, we've got to go," Tariq said.

"Yes, yes, of course," she fluttered her hands and smiled at Calvin. "I had a wonderful time with you today. I hope we get to do it again soon."

"So do I, Professor," he answered. "Thank you."

She left them at the door.

Calvin turned towards the camera.

"You're not Tariq," he said.

"No, I'm not," looking like himself again, Zeke answered.

"But I know you. I saw you before." Calvin narrowed his eyes.

"Yeah, you did. How did you do that?" Curiosity hushed Zeke's voice to a bare whisper.

"Who are you?" Calvin backed up towards the door and put a hand on the handle.

"I'm Zeke. I'm like Evie," Zeke replied.

"No, you're not. Not really. You're more just dark blue. I don't think I like you." Calvin pressed his back against the glass door of the Center.

"My energy is a little different, but underneath, she and I are pretty much the same." Zeke reached for the child. Calvin shrank away from him. Zeke squatted down until he was at eye level with the child.

"Evie and I need your help," Zeke said. "Come with me," he said. "Tariq is in trouble, and he's going to need you."

"Tariq's in trouble?" Calvin's eyes widened.

"Yes, and I need you to come with me so you can help your brother."

"Okay," Calvin placed his small hand in Zeke's, and the two left the Center.

The video ended. Tariq closed his eyes and sent a prayer to his grandmother to watch over Calvin.

"Do we understand each other?" Zeke asked.

Tariq met Zeke's eyes. He drew in a shaky breath.

"Don't hurt my brother," he whispered. "I'll do whatever you want. Just don't hurt him."

"How Calvin comes out of this will be entirely up to you, Tariq," Zeke smiled and slipped the phone back in his pocket. "Now, let's get down to business."

DANIEL

Daniel pressed the "Submit" button on his latest story on resources for homeless people in the five boroughs.

"Hey Tommy," Daniel called. "Where did you learn to edit?"

Tommy entered the small room drying his coffee mug. Coffee bowl was a more fitting description since it more resembled a huge salad bowl than it did any sort of cup. Tommy lived on coffee. Daniel supposed it was his way of keeping himself from reaching for alcohol.

"Believe it or not, I learned in high school," he poured himself a full bowl and plopped down in his chair. "I was the editor-in-chief of an underground paper. One of my teachers got wind of it, found a copy, and decided to help me learn how to edit. And I loved it. Heh, who knew I'd ever love doing anything but drinking and screwing?"

Daniel smiled and remained silent.

Tommy flipped on his monitor and scanned Daniel's latest story. His brow furrowed, and he emptied his cup in one long swallow.

"These are good," Tommy said after he finished his scan. "I think, though, that I want a rewrite on the last two paragraphs. We want people to realize that there's still a homeless population in this city that needs help, but we don't want the story so on-the-nose that they stop reading before your clincher." He pointed to the photo of a woman who stood holding the hand of her daughter. The woman's determined eyes focused on her child with the ferocity of a lioness prepared to defend her cub.

"That's the money shot," Tommy said. "They need to get to that image to understand what's really happening in this city." He slid his chair back a few feet and looked at the monitor. "Damn," he said.

"What?" Daniel asked. "Is something else wrong with the story?"

"No," Tommy replied. "The rest of it is great. I was just thinking that if my father took even ten percent of his net worth and put it towards helping the homeless population, we could get a huge number of these problems addressed."

"Do you think?" Daniel leaned on Tommy's desk and crossed his arms.

"Hell yeah." Tommy stood and paced around the small room. "He could set up food centers. He could fix up the shelters and build low income housing that actually works for the people who live in it. He could start some local business that could increase jobs in the city. And it wouldn't even cost him very much."

As Tommy talked, Daniel picked up a pad and noted the bullet list Tommy had created.

"Then, we could also have job training for younger people too." Tommy slapped the air with his hands to illustrate each point. "And let's not forget about the arts. Kids need to have exposure to art, writing, photography, and music." He ticked each one off on his fingers. "Oh no," he smacked his desk with the same hand.

"What?" Daniel straightened in concern.

"Speaking of music, I forgot I have to go to this thing tonight. My father's going to this fundraising gala and he wants me and Nadia there, too." Tommy's eyes lit up. He pointed to Daniel. "And you're coming with us."

"What? No, I can't," Daniel evaded. "I have to finish this rewrite, and then I have another bunch of ideas I need to develop. Plus, I wanted to spend some time in my dark room, and I can only do that at night."

"Yeah, because your darkroom is your bathroom. Honestly, Daniel. I think you might want to get an actual darkroom space." Tommy angled around the desk and stood next to him. "But, you're not going to get out of this. You should come with us. A, it's at the Plaza, and you can't pass up a chance to go to the Plaza. B, it's for a great cause, a Youth

Center's music program. And C, you need to get out and do something that isn't either work or working out." He eyed Daniel. "Not that it's not doing you good. You look hot." Tommy blew a low wolf whistle.

"I'm not training to look hot," Daniel bristled. "I'm training to know how to defend myself."

"Simmer down, sweetie," Tommy purred. He touched Daniel's forearm. Sympathy shone in his eyes. "I'm just poking a little fun at you."

"Sorry," Daniel sighed and ran his fingers through his hair in frustration. He had not made any sort of peace with what happened to him. "Sometimes, I feel like things will never be normal again," he said.

"Well," Tommy leaned against the desk. "Maybe you need to make this your new normal. And what's more normal than going to the Plaza, eating canapés, and flirting with inappropriate women?"

"That might be normal for you, but that's far from my idea of normal," Daniel laughed.

"My idea of normal would be to flirt with inappropriate men, but you can flirt with the ladies."

"I don't know if I know how to do that stuff," Daniel roamed around the office. He needed a distraction and settled on checking his camera equipment, yet again. He unpacked and repacked it as they talked.

"How do you know until you try? Come on, Daniel. It will do you a world of good to get out of your own head for a little while. What do you say?" Tommy cajoled.

"Okay, okay, I'll go," Daniel acquiesced.

"Excellent!" Tommy raised his arms in a victory salute and handed Daniel a card. "This is my tailor. Call and tell them I sent you, and they'll squeeze you in."

"I have a suit," Daniel said.

"I've seen your suit," Tommy's voice was not unkind. "And while it might work for regular life, it simply won't do for the Plaza. You'll need a tux. It's too late to have them make you one, but you're a pretty standard size so I'm sure they'll have something off the rack for you."

Daniel rolled his eyes but took the card. He sat back at his desk.

"What do you think you're doing?" Tommy cried. "Go, go. They can get you a suit, but they'll need a little time to get it together. They're not miracle workers, you know."

"Okay, okay, I'm going," Daniel laughed and headed towards the door.

"I'll tell them to expect you," Tommy said lifting his phone. When a voice barked at the other end of the line, Tommy said, "You asked me to call, Father." He listened for a few seconds. "Yes, Daniel will be at the gala tonight. I made sure of it. He has no other plans."

He ended the call and dialed a second number.

"Georgio," he crowed. "I have a challenge for you. I've sent him over. No, no, he's beautiful and should be easy to fit. But I need you to make him shine. When? This evening. I know you can do it Georgio. If anyone in the world can do it, it's you." He rang off and slumped in his chair.

"Oh shit!," he leaped back out of his chair and streaked towards the door. "I need to figure out what I'm going to wear."

CHAPTER 27

EVIE

The Plaza Hotel was a New York institution. I still had no idea how the Professor had managed to secure the Grand Ballroom for the gala, and on such short notice, but I wasn't looking into any horses' mouths on this one.

"Wow!" I breathed as we entered the gilded space. Numerous golden arches lifted to filigreed ovals all around the rectangular room. Two enormous chandeliers hung suspended from the ceiling one-third and two-thirds down the space. Their thousands of crystals reflected sparkling rainbows to every corner. The wooden dance floor took up close to two-thirds of the room and a rich magenta and gold carpet covered the rest.

"Nice," Margaretha drawled behind me. She hefted a case of champagne and carried it with ease to the dark wooden bar she had conjured on the side of the room opposite the stage. The stage held my beautiful Baldwin piano from the Youth Center. Yes, I had conjured it here in the dead of night, and no, I wasn't sorry I'd tricked the hotel manager into thinking I'd had someone bring it in the day before. I didn't have money to rent the hotel's piano, and I had too few funds to hire anyone to move mine. This whole new Level 4 FG "Earn it yourself," paradigm was for the birds. While I was willing to do most things according to those antiquated rules, I wasn't about to do it with this gala. We needed all the money we could get to outfit the music room and to throw a little something to the Youth Center, too. The rules could be bent in the service of that. I hoped.

We piled into the room and commenced decorating. The Professor hadn't arrived yet so we had time to fast track some of the work. Mar outfitted the bar with a few flicks of her wand. A variety of bottles of liquor, wines, and liqueurs covered every spare surface. The army of glasses, flutes, and other drink accouterments was lined up in razor straight rows on a temporary counter along the back wall. Ice buckets sat below the front bar.

Round, wood tables were upended and stored against one wall of the space. Wisteria opened them and lugged them in an oval around the dance floor. She could have used magic to do it, but as usual, she took the more arduous path and did it all with muscle. She then unfurled the magenta tablecloths and threw them Frisbee style onto each of the tables. To a one, they billowed out across the room and landed perfectly centered on each table. She gave a crisp nod and started carting chairs around each table. I shook my head at her and got on with my own work.

I suspended silver and crystal instruments a few feet below the ceiling. Crystalline violins, cellos, trumpets and others floated on the room's air currents. A few of the smaller fey in my acquaintance had agreed to come and float inside them for the evening. A couple of titters overhead told me a few had arrived early and had already started dipping into the mead Mar had opened for them. I gazed up at them and sighed. I hoped they wouldn't get too drunk.

The Professor entered carrying several sheafs of paper piled on top of several large cardboard boxes.

"How lovely!" She exclaimed.

"Hey, Professor," I hid my wand in my messenger bag. I rushed over to take the boxes from her. "What are these?" I asked. We walked over to one of the tables Wisteria had not yet surrounded with chairs and laid the boxes on them.

"These are for the silent auction," she answered. "I asked a few of my friends and colleagues to donate some items that might be of interest."

"Are they coming tonight?" I asked.

"Several will be in attendance, I believe." She smiled. "And I have a feeling many might end up bidding on the very things they donated so we might have a war on our hands." She arranged the items into a pleasing array on the table. I left her to her decorating. Composition and aesthetics make me cross my eyes.

A bright spark in one of the chandeliers caught my eye. I walked under it and took my out phone.

"Hey Torlyn," I pretended to talk into the phone. The Fire Elemental above me giggled.

"Hi Evie." She replied. "We're all set up here. We'll get everything started shortly before the guests arrive."

"That sounds great," I continued speaking into the phone while looking up at the chandelier. "It'll be a great surprise for everyone. I'll see you later." I hit my phone's End button.

We all worked until it was time to go and get dolled up for the evening. Everyone except Wisteria was going to glam up. She would wear her customary black and resemble a menacing Dante Gabriel Rossetti painting.

Mar, Wisteria, the Professor, and I gathered in the center of the dance floor.

"It looks great, everyone," I surveyed the ballroom. "I can't thank you enough for everything you're doing for the Youth Center."

"It is our pleasure, Evie," the Professor replied.

"Yes," Mar agreed. She elbowed Wisteria who huffed out a breath.

"Yeah," Wisteria nodded. "This looks pretty good."

I smiled at her and then included everyone else in my grin.

"We're going to rock the house tonight," I shouted.

"And we will not only raise the necessary funds to outfit the music room with instruments and other vital materials, we will have sufficient funds to assist the Center at large." The Professor asserted. "I guarantee it."

We all clapped at her pronouncement and then parted company.

ZEKE

Zeke sat at his desk and pretended to work. He rolled his eyes to the heavens. He pressed his fists against his ears. The constant staccato "Rat-tat tat," of the kid's shoes on the legs of his chair were boring a hole in his skull. The tapping had no rhyme, no reason. If it had been some sort of pattern, Zeke might have ignored it. This kid's sense of rhythm must have come from the trickster gods themselves. Powerless, he craned his ears for the tap. Damn! The wait was excruciating. Zeke's level of tension ratcheted up another notch. The kid tapped on the chair leg and then tapped again. He tapped the famous, "Shave and a hair cut," rhythm, but stopped short of tapping out the "Two bits," part of the rhythm. This is like Roger Rabbit, Zeke thought. Any second now, that crazy, cartoon rabbit would run into the room and yell, "Two bits." Crap! Now, I'm quoting movies like Evie, Zeke thought as he rubbed his eyes.

"Can you stop that?" Zeke muttered to Calvin.

"Can you take me home?" Calvin countered.

"No," Zeke answered. "Not yet."

"Okay," Calvin tapped on the chair.

"Okay, what?" Zeke yelled.

"Now we both have our answer," Calvin's answered. "I'll stop when you can take me home." Frowning, he continued tapping.

The barest tremor vibrated the floor. Zeke's head snapped up. He searched Calvin's face, but the kid seemed oblivious.

"You're not a typical kid," Zeke ran his fingers through his dark hair.

"Do you spend a lot of time with typical kids?" Calvin raised his eyebrows.

"No," Zeke replied. He gazed at the floor and walls as the tremor ceased. He studied Calvin again, but again he appeared unconcerned.

"Then how do you know if I am one?"

"Good point," Zeke inclined his head in acknowledgement.

"Thank you," Calvin said. "I'm hungry."

"What do you want?"

"Pizza. And French Fries. And Macaroni and Cheese. And Ice cream."

"Are you serious?" Zeke was incredulous. "There's no way you're going to eat all that."

"You asked what I want."

Once again, Zeke inclined his head. The kid might only be six years old, but you couldn't fault his logic.

"Okay," he said. "Pizza, french fries, macaroni and cheese, and ice cream, coming up."

"And chocolate milk," Calvin added.

"And chocolate milk." Zeke stepped out of the office to conjure up food.

The kid would be fine there for a couple of minutes. Just in case, he turned off the computer and the office phone remotely. After the kid ate, he would need to stash him somewhere. The gala started at eight. He would need to make sure the boys had left for their runs on schedule and then make it to the gala without arousing anyone's suspicions. Tariq, especially, might need a little extra motivation, and the picture he had taken of Calvin ought to do the trick. He paused. That kid was something special. When he took the boy, it was only to squeeze Tariq. But he might need to amend his plans. He might have to keep both him and his brother after this was over. Luckily, he had leverage.

He patted his phone. That little baby contained all sorts of information he would need as he put his plan into motion. He smiled in anticipation.

"This was good," Calvin said as he finished the last mouthful of macaroni and cheese. He sat back and patted his belly.

Zeke studied him like he was some sort of exotic animal. The kid should have been terrified, but he seemed only a little put out that he was not at home. Zeke parted his lips in what passed for a smile. "I'm glad you enjoyed it."

"I did," Calvin said. "But I still think you should take me home."

"Soon," Zeke answered. "We have some other things to do before that can happen."

"You said that before." Calvin gazed at him with serious brown eyes. "But you haven't kept your promise. That makes me think you are not an honest person."

"It does, does it? What else does it make you think?" Zeke smiled, straddled his chair, and sat.

"My grandmama always said that if someone means to keep his word, he'll make it happen. And if he doesn't mean to keep his word, he'll make an excuse. Which are you going to do?"

"Are you sure you're only six?" Zeke narrowed his eyes and gazed at him.

"I would like an answer," Calvin slid off his chair and stretched to his full height. He faced Zeke.

"You're not going to get one," Zeke shot to standing and knocked the chair over.

Calvin did not flinch.

"There's a lot more going on than you can understand," Zeke ranted. "So, you're just going to have to wait."

"I don't want to wait. I want to go home now," tears spilled as Calvin started to weep.

"Oh, no you don't," Zeke shouted. "Stop it. Right now." He raised his hand inscribed a sigil in the air above Calvin's head. "Sleep," he intoned the one word. Calvin crumpled to the floor.

"Shit!" Zeke muttered. This had not been his plan. Hell, none of this had been his plan. He ran his fingers through his hair, then stooped to pick Calvin up off the floor, placing him back in the chair. If things were going to go down like this, he would need to make some modifications. He made a call.

"I'm going to need you at the rendezvous point early," he said.

"When?"

"Now!"

DANIEL

Daniel entered the Newsblitz office. His tuxedo fit well, but the bow tie had been his undoing. He had assured the tailor he would be able fasten it himself, but it had confounded him.

"Daniel! You clean up very well." Tommy sent a low wolf whistle in his direction.

"I need a little help." Daniel showed his friend the crumpled bow tie.

"No problem," Tommy laughed and tied it for him. "Are you ready?" He asked.

"Almost," Daniel grabbed a small camera out of his desk drawer and stored it in a pocket.

"Never fully dressed without at least one of them, huh?" Tommy asked.

"I guess not," Daniel admitted.

"Okay, the limo's waiting." Tommy said.

"Limo?"

"Honey," Tommy said as they left the office and jogged down the steps to the street. "You don't arrive at the Plaza in a cab."

"Oh, I didn't realize that." Daniel got into the long, black limousine and found himself staring at a long expanse of thigh.

"Hello, Daniel." Nadia waved a glass of something on the rocks in his direction.

THE PIANO'S KEY

"Nadia, you look beautiful," his voice cracked. She was the most stunning woman he had ever seen in real life. That he remembered, he corrected himself.

Her silk gown of deepest midnight blue adorned her like a second skin. Her long hair was loose and tumbled about her shoulders in cascading waves. She laughed and crossed her legs. He bit back a moan.

"Don't worry about your lascivious thoughts," Tommy settled in beside him, and the car moved forward. "Nadia specializes making everyone around her have them. It's been happening since we were teenagers, and it's gotten a lot of my friends in trouble. So, don't let her tempt you."

"I won't," Daniel answered.

"Are you sure?" Nadia leaned towards him.

"No," Daniel smiled into her eyes and retreated against the seat. "I'm not sure, at all."

When they arrived at the hotel, the gala was already in full swing. Several couples swayed on the dance floor while others sat at the tables or gazed at the various items up for the silent auction.

Nadia studied the gathering. "I need a drink," she announced and headed towards the bar at the far end of the room.

"We'll join you in that," Tommy responded.

After Nadia had ordered, she moved to a group of their father's friends and soon disappeared from their view.

"Good evening, what can I get you?" The bartender smiled at them both. Her long salt and pepper dreadlocks were pulled from her face but her mocha colored face looked ageless.

"A water on the rocks in a tumbler, please," Tommy ordered. She paused for a second and gazed at him. Then she gave a swift nod of understanding.

"And for you, Daniel?" She asked.

"The same, please," he answered then paused. "Wait, how do you know my name?"

"We've met," she smiled at him.

"When?"

"This isn't the only place I tend bar." She filled their orders.

"Ah," Daniel pretended to understand.

"Mar, I'd like more water," Wisteria appeared at the bar. The bartender handed her a tall glass of water.

"Wisteria, what are you doing here?" Daniel smiled at his sensei. She wore her customary black commando pants and tank top. This time she also wore a black blazer with various pockets.

"I'm providing security for the event," she said by way of explanation.

"I didn't realize we needed to worry about being in danger tonight," Tommy laughed.

"Prepare now … " Wisteria began.

"'And you won't need to worry later,'" Daniel finished the saying with which she ended every class at the YMCA.

Daniel introduced Tommy and Wisteria.

"You're gorgeous," he said. "I'd say where have you been all my life, but …."

"You're gay," she finished for him.

"As the day is long," he winked.

The clinked glasses and laughed.

Daniel gazed out at the crowd and his gut clenched low and tight. Evie walked towards him. Her auburn hair fell long and wavy on her shoulders. Her blue eyes glistened as their eyes met. She wore a gown of deepest purple. It flowed and shimmered around her. He stared at her lips and fought the urge to kiss her. His hands clenched with the desire to put them on her, everywhere. He wanted her under him. He wanted to be inside her. A part of him screamed at him to walk away, anywhere, before she spoke. He stayed rooted to the spot and watched her approach. Her steps faltered. She grinned and approached the bar.

EVIE

Where was Tariq? I craned my neck and looked around for him again. The party was in full swing. Lots of beautiful people in glittering clothes flowed through the room. Each one had paid a thousand bucks to attend the evening, listen to music, and drink. Speaking of needing a drink, I could use one. Of course, Mar was tending bar, and that meant I'd end up with a soda and soda instead of a scotch and soda. Hope sprang eternal, and I approached the bar. The tall, lean, hot guy standing in front of it turned towards me. Daniel! My heart skipped ten beats, and I tripped over my own feet.

Oh no! This would not do. I needed my head about me. Daniel normally distracted me from my goals, because I thought he was adorable. Daniel in a tux looking like he wanted to eat me with a spoon? I couldn't resist that. I pasted a grin on my face and made my way towards him.

"You look beautiful," he smiled into my eyes.

"Thanks," I breathed. "You do too, look handsome, I mean." What the hell! I was three-hundred and six! I had exchanged witty repartee with some of the greatest and cleverest minds ever born. Why was I stuttering like I was the geek in a John Hughes movie? I looked at him again and appraised the tall, lean man before me. Something had changed in the last few weeks, and it wasn't just his memory. He looked tougher, harder somehow. And he filled out that tux jacket like he was a young "Bond, James Bond." Instead of being sorry for what was gone, I wanted a taste of who he had become. I stood on tiptoe to brush my lips against his.

"Hello, lover," a husky voice purred near my ear. A tall, lithe model who had just escaped from a photo shoot of barely-there apparel stood next to us.

"Jordan," he jerked away from me.

"Now, we know who I am," she leaned into Daniel. "Who is this?" She looked down her perfect nose at me.

"This is Evie," Daniel answered. "She's my ...." He paused and quieted.

"Friend," I finished for him. At least for now, that was the truth. I glanced from one to the other. "And you're Daniel's ...."

"Let's just say we're sparring partners," she watched me as she wrapped her arm around his waist and kissed him. He kissed her back.

"Right! I see," the pain lanced through me. I turned and fled.

"Wait! Evie," Daniel called from behind me. I sped out the doors of the ballroom.

I ran towards the nearest bathroom, careened into a stall, and collapsed against the door. I doubled over and cried. I sobbed until I was dry. I wanted to curl up and die. I wanted to torture Jordan until she came apart in tiny pieces. I wanted to find the freezer and drown my sorrows in Mama Brader's ice cream buckets. Crap! I had responsibilities out there. Instead of any of those promising alternatives, I was going to fix my face and repair whatever damage this jag had done to my hair, eyes, makeup, and soul, and get back out there. I sighed.

"She's not human, you know." Wisteria said from the other side of the door.

"What?" I marched out of the stall. Wisteria reclined on the long gray marble counter of the sink fixture. One leg swung to and fro' as she watched me. She appeared relaxed, but I had a feeling every part of her was on high alert.

"Jordan," she said. "She's not human. She's a Bane."

"What?" I was starting to sound like a drunk parrot, but I didn't care. "Is she your Bane?" Every Godparent had a Bane. It was like some cosmic chess match. As soon as a Godparent got his or her stripes, a Bane was assigned to thwart their every move.

"No," Wisteria shook her head. "Her sister was, but she's gone now."

"Did you kill her?"

"That was a long time ago," Wisteria hopped off the counter. "And it's not important. What is important is that you're letting her win. And you can't."

THE PIANO'S KEY

"I'm not letting her win anything," I grumbled. "Daniel doesn't remember me. And he's chosen her. He's moved on." I sounded pathetic, but I didn't care. I'd bucked a lot of tradition and broken a ton of rules to be with him. But mostly, I hurt.

"Get over yourself, Songbottom," she snapped. "If you want him, go fight for him, but stop this sniveling. It's pathetic. You're pathetic. I knew you couldn't handle it. I told them you would crap out in the clinch, and I was right." She stalked towards the door.

"Couldn't handle what?" I asked. I caught up with her and swung her around. "Couldn't handle what?" I asked again.

"Any of this," she waved her arms. "The Youth Center, helping kids, the music, being a Level 4, living on Earth full time. You name it."

"But, I can handle it," I defended myself hotly.

"Then, prove it," her green eyes flashed fire. "Go out there and kick some ass."

"Yeah, I will!" I stormed towards the door. In the doorway, I turned back to look at her.

"Hey, Wisteria?"

"What?"

"Thanks."

"My pleasure," she followed me out. We approached the ballroom together. "You need to know some things. First, he tried to follow you, but Jordan stopped him. Second, something else is going on."

"What?" I asked. We stood in the arched doorway to the Ballroom. The whirl of couples on the dance floor took my attention for a moment.

"I don't know yet," she answered. "But something else is going on."

"What, is your 'spidey sense' tingling?" I laughed.

"Something like that," she said, her eyes gleaming. "I'm going to go find Jordan. We're going to have a talk."

I raised my eyebrows in her direction. When Wisteria used that tone, someone was about to suffer. I spent a guilty second feeling bad for Jordan. Then, I smiled. Jordan was a Bane. She had deliberately tried to separate Daniel and me. And she was up to something. Banes were always up to something. On second thought, I didn't feel bad for her at all.

Now, where was Tariq? The Professor would need to introduce him soon. I hoped nothing was wrong with Calvin, because that was the only reason I could think of that would keep him from playing - well, that and the fact that he was terrified. No, I shook my head. He would rise to the challenge. I knew it. So, that brought me back around. Where was he?

TARIQ

Tariq found the door marked "Authorized Personnel Only" and pulled it open. It screeched as it opened, but the evening crowd hurried by and paid him no mind. He flipped on his flashlight and gazed around. Like the plans had said, the long hallway led to a set of metal steps. He passed huge spools of cables, abandoned subway seats, brooms, and shovels, and climbed the stairs. He doubled back until he stood over a grill in the floor. Below the grill, Saturday evening commuters milled back and forth towards the many trains that Grand Central station served.

He donned the surgical mask and gloves that Zeke had provided. He removed the jar of Heaven, unscrewed the lid, and placed the jar on the grill. He stood over it with his palms pointed up and his arms spread wide.

"To-tanicum Potariuate," he sounded out the unfamiliar words phonetically. He had no idea what they meant, but Zeke had told him they must be said perfectly or everything would blow up in his face.

"To-tanicum Dunabeelay Dunabeelay," Tariq formed a complicated steeple out of his fingers with his forefingers and thumbs interlocking and forming a crude sideways eight. He moved his entwined hands in a complicated sigil in the air as he repeated the phrases three times. He culminated his actions by making the same sideways eight sign in the air with the tips of his fingers. As he completed the sign, a ghostly shadow hung in the air where his hands had been.

"To-tanicum Protarium," he intoned the last phrase as he pointed his fingers at the jar that held the blue powder. Before his eyes, it disappeared.

"What the hell," he breathed. He leaned down and studied the jar. The powder was still there, but it had become transparent. He lifted the jar and in a sweeping motion, poured the powder down through the grill and onto the floor of Grand Central Station. It landed on a few of the people who passed under the grill. Most people walked through it and carried it on their shoes. Before long, everyone who walked through this spot would be exposed. Tariq had no idea what the powder would do. He hoped it wouldn't be too awful, but in the end, he cared more about getting his little brother back.

He pulled out his phone and dialed Zeke.

"Okay," he said when Zeke answered. "I've done it. Now where's Calvin?"

"Did the powder become transparent?" Zeke asked.

"Yes," Tariq answered. "Now, you bring Calvin back to me."

"All in good time. I have a few other things." Zeke replied. In the background, classical music, the kind that Evie liked so much, drowned out the rest of his words.

"Where are you?" Suspicion darkened Tariq's voice. "Are you at the gala?" What the hell was Zeke doing there? Tariq knocked his head with a fist. Something really messed up was going on.

"I am at the gala," Zeke answered. "And if you hurry, you might even get to play your little solo."

"I don't give a shit about my solo," Tariq shouted. "I want my brother back."

"And you'll get him back, but don't overstep." Zeke replied. "You do exactly as I say, and you'll have Calvin back in no time. Do anything else ...." The silence hung heavy between them.

"Fine," Tariq closed his eyes. "What do you want me to do?"

"Get to the Plaza and play your solo," Zeke said. "After that, I'll let you know."

Tariq ran down the stairs and out into the body of Grand Central Station. He exited and sprinted towards the Plaza Hotel. He slipped in through the front doors while the doorman helped an elderly woman into a taxi. He skidded to a stop on the cream-colored marble floor and swung around to take in the view. The open foyer held a plush seating area. The twenty-foot high ceiling held cream-colored curtains. Dark, red wood paneling lined the walls at the front desk. He gave a low whistle and marched to the front desk.

"Excuse me, I need to get to the Grand Ballroom," he said to the woman behind the desk.

"Tariq Wilson?" She asked.

"Yeah," he backed up a few steps and prepared to run.

"Perfect!" A smile lit her face. "They've been expecting you. Please follow me." She spoke to one of the other people behind the desk for a moment and then stepped out in front.

"I hear you are the entertainment this evening," she said as they walked.

"Yeah, well, I'm supposed to play piano."

"I'm sure you'll knock 'em dead." She led him to the main entrance and opened the door.

"Break a leg," she called as he walked into the room.

"Huh?" He turned back.

"That's a way of saying 'good luck,'" she said.

"Thanks." He searched the room for Zeke, but too many people were whirling around the room. To his right, the small bar was doing a brisk business.

"Hey," he said to the bartender with the salt and pepper dreads. She wore black pants and a vest over a white shirt, and she seemed to have plenty of time for every person in line.

"Can I get a coke?" He asked.

"Nope, but you can get some water," she answered. A tall glass of water appeared in front of him as if by magic. He squinted at her. She stopped moving and squinted back at him.

"Do I know you?" He asked.

"Nope," she answered with a laugh. "But I know you. And you're running late." She pointed to the stage on the other side of the ballroom. "Don't you think you should get yourself up there and play?"

"Do I have to?" His voice trembled.

"No. You don't." Her voice got quiet, serious. "You don't have to do anything you don't want to do. Thing is, I think you do want to do this. Now, how about you get up there and show 'em what you can do."

"First, I need to find someone." Tariq answered.

"Who?" the bartender asked.

"This guy," Tariq craned his neck for Zeke again but still could not see him in the crowd. "He's tall and has weird silver eyes. His name is …."

"Tariq!" Evie cried. She ran up and hugged him. "I was getting worried. Are you ready to play?"

"Give the boy a minute, Evie," the bartender spoke up. "At least let him finish his water." Another water glass appeared on the bar in front of them.

He gulped the water and looked for Zeke over the rim of his glass. At last, he could not avoid it. He would have to go play.

"I'm ready," he replaced the glass on the bar.

"You're going to do great!" Evie cheered. "Just go on up there and do your thing, and you'll knock 'em dead."

"I hope so," Tariq wanted nothing more than to find his brother, but Zeke had said this was part of the plan. And until he got Calvin back, he would do anything Zeke said. He approached the raised stage, but the Professor beat him to it.

"I'm pleased to see you, Tariq," she said. "Where is Calvin?"

"He's," Tariq choked on the words and tried again. "He's with a friend this evening."

"I'm sure he's sorry to miss hearing you play," the Professor smiled. "Are you ready?"

"As I'm gonna be," he whispered.

She ascended the few steps to the microphone set at center of the stage and raised her hands for quiet. The music silenced and the couples stopped dancing.

"Ladies and Gentlemen," she called to the crowd. "Thank you all so very much for joining us this evening to support such a worthy cause. The Music Program at the 127th Street Youth Center will certainly be successful with your generous contributions. In fact, we might expand to some of the other Centers all across the City. We dream big and with your help, we will achieve those dreams," she declared. "We wanted you to see for yourselves just how much difference this program will make in young people's lives. One of our gifted young people has consented to treat us to a performance. Please welcome, Tariq Wilson."

Tariq ascended the steps and walked over to the Professor.

"Do I have to say anything?" He whispered.

"Not unless you want to," she replied.

"No," he answered. She left the stage while he sat at the piano. He placed his fingers on his starting note, took a deep breath, and struck the key.

CHAPTER 28

DANIEL

Along with the rest of the gathering, Daniel clapped for the young man as the Professor introduced him and left the stage. Something about the young man on stage tickled the back of Daniel's head. He looked familiar, but Daniel couldn't place him. He sighed. So many things seemed just out of reach.

He moved to the bar and asked for a whiskey. The bartender handed him a glass of water.

"Trust me," she said. "You'll want to be sober tonight."

"Okay," he said dubiously. Strange bartender, he thought. He nodded his head in Tariq's direction.

"Do you know him?"

"Not well," she answered. "But I have a feeling we'll all know him before too long."

The room quieted as Tariq struck a single note. One by one, he played the simple, quiet melody of the first phrases of "Mood Indigo." He used to no artifice, no ornamentation. He played the notes softly as befit a velvety night of sorrow. As he repeated the phrase, he added a single note harmony with his left hand. The notes merged and struck against one another in dissonance and consonance by turn. The third time through the introductory phrase, he let loose a waterfall of notes. Liquid, fluid, cascading, yet still slow, dark, and deep, the phrase reminded Daniel of a low, burning sorrow, quiet heartache, and whiskey. He leaned against the bar and let the music wash over him.

An opening door and a rumble of footsteps shattered the quiet. Mitchell St. James, Tommy, and Nadia breezed into the room. They were flanked by Jordan on one side and that guy, Ezekiel, on the other side. They paused at the entrance. Jordan glided up next to St. James, leaned close, and pressed her lips to his ear. He ran a slow hand along her cheek and then patted it. He turned to the man at his other side and said a few words. He gave a curt nod and slipped away.

Elusive memories skated by Daniel's consciousness. He could swear, he had known Ezekiel, from before, but the memories slithered away. Damn! He had to figure it out. He would, but for now he turned back to Tariq and immersed himself in the music.

Tariq ended the last phrase on a run that sent him from the very bottom to the very top of the keys. He began a syncopated rhythm where he caught the upbeats of every phrase and added them to the downbeats of every subsequent phrase. He played with the timing until the song barely resembled its usual, melancholy self. He modified the mood into a sparkling dance tune and then morphed it into a Broadway show-stopper. Just as suddenly, he pulled back until he played a single phrase using one finger. He held the entire audience on the precipice as he sustained one last note. They held their collective breath while he held them at the breaking point for endless seconds. He waited to give them resolution until they could stand it no longer. One note, held, lengthened, and gave birth to a poignant silence.

A glass crashed the marble floor and shattered it.

MARGARETHA

The glass flew from her nerveless fingers. She stared at St. James.

"You!" she seethed.

St. James turned his leonine head in her direction. His eyes widened. He approached the bar.

"You haven't changed much, Margaretha," he sneered. "Still a servant, eh?" He smiled. "I'll have Scotch, neat," he ordered.

Mar folded her towel and angled around the bar to stand before him. She steepled her fingers into a complicated structure, pointed at him, and said one word.

"Die."

A jet of red flame spurted out of her fingers and struck him full in the chest. He staggered back but recovered. His suit smoked where the flame had hit it, but otherwise he appeared unhurt.

"You're rusty," he nodded. "Too bad. It would have been fun to try you out again." He waved his fingers at her and an inky black mass covered her from head to toe in an instant. She shook her head and the mass dissipated.

Evie ran up to them and placed herself in front of Mar. She held her conductor's baton aloft and faced St. James.

"What the hell is going on here?" She demanded.

"Evie," Mar kept her voice quiet. "This is not your fight."

"The hell it isn't," she spat at the man. "I don't know who you think you are, but you'd better leave."

"Using babies as your shields?" St. James' voice dripped with contempt. "It wouldn't be the first time. I seem to recall Amelia served as an excellent one." He paused. "For a little while, anyway."

"Don't you say her name," Mar snarled. "You killed her. You don't deserve to say her name."

The crowd had finally noticed the commotion and people formed a ring around them.

Mar whispered a complicated incantation. A livid ball of flame appeared between her hands. It grew in size and intensity until everyone shaded their eyes from it.

"Daddy?" Nadia approached them and stood next to St. James.

At the same instant, Mar threw the ball towards him. He stepped behind Nadia. She took the full force of the energy bolt in her chest and crumbled to the floor.

"Coward!" Mar shouted. She rushed him and grabbed his arms. Electricity sizzled over and around them. The air crackled. With a loud pop, they disappeared.

EVIE

"Shit!" I rushed towards the fallen woman. Daniel ran towards us and fell to his knees.

"Is she okay?" Daniel asked, as I checked for a pulse. There wasn't one.

"No," I whispered.

"Nadia?" Tommy St. James collapsed to his knees before us. "What just happened?" Shock hushed Tommy's voice. "What was that? Did he just use my sister as a shield? I knew he never loved us, but this...." Tears streamed down his face. He turned to Evie. "Save her," he whispered.

"Get him out of here," I muttered to Daniel. "He's not going to want to see this." Daniel nodded.

"Come on, Tommy," he said. Daniel led Tommy off towards the stage.

Wisteria joined us in the center of the circle.

"This is a national security matter. You will all leave and go to the lobby," she barked. "You will remain there and not talk to anyone until we get you. Is that clear?"

"Yes, Ma'am," several people who had obviously been soldiers responded to the command in her voice. They herded the rest as the group shuffled out of the ballroom.

"I just bought us some time," Wisteria whispered to me. "But we need to deal with this now."

"We need to heal her," I said. "You're going to have to do it. I can't. I don't know how."

Wisteria looked at the far end of the ballroom and shook her head. "No, it's yours to do. I have other business."

"What other business? She has no pulse. She's going to die."

"Then I guess you'd better get her heart started." Wisteria rose in a fluid motion and jogged to the far end of the room.

"Shit!" I cried. "How am I supposed to do this?" I fought to get my breathing under control. I threw everything but the task before me out of my head. In my mind, I envisioned a blank, white movie screen. I was sitting in a theater by myself and my favorite movie was about to start. It was the one where I had the patience, knowledge, and wisdom to save someone's life.

I reached out with my senses and called on the power of the sun, the stars, the moon, the leaves on the trees in Central Park, the water flowing down the Hudson, the bedrock of the Earth herself. A tendril of power answered my call. Then, another added to it, and then anther joined them. Within seconds, a ball of energy had blossomed between my fingers. I focused the energy in my hands towards one goal - that Nadia's heart would start to beat. With a cry, I placed my hands over her heart. I saw her heart. It was already starting to cool. It had lost its battle and after a lifetime of working constantly, it felt it had earned its rest.

"No, you don't," I cajoled. I imagined it beating her life's blood around her body. I imagined it new, juiced up, and ready to go for the next sixty years. I visualized this with every fiber of my being. I coaxed her heart with licks of energy. I tantalized it with earth, air, fire, and water. I bargained with it. I presented it with the limitless energy in my hands and asked it to start again. Under my hands, her heart jerked once and stilled. Then, as if it changed its mind, it beat a second time. Then, it contracted a third time. Within seconds, it was pumping as if she had never been in any danger. Her body expanded with its first breath. Her startling blue eyes opened.

"What happened? Her voice was hoarse.

"You had a fall," I said. "But you're going to be fine."

"Nadia?" Tommy ran towards us. He kneeled before us and gathered her in his arms.

"Thank you," he said through his tears. "I don't know what you did, but thank you for saving my sister."

I swiped at my own tears with my hands and stood.

"I don't know what I did either," I admitted. "But I'm glad you're okay."

A rhythmic clap from the doorway drew our attention.

"Well done, you," Zeke gave me a small salute.

"Zeke!" I cried. "You'll want to leave. Right now." I commanded with more power than I had. I had debilitated myself with that healing spell.

"Oh, I'll be going," he smiled. "But, I think you'll want to talk with me soon enough." He smiled at me and disappeared.

A thunderous crash drew my attention from the other side of the room.

"Shit!" Tariq cried as he tumbled off the stage and to the floor. Wisteria and Jordan squared off on the stage.

"What is going on?" I shouted. I ran to Tariq and helped him stand.

"Where did Zeke go?" He panted.

"You know Zeke?" I grabbed him by the shoulders. "How do you know Zeke?"

"Never mind that," he yelled. "He has my brother. He has Calvin."

"What do you mean, 'he has Calvin?'"

"He took him, and he told me if I didn't do exactly what he said, I'd never see Calvin again."

"Ack!" I let him go and yanked at my hair. I'd missed everything. "We need to find Calvin and Zeke. When I get my hands on him, I'm going to…."

"Jordan, where are they?" Wisteria said to the other woman.

"I don't know," she replied. She backed up a couple of steps. Her arms came in front of her in a martial arts ready stance.

"You're kidnapping children now?" Wisteria dropped into a crouch.

"Hey, that wasn't my doing," she replied. "I'm just here for Daniel." She mimed a kiss in his direction and then looked right at me.

"Wow!" Wisteria shook her head. "That's your big plan? To make her jealous?"

"Wait!" I cried. "Make me jealous about what?" I asked.

"Let's just say we christened the mats at the Y," Jordan's smile was predatory.

I rocked back as if she had slapped me. And then I regrouped and filed this crappy feeling away with the remnants of my crying fit for when I had time to feel it. I had bigger problems than where Daniel had been having sex.

"Evie," Daniel approached us. "I'm sorry."

"We're not together, Daniel," I managed to keep my voice level. "You don't owe me any explanations."

"I don't?"

"No," I turned away from him. "Besides, I have more pressing things to deal with." I turned to Tariq and saw him looking at Daniel with huge eyes.

"What's wrong?" I turned him to face me.

"He's okay." Tariq swallowed, hard. "You're okay."

"You know Daniel?" I asked.

He shook his head and backed away from me.

"Of course you do," Jordan hopped off the stage and glided towards us. "You helped beat the shit out of him."

"You did what?" I advanced on him. Rage choked me. My vision rimmed red around the edges. He hurt Daniel. He was going to pay.

"Evie," Wisteria stepped between us and held her hands up in a placating gesture.

"Get out of my way," I growled. I tried to edge around her. She flicked out a hand. I landed in a heap ten feet away from her.

I rolled to standing and rushed her.

"Stop!" She commanded.

I skidded to a halt. The breath heaved in and out of my lungs.

"Stop and think," her voice quieted but lost none of its urgency. "Don't you think he must have had a good reason?"

"It doesn't matter," I shot towards her. She connected with my forearm, flicked her wrist again, and again sent me sprawling on the wooden dance floor.

"He hurt Daniel," pain twisted me from the inside out. I glared at her from the floor. "I trusted him, and he hurt Daniel."

"But, I'm okay, now," Daniel walked to me. He extended a hand and helped me up. "I'm okay."

"But you're not my Daniel," I swiped at the tears that threatened to spill over. I moved away from him.

"No, I'm not," he stepped towards me. "But I'm me, now, and that's what I'm going to have to be. I'm okay with that." He put a under my chin and tugged until my eyes met his eyes. "Can you be okay with that?" He asked.

I closed my eyes for a few seconds and took a deep breath. I nodded.

A murmur drew my attention.

Jordan was prepping an incantation.

"Oh no you don't," Wisteria flew over to Jordan and grabbed her. "We need some answers." She grabbed the Bane's arms.

Jordan glanced down at where Wisteria gripped her then met and held her eyes. "You'll want to let me go," she said.

"Not until you tell us where Zeke went," Wisteria tightened her grip.

"And more importantly, Calvin," I jogged up to them. I stared from one to the other. I crossed my arms over my chest.

"I don't have to tell you jack," Jordan said.

"No, but you're going to anyway," Wisteria circled Jordan as she moved. Jordan lowered to a crouch but otherwise remained still. Her eyes followed Wisteria's every movement. I suspected if her eyes could have reached all the way around, she would have not let Wisteria out of her sight for a nanosecond.

"Just tell me where Calvin is," I advanced on her.

"You know where he is?" Tariq inserted himself between us.

"Get away from here, Tariq," I snarled. "You don't know what she's capable of."

"I don't care," he insisted. He grabbed her arm. "Tell me where he is."

"He's at the New Amsterdam Gladiator Arena," she said.

"There's no such thing," I cried. "Enough is enough!" I raised my hand and my wand appeared in it. I pointed it at her chest and cried the incantation for the most powerful fireball I could make.

"Evie, no." Daniel reached for me.

"Screw this!" Jordan clapped her hands once and phased out. We phased with her.

"Shit!" Wisteria cried. She raced towards us.

Stuck to Jordan like burrs on her clothes, we shifted locations with her. The Grand Ballroom disappeared in front of our eyes and a rounded, brick arena appeared around us. We stood behind a small, hexagonal pavilion inside the arena. Jordan wrenched herself away from us and rolled under the awning covering the inside walls. She disappeared from view.

A cannon shot boomed behind the pavilion. A zap of electricity zinged in response.

"What the hell? Where are we?" Tariq found his voice first. We huddled against the pavilion as more bombs pounded in the arena.

"Oh!" I realized where we were. "We're at Castle Clinton."

"The old Fort at the park downtown?" Daniel asked. We all ducked our heads as another explosion rocked the pavilion.

"Yep." I answered. "Stay here," I admonished them both. I crouched and worked my way around the pavilion. The explosions were bad, but the searing lasers streaking over my head were the real problem. I craned my neck and tried to glimpse the action. All I saw was the sandstone that made up the Clinton's main body. A bolt of lightning seared over my head. I dropped to the ground and belly-crawled forward. I should have known they would choose this as the battlefield. For many years, Clinton was the main entry point for

European immigrants. And they were often cruisin' for a bruisin' as they say. The history books say that the Fort never saw any battle, but they don't have the whole story. It never saw any human battles, but we magic folk have been using this as the arena to solve our disagreements since the Fort was built.

"Children?" Mar shouted over the din of the battle. "You're taking children?"

"I took no one," the answer roared back. "I had nothing to do with that. That must have been Zeke. What can I say? You can't get good help these days."

Zeke! I rocketed up. If he was working for this guy, he might be here. And if he was here, Calvin might be, too.

"Calvin!" Tariq came charging around the pavilion. I grabbed his arm and swung him around.

"Let me go!" His eyes wild, he tore himself free.

"Tariq. Tariq!" I pinned his arms to his sides and held him to me. "Listen to me. Do you hear that?" I pointed out to the bigger space where explosions rocked the walls every few seconds. "If you go out there right now, you're going to get hurt or killed. And then who's going to take care of Calvin?"

He stopped struggling, but he trembled in my arms.

"Let me take care of this," I said in his ear.

"Get my little brother," Tariq whispered. "Please bring him back to me."

"I promise," I said.

We shimmied back around to the other side of the small pavilion where Daniel waited.

"I need you to stay with Tariq and make sure nothing happens to him," I said. "Can you do that?" I knew what I was asking, but I didn't care.

He straightened and gazed down at me. For a long moment, all was quiet as we searched each other's eyes.

"Yeah, I can do that," he said.

"Good," I nodded. "You two stay out of sight." I darted out into the open.

THE PIANO'S KEY

ZEKE

Protected from view by the low-hanging awning, Zeke watched the battle unfold in front of him. Fireballs and laser bolts flew across the arena. They lit up the evening sky as if the July fourth fireworks had come three days early. Margaretha and St. James were evenly matched, but he had his money on Mar. She had heartbreak on her side and nothing gave your battle magic that extra zing like a broken heart. She zapped a nasty fireball at St. James' head. He deflected it with ease but missed the follow-up. It struck him squarely in the chest and blew him into the circular wall of the fort.

St. James recovered and lobbed a net made of flaming barbed wire at Margaretha. She caught it in one hand, spun it around her head and tossed it back at him.

"Nice!" Zeke whistled his approval.

"What's nice, man?" Darnell, Wayne, and the others approached him from one of the two arched doorways. "Damn!" Darnell breathed as a fire ball scorched the sky overhead. They ducked their heads and retreated to the back wall.

"What you need us for?" Darnell asked as they hugged the back wall.

"Tariq is here," Zeke answered. "And so is his little brother." He pointed to a small wooden bench a few yards away. A pile of sheets and tarps lay on the bench.

"Calvin's in there?" Wayne's voice quaked.

"Yes," Zeke barked. "And I need you to get both him and Tariq out of here. Don't let either of them get hurt. Got it? Now get out of here, do your job, and take them both to the new warehouse."

"All right, man," Darnell held up placating hands. "We can do that, but where's Tariq?"

Zeke motioned towards the pavilion on the right side of the arena. "He's over there."

Darnell pointed to the center of the fort. "We ain't going out there, man. I don't know what they're shooting, but it don't sound like friendly fire to me."

"It's not," Zeke spat through gritted teeth. "And you're going out there anyway." He grabbed a fistful of Darnell's shirt and hoisted him up to his eye level. Darnell's toes brushed past the ground as Zeke stared into his eyes. "You get Tariq and take care of Daniel."

"Daniel?" Darnell squeaked.

"Yes. You didn't do a good enough job last time. This time, you kill him. Do it or I'll kill you. Do I make myself clear?"

"Why don't you just kill him yourself?" Wayne muttered from behind them.

"Because I can't," Zeke snapped. "So, you're going to do it for me." He pulled Darnell off the ground completely. "Got it?"

"Okay, okay," Darnell whimpered. "We got your back."

"No one's got my back," Zeke said. "But you'll still do what I tell you."

Darnell, Wayne, and the others crouched and dodged their way to the pavilion.

Zeke turned his attention back to the fierce battle in the center of the arena. Margaretha fired bolt after bolt at St. James. His shields had worn away, and each hit now left its mark on his body. Zeke's lips pulled back from his teeth in a feral grin.

DANIEL

The battle raged around them. Daniel and Tariq hugged the wall of the small pavilion and tried to keep from being blown up.

"Looks like the party's just getting started," Darnell said from right next to him.

Tariq sprang up and grabbed Daniel's arm.

"What the hell are you doing here?" Tariq cried.

Daniel lowered his center of gravity into a "Ready" stance. He glanced at the four men who stood before him. Three were unarmed. The other held a bat. "Tariq, get behind me," Daniel instructed.

"Yeah, Tariq, you pussy. Get behind him," Darnell taunted.

One of the others, a guy almost as wide as he was tall, reached around and grabbed Tariq's wrist. He clamped a vice-like grip on Tariq's fingers and squeezed.

"Not my hands, man," Tariq whimpered.

"Yo, man," Darnell interceded. He chuffed his friend on the back of his head, and he released Tariq. "You leave his hands alone. Zeke said not to hurt him." He turned to Tariq. "Why don't you go get your brother, boy?"

"Calvin's here? Where is he?"

"He right over there," Darnell jerked his head in the direction from which they had come.

Daniel and Tariq exchanged a long look. Daniel nodded.

"Go," he said. "Go get your little brother. I've got this." He turned and faced the four football players.

"I'm sorry, man," Tariq said. He ran towards the interior wall of the Fort and disappeared from view.

"I think it's time we finish what we started," Darnell said. "Looks like you healed pretty good." He clenched his ham-sized hands into fists. Daniel kept his back to the wall. The four of them flanked him. With a deep breath, Daniel entered the meditative state Wisteria had taught him to cultivate. He became aware of all sounds, sights, and smells around him. As an objective observer of his own status, he picked and chose which stimuli needed his attention. He released his awareness of the booms of battle raging behind him and his concern for Tariq and his little brother. He would seek them out afterward, provided he had an afterward.

He maintained his awareness of the sights and sounds of the four men he faced. One was trembling with fear of the fire balls. The one with the bat was smacking it into his palm every few seconds. The third licked his lips in a nervous habit. Each looked formidable, but Daniel sized them up and saw they were all followers. His main concern would have to be Darnell, the leader. He faced Darnell just off-center. He kept his knees slightly bent and his shoulders relaxed. He softened his gaze so he could sense any change in the visual patterns he was seeing.

The bat whistled as it sliced through the air towards his head. He shifted his weight to his back foot and dropped to one knee. Darnell rushed him. He swung an arm up and connected his hand with Darnell's arm. He pivoted again, shifted weight, and stepped just to the left Darnell's trajectory. Darnell lost his balance and careened into the wall of the pavilion. His breath huffed out of his lungs, and he lay still. The guy with the bat swung again. Daniel ducked. As he straightened, he brought his right foot in towards his left knee. He kicked out at an angle. The pop of ripping ligaments rivaled the fire balls and bomb blasts. The guy dropped. He cradled his knee and whimpered.

The third guy raised his hands in an "I surrender" gesture and sprinted towards the exit. Wayne, who resembled a refrigerator, lumbered up to him, grabbed him in a bear hug, and squeezed.

Daniel struggled against Wayne's vise-like grip. Wayne smashed him into the Pavilion wall. His head cracked on the sandstone, once, twice, three times. His head exploded with pain. A vivid light sliced through him. He screamed. Visions, memories, knowledge poured into him as his memory flooded back.

He slumped as the gates in his mind crashed open. For a few seconds, he was limp as all he had forgotten swirled in his mind and realigned with who he was now. His two selves filled his mind to bursting and then exploded into every fiber of his being. Oblivious to the battle raging around him, he screamed under the pressure behind his eyes.

His unexpected dead weight surprised Wayne, and he loosened his grip. The two men staggered in a macabre dance. Daniel shook his head to clear it. He clenched his hands into fists and boxed Wayne's ears in a simultaneous downward strike. Wayne cried out and dropped him. Daniel rolled to standing. He grabbed the fallen bat. He swung and cracked Wayne once on the head. Wayne crumpled and lay still.

"Shit! Evie," Daniel gasped. He gripped his head as his memories reconciled and integrated. He remembered her. He loved her. He had cheated on her. "Shit!" He swore again. He searched for her through the haze fire and smoke at the center of the fort. Where was she?

EVIE

Mar and St. James stood on opposite sides of the round arena. She was supporting herself with some sort of stick. She cradled her left arm against her stomach. She had no shields left.

He bled from several wounds in his chest and right arm. A cut spurted just above his left eye. He wiped at it with his left hand. He threw the droplets of blood into the air said some ancient word and the droplets transformed into three scarlet dragons. They sliced through the air with their razor-sharp claws and scales. Their inky, black eyes darted around the arena as they searched for prey. Gold tongues licked the air as they floated above our heads and waited. St. James sliced his hand in a downward motion, and they rocketed towards Mar, angling in from three sides. As they neared her, flames erupted from their mouths.. She was trapped. They would incinerate her.

"No!" I screamed as I ran forward.

As one, they turned their attention to me. Like a school of piranha they turned in formation, banked, and streaked straight towards me.

"Come on, you overgrown tea lights," I shouted. "Come and get me!" I had no idea what to do since those nightmares were way above my pay grade, but I was damned if I was going to let anything happen to Mar.

On the other side of the arena, Mar raised her arms. She started some sort of low chant in yet another language I didn't know. Her mocha colored skin glowed golden from within. Her hair looked alive like snakes were moving through it. Her brown eyes glowed violet as she chanted.

"Mauy Riuchi Dandrobue. Mauy Riuchi Dandrobue," she repeated the phrase louder each time until she was screaming it. The dragons stalled in mid-air and shuffled around as if they didn't know which way to go. Mar raised her hands and shouted the phrase one last time. She chopped both arms down in St. James' direction. The dragons careened towards him.

"Master, no!" Jordan sprinted onto the field and rushed Mar. With a flick of her hand Mar redirected Jordan's leap fifteen feet away. Jordan landed in a heap, rose, and blazed towards Mar again, only for Mar to levitate ten feet in the air and swoop toward St. James. She pointed the tip of her staff towards his heart.

"Ah, ah, ah," Wisteria appeared in front of Jordan where Mar had been and blocked her progress. "That's not your fight."

"The hell it isn't," Jordan panted. "He's my Master, and that bitch needs to die."

"If it is her time, so be it," Wisteria agreed. "But it won't be at your hand."

Jordan feinted right and tried maneuver around Wisteria. Wisteria zapped to right in front of her again. Jordan drew a gun and leveled it at Wisteria's heart. Wisteria raised her hands towards her shoulders and backed up twenty feet. She withdrew a knife from a holster on her back and held its business end pointed down.

"Wisteria, did you really just bring a knife to a gun fight?" Jordan laughed.

Wisteria tossed the knife into the air. It rotated halfway. She caught it by its tip and winged it at Jordan. The knife slammed into her gun and jammed the safety on. It continued on its arc and embedded itself into the sandstone wall.

"You were saying?" Wisteria raised an eyebrow. She softened her knees and kept her arms relaxed at her sides.

"Dammit!" Jordan shouted. She dropped the gun and ran towards Wisteria. She caught the taller woman by the waist and they fell to the ground. For a couple of seconds, they grappled and rolled on the packed earth floor. Jordan straddled Wisteria's waist and landed a few solid punches to Wisteria's face and torso. A cut opened above Wisteria's eye, and she grunted. She kicked her legs up and hooked them over Jordan's head. She arched her back. Jordan hit the ground with a shattering thud. Wisteria kipped to standing and resumed her ready stance. Jordan rolled to standing and attacked with a flying sidekick to Wisteria's head. Wisteria stepped back. As Jordan flew by her, Wisteria brought a downward elbow strike to the side of Jordan's knee. Jordan howled in pain and landed in a heap.

Wisteria again resumed ready stance and waited in stillness. Her eyes were half closed and her breathing looked deep and regular. How did she do that?

With a great battle cry, Jordan attacked once again. She rushed towards Wisteria and tried to land a combination of hooks and jabs to Wisteria's face. Wisteria back-stepped, side-stepped, and feinted. I realized none of Jordan's punches were landing. Wisteria seemed like she would be where the next punch would land, but when the punch would have connected, Jordan was just whistling through the air. She struck nothing.

Jordan heaved an inarticulate cry and attacked again with a volley of kicks. She connected with one vicious roundhouse to the side of Wisteria's head and Wisteria dropped to the ground.

Jordan kicked Wisteria's belly and torso. She landed three kicks. On the fourth, Wisteria caught her leg and rotated it over her own body. Jordan splayed in a sort of splits. Wisteria levered her legs up and twisted her body around until her legs were even with Jordan's chest. She rolled herself up Jordan's body until she sat with her legs scissored around Jordan's neck. She squeezed.

Strangled sounds escaped Jordan's throat as she collapsed. She thrashed in an effort to free herself. Wisteria held her immobile and stilled.

"You're going to kill her," I whispered. Banes were notoriously tough to kill, but strangling one and then burning the body before they came back to life was an effective method.

"Only if she doesn't stop struggling," Wisteria said it to me, but I was sure she meant it for Jordan to hear. "Are you ready to stop struggling, Jordan?"

Jordan re-doubled her efforts to free herself.

"Very well," Wisteria sighed. "We do this the hard way." She held Jordan in a death grip until her struggles ceased. For an instant, everything was silent.

Huh? Silent? I looked at Mar and St. James. They faced each other without moving. Each had a palm pointed at the other's heart. They both trembled with silent effort. Blood flowed from their eyes and ears. A wild, reckless energy built between them. Electricity flared around them. The electric storm brought a thunderous vibration that shook the walls of the fort. Cracks in the sandstone formed and spread.

Mar gasped as blood poured from her mouth.

"Mar, no!" I shouted.

"Stay back, Evie," Mar yelled. "This is not your fight."

"Why is everyone always saying that?" I cried. "Let me help."

"You can't help her," St. James rasped. "No one can. You've failed, Margaretha." He rumbled. "You will always lose to me, and after I'm through with them, they will curse your name for bringing them to my attention."

"Not again," she snarled. "Never again!" She ran to him and grasped him in her arms. A tornado whirled above them. The electrical storm slashed through them. Lightning bolts seared the walls and floor around them. Thunder roared throughout the fort and blasted us thirty feet away. I sprawled on the ground and could do nothing but watch. A blazing light erupted from them and then contracted back to where they held each other chest to chest. They exploded into a thousand shards of light and disappeared.

The fort stood silent and dark.

"What happened?" I found my voice first. "What the fuck just happened?"

Wisteria extricated herself from Jordan's prone body and approached me. "You don't want to know," she said. "You're not ready to know."

"Is Mar dead?" My voice trembled.

"Death has many forms," Wisteria answered.

"That's not any kind of answer," I shouted.

"Ask a question I can answer," she said. "And I will."

"Fine. What about her?" I pointed to Jordan.

"Yes, well, I'll need to take care of her," Wisteria walked back to her and hoisted her up in her arms. "And you, Evie, will need to take care of everything else," she admonished me. "Your work's not done."

"What are you going to do?" I indicated Jordan with my chin.

"She is a warrior," Wisteria answered. "She deserves a warrior's death."

"But, she's also a Bane," I pointed out.

"A warrior is a warrior regardless of politics."

"So, you're going to give her, what? A Viking burial. For a Bane?"

"Yes," she said.

"And what, was she just following orders when she slept with Daniel?" I snarled.

Wisteria sighed. "It might be good to figure out exactly who you are mad at about that. Jordan owed you no loyalty." She paused. "But then did Daniel?"

I nodded at her point. Jordan never owed me anything, and Daniel and I weren't together when it happened. Shit. I had all this hurt and no one at whom I could throw it. I tugged at my hair for a few seconds. Somehow, I was going to have to let this go.

"So what are you going to do with her?" I asked.

"I have a debt to pay to her sister. Jordan will not die a dishonorable death."

I shook my head. "I guess I have a lot to learn about being a warrior."

"Yes, you do. Now, go learn the next lesson," Wisteria said. With a nod of her head, her knife flew into her holster. She, Jordan, and her knife disappeared. For a few seconds, an eerie quiet pervaded the space. I stared at the spot she had been standing. Damn! She was strong. That entire time, Wisteria had been holding Jordan in her arms like she was Calvin.

"Oh shit! Calvin!" In the silence, my voice rang out like a shot. I clamped my hands over my mouth. "Way to be a warrior and broadcast your location to everyone around, Songbottom," I mumbled. I gazed around but no one seemed to have heard me. I jogged back to where I had left Daniel and Tariq. They were gone.

"Daniel! Tariq!" I hissed. I sprinted under the awning and ran around the inside of the Fort. As I skirted a small shed tucked against the interior wall, a hand shot out and clocked me on the side of the head.

"Ow!" Stars shot through my vision. I landed on my ass.

"Crap! Sorry, Evie. I didn't know it was you." Daniel knelt before me. He cradled my face in his hands and touched his lips to mine. "Are you okay?"

I shook my head to clear it. "I'll be fine. Wait, why did you just kiss me?"

"I remember everything," he said.

"You remember?" I shouted. "Now you remember?"

"Yes, and I'm sorry."

"You know what? I can't deal with this right now." I hoisted myself up. "Where's Tariq? Did you find Calvin?" I asked.

"Yes, we did. But Evie, something's wrong." Daniel and I jogged to the bench where Tariq sat holding his brother.

"What happened?" I knelt before them.

"I don't know, Evie." Tariq mumbled through his tears. He held the little boy in his arms and rocked him back and forth. "I can't get him to wake up."

"And he won't until I wake him." Zeke stepped out of the shadows.

THE PIANO'S KEY

"Shit!" I swore. I stepped in front of Daniel and the boys. My wand appeared in my hand. I softened my knees and kept my hands loose at my sides.

"Nice 'ready' stance," Zeke raised a sardonic brow.

"Daniel, get the boys out of here, now," I didn't look back but kept my eyes riveted on Zeke.

"I'm not going to leave you," Daniel spoke from right behind me. Shit. Now wasn't the time for misplaced heroics.

"This isn't your fight," I smiled, because I finally realized what that meant. "Besides, I need to know those boys are safe, and you're the only one I'd trust to make sure of that."

Daniel retreated from us, and I heard some shuffling as he lifted Calvin into his arms.

"Come on," Daniel spoke to Tariq. "We need to go."

"What about Evie?" Tariq's voice sounded small and young.

"Evie will meet up with us later."

"Are you sure?"

"I'm sure." Their voices receded.

I waited until I couldn't feel them in the fort. Then, I dropped into a crouch and circled Zeke slowly. I had no idea what I was going to do, but I was not letting him anywhere near those kids ever again.

"It's just you and me now," I stated. I shifted my wand from hand to hand as if it was a stiletto.

"Don't you get it, Evie? It's always going to be just you and me," Zeke smiled.

"Get that smirk off your face," I rasped.

"Or, what?" He asked. "Or you'll kill me? If you could kill me, I reckon I'd already be dead."

"You kidnapped Calvin! Just how low were you planning to go?" I raised my wand.

"We have a lot farther to go together," Zeke said. He sidestepped a wide circle around me.

I kept the business end of my wand on him. He was far better at Battle Magic. I wouldn't kid myself that I could beat him in a fair fight. So, I was going to have to fight dirty.

Wisteria would be pissed that I resorted to tricks and shenanigans rather than being all scrupulous about it. I could live with that.

I shot a fireball at life side of his chest. At the same time, I dove for cover to my right. As he dodged to the right, I shot another one right where he was about to be. It slammed into him and knocked him back a good six feet. Good!

"So, that's how it's going to be," he gasped. He grinned. "This is going to be fun." He leaped into the air and float-rolled behind the same pavilion Daniel and Tariq had used as their hiding place.

I scanned the perimeter for anything Zeke might throw at me. I belly crawled to the other side of the pavilion and squatted against its round wall. I strained my ears for any sounds. Nothing.

A bright spot light blinded me. I raised my hands to shield my eyes. The wall against my back vibrated and crumbled, and several blocks of sandstone pummeled me as they fell. In seconds, they engulfed me. They were too soft to do much damage, but they battered and bruised my legs and arms. I lay covered and smothered. Somehow, I still held my wand. I sent a prayer of thanks that it hadn't shattered. I inscribed a sigil in the air with a couple of flicks my wrist and the sandstone lifted off me. I pulled myself to standing and pivoted three-hundred and sixty degrees. Zeke was gone.

"Where the hell are you?" Frustration spiked my voice.

"Right behind you," he whispered in my ear.

I swung around and threw every bit of my weight into a punch to his gut.

He whuffed out a breath and doubled over. I connected with a heel strike to his chin. His head snapped back with a crack. He fell backwards and rolled a back somersault to standing. I shot off a bolt. It glanced off his shoulder and careened towards the far wall. It burned and sizzled before it winked out. The flame left a burned, black crater in its wake.

He looked at his shoulder and said a quiet word. It mended before my eyes.

"I expected more from you, Evie. I don't think you're in it to win it this time," he said. He flicked his hand at me and a net appeared over my head. It dropped. I threw myself to the side and lashed at him with another fireball. I pummeled him with flame after flame while he stood there with his eyes closed. A few more and I'd break through his defenses.

"Evie?" The child's voice sliced through my concentration. Calvin had walked into the arena. He ambled towards us.

"Calvin, get out of here," I shouted. The net wrapped around me. Calvin disappeared.

"What the hell?" I screamed at Zeke. "What did you do to him?" I struggled against the net, but the more I struggled the tighter it bound me.

"Me? Nothing," Zeke answered. "I don't even know where he is." He walked towards and clucked his tongue in disapproval. "Wisteria would be so disappointed to know you failed her most important lesson. If you can't accept your situation and maintain focus, you will die," he mimicked her.

I ceased my struggles. I stopped everything except my breath. As I inhaled, I felt the floor below me. As I exhaled, the balmy night sky welcomed me. A sort of peace descended on me as I breathed and accepted my situation. "Get up, and I'll get you free," a voice whispered in my ear. "All you have to do is get up, and the sky is yours." In my peripheral vision, I spied Torlyn.

"Torlyn, get out of here," I whispered. "This isn't your fight."

"The hell it isn't," she whispered back. She had tamped down her inner flame until it was nothing more than the glow of a firefly.

I willed my bones into a fluidity I didn't feel and sat up. She blew a flame around me that seared through the net. I rocketed up and faced Zeke, shooting another bolt at him. He parried and deflected it back on me. It seared the skin on my belly, and I dropped like a stone, curling around my burned stomach. Tears of pain escaped my eyes. I tried to stand. Shit!

My gasps and cries sounded like canons in the quiet of the arena.

"You asshole," Torlyn blazed into her full glory. She had the brightness of a tiny sun. She sent bolt after bolt of flame at Zeke. He deflected each one.

"You can't hurt me," he said to the Fire Elemental. "I come from you."

"Shit!" Torlyn shouted.

Zeke stood over me as I writhed on the ground.

"Go ahead, you bastard," I gasped. I willed my charred and broken body to sit up. "Get it over with."

"Killing you isn't part of my plan. It never was," Zeke said. "I'll be seeing you." He stared into my eyes for a long moment and disappeared.

"Ow, ow, ow, ow, ow," I collapsed back on the ground. I curled around my belly and retched everything I'd ever eaten.

"Oh, Evie," Torlyn wrung her flame hands together. "What can I do?" She billowed into a small explosion. "I can't heal burns," she apologized.

"It's okay, Torlyn," I panted. "I'll be okay."

I had no energy to heal the multiple cuts, bruises, contusions, and burns. I made it onto my hands and knees. I crawled over to the nearest wall and pulled myself to standing.

Torlyn lit the way as I limped to the exit. At the arched doorway, I turned around and glanced back at the field of battle. It looked clean and pristine and ready for tomorrow's tourists. What the hell! I cocked my head to the side and set off a cacophony of pain alarm bells.

"Okay, okay. I'll never move again," I moaned.

"Sorry," Torlyn apologized again. "I had to call the cleaners, or someone would have gotten suspicious."

One thing I'll say for those cleaners. They're efficient.

"Thanks, love," I said.

"Anything else I can do?" Torlyn asked.

"No," I answered. "You don't want to piss off the Fire Lords anymore than you did tonight by working against one of your own."

"But he's a Bane," she pointed out. "And he's an asshole. That's got to count for something."

"Boy, I wish it did," I agreed. We made our goodbyes, and I stumbled out into the New York night. I lucked out and hailed a lone cab.

"Take me home," I mumbled through cracked and bleeding lips.

"Sure you wouldn't rather go to the hospital?" He asked.

"No, home will do." I gave him the address.

"Don't bleed on the upholstery," he said, as he took off for Juilliard.

CHAPTER 29

EVIE

My room at the Rose Building was buzzing with commotion as I shuffled in.

"Evie!" Daniel cried. He rushed to me and helped me onto the couch.

The Professor poked her head of out Joanna's bedroom.

"Evie," she cried. "You look terrible."

"I know, but it's not as bad as it looks," I lied. I hadn't seen myself, but I was pretty certain it looked a lot better than it felt. "Where are Tariq and Calvin?"

"In there," the Professor motioned with her head.

"Has Calvin woken up, yet?" I asked.

Her eyes rimmed with tears. "Not yet," she sighed. "Those poor boys," she wrung her hands. "Those poor, poor boys."

"We ran into the Professor as we pulled up," Daniel offered by way of explanation.

"And I insisted on helping," she continued for him.

"I'm sure you want to know what happened," I said to her. "But honestly, I'm not sure I can even begin to tell you."

"I don't need to know what happened," she straightened to her full, formidable height. "I only need to know what I can do to make sure it doesn't happen again."

I stared into her determined eyes and sent a prayer of gratitude for strong women who took no bullshit.

"I'm glad you're here, Professor," I leveraged myself off the couch and shuffled towards my bedroom. "I need a minute."

I closed the door to my room and resisted the urge to collapse on my bed and cry for my mommy. Instead, I grabbed my wand and made a call.

"Doc," I spoke into the intercom system. "I need you. Please come." I gasped the last few words as a wave of pain engulfed me.

"What is it, Eveningstar? The Doc stood in front of me. She carried her big, black healer's bag. She clucked her tongue and shook her head. "This looks bad," she diagnosed me with a glance. "Can you not heal it yourself, though?"

"I can, and I will," I replied. "But I wasn't asking for myself."

The Doc froze for a second while she scanned the suite's other the occupants. "There are some bumps and bruises, but otherwise, everyone seems fine."

"But they're not fine," I cried. "Calvin won't wake up."

"What?" She stared at me. "I didn't sense anything like that at all."

"We can't get him to wake up," I repeated. "Zeke did something to him, and now he's asleep and won't wake up."

"Take me to him," she commanded.

We marched into Jo's bedroom. Tariq sprang from the bed and placed himself between us and his brother.

"It's okay, Tariq," I said. "This is the Doc. She's kind of like a Doctor. She's going to make Calvin better. Aren't you?" I turned to her.

"I'm certainly going to try," her voice softened as she looked at Tariq with wise and kind eyes.

She stood over Calvin and placed her hands a few inches from his body. A low hum emanated from nowhere and everywhere. She waved her hands from his head to his feet and settled on his head. Little electrical flicks flew from her fingers. After a few seconds, several flicks flew in the opposite direction and hit her hands.

"MmmHmm," she nodded. "He is on 'walkabout.' I will need some time alone with him to see if I can coax him back." She extended a hand to Tariq. "I swear to you. He will be okay with me."

"I would rather stay here." He held her hand.

"I understand, but in order for me to do my work, I will need to use what to you will seem like unorthodox methods. He won't be hurt by anything I do. I promise you that."

After a long moment, he nodded.

"I think what she's trying to say is that it's better if we don't watch this part," I said to Tariq as we moved out of the room.

"Is she like you?" He asked.

"Oh, no," I looked back at the Doc as she prepared to bring Calvin back from wherever it was he had journeyed. "She's a healer. She's way more powerful than I'll ever be."

"Can she help you?" Tariq asked as we made our way back into the main room of the suite where Daniel and the Professor waited. Daniel sprang up off the couch. His brown eyes radiated concern. I couldn't make myself look at him and so focused on Tariq.

"She can," I said to him. "But she was my healing arts teacher, so I think I'd disappoint her big time if I couldn't help myself."

I put my hand on his shoulder. "She's going to need some time to heal him," I said. "You can go eat or make use of that horrible couch. Whatever you need." I made my way towards my bedroom. "I'll be back in a little bit." I made it into my room and shut the door. I grabbed my wand and prepared to use every single bit of healing knowledge I'd eked out in class.

THE PIANO'S KEY

TARIQ

Tariq moved towards Daniel and the Professor. He perched on the couch near the Professor. He avoided Daniel's eyes. After a long moment of silence, he took a deep breath.

"Daniel, I'd like to talk to you," he murmured.

"Now, where was that hairbrush?" The Professor opened her purse and searched inside. Tariq sent her a grateful smile for trying to give them some privacy in the tiny room. She looked at him out of the corner of her eye and winked. She returned to rummaging in her bag.

"Okay," Daniel said. He pivoted on the couch and looked at Tariq.

"I guess you got your memory back." Tariq broached the topic.

"I did," Daniel replied.

"So you remember everything?" Tariq shifted and looked away.

"I do," Daniel said.

"Man, can you please answer me with more than two words?" Frustration pitched Tariq's voice high and tight.

"Are you asking if I remember you from before?" Daniel asked.

"I figure you must remember me, or you wouldn't have asked that just now." Tariq massaged his injured hand with the other as he talked.

"Are you okay?" Daniel asked.

"I guess that's what I want to know from you," Tariq replied. He swiveled on the couch until he faced Daniel. "Are you okay?"

"I'm okay," Daniel answered.

"Is there anything I can do to make up for what I did?"

"Yeah, you can tell me why," Daniel met his eyes.

"I needed the money," Tariq answered. He stood and paced in front of the couch. He hadn't articulated his motivation for anyone, least of all himself, because it had been too painful. But he knew Daniel deserved an explanation. "After my brother Jerome split, it was just me, my grandmama, and Calvin. And we were getting by okay, I guess." He risked a glance at Daniel. "But then, my grandmama died, and it was up to me to take care of Calvin. So, I did what I had to do. Jordan found out that it was just me and Calvin, and she offered me a deal. If I worked for her with Darnell and those guys, I could make some money, and she wouldn't turn us in."

"Wait a minute," Daniel interjected. "You've been the only one taking care of you and Calvin this whole time?"

Tariq shook his head and shrugged.

"Veronica helped with babysitting and shit, but that still doesn't excuse what I did to you. It doesn't make it right," Tariq hung his head for a long moment.

"You did the best you could in a crappy situation," Daniel said.

He raised his eyes. "I'm sorry, man. Really, sorry. If I'd known they were going to want to hurt someone, I wouldn't have done it." He looked away.

Daniel stayed silent behind him for what seemed like an eternity. "It's okay," he touched Tariq's arm. "We all do things we're not proud of," Daniel stood as Evie entered the room. "I guess it's how we deal with the consequences that's the important thing."

DANIEL

Evie entered the main room looking less damaged. Her swollen lip had receded almost to its normal size. The bruises on her face and arms were already fading. She cradled her arms around her belly, but for the most part she looked okay. Daniel exhaled a breath he had not been aware of holding. She was okay. That made everything a thousand times better. But now, he had to do his own apologizing.

"Evie," He managed. He ached to rush to her. He wanted to run his hands all over her body to make sure she was all right. He remained rooted to the spot.

"Tariq," the Professor stood and held out a hand to the young man. "I'd like to speak you privately." He stood and walked over to her.

THE PIANO'S KEY

"Evie," she continued. "May we use your room?"

"Sure, thing, Professor." Evie smiled. Tariq and the Professor left them alone.

"Wow, she's smooth. She slid right out of here," admiration filled Daniel's voice.

"Yeah, no moss on her," Evie laughed and then quieted.

"Are you okay?" He asked.

"Considering I was charbroiled not more than an hour ago, I'm fine," she replied.

"Evie-"

The door to Joanna's room swung open. Calvin raced out of the bedroom and into Evie's arms. The Doc remained in the doorway. She mopped her brow with a handkerchief, nodded once, and closed the door.

"Hey, Handsome," she hefted him up. "Are you back from your 'walkabout?'"

"Sure am," he answered. "But I'm going to have some questions for you as soon as I think about some stuff first."

"I'm all yours," she said. She swung him around in a wide circle. "I'm glad you're back, Tiny Buddha," she said.

"Me, too, Rainbow Lady."

They laughed at the shared joke.

"Calvin!" Tariq rushed into the room followed by the Professor. Evie handed Calvin to Tariq who took his own turn at swinging him in a wide circle.

"Calvin, are you okay?" The Professor wrung her hands.

"Yes, Edith," Calvin replied. "I'm fine."

"Calvin, I know this is kind of sudden, but I need to talk to you," Tariq pointed to the Professor. "Edith would like us to come live with her, but only if you want to."

"I want to," Calvin looked from Tariq to the Professor. "And you have a piano at your house so Tariq can play whenever he wants."

"How did you know I have a piano at my house?" The Professor smiled.

"You teach piano. You love piano. You couldn't not have a piano," Calvin's explanation raised everyone's eyebrows, but everyone nodded their assent at his logic.

"Then, it's settled!" The Professor sighed and grinned.

"This calls for a celebration," Evie cried. "Grape juice and cookies for everyone!" She ran into her bedroom and reappeared immediately with a tray laden with Veniero's cookies and glasses of grape juice.

Daniel scooted towards the door as everyone else grabbed glasses of juice and dug into the cookies. He took a last glance at them, exited, and closed the door behind him. He felt like crap. Unlike Tariq, he had no real excuse for cheating on Evie. Sure, he hadn't had his memory, but he had known there were unresolved issues between them.

"You should have kept it in your pocket, Evershed," he scolded himself. "Come on," he jammed the elevator down button again. It was taking forever. The doors finally slid open.

"Hey, Daniel. Good to have you back," Torlyn floated out of the elevator.

"How did you know I got my memory back?" Daniel started in surprise.

"Word travels fast," she answered.

"Why did you take the elevator?" He knew all she needed to travel was a candle flame or a sunbeam, or air for that matter.

"Sometimes, I like to ride it and stop on every floor," she deadpanned. "See ya." She flicked out like an extinguished candle.

"Daniel? Are you leaving?" In the smoke of Torlyn's wake, Evie jogged towards him.

"I didn't think it was appropriate for me to stay. This is a time for family," he said.

"What do you mean? You're family."

"How can you say that? After what I did?" He ran his fingers through his dark hair.

"And what did you do?" She asked.

"I was shitty to you and on top of that I screwed someone else," he shouted. "I wouldn't forgive me, so I don't know how to ask you to do it."

"So, what? You're just going to give up?"

"What else can I do? It was a shitty thing to do and not having my memory is no excuse." He turned away from her and stared down the long, empty hallway.

"Actually, a surprisingly wise pain in my ass showed me that it's a damn good excuse." Her voice was as tender as her touch on his arm. He ached to reach out to her but held himself in check. First, he needed to know something.

"There's something I need to know," he turned to her. "Do you still love me? Is there any hope for us, at all?"

"Daniel," she stroked her fingers across his cheek. "I'm a fairy. Bottom line is, once we love, we love forever." Her eyes clouded over, and she smacked her own forehead. "Oh! That's why they have so many rules about us falling in love with humans." she realized. She sobered. "Now, I get it. I'll outlive you and then some. And if you're only one I ever love, then, I'll love you long after you're gone."

"Maybe I'll live a really long time," he murmured.

"And I'm already 306, so between us, we might balance out okay," she smiled. He took her hands. He lowered his head and touched his forehead to hers. They stood like that for a long time.

The sky lightened with the dawn at the far end of the hallway when they finally kissed. Something slid inside him as if the enormous machine that ran the universe clicked into place. He wrapped his arms around her and lifted her off her feet. He touched his lips to her eyes, her cheeks, her nose, and last her mouth. He lingered there and tasted her sweetness.

"Evie, do you love me?" He whispered against her mouth.

"Yes." Her reply was languid

"Will you marry me?"

Her eyes snapped open. A smile bloomed on her face.

"Yes!" She shouted. She pressed her lips into his throat and inhaled his spicy scent. Then she giggled. "Oh boy. The

Head Office is going to have a conniption. We're breaking like forty-five rules just talking about this."

He held her to him and laughed. "What? Are they going to throw Godparent Handbook Rule Number three-hundred sixty-eight, section six, paragraph B that lists all the reasons why we can't get married at us?"

"Yes, but to hell with the rules," she cried as she smacked her lips against his in a satisfying kiss. "We're getting married!"

EPILOGUE

Zeke stood on top of World Trade Center Tower One. Safer places to do this work existed, but he couldn't ignore the poetry of this place that had seen such tragedy and courage. To achieve his goal, he would need to call on the strength of the people who fought and died on this sacred ground. Some survived. Many died. Many gave their lives so others could live. Tears streamed from his eyes as he remembered the fallen heroes and those they saved. He had not wanted any part of that plan to destabilize the Earth, but as usual he'd had no choice. That was the moment that had decided his fate, his life, and perhaps his death.

Life and death - the presence of both surrounded him. He braced himself against the stiff westerly breeze as he waited for dawn. The entire city lay spread out before him. He couldn't see the buildings of Juilliard from his perch, but he sensed Evie was there.

He would have only two minutes to complete his mission, his vision. As the sun broke over the East River, Zeke unscrewed the cap of the first jar he held. The blue powder inside it reflected the burgundies and violets of the morning sun. He lifted it in salute to the general direction of Juilliard. "To you, Evie," he lifted a sardonic eyebrow and brought the mouth of the jar to his lips. He poured the powder down his throat. He gagged and retched but persevered. He had no idea if his gamble would work. He would succeed, or he would be dead. Either way, go big or go home, he thought. He opened the second jar and swallowed its contents. He consumed the last of it as the sun rose over the horizon.

Spasms pounded through him. He collapsed on the floor and writhed. He gazed at the lightening sky until it faded, and he saw nothing more. All decisions now lay beyond his grasp. Others more wise than he would choose his fate.

Leili watched Zeke's collapse from the first ray of the sun. Her fiery face burst into a fierce grin. Zeke was responsible for everything that had happened to her over the last year, and now, it was her turn. She faced the rising sun and paid her respects to her Mother.

"It's on!" She said.

ABOUT THE AUTHOR

Born in Moldova in the former Soviet Union, Izolda grew up steeped in the rich heritage of Eastern Europe. After her family immigrated to the USA, she graduated from the University of Michigan with a BA in English. She followed her love of travel and education and worked for the National Geographic Society and then traveled the world as an environmental educator for NASA. Her first book in the Fairy Godmother Diaries series, "The Fiddler's Talisman," was released in 2011. Izolda wrote and directed the NASA air quality movie, "Breathable." She also wrote the "Today's Tarot" iOS app and the self-improvement book, "Life Elements." She practices and teaches Tai Chi and has her first-degree black belt in aikido. She also performs music on the college circuit. She and her husband reside in Greenbelt, MD, USA with their dog and three cats, and a house full of books, movies, and musical instruments.

Connect with Izolda at IzoldaTWriter.com

ALSO AVAILABLE FROM IZOLDA TRAKHTENBERG

"The Fiddler's Talisman"
Book One of the Fairy Godmother Diaries

New York City is only a hop, skip, and Ley Line jump away from the Fairy Lands. And if anyone can make it there, it's Level Three Fairy Godmother, Evie Songbottom.

Evie isn't your childhood Fairy Godmother. She prefers whiskey to glitter, movies to wishes, and music to just about anything.

Joanna Brennan, a violin prodigy with a magical edge, is a student at Juilliard School of Music, and she's having a rough term. She caught her boyfriend playing "hide the salami" with her own roommate. Now, her grief is turning magical creatures mundane. Her very own Fairy Godmother, Evie rides in to help, but she must do so before Joanna's agony results in the end of everything.

COMING SOON
"The Player's Crossroads"
Book Three of the Fairy Godmother Diaries

Made in the USA
Charleston, SC
23 April 2016